Rebecca's Rose

Forever After in
APPLE LAKE

Rebecca's Rose

JENNIFER BECKSTRAND

summerside
PRESS™

Summerside Press™
Minneapolis 55378
www.summersidepress.com

Rebecca's Rose
© 2012 by Jennifer Beckstrand

ISBN 978-1-60936-558-5

All scripture quotations are taken from the King James Version of the Bible.

This is a work of fiction. Any resemblances to actual people or events are purely coincidental.

Cover design by Lookout Design | www.lookoutdesign.com
Interior design by Mullerhaus Publishing Group | www.mullerhaus.net

Summerside Press™ is an inspirational publisher offering fresh, irresistible books to uplift the heart and engage the mind.

Printed in USA.

Dedication

To my mom, Anne Gappmayer, who is the
perfect example of everything a mother should
be. I learned unconditional love from her.

To my dad, Richard Gappmayer, who made me
believe I could do anything I wanted to, and
who got me through high school Calculus.

And to my husband, Gary, who believes in
me even when I don't believe in myself.

Acknowledgments

I am inexpressibly grateful to Lindsay Guzzardo, my editor, who has a knack for knowing what should go into a story and what should be left out. Her talent has been invaluable to me. Thanks always to Priscilla and Levi Stoltzfus and the Riehl family, who have helped me understand what real Amish people are like. My gratitude also goes out to my sister, Dr. Allison Sharp, who gives me sound advice. And Mary Sue, thanks for getting me started.

Chapter One

Rebecca didn't see the section of crumbling pavement before it was too late. She landed on her hands and knees with a thud and a groan and watched as the skateboard persisted for another twenty feet before burying itself under a thick bayberry bush growing against the south wall of Patton City Hall.

The little boy perched on the corner ignored Rebecca completely and bolted after his skateboard as if it were a stray dog that might run away at any second. Rebecca pulled herself to the curb. Her knees throbbed and her right elbow stung something fierce. A long rip in her sleeve exposed a deep gash in her elbow, and blood already stained the fabric. She growled to herself. *Ach*, how she hated mending!

Examining the bleeding elbow with her finger, she gasped in pain and annoyance. Holding her breath, she firmly dug a small piece of glass from the wound. *That* would leave a scar. She pulled a handkerchief from her pocket, but it soaked clear through with blood in less than a minute.

"You okay?" said the boy, who had retrieved his skateboard and apparently decided it was his duty to check on the Amish girl bleeding on the sidewalk.

"*Jah*, I am all right," Rebecca said, trying to put pressure on her elbow and smile blithely at the same time. "*Denki* for letting me try it out. It is different from a scooter."

"Yeah, with a scooter you have more balance. But with a skateboard you can go faster." The boy grinned and sauntered away, his skateboard tucked under his arm.

Rebecca's black bonnet had escaped her head fifty feet ago. She put her hand to her head and felt for her *kapp*. Still in place. Anchored with about a dozen pins, the prayer kapp couldn't be blown off her head by a tornado.

Feeling a little silly sitting in the middle of the sidewalk, Rebecca tried to stand. Her knees screamed silently at her. As discreetly as possible, she lifted her dress. Both knees were scraped and red, but the fall hadn't drawn blood. The bruising, unfortunately, made it nearly impossible to put weight on her legs. She sat again and stared at her banged-up kneecaps. Would she have to crawl home?

"Can I help?"

She hadn't seen him standing there. A young man, an *Englischer* with finely sculpted arms, looked at her with some concern.

Excruciating pain or not, Rebecca jumped to her feet and immediately proceeded to lose her balance. The young man grabbed both her elbows to steady her, and she involuntarily cried out. He pulled his hand from her injured arm and discovered the plentiful blood.

"Wow," he said, "you really got yourself good."

Rebecca tried to pull away. "I am fine. I just fell on a piece of glass."

He didn't let go. "Come into the store. I've got a first-aid kit. You might need stitches."

"You want to give me stitches?"

The hint of a grin played at the corners of his mouth. "I operate on all the girls who crash in front of the store. Car crashes are the worst, but those skateboards can be deadly."

"Are you a doctor?"

"No."

"Then you're not touching me."

The young man laughed. "I'm joking, kid. I can fix you up with Neosporin and a bandage. That's about the extent of my skills. But that elbow looks bad. You don't want to leave a trail of blood all the way home, do you?"

Mamm would have a fit if she saw the damage. Rebecca shook her head.

"Good, then. Lean on me, and I'll help you in."

Rebecca didn't want to appear weak, but the throbbing in her knees made plain how futile it would be to try to journey anywhere by herself. Still, she hesitated.

"I saw the knees," he said. "This is no time to be proud." He winked and flashed a set of very white teeth.

Rebecca frowned. "Don't make fun of me, or you can forget it."

He kept grinning and shook his head. "I would never laugh at a girl who is brave enough to ride a skateboard full-speed into the bushes."

She pulled away from him. "I'll be fine."

He held out his hand to her. "I'm sorry. I didn't mean to make you mad. Most of the girls I know wouldn't be caught dead on a skateboard. I thought it was kind of cute."

"Cute?"

He cleared his throat. "Or, rather, daring and courageous of you to try the skateboard."

He was trying so hard not to offend her. It was her biggest weakness—taking offense when none was meant. Why did she find it so hard to be laughed at?

"Besides," he said, "most girls who took a fall like that would be crying their eyes out. You're pretty tough."

She grabbed onto the young man's arm and nudged him forward. "I should cry about the rip in my hem. *Mamm* will scold me for a week when she sees it."

"Then after I sew up your elbow, I'll sew up your hem. I need to practice my surgical skills."

"But you're not a doctor."

"No."

"Then you are not touching me."

"I can sew your hem."

"Are you a tailor?"

"No."

"Then you are not touching my dress."

He laughed.

She cracked a smile.

The young man led her into the sporting goods store, and Rebecca was pleased to discover that the pain in her knees subsided with each step. She might manage to get home.

Still clutching her elbow, he led her to a back office with a soft, rolling chair. "If you could manage not to bleed on the furniture, my boss would appreciate it," he said, walking out of the room.

He reappeared shortly, toting an unusually large white box. It must have been heavy. Rebecca could see his muscles flexing under his crisp white shirt. "First-aid kit," he said. "The boss thinks he's going to have to remove someone's appendix someday right here in the store, and he wants to be prepared." He unlatched the box and opened it flat on the desk. It was indeed an impressive collection of colorful boxes and bottles and crinkly paper packages.

"I bet there's nothing you won't find in this box," the young man said. He rummaged through the supplies and pretended to read labels. "Swine flu vaccine, nose-hair trimmers, vascular clamps, the last living smallpox virus. Ah, here's what I'm looking for. Needle and thread."

Rebecca jerked her head up and glared at him. "No stitches."

"You've got to lighten up, kid."

"I cannot be that much younger than you. Why do you call me *kid*?"

He began pulling supplies from the box. "Because you haven't told me your name yet."

Rebecca's heart skipped a beat. Why did she care that he wanted to know her name? Clearing her throat, she increased the pressure on her elbow. "Rebecca Miller."

"Rebecca. Nice to meet you. I'm Levi."

Rebecca only nodded. His brown eyes made her heart skip another beat.

"You live here in Patton, or are you from Cashton?"

"A few miles in the other direction. Apple Lake."

Levi took two bags from the first-aid box and squeezed them until it sounded like something inside them snapped. He shook the bags vigorously then knelt beside her chair. "I'm not trying to get fresh here," he said. "But you need some ice on those knees, or you'll be a cripple for weeks." She flinched slightly as he wrapped his hand around her ankles and pulled them toward him, straightening her legs slightly. He placed one bag on each knee over the fabric of her dress, balancing them there. She immediately felt the soothing coolness on her throbbing joints.

Levi stood and unwrapped a gauze pad. He poured some liquid on the pad and held out his hand. "Okay, kid—Rebecca—let's have a look."

She pulled her useless hankie from the cut and pushed her elbow toward him.

Gently, almost with a caress, he held her upper arm and studied the wound. "Good job with the pressure. The bleeding's almost stopped." Slowly, he worked his way over the cut, first around the edges of the gash and then to the middle. He went through several gauze pads, thoroughly cleaning the entire area. He glanced at her periodically, making sure he wasn't hurting her. But even though it stung like crazy, she didn't betray any sign of the pain. She knew how to be tough.

"Do you ski?" Levi asked.

"Ski?"

"You like to look at the skis. In the store."

"You… How do you know?"

"I've seen you in here a few times. You slink around the edge of the store until you make it to the back wall, and then you stare at the skis."

"I do not slink."

"Afraid someone will see you?"

"I am not afraid of anything."

"Apparently not." His eyes twinkled. "Rebecca Miller, the skiing Amish girl. Sounds like a good name for a punk-rock band."

"I do not know how to ski. I want to learn."

"Really? Why does an Amish girl need to know how to ski?"

"It sounds exciting. The Amish life is not very exciting."

"I don't know about that. I'll bet milking cows has its appeal," Levi said.

"Only the first hundred times or so."

Rebecca had almost forgotten the pain in her elbow when Levi's probing uncovered another shard of glass embedded in her skin. As the gauze pad scraped against it, she cried out and pulled her arm away.

Levi grimaced. "I'm so sorry. Did I push too hard?"

She cradled her head in her hand and tried to keep the room from spinning. "I think there's another piece of glass."

"Let me see."

With her eyes closed, she took a deep breath and showed him her elbow.

"Ouch," he said. He handed her the gauze pad to stanch the blood. "Tweezers. I need tweezers."

Levi looked through the first-aid kit and produced a pair. "This will hurt," he said.

"I've had worse," she said.

"I'll bet you have."

The piece of glass had lodged rather stubbornly under Rebecca's skin, and Levi tried four times to get a good grip before he succeeded in pulling it out. Rebecca gasped only once and stifled any emotion she was sorely tempted to show. It was a thin half-inch shard, and her cut bled anew when Levi removed it.

He took another gauze pad, poured some antiseptic on it, and gently pushed on her cut. "Any more foreign objects?"

Rebecca shook her head and took a deep breath.

"I still think you need stitches, kid."

"I'll be fine. And my name is Rebecca. Unless you want me to start calling you *lad*."

Levi chuckled. "Sorry, Rebecca. I stand corrected."

He took more gauze pads from the box, along with a roll of white tape and a small yellow tube. "Now you will get to see my skill in dressing a wound."

"Do you think you can do a good enough job? I do not want you cutting off my circulation."

"If your arm falls off, I'll gladly refund your money."

He smeared the clear paste on her cut then laid gauze pads over the broken skin and taped them securely. His movements were as gentle as if he were working on a newborn baby. Finally he wrapped a good portion of her arm with a flexible bandage.

"This should keep the gauze in place but still let you move a bit. No skateboarding for at least a week, though. And no skiing, either." The playful lilt of his voice assured Rebecca that he wasn't making fun of her, at least not in an unkind way.

"Do you know how to ski?" she asked.

"Sure. But Wisconsin skiing is only fun if you've never skied in Utah or Colorado."

Rebecca swallowed the very big lump in her throat and charged ahead. "Could you teach me how to ski?"

"Me?"

"Not one person I know can ski except for Jacob Glick, and I refuse to let him take me anywhere. You seem smart enough, and I really need to learn."

Levi sprouted a peculiar look on his face and folded his arms across his chest. "Now, wait a minute, kid. We only just met. How do I know you're a fun date?"

"Date? I don't want a date." Ach, she almost shuddered at the thought. "I want to learn how to ski. I can pay."

"I don't want your money. If I take a girl skiing, it's a date. I won't take a day off work for a gal pal. I have a reputation to live up to."

"All right, then, it will be a date. How about in November? When it snows."

"How about this Friday at the Cowtown Grill? I need to get to know you first, see if you're a good prospect for skiing lessons. See if you've got what it takes to be my date."

"How will you…what do you want me to do?" Rebecca said, balling her hands into tight fists.

"Meet me there and we can talk. Maybe catch a movie."

A movie? What if it was something inappropriate? She'd cross that bridge when she came to it. "And then you will take me skiing?"

Levi looked up at the ceiling and considered the question. "It might take three or four dates to really figure you out. Are you up for it?"

Rebecca's mind raced. She was foolish to think she could spare even a minute. Chores at home demanded all her time, and *Fater* would never approve. But she knew she would have to go behind his back to do the skiing anyway. What would a few outings with Levi matter?

She needed experiences—the kind she wouldn't find on her little farm in Apple Lake. Before they even went skiing, she might be able to convince Levi to take her places she'd never be able to manage by herself and help her check things off her list. She really wanted to finish that list and fulfill her promise to Dottie Mae.

She would simply make time, even if it meant sacrificing sleep to do what must be done.

The downside? He'd expect something in return, like all Englisch boys did.

"What's in it for you?" she said softly, almost in hopes that he wouldn't hear.

He looked confused for a minute and then shook his head. "No strings attached, kid. You want my help, and I'm a nice guy. Maybe you can help me make a few girls jealous before we actually go skiing."

"Okay," she said, more doubtful than ever. "I will meet you on Friday night. But only because I want to help uphold your reputation."

He sprouted a grin that seemed brighter, contrasted with his tan face. "Thanks for your help."

She handed him the ice packs from her knees. He took her hand as she gingerly rose to her feet.

"Better, kid?" he asked.

"I will be able to walk home well enough, lad."

He threw back his head and laughed. "Sorry. I'll try not to do it again." He supported her as she took a few steps. "You're not walking home."

"Jah, I am."

"I'll drive you. We have to stop off at the health clinic first anyway. I refuse to date a girl with lockjaw. You're getting a tetanus shot."

Chapter Two

"Levi, get up."

Levi heard his sister's voice, but it sounded as if his head were submerged in a tub of gelatin. He rolled over in bed but couldn't seem to open his eyes. Groaning softly, he wrapped his pillow around his ears.

"It's two thirty in the afternoon," Beth said.

Levi opened his eyes to slits and tried to focus on Beth. She pulled up the blinds, and he screamed like a vampire caught in the glaring sun.

Beth put her hands on her hips. "Don't mess with me, Levi Cooper," she said in that exasperated tone she used with him when he really screwed up.

He rolled onto his stomach and turned away from the window. "Five more minutes," he mumbled.

Beth sat on the mattress and bounced up and down.

Levi moaned. "Don't, don't. My head weighs a ton."

Beth kept bouncing while Levi grunted and groaned. "What time did you get in last night?" she asked.

"I can't remember."

"You were in bed when I left for school this morning."

Levi turned onto his back and made his eyes focus on his sister's face. He gave her what he hoped passed for a smile. "Why are you still going to school? You're supposed to skip the last week of class during senior year."

Beth grinned at him sheepishly. "I'm going for a hundred percent attendance."

"Always the overachiever. I skipped my entire last semester."

"It's a miracle you managed to graduate."

"They felt sorry for me."

"Well, nobody feels sorry for me, and somebody has to uphold the family name."

Levi sat up in bed and cradled his head in his hands. "I gladly give that responsibility to you."

Beth reached over to the small table next to Levi's bed and picked up the glass of water that had been sitting there for a week. He glanced at it and shook his head.

"Do you want some Tylenol?"

Again Levi shook his head.

"You didn't miss work today, did you?" she said.

"I don't work on Wednesdays. Don't worry, I haven't missed work yet because of a hangover."

"I'm afraid it's only a matter of time," Beth said, patting her brother on the arm.

"Ouch. Even my skin hurts."

"Oh, stop, you big baby. Get up before Mom sees you like this."

Levi sank into his pillow. "I always time it perfectly so that when Mom walks through the door at five-seventeen, I am showered, shaved, and looking like the model son. She has no clue of my undercover work as an international spy."

"Is that what you do till all hours of the night?" Beth said. "And here I thought you went out drinking with Tara."

Levi pressed his hands to his eyes. "We broke up."

Beth, ever calm and levelheaded, folded her arms and studied Levi's face. "When did this happen?"

"Last week."

"Your idea or hers?"

"Mine. I caught her with Eddie Manville in the back of his truck. Don't tell anybody. She was pretty mad about it."

"After she was the one caught?" Beth stifled a grin. "Well, good.

She's a player, and she was using you." Beth jumped off the bed and clapped her hands together. "I think we should celebrate your breakup."

"You'll regret acting so happy if I get back together with her."

Groaning, Beth sank back onto the bed. "You're not going to be that stupid, are you? After how she's treated you?"

"That's the way Tara is with guys. It doesn't mean anything."

Beth scowled. "You're twenty-one years old and yet still so gullible."

Levi couldn't meet her gaze. His reasons didn't sound very convincing even to him. "I broke up with her because I want her to feel sorry enough to come groveling for forgiveness. Teach her a lesson. Make her jealous and show her what she's giving up for Eddie Manville and his truck."

"Sounds like a good plan. Make sure she knows you're going to break up with her every time she makes out with another guy. That'll show her who's boss."

Levi looked away then brushed off the scolding. He knew what he was doing. "Hey, be nice. I'm just coming off a relationship, and my feelings are very fragile right now."

Beth cracked a smile. "Oh, give me a break. I haven't seen you cry yet, and you always cry." She stood and pulled on her brother's hand. "Will you at least get up and help me clean the kitchen before Mom gets home?"

"That little four-by-six-foot space with a fridge in it? You can do it yourself in about three minutes."

"Levi, flake out on me and you'll end up with your hands in a bowl of warm water while you sleep."

Levi sat up and put his feet on the floor. His head throbbed painfully, but he wouldn't indulge the urge to lie back down. The cloudy head and roiling stomach were natural consequences of drinking too much, but he wouldn't give up liquor anytime soon. Alcohol dulled a worse pain.

"I'm coming," he said. "Just let me throw up first."

Beth stood in the doorway with her hand on the doorjamb and eyed her brother. "Mom knows about the drinking, by the way."

Levi put his face in his hands and focused his blurry vision on the threadbare carpet. "I know," he said.

By the time their mother came home, Levi and Beth had the kitchen as clean as it would ever be. The forty-year-old cabinets and moldy caulking around the kitchen sink could only be made to look so good.

Levi swiped a towel across the counter as Mom walked through the door. She threw her purse on the small table and plopped onto the sofa in her scrubs without even looking up.

"Hey, Mom," Levi said.

Instead of answering, she frowned as her eyes moved back and forth across the sheet of paper she clutched in her hand.

"Is anything wrong?" Levi asked.

She stared at the paper and took a deep breath.

Both Beth and Levi marched to the sofa and sat on either side of their mother. As if noticing both her children for the first time, she dropped the paper facedown in her lap and smiled weakly. "Everything will turn out right, Lord willing."

"What does it say, Mom?" Levi asked, putting his arm around her.

"It's from your father's attorney." She handed Levi the paper and looked up to heaven before pinching the bridge of her nose, the place where her headaches usually started. "We knew this would happen. Beth turns eighteen in three weeks."

"'The last child-support payment for your daughter, Beth Cooper, is enclosed,'" Levi read. "'My client regrets to inform you that he is unable to support your daughter in her college studies, and all financial obligations end with the receipt of this payment.'"

Beth grasped her mother's arm. "You asked him to pay for my college?"

Mom sighed. "I thought it was worth a try."

Levi crushed the letter into a ball and chucked it across the room. "You shouldn't have wasted the paper."

"Your father has his own finances to worry about," Mom said. "We can't expect him to—"

"Why are you always defending him?" Levi said. "The guy is stinking rich. He left us. He left us and then got a really good lawyer who managed to bleed us dry because you didn't want a fight."

"I thought that if it turned nasty, you children would be hurt."

Levi leaped from the sofa and slapped the nearest wall loudly. "You don't have to justify yourself, Mom. Dad knew how you would react. He took advantage of your good heart because his new girlfriend didn't want you to get a cent in the divorce. I hate him."

Mom, who was all of five feet two inches, got up and wrapped her arms around Levi's waist. She had given up years ago in trying to reach her arms around his neck. He stood a full foot taller. "Come," she said. "Sit, and we will talk."

"I don't want to talk, Mom."

"You don't have to carry this."

He pulled away from his mother's arms, resisting her efforts to comfort him. "You've talked at me until you're blue in the face, Mom. I've heard it all before. It doesn't help."

"The weight of unforgiveness is crushing you," Mom said. "You've got to forgive your father, and you must forgive yourself."

"My so-called dad doesn't deserve forgiveness. If I forgave him, it would be like pretending he didn't do anything wrong."

His mom didn't reply, just giving him that sad sort of pitiful look that usually buried him in guilt. But today the anger won out, and he couldn't muster an ounce of remorse.

Beth tried to smooth things over, as usual. "He's not even our real dad, Levi. He doesn't have the same obligation to us."

Levi stretched out his arm and leaned against the wall. "He raised us since we were little. He adopted us. I think that's enough to expect something from him."

"It is," Beth said, lowering her eyes. "But lots of kids support themselves through college. I can do it."

Levi frowned in disgust. "With what? We were both cleaned out, trying to make the house payment. You can barely afford a cell phone."

"I could live at home and go to the community college. It's cheap."

"And forget about Northwestern?"

"It will be okay," Beth said, even though tears brimmed her eyes.

Levi sat on the arm of the ancient overstuffed chair and brushed his hand over his face. He thought of his plump little *mammi* with the laugh that could cheer up the dead of winter. "Mom, have you asked your family for help?"

Deflated, Mom plopped next to Beth and threaded her fingers together. "I wrote to them right before we lost the house. Counseling seemed to be helping all of us. We needed therapy more than we needed a house."

"They wouldn't help?" Levi said.

"They have shunned me for fifteen years. I didn't expect they would." She let out a long breath and put her hand over her face. "I never should have left."

Levi bristled. It was a regret he'd heard from Mom a thousand times since Dad abandoned them.

I never should have left. Oddly, Levi found himself wishing the same thing sometimes.

That was nonsense. Life was carefree for a seven-year-old Amish boy. It only got complicated once the boy grew up.

Levi rammed his hands into his pockets to avoid hitting the wall again. "Do they have to be so rigid about shunning?"

"It was my choice, Levi. They have to keep the church pure."

"It seems to me they would practice Christian kindness to one of their own."

Mom's voice took on a scolding tone, one Levi rarely heard from her. "How can you say that, when they were so kind and forgiving after the accident?"

A sledgehammer to the chest couldn't have hurt any worse. He stood and quickly retrieved his phone from the counter. "Every conversation comes back around to the accident, doesn't it?"

More quickly than he could have guessed, his mother was by his side. She clutched his hand and refused to let him pull away. "I did not mean to make you feel guilty. The accident was over four years ago." She grabbed his arms. "I hate to see how it haunts you. Please let go of it."

Levi shoved the phone in his pocket and headed to the door. "I will let go of it, Mom. When God sees fit to bring that little girl back, I will." He opened the door.

"Where are you going?"

"Don't worry," he said over his shoulder. "I'm not driving." He bounded down the stairs of the apartment building.

I'm going out to get stinking drunk, Mom, because alcohol is the only thing that takes the edge off the pounding, relentless guilt. But don't cry for me. By tomorrow morning I'll have put on my happy face and no one will see anything but the cheerful and pleasant Levi Cooper. With a cement box around his heart.

Chapter Three

It took Levi a few minutes to spot Rebecca in the corner booth at the Cowtown Grill. The place was crowded, as usual, and he was a little late. His eyes passed right over her at first because she wasn't wearing her Amish dress or kapp. She wore jeans and a light yellow T-shirt that accentuated the golden highlights in her hair. The effect was a halo surrounding her face. Her silky hair cascaded over her shoulders and down her back, almost to her waist. His fingers ached to play with it.

Surprised at his own reaction, Levi folded his arms across his chest. How could he even think about running his fingers through an Amish girl's hair?

He smiled as she eyed her surroundings tentatively. Rebecca was one of those girls who didn't need makeup to look beautiful—a nice bonus if you were Amish.

He shook his head. What was he doing here anyway? What in the world had compelled him to ask Rebecca for a date?

To make Tara jealous, what else?

He surveyed the crowd of college kids at the restaurant. One of Tara's friends was bound to see Levi with Rebecca, and the news would get back to Tara before he ordered his first Coke.

Eyeing Rebecca again, he admitted that getting back at Tara wasn't the only reason for the date.

Fascination and guilt warred with each other as he gazed at Rebecca. Fascination for a girl who represented a life he used to know—so long ago but so close in his memory.... And the ever-present guilt. Guilt for his part in the accident that had taken an Amish girl's life.

That's why he'd agreed to take Rebecca skiing. He felt like he had to make it up to the whole Amish community for something that happened to a random Amish girl four years ago. His guilty conscience got the better of him.

And yet, he knew this wasn't entirely the reason either. Rebecca intrigued him. He might even say he was attracted to her, but not in the usual way. Most of the time, Levi didn't even need to work up a sweat to persuade a girl to go out. He knew how good-looking he was, and girls practically lined up to be with him. In high school, they'd hung around outside the locker room after a game for the star football player.

No, Rebecca possessed an attractive innocence and reckless naïveté that Levi found oddly adorable. He was curious—that was all. Just wanted to see what going out with a girl like Rebecca would be like before he got back together with Tara. But no matter how things worked out with Tara, he'd still take Rebecca skiing. He didn't intend to go back on his promise.

Rebecca pulled a sugar packet from the square dish at her table, ripped it open, and poured the sugar into her mouth. *She must be getting bored.* Levi stopped staring and dodged around the tables to his date.

Sliding into the booth, he smiled at her. "Hungry?"

Blushing, Rebecca hurriedly crumpled the empty sugar packet into a tiny ball and hid it in her fist. "You are late. I thought I would get started with the appetizers."

"You look nice," Levi said. He sincerely meant it.

Rebecca looked away and tucked a lock of hair behind her ear. "For a few dollars at the thrift store, it is easy to look like the average American teenager."

Levi reached over and laid his hand lightly on Rebecca's wrist. "How's the arm, kid?"

She stared at his hand for a moment. "Sore and stiff. I should never have let you talk me into the shot. I could barely move my arm for three days."

"Better than being dead, I always say." He squeezed her hand and tugged her forward. Smoothing his fingers along the crisp white bandage around her elbow, he said, "Is the cut better? Are you watching for infection?"

She shifted in her seat but made no attempt to pull away from his touch. "It's amazing how someone like you could have managed to do such a good job on the first aid."

"I'll have you know, I'm a highly trained Boy Scout. I got my First Aid merit badge," he said.

A gum-chewing, ponytailed waitress came to the booth. She took one look at Levi and completely ignored Rebecca. Levi had seen it before. Girls were attracted to him, plain and simple. Rebecca was very lucky to be out with the best-looking guy in town, and she should appreciate it.

"What do you guys want?" the girl asked, staring at Levi. "We've got new flavors of lemonade. Raspberry, peach, mango, and passion fruit."

"I will have a glass of water," Rebecca said. "That is all."

Levi looked up from his menu. "Don't you want a burger or something?"

"I did not bring any money."

"This is a date, remember? You bought an attractive new outfit for the occasion. I'll pay for the dinner."

"*Nae*, you won't want to go out with me again if you have to pay my way for everything."

"What kind of guy would I be? Only a flake lets the girl pay. How would it look, you sitting here with your glass of water while I'm pigging out?"

"You get a free drink if you order cheese fries," the waitress said, as if this would solve all their problems.

Levi winked at her. "Thanks, but I think we'll have two bacon cheeseburgers with onion rings and a couple of Cokes."

The waitress wrote it down. "Do you want special sauce or—?"

Rebecca snatched Levi's menu. "Did you just order for me?"

"Since you're not going to order for yourself."

She glared at him. "You cannot order for me. How do you know what I like? Maybe I am allergic to cheese or hate bacon. Why do you think you can take charge of my dinner?"

"I'm paying."

Rebecca folded her arms and lifted her chin. "Then I'll have water."

Levi threw up his hands. "Okay, okay, I didn't mean to offend you and all your ancestors. I want you to order whatever you'd like."

Rebecca opened her mouth to say something.

"Except water. I forbid you to order water," Levi said.

"Would it be all right with you if I ordered water *and* a pizza?"

"No, get a Coke or something." She needed to put some meat on those bones.

"I can come back later if you need more time," said the waitress, still friendly but glancing with concern at the roomful of crowded tables.

"I'll have an eight-inch barbecue chicken pizza with a glass of water," Rebecca said, daring Levi to contradict her.

Levi stifled a convulsion of laugher. "I want a bacon cheeseburger with onion rings and a Coke. And bring us an extra peach lemonade and an order of cheese fries in case she changes her mind."

The waitress jotted down the order and sped off to another table.

Levi glanced at Rebecca. She sent daggers back at him.

"I hope you like peach," he stammered. Why was she so irritated? Didn't she recognize gallantry?

"Is this always your habit?" she said.

"What?"

"To think you know what I want better than I do and disregard my wishes."

"How can this be a habit? This is our first date."

"I mean, in general. You are used to getting your way, doing exactly what you want."

Levi chuckled. "You're psychoanalyzing me because I ordered cheese fries?"

"I do not know what that word means."

"I'm not trying to get my own way or anything. I just thought you might like to try the cheese fries. They've got like three thousand calories a serving. They're called a 'heart attack on a plate.'"

Rebecca cracked a smile.

Levi nudged her foot under the table. "Hey, you get a free drink with the cheese fries. And you can have the lemonade without feeling guilt-ridden, because I technically don't have to pay for it," he said.

Some of the ice melted. "I would hate to see a perfectly good peach lemonade go to waste."

"And you'll feel terrible if the cheese fries don't get eaten. I'm paying for those."

Rebecca had a really cute smile when she showed it. "I know I shouldn't give in."

"Yet you feel powerless to resist." She was on to him, but he didn't care. He'd gotten his way.

In all his dating experiences, Levi had never seen a girl actually finish her meal. Tara ate like a bird, and the cheerleaders he'd dated in high school took a few bites of whatever they ordered and left the rest on their plates to be eaten by him once he tucked in his own food.

Rebecca was not one of those girls. She polished off her pizza, the peach and a mango lemonade, and more than half the cheese fries. She ate with impeccable manners but cleaned up an amazing amount of food. It was kind of cute, and he couldn't help smiling at her enjoyment. He should have brought his camera to capture her expression, even though he knew she wouldn't have appreciated it.

She caught him staring as she popped the last cheese fry into her mouth and lowered her eyes self-consciously.

"I told you you'd like them."

She blushed. "It has been awhile since I ate out."

"I thought Amish people loved to eat out. There are four or five buggies at that Denny's across from the sporting goods store all the time."

"My *mamm* doesn't feel good most days, and I am not about to take my little brothers anywhere in public by myself."

"That bad? How old are they?"

"Twelve and fourteen. Getting them to sit still is like trying to milk a bull—painful and impossible."

"Any other Millers at home?"

"I have a younger sister, Linda Sue. She is almost seventeen. I cannot get her to do chores, but at least she doesn't give me trouble like the boys do."

"So your brothers are rambunctious."

"I don't know what rambunctious means, but if it explains why Max has almost been kicked out of school twice, I guess they are. I had to promise the teacher that I would sit in class with him every morning for two weeks before she agreed to let him stay. Ach, it is irritating."

She hadn't said anything about her dad. Was he dead? Levi didn't ask. But he knew that there was no such thing as divorce in the Amish community. Levi envied the stability of the Amish family—the dad didn't wake up one day and decide to abandon his wife and rip out his son's heart because he "couldn't stand to live like this anymore."

"Hey, Levi."

Levi looked up. Megan Donelly and Cassie Can't-Remember-Her-Last-Name gave him the eye from across the room. Megan, in her characteristic short skirt, winked and smiled at him, while Cassie played with her hair and tried to look demure and available at the same time. He should have been happy to see them. They'd be sure to inform Tara that they'd seen him with a beautiful blond at the Cowtown Grill. But he wasn't as pleased as he thought he'd be.

He glanced at Rebecca then waved back casually, hoping she didn't make anything of if. He didn't want to hurt her feelings.

Rebecca eyed the girls with apparent indifference before folding her arms and staring out the window.

Levi guzzled the rest of his Coke then thumped his glass on the table. "Okay, kid. I've got more excitement planned for the evening. Have you ever seen a movie?"

"Lots of Amish kids go to movies before baptism."

"But have *you* ever seen a movie? In a theater?"

Rebecca played with her straw. "Nae. I've lived a very dull life."

"No money?"

"I work one day a week cleaning for an Englisch woman so I can pay for prescriptions and my cell phone. There is not much left over for anything else."

"You have a cell phone?"

"Mamm is not happy about it. She thinks it will pull me to the world. But I have not been baptized."

"So anything goes until you're baptized?"

"No. All good parents want to keep their children from doing destructive things. *Rumschpringe* or not, we try to live lives of duty to God and our families—though some experiment more than others. I do not think God smiles on immoral behavior simply because someone has not been baptized yet. The consequences are certainly worse after one has committed to God, but sin is sin whether before or after baptism."

Her earnest expression made him smile to himself. "So is that a yes or a no to seeing a movie?" he said.

"What movie?" Rebecca said.

"Well, if you're brave enough to ski, you should be brave enough for *The Fleshies*. Can you handle zombies?"

"What are zombies?"

"You'll find out. But I warn you, it's supposed to be terrifying," Levi said.

"I am not afraid of anything."

He didn't know why, but Levi had the sudden, almost irresistible urge to lean over and kiss her. She was so cute with her unfailingly proper manners and her ready-for-anything facade. A girl couldn't fake such endearing behavior. Up against Rebecca, Tara seemed kind of hardened.

He shook his head back and forth a couple of times to clear his thoughts and plopped some cash on the table. "Then let's get out of here."

* * * * *

Zombie movie. Best idea ever.

As the blood and guts exploded on the screen, Rebecca seized the armrests on either side of her and gripped them until her knuckles turned white. Levi inched his warm hand on top of her ice-cold one. She pulled away as if she had been burned.

Okay, she didn't want him to touch her during the movie, but she would definitely melt into his arms as soon as the danger was over. A scary movie did that to a girl.

She pressed her head against the back of her seat but never closed her eyes or looked away from the screen. She might be terrified, but she seemed determined to take the horror with both eyes wide-open.

Her lips, pursed in distress, were achingly tempting. Maybe he would give her a post-movie kiss. Just to make Tara jealous.

After the military blew the last zombie's head off and the credits rolled, Levi moved in to comfort Rebecca. Lowering his head, he locked his eyes on hers to prepare her for what was to come.

Instead of puckering up, she produced three whole sticks of gum from her pocket and stuffed them into her mouth. He waited for her to chew them into submission then closed in again, cupping her chin in his hand and turning her toward him. Her eyes, deep pools of emotion, pled with him to lay one on her. He tilted his head slightly.

"Don't kiss me," she said, loud enough for the guys three rows in front of them to hear.

Levi almost choked on his astonishment. "What?"

"Don't kiss me."

"Why not?"

"Thirty-four people are dead and you expect a kiss?"

"It's just a movie."

"I have never been kissed before, and if you kiss me now, I will forever associate kissing with creepy men with skin peeling off their faces. How could you do that to my future husband?"

Levi pulled back. "It's not real. Can't you just forget—?"

"Nae, I cannot just forget."

"But I want to kiss you. That's what people do on dates."

Rebecca held up her hand in case Levi tried to break through her defenses. "No kissing."

Surprised at the depth of his disappointment, Levi backed off.

Zombie movie. Worst idea ever.

Chapter Four

Rebecca tucked the six twenty-dollar bills into her apron pocket and took her black bonnet from the hook by the front door.

"I will see you next week, Mrs. Johnson," she said, deftly fastening the bonnet ties into a bow under her chin.

Mrs. Johnson, who was perched in her lounge chair in front of the television set, nodded inattentively. "Put some ointment on that elbow. And put the garbage out on the street, will ya?"

Rebecca cleaned house for Mrs. Johnson one day a week, twelve hours a day, every day the same. She scrubbed bathrooms, vacuumed floors, washed windows, and wiped walls, then made two casseroles for Mrs. Johnson to freeze for meals during the week. The work was hard, but Mrs. Johnson paid well. A hundred and twenty dollars a week funded Rebecca's cell phone and two prescriptions for Mamm. She stashed the few surplus dollars every month for emergencies, like anticipated amusement park trips and future ski rentals.

Although she earned good money, Rebecca dreaded Tuesdays. Even after work, her labor didn't end. Once she got home she would clean up her siblings' messes, do a batch of laundry, mop, and milk. And look after Mamm. She was usually up past ten o'clock.

Every week, Rebecca caught a ride home with Marvin Yutzy, who passed by Mrs. Johnson's in his buggy at precisely six o'clock in the evening. Marvin was already baptized and eagerly looking for a wife.

And Rebecca eagerly hoped that Marvin did *not* consider her a possible future companion.

The man would put his poor wife to sleep every night with his monotone voice and long recitations of the latest weather patterns. Rebecca thought of him as the human sleeping pill—a very uncharitable notion indeed. How could she ever hope to join the community of Christ with such wicked thoughts filling her head?

Unfailingly prompt, Marvin guided his horse in front of Mrs. Johnson's mailbox just as Rebecca put the garbage bin at the street. With more energy than he ever exhibited in his conversation, he nimbly leaped from the buggy, ran around to the other side, and helped Rebecca into her seat. She thanked him sincerely. If it weren't for Marvin, Rebecca would have to walk the four miles home every Tuesday.

"*Gute* day at work today?" Marvin asked as he prodded his horse into a slow trot.

"Jah. Mrs. Johnson's back was acting up, but she can still walk around fine."

"She is a nice lady."

"Jah, very nice. Gute day for you?"

"Me and Davie today was disagreeing over which breed of Jerseys or Holsteins is best. The Jerseys are smaller and easier to handle, but Holsteins give more milk. I think the Jerseys are a better breed for the cream. The milk is richer, and with Samuel making more cheese than anything else, he needs the higher fat content."

Rebecca smiled and nodded politely. She had heard Marvin debate with himself about Jerseys and Holsteins no less than six times. She wondered what he would say if she asked for his opinion about skiing versus skateboarding. Or zombies versus aliens. Not that she would ever seek out that disturbing zombie experience again. She could proudly say she'd seen a zombie movie and check that off her list of things to do before she died—but there was no need to distress herself like that ever again. As Levi would say, "Been there, done that."

"...and ice cream. Do you think Samuel would try that?" Marvin turned to look at Rebecca. He seemed intensely curious about what she had to say. She couldn't bear to hurt his feelings and admit that she hadn't been listening.

"I—I do not know," she stammered. "Samuel has a gute head for business." Rebecca held her breath, hoping this answer would suffice.

Marvin nodded. "I agree. He will make the right decision. Ice cream is more expensive to transport."

As the buggy rounded the corner, her house came into view and Rebecca caught sight of her brothers wrestling in the front yard. Had they finished the milking? Her heart sank. More likely, they hadn't even started.

"Will you come to the gathering tomorrow night, Rebecca?" Marvin said. "My parents are hosting."

Rebecca pried her glare from her brothers. "Nae, Fater won't be home until Friday and the chores are piling up."

Marvin actually reached over and placed his hand on hers. "You are nineteen years old, Rebecca. How will you find a husband if you don't go to the gatherings?"

A husband? The question pricked her temper, and she answered more adamantly than she meant to. "I already have three siblings and my mother to look after. Why would I want another mouth to feed?"

Marvin furrowed his brow. "Is that all a husband is to you? Another mouth to feed?"

Jah, Rebecca wanted to snap. *What would I be but a maid and servant to one more person in the house? A person who would claim some sort of authority over my life.*

That was how her fater treated her. He used their home as a boardinghouse, sleeping over on weekends before leaving town for another job as far away as possible from his ailing wife and burdensome children.

Rebecca swallowed the resentment that Marvin didn't deserve and shook her head. "Of course not," she said. "I didn't mean it to sound that way. I have plenty of work to do here. How could I abandon my family for a husband when they need me so much right now?"

Marvin stared at her for an uncomfortably long time. "You have a gute heart, Rebecca, to take such care with your family."

"Denki, Marvin. I complain too much."

"I have never heard you utter a word of complaint."

In my heart I grumble constantly, thought Rebecca. *Gute thing Marvin or anyone else cannot see my rebellious spirit.*

Dottie Mae saw what others did not, but she never rebuked Rebecca for her complaining. There would never be another bosom friend like Dottie Mae, ever, in the entire world.

Marvin didn't feel the need to open the door for Rebecca a second time. With her shoulders slumped, she trudged to the house, ignoring her brothers and drawing up a mental list of things that must be done before bedtime.

Peeling off her bonnet, she tiptoed down the hall to the room she shared with Linda and peeked inside. Linda was not in her usual place, sprawled on the bed looking at magazines or filing her nails. Rebecca hastily entered the room. With the door bolted behind her, she walked to the window, where she pried the windowsill loose and laid her money in the space beneath. She shuffled through her cash to make sure nothing was missing then repositioned the board to appear as if it hadn't budged since the house was built.

The profound silence shattered when someone pounded on the door. Rebecca jumped out of her skin.

"Hey, why is the door locked?"

Rebecca hurried to the door and slid the bolt from the fastener. Linda burst into the room and launched herself onto the small double bed with a dramatic groan.

"Mamm needs you," she said, fluffing a pillow and preparing to make herself comfortable.

"Has she been asking for me?"

"Nae, but I can tell when she is tired of me." Linda repositioned a pin in her kapp. "I do not have the patience to be a nurse. It's so boring, watching after a sick person all day long. I need to use my brain. Hannah said I was one of the top in the class in eighth grade."

"How did Mamm do today?"

"I don't know. Like she always does, I guess."

"Did she get up?" Rebecca said.

"After breakfast she walked outside to tell the boys to weed the garden, which they did for about three minutes before running off."

"I did not see any clothes on the line."

Linda rolled onto her side and propped up her cheek with her hand. "I did not have time to start the wash."

Rebecca sighed in exasperation. Getting her sister to do anything but the bare minimum was like expecting Marvin Yutzy to develop a personality. "Linda, the wash is the one and only thing I asked you to do today."

Linda stuck out her bottom lip. "I read to Mamm, practically the whole morning, and I made her a sandwich. I fed the boys too."

Rebecca wanted to stomp around the room and scream at the top of her lungs, but what good would it do? It would only upset Mamm. Linda and those two troublemakers wrestling on the front lawn were plain lazy—as lazy as the day was long. And with an absent father and an ill mother, Rebecca had all the work and none of the authority. She couldn't make her siblings do anything, and when she tried, she got so angry she thought her head might explode like one of those zombies. So she soldiered on, doing her best to run the household without much help from anyone, keeping her emotions buried deep so Fater would not find fault with her—and so she would not crack into a million pieces.

But even as the rage swirled inside her, she tried to quell it, to ignore it, and, if possible, to refuse to give it power. Rebecca had no desire to play the martyr. She could rail against her lot in life and be completely miserable or accept reality and make the best of it. She tried—oh, how she tried—to cheerfully make the best of it, but some days the weight of her responsibilities overpowered her resolve.

Rebecca couldn't think of anything nice to say to her sister. Not even an insincere "Thank you" escaped her lips. She tromped into the kitchen, pulled the flour and some spices from the cupboard, and began mixing a coating for the chicken. Heating an inch of oil in a frying pan, she smeared the chicken legs with egg and coating mix and arranged them in the hot skillet. Then she made her way down the hall to Mamm's room. She had five minutes to spare before she needed to turn the chicken.

Her mamm, fully clothed except for her shoes, lay on her side on top of the intricately appliquéd quilt on her bed. Her eyes were closed, but Rebecca could tell that she was not asleep.

"How is the pain today, Mamm?"

Mamm opened her eyes. "I've had worse."

Rebecca shook her head. Mamm only said that on especially bad days. "Knees and hands?"

Mamm gingerly rolled onto her back and winced. "Ach, *heartzly,* everything is worse today." She held out her arms. "*Cum,* give me a hug. I hate it when you are away from home."

"Jah, I should be here to take care of you."

Mamm patted Rebecca lightly on the cheek. "I am sorry you bear this burden of nursing your invalid mother."

"It is no burden, Mamm."

"I like you here where it is safe. I worry when I send my babies out into the world."

Instinctively, Rebecca placed her hand on her elbow. No one but Levi Cooper knew about the three-inch gash hidden under her long sleeve. Well, Levi and the unsympathetic nurse who'd administered the tetanus shot. If Mamm found out, she'd have Rebecca on three different antibiotics before bedtime and probably take a turn for the worse herself. Being upset only made Mamm sicker.

"You look as if you have a headache," Mamm said. "Take some gingko. There's a bottle in the bathroom."

"No headache, Mamm. I feel fine."

"The feverfew helps, just in case you are coming down with a headache. Better safe than sorry."

"I must turn the chicken," Rebecca said, slipping from her mother's arms. "I'll bring in some supper and rub your legs."

Putting her hand to her heart, Mamm sank into her pillow. "I told Linda to put the chicken on. But she had a headache and said the ibuprofen didn't help." Mamm frowned. "If tomorrow I could rise from this bed for good, I would see to Linda right quick."

"Don't worry, Mamm. You mustn't upset yourself. I am fine to cook the chicken. Linda would only burn it."

"That's my gute girl. I feel better when you are home to take care of us."

Rebecca turned from her mother and felt the familiar tightness in her chest. They depended on her so desperately. She mustn't fail in her duty.

The guilt pressed on her chest until she found it hard to breathe. She marched down the hall into her room and retrieved her cell phone from her top drawer. Her thumbs hunted awkwardly for the right buttons. She was still very slow at texting.

Levi, I am sorry. I will not be able to see you on Friday.
Let's forget the whole thing.

Her place was here, at home, with no time to waste on Englisch nonsense. But before she pushed SEND, she hesitated and put her hand on her pocket, where Dottie Mae's list rested. She fingered the paper and in her mind saw Dottie Mae's chunky handwriting on the page.

Wasn't she willing to sacrifice for her best friend?

Jah, anything.

She took a deep breath to clear her conscience and pressed the DELETE button instead.

Anything for Dottie Mae.

Chapter Five

"Smile, Rebecca. Your horse can smell fear," Levi said.

Rebecca didn't take her eyes off the back of the horse's head. "Is that what that smell is? I thought it was the perfume you are wearing."

"Guys don't wear perfume, kid. It's called *cologne*."

"Oh, sorry to offend you, laddie."

Levi laughed and shook his head. "I know you hope to irritate me with that nickname, but I rather like it. It makes me feel like some manly Scot warrior in a kilt."

Rebecca glanced at Levi. "I will have to give more thought to finding you an annoying nickname. Nothing I've tried so far seems to be just right."

"*Kid* seems to do the trick for you," Levi said. "But is there a nickname you like? I hate to keep offending you. How about *Fred*? *Fred* is kind of cute."

"You want to be seen with a girl named Fred?"

"I like *Bec*. You like that?"

She shrugged. "It's okay."

"*Becky*?"

Rebecca's face clouded over. The expression was even more concerning than the sheer panic from a few moments ago. "Don't ever call me that."

Her reaction spoke for itself. This went beyond discussion, beyond joking. Levi knew without asking that if he ever called her *Becky*, she'd ride off into the sunset and he'd never see her again.

Jack Pittford, the owner of the two horses, finished tightening the cinch on Rebecca's saddle. "Okay, Levi, you're all set. Rebecca's horse is real gentle. Shouldn't give you any trouble."

"Thanks, Mr. Pittford," Levi said. "We'll have them back by four."

"No hurry. I know you'll take good care of 'em. There's plenty of places to water them along the way if you stick to the trail." Mr. Pittford patted Levi's horse on the neck. "Come by the house after, if you want. Millie would love to see you."

Levi thanked Mr. Pittford a second time and checked that the reins were even. He loved riding horses. It always brought back memories of helping his *dat* hook up the buggy for *gmay*.

He would have given Rebecca a reassuring wink, but she had her eyes glued to the spot exactly three inches below the horse's right ear. Her hands gripped the saddle horn so tightly, her knuckles were white. She wore the same jeans and yellow T-shirt from their first date, and she looked even prettier than before, even with that look on her face.

"You remember what to do?" he asked.

She nodded slightly as if any unexpected movement might catapult her off her mount. Was she even breathing?

"It's going to be okay," he said. "Loosen your pull on the reins and give the horse a gentle nudge in the flanks with your heels. That's right."

Rebecca let out a muffled squeak when her horse actually moved, but she didn't panic. After the horse took four or five steps forward, Levi saw Rebecca take a breath. Good. She might not hyperventilate after all.

"See," he said, "nothing to be afraid of."

"Did I say I was afraid?"

"No, absolutely not. That thought never even crossed my mind. I mean, Amish girls are around horses so much, they probably understand their language."

Levi heard Rebecca breath again. Twice in the last minute. This was progress.

"A lot of Amish ride horses. I just never got the chance. Mamm thinks it's too dangerous." A sigh unconsciously escaped her lips. "Did you have to pay Mr. Pittford to use the horses?"

"Nah, I help him in the stable once in a while, so he doesn't mind."

"He likes you very much."

Levi chuckled. "He wants me to marry his daughter."

"He does? Is she your girlfriend?"

"We hung out a couple times in high school. I got to know her dad because we went riding sometimes."

"Do you want to marry her?" Rebecca said, more interested in staying on her horse than in anything Levi might say.

Grimacing, Levi spurred his horse even with Rebecca's. "Why would I want to do that? She's pretty but not real smart." He thought about his entire high school and post-high school dating experiences. That description fit just about every girl he had dated, including Tara.

"So you prefer smarts over beauty?" she said.

Levi glanced at Rebecca. Considering she was only giving him half her attention, her question seemed like the beginning of a deep conversation, and he was tempted to make a joke. He wasn't particularly eager to share his girl experiences with Rebecca. She'd think badly of him.

Why should he care if she did?

Despite his inclination to make light of her question, he cleared his throat and said, "Cornflake girls."

"What?"

"That's what I call them. Pretty on the outside but with cornflakes for brains."

He wanted to laugh at her expression. The tight-laced Amish girl thought *he* was strange.

"So Mr. Pittford's daughter is a cornflake girl?"

"Pretty much."

Rebecca pried her gaze from the trail and looked at him with those eyes that reflected so many different colors at once. "You have dated many cornflake girls, like as not? I suppose the Englisch girls claw out each other's eyes to get to you."

"Claw out their eyes?" Levi sputtered then laughed. "That has never happened."

"But they like you."

He cocked his head to one side. "Sure they do. What's not to like?"

Rebecca rolled her eyes while still clutching the reins like her horse might bolt at any minute. "Pretty is as pretty does."

Levi's heart sank. How could she make him feel like his good looks were a liability? "It's true," he said. "Beauty will only get you so far."

Rebecca furrowed her brow and nodded. "My mamm is pretty."

Why did he suddenly feel so concerned about that look on her face? He wanted to put his arms around her and tell her it was going to be okay—whatever *it* was.

Too soon for that. It was none of his business.

"Are you up to going a little faster?" he said.

She breathed rapidly, and beads of sweat appeared on her forehead. "Jah, of course. I want to run."

"Running might be beyond your skill level at the moment. Let's try a brisk walk first."

He showed her how to prod the horse into a trot. The look of sheer terror grew with the speed of her horse, but she made no attempt to slow down. On the contrary—she urged a faster and faster pace. It seemed the more frightened she became, the faster she wanted to ride.

They rode up the trail, cresting the low hill at a trot. He insisted they slow the pace down the other side. No use in breaking her neck on the second date.

At the bottom of the trail, they stopped to water the horses at the small stream that crossed their path. She held onto the saddle horn for dear life as her horse bent its head to drink, and she was doing that breath-holding thing again. Levi hated seeing the look of panic in her eyes. Why did she want to ride a horse if she was so obviously traumatized by the experience?

"You're doing really well," he said, leaning over and patting her horse's neck. "I've never seen Sandy lose a rider yet."

Rebecca forced a smile. "It is really fun."

Levi wanted to laugh out loud. Clearly, she was having a miserable time, and he was dying to know what she would truly find enjoyable. Unable to suppress a chuckle, he coughed to cover it up. Then he pointed down the trail. "Past those trees is a long stretch of trail where we can let the horses run. Then we'll go up through the meadow to a really nice spot for a picnic."

Rebecca panted as her horse bent for another drink. "You've been on this trail a few times."

"With Ashley Pittford. And Brittany."

"Brittany?"

"Ashley's sister," said Levi. Levi had been in high school at the time, and she was a college girl. He'd never met a girl as brazen as Brittany Pittford. Everything about Brittany, from her low-cut halter tops to her skull tattoo, broadcasted the type of girl she was.

Levi studied Rebecca's face. There was something so much more appealing about a girl like her—someone whose love couldn't be had so cheap.

He frowned. He was thinking too deeply about this Amish girl.

Levi spurred his horse forward in a gallop. "Come on," he called. "The trail follows the water."

After cantering a hundred yards down the trail, Levi slowed his horse to a trot to let Rebecca catch up with him. She followed surprisingly close behind, still with that scared-spitless expression on her face but riding fast enough to quickly pull even with Levi. When she caught up to him, she slowed her pace to match his while gulping gallons of air into her lungs. She really would hyperventilate.

"Okay, stop for a minute," he said. He brought his horse around so that he faced her, and he nudged his foot against hers in the stirrup. "Catch your breath, kid," he said. "You sound like you're having an asthma attack."

"Really, I am gute."

"Okay, then, *I* need to catch my breath. Do you mind?"

She screwed her mouth into a funny little smile and shook her head. "Take all the time you need."

He motioned for her to follow, and the horses ambled leisurely down the trail until Rebecca's breathing slowed from "utter panic" to "mild fear."

"Okay," Levi said. "You see where the trail is real smooth? We'll do some cantering through there up to that stand of trees on the other side of the meadow."

Fear flashed in Rebecca's eyes, but she nodded enthusiastically.

"But don't—don't—go faster than I go. An inexperienced rider can injure herself and her horse. So keep my pace but no faster." He stared at her until she met his eyes. "This is important, Rebecca. Do you understand? Don't do anything to put the horse at risk."

Again she nodded, sufficiently humble.

Levi spurred his horse into a canter. He wasn't about to burst into a dead run. Rebecca matched him stride for stride. Good enough. She'd regained the terrified look on her face, and she should be satisfied with her speed.

Suddenly she dug her heels into the horse's flanks. The horse bolted in surprise and took off through the meadow at breakneck speed.

No! Levi wanted to scream at her, but fear that she would spin around to look at him and fall off the horse stopped the word in his throat. He watched helplessly as she rode hell-bent over the trail, hoping and praying she wouldn't end up wrapped around some tree with the horse dead beside her.

To his relief, she somehow pulled up and stopped her horse just before diving into the thick growth of pines. As soon as the horse was stationary, she swung her leg around and practically jumped off her mount. After taking a few unsteady steps, she plopped to the ground and buried her head in her hands.

Levi raced his horse next to hers and dismounted. He tethered both horses to a tree branch and fell to one knee beside her. "Are you okay?"

"Jah," she mumbled behind her hands.

"Are you hurt anywhere?"

"Nae, I am gute."

Relief washed over Levi, followed close behind by unbridled outrage. "What were you thinking?" he yelled, twelve inches from her ear. "A mere three minutes ago, I told you not to do that!"

She lifted her head and stared at him with glassy eyes. "I did it. I never have to do it again, but I can say I did it."

"Yeah, congratulations. It could have been the last thing you ever did."

She blinked and grinned. "At least I would have gone out with a bang."

"More like a thud. And a splitting headache—literally. Look," he said, helping her to her feet, "how you want to die is your business, but I'm responsible for the horses, and shame on you for risking a broken leg or torn ligament. We'd have to put her down."

Frowning, Rebecca brushed the hair from her eyes. She walked to her horse and patted it on the neck. "I'm sorry," she said. "That was selfish. I needed...I wanted to be able to say I did it."

"You already said that. What have you got, a list of a thousand dangerous things to do before you die? Or an adrenaline-junkie death wish?"

"I want to live before I die."

"Well, it's a good idea not to kill any small household pets, horses, or people while you're fulfilling your destiny. Do you understand?"

"Jah."

"Because if I am going to take you skiing, you'd better learn to do exactly as I say in situations like this. I know stuff, kid. Don't treat my advice lightly."

"Yes, sir, laddie," Rebecca said. "You're right and I was wrong. I promise not to be so *deerich* again."

"Foolish, yeah, try not to make a fool of yourself."

The adrenaline still pumped through Levi's veins, and judging by Rebecca's trembling voice, she hadn't recovered her composure either.

"Come on," Levi said, grabbing her hand and leading her down a narrow path through the trees. It was a casual, natural gesture that he'd done a hundred times before with dozens of girls, but for some reason, he suddenly became aware of her soft hand clasped in his. Her hand, ice-cold and feather-soft, fit perfectly in his as if it belonged there. He couldn't resist rubbing his thumb back and forth across the back of her hand, savoring the pleasant sensation when he touched her.

He cleared his throat. "There's a place over this way where we can have our picnic," he said. "Nice shade with soft ground."

They emerged from the tangle of branches into an idyllic clearing with a canopy of leaves overhead and two or three fallen logs arranged for comfortable seating. He and Ashley had made out under these trees once.

Why did that memory intrude today?

Because those were the only types of memories he had with girls, even his supposed girlfriend, Tara. Nothing significant or heartwarming—just meaningless encounters. He felt a stab of regret. Were all his past relationships that empty?

Rebecca let go of his hand and sank onto one of the fallen trees. "My legs feel like jelly."

"It's a letdown after the adrenaline rush," he said. "You sit, and I'll go get the food."

Levi led the horses to a place in the meadow where they could graze and drink. "No more running today," he told them. From the saddlebags, he retrieved the makeshift picnic lunch Beth had helped him make. Okay, Beth had actually prepared most of it. She made a mean tuna sandwich. He couldn't boil water.

When he returned to the clearing, Rebecca lay on the ground asleep, her head propped against a log. Her hair tumbled around her head like a waterfall, and Levi had to clench his fists to avoid the temptation to stroke it. Again. What was it about her hair that hijacked his senses every time he looked at it?

She must have heard him as he plowed through the underbrush. She opened her eyes and bolted to an upright position.

He sat next to her with his bagful of goodies. "A hard day's ride'll wear you out."

"Late night," she said.

"Let me guess. An Amish all-night drinking party?"

Rebecca gave him a half smile and smoothed her hair back over her shoulders. "I had some chores to finish."

"And your brothers are too rambunctious to help?"

"Some days they work gute. We all have extra chores when our mamm does not feel well."

"Is she sick a lot?"

"Rheumatoid arthritis."

Levi grimaced. "My neighbor had that, and he was always at the doctor. Does she take medication?"

"Several," Rebecca said, frowning. "One that makes her hair fall out and one that they said might cause her to go blind."

"I'm sorry. I bet she's miserable."

Rebecca wouldn't look at him. "They say it runs in families."

He moved close enough to nudge her with his elbow. "Maybe. My mom's a nurse, and she says that just as often as not things like that don't get passed down." He tilted his head and looked at her until she met his eyes. "I'd hate to worry my life away about it."

She attempted a smile. "Jah."

Giving in to the urge, Levi pulled a leaf from Rebecca's hair and caressed her golden locks with his fingers—for just a second. No good lingering over temptation. "What I'd really like to talk about is how stunningly beautiful you look. You take my breath away."

"Ach, you are handing me a shovelful of manure. How many corn-flake girls have you said that to?"

Levi looked to the sky and pretended to be adding numbers in his head. "Seven. Maybe eight. But, Rebecca, you should know by now that it is impossible to resist my charm. You may think it's manure I'm shoveling, but something compels you to take it. Isn't that true?"

She screwed her mouth into that adorable little smile. "Well, manure is really gute for the garden. It makes all sorts of things grow. There are lots of worse things than manure."

"I like to see a good attitude."

"What's in the sack?" Rebecca asked.

"Lunch. I hope you like tuna." Levi handed Rebecca the stash of food as he produced it from the bag. "Scooby-Doo fruit snacks, Dora-the-Explorer juice boxes, SpongeBob cookies, and non-trademarked apple slices. I'm guessing you've never seen any of those TV shows."

"The lady I work for loves SpongeBob. But the others? No."

"Me neither. We don't own a TV."

"Really?"

"Really. Mom wants to protect us from the world's corrupting influence." He handed her the sandwiches. "I don't think she succeeded, except I still think TV is boring. I'd rather go out and throw the ball around or work on my car."

Without fanfare, Rebecca closed her eyes and bowed her head. She fell silent for a moment then lifted her head and held up the sandwich bags. "Do you want tuna with pickles or without?"

* * * * *

How did someone eat so much food and stay so skinny? Levi couldn't comprehend it. Rebecca polished off one sandwich and then ate the extra one when Levi insisted he was full. This girl had a healthy appetite.

"I think I will write to Dora the Explorer and thank her for the juice. Very gute," Rebecca said.

"I'm sure Dora will be pleased to hear from you."

"This is a beautiful spot. So many wildflowers." She pointed to a bright red cluster of flowers growing just off the path. "That's a cardinal flower. Sometimes I walk through the pastures and groves by our house and see how many different colors I can find."

"I've always liked this spot," Levi said. "Good shade, far from the beaten path."

"Denki for taking me riding today. I've had a wonderful-gute time."

"In a near-death-experience kind of way." Levi shook his almost-empty packet of fruit snacks, and the last snack tumbled out into his hand. He gave it to Rebecca, who snatched it up and popped it into her mouth. "I've been thinking about our next big adventure. And I'm wondering if you're going to wear these clothes for every date."

"I have one Englisch outfit and this is it. Or I could wear the apron and kapp."

"Don't get me wrong, I love the Englisch clothes. The T-shirt really brings out the yellow in your hair. It practically radiates heat."

"No manure."

"I'm being sincere, kid. But will you wear the same thing if we go swimming? Jeans tend to absorb water and drag a person to the bottom of the lake."

Rebecca eyes flashed with fear, and she momentarily held her breath. "Swimming?"

"We don't have to. If you're afraid of the water—"

"Nae, swimming is perfect. I want to do it. My fater used to take me to the lake, for fishing."

"Do you own a swimsuit?"

"I will find one," she said, and Levi knew she wouldn't let something as trivial as procuring a swimsuit keep her from her next adventure.

Rebecca meticulously began to gather up the trash and stuff it into the empty bag.

"I can do that," Levi said. "You're the date."

Rebecca hesitated and handed him the bag. "I am sorry. Linda says I am such a Martha."

"A Martha?"

"There is a Bible story about two sisters, Mary and Martha."

"Martha gets a bad rap, if you ask me."

"You know the story?" Rebecca said.

"Don't look so surprised, kid. Mom read to us from the Bible every day. I know those stories better than I know my own name. Jesus was at

Martha and Mary's house, and Martha was serving dinner while Mary sat there listening to Jesus teach. So Martha asked Jesus to tell Mary to help her serve. And Jesus told Martha that she was too anxious about things and that Mary had chosen the good part."

Rebecca nodded. "I am not sure what the 'good part' is, but Linda must think it means sitting around the house all day. She wants to read, and I make her get up and work."

"Sounds like Linda uses a perfectly good Bible story as an excuse to be lazy."

"Jah. You hit the nail on the head."

"I've never understood that story," Levi said. "Why was Martha doing something bad? People have to eat."

"Maybe her complaining was wrong. Do you think she was trying to get the Lord to choose sides?"

Levi had no answer. Instead, he studied her expression—so beautiful in deep contemplation.

She leaned toward him and her arm rested lightly against his—an unconscious gesture. Still, that didn't stop his heart from picking up its pace.

"It is better to do the chores by myself than to complain at what will never be," she said.

"So you get stuck doing all the work because you think that if you ask for help, it will be a sin?"

"I can manage things well enough. And my sister and brothers put up such a fuss, most of the time it is easier to do it myself."

"You shouldn't let them get away with that."

"It is no use wishing for what will never be."

Levi crumpled the bag. "You don't sound like a Martha to me. More like Paul. That guy traveled and wrote and preached like he didn't ever sleep." He gave her shoulder a playful nudge with his fist. "But I've seen you sleep. Every time there's a lull in the conversation, you nod off."

Rebecca grabbed the crushed bag from Levi and threw it at him. "I do not."

"You have no idea the pressure on me to be entertaining enough to keep you awake."

"I stayed up late last night finishing chores so I could come riding today. I will try to stay alert for the rest of the date." She grinned at Levi and leaned back against the fallen log. "I like being compared to Martha. Martha is the one who trusted that Jesus could raise her brother from the dead. She said, 'I believe that thou art the Christ, the Son of God.' She knew. I want to be that strong in my faith. Worthy of His name."

Her gaze locked onto his with an alarming intensity. He hadn't expected a sermon. He hadn't expected to be touched by one. What kind of strange, unnerving power did this little Amish girl have over him?

He reached over and cupped her cheek in his hand and stroked the flawless skin with his fingers. She held perfectly still as he raised his other hand and held her face between his palms. He moved close enough to feel her breath on his cheek. After pausing for a moment to look into those brilliant hazel eyes, he closed his eyes and puckered his lips.

"Don't kiss me."

Levi pulled back as if she'd thrown a bucket of ice-cold water on his head. "What?"

"You smell like a horse. Don't kiss me."

"You smell like a horse too. A sweaty horse."

"If you kiss me now, I will forever associate kissing with stinky horses. You would not want to do that to my future husband."

Levi groaned and fell backward on the ground. "Isn't kissing a guy on that list of things you want to do before you die?"

"I have plenty of time for that. I will be kissing my husband every day for the rest of my life."

Lucky guy. "But what about kissing a mysterious Englisch stranger before you settle into the dull Amish routine?"

"Hmm. I will give that idea some thought," she said. "But do not hold your breath. The thought of kissing you does not appeal to me."

Levi laughed as he pretended not to be deeply disappointed.

You don't want to kiss me? What's wrong with you, kid? What's wrong with me?

He swallowed his embarrassment, jumped to his feet, and pulled her up with him. Stepping on both her feet, he playfully pushed her backward then tugged her toward him so she wouldn't fall over. She gasped and cuffed him on the shoulder.

Mustn't let her see she'd struck a blow to his pride. He forced a smile.

"We'd better head back now, or we won't get home 'til midnight," he said.

"It took us less than an hour to ride this far."

"I know, but on the way back we'll be walking. I'm not letting you get on a horse ever again."

Chapter Six

Although Levi offered to drive her right up to her front door, Rebecca insisted that he drop her off around the bend from the house. She ducked into the bushes just off the road and disappeared from the sight of curious eyes. Keeping close to the cover of the trees, Rebecca quickly made her way to the safety of the toolshed at the back of her fater's property.

Even though she was an hour late—even though she would be up past midnight finishing the chores—she couldn't stop smiling. The horseback ride was horrible, simply horrible, but her riding companion had been surprisingly pleasant. She knew she shouldn't let his good looks sway her. As Levi himself had said, beauty would only get him so far. But she liked the fact that he was nice to look at. She was also certain that if his handsome face were his best quality, she wouldn't be enjoying herself so much.

Although he probably didn't realize it, Levi developed an uneasy grimace whenever she betrayed signs of distress. She'd tried to hide her panic, but her attempts obviously hadn't worked. She found his concern for her feelings endearing. Rebecca suspected that nothing much could ruffle his feathers—except when the Amish girl tried to break her neck on a horse.

Guilt momentarily caught hold of her. How could she justify enjoying herself while Mamm suffered in bed? Fater would be furious if she hurt herself and was unable to take care of her mother.

She slid her hand into her jeans pocket and pulled out a piece of paper that had been folded and unfolded so many times, light passed right through the creases. She looked at the first item on the list, written in Dottie Mae's handwriting: *Go skiing.*

For her mother's sake, she would be cautious. But for Dottie Mae's sake, she would be persistent.

Rebecca slipped through the shed door, making sure to open and close it carefully. She saw to it that the toolshed had the best-oiled hinges on the farm—probably the *only* oiled hinges on the farm.

Rebecca sighed. The property was falling apart around her. The barn doors hung by a thread. One of the buggy wheels had cracked last week. Fences and gates were missing slats and a good coat of paint, and the house desperately wanted a new roof. How ironic that her roof leaked when her fater roofed houses for a living.

Rebecca wedged a rake firmly under the door latch then untied the knot in her blue canvas bag. With a speed that could only be developed by frequent practice, Rebecca peeled off the Englisch clothes and slid into her dress and kapp. The jeans and T-shirt went into the bag, and the bag went behind a crate of seeds on the top shelf of the shed. She would wash the clothes later tonight while the others slept.

Rebecca's heart performed a tiny flip. Levi liked the yellow T-shirt. She was glad she'd chosen it instead of the red one. Although he probably would have told her how much he liked the red one if she'd bought it. The boy certainly had a silver tongue.

She growled quietly. Levi was extremely kind, while she couldn't hold her tongue. Plainspoken and harsh, Fater said. Rebecca felt her face grow hot. Although Levi tried to make light of her remark, it was obvious she had hurt his feelings when she told him she didn't want to kiss him. She wanted to kick herself for being so blunt. *"The thought of kissing you doesn't appeal to me"*? She might as well have said, *"I find you repulsive."* That was not how she meant it, but that was how he heard it. Truth to tell, she found him quite attractive, but kissing was a line she would not cross. Too many undesirable things could happen once she opened that door—especially with an Englisch boy.

Still, she regretted hurting his feelings.

Emerging from the shed, fully restored to her Plain self, Rebecca saw fourteen-year-old Max tromping out of the barn and carrying a full pail of milk.

"Max," she called. He turned at the sound of her voice. "You did the milking. Oh, denki. You are a gute brother."

Max pursed his lips and looked past her. "Fater is home."

Rebecca's heart sank to her toes. "Where is he?"

"In the house."

Hours earlier than expected. Fater's presence explained why Max had actually milked today. The brothers snapped to attention whenever Fater was around.

Rebecca trudged to the house, though she really wanted to run the other way. She never should have gone out on the day of Fater's return, but she had been certain she would have time later to finish the chores.

Best do what she could to placate Fater before he took his irritation out on the other siblings.

Even if Max hadn't told her, Rebecca would have known her fater was home as soon as she came in the front door. Linda stood at the sink peeling potatoes and wiping tears from her face. She didn't look at Rebecca but sniffed loudly as she passed.

Down the hall, Fater yelled at Danny: "...to see you can't even make your bed. This better be spotless by the time I come back, or you can forget about supper."

Rebecca met her fater in the hall as he marched out of Danny's room. The irritated scowl plastered across his face was how she would always remember him. "And where have you been?" he said.

"You are home earlier than we expected, Fater," she said.

"I told you I was coming home on Wednesday this week," he said.

"I meant a few hours earlier."

"Be that as it may, I should not be greeted by such a mess. The stalls need mucking out, the weeds are three feet high, the floors are sticky... and you—nowhere to be found. I leave this farm and this family in your care, Becky, and you have proven yourself a slothful, selfish girl like your sister."

Rebecca massaged a spot on her forehead above her eyebrow. "I will catch up on everything tonight. It would have been done if you had not come home early, and then you never would have known the difference."

"So you wile away the time and think you can rush to get things done before I return? Don't you care what your mamm suffers while you are idle?"

Rebecca had heard Fater's tirade before, weekly almost, and every word still stung like a swarm of hornets. But the accusations about Mamm sliced closest to Rebecca's heart. Truth be told, she felt a stab of guilt every time she left Mamm's side, even on the days she worked for Mrs. Johnson. The two outings with Levi plagued her conscience. She cared for Mamm more than anyone else in the world.

Rebecca was the one who could loosen the knots in Mamm's shoulders or rub her feet to help her relax. She knew how to soothe her mother's anxious thoughts with a song or a reading from the Bible. Rebecca remained her mamm's one comfort, and they both knew it.

"Linda takes care of Mamm when I am away."

"Linda can't even care for the horse. You think she can nurse your mamm properly? You are the one who should be here, Becky. You forget how much Mamm needs you. Why are you so selfish?"

Rebecca sucked in her breath and held it. She worked hard for her family. Hard—every day. Almost single-handedly, she scrubbed the house from top to bottom—bathrooms, floors, kitchen. She tended the garden and the animals, milked, gathered eggs, watered the grass, cooked meals. It would take three hired servants all day to do the work she did. The thought of a life stuck in Mamm's tiny little room in this suffocating house almost choked her. She had to live before the inevitability of her future life sucked her in with its endless days of drudgery, slaving for her siblings, watching her mother suffer, and enduring her fater's bad temper.

Marriage held no escape for her either. She felt too guilty about leaving her mamm to wish for a husband.

Rebecca should have bitten her tongue, but she did not. "I could quit my job if you want me here more often, but the money I make from Mrs. Johnson pays for Mamm's new prescriptions. And unless you bring home a bigger paycheck, I need to work."

The blood vessel in Fater's neck pulsed visibly. "Are you saying I cannot provide for my family?"

"Nae, we are all doing our best," she said, in a tone she hoped would placate him. Why did she feel compelled to speak her mind? She'd be able to keep the peace if she could just shut her mouth.

"I work harder than any man I know. Do you think it is easy, spending ten hours a day on a hot roof installing shingles? I take on jobs out of town for extra money."

Rebecca lowered her eyes and stared at a dust bunny in the corner. "I didn't mean... You work very hard."

"Jah, I do, and I should not have to come home and work doubly hard because my children are too lazy to keep up the farm. I am entitled to rest for a day before going out again. Is that too much to ask?"

Yes! Rebecca wanted to scream, but for once she managed to swallow it. Let Fater release his tirade when he came home from a long week of construction work. At least they were in peace while he was away.

Rebecca turned from her fater and headed down the hall to the kitchen. "I will help Linda with supper while you look in on Mamm."

While Linda tended the bubbling soup, Rebecca, Danny, and Max weeded the garden. Rebecca had planted two extra rows of peas this spring plus tomatoes for fall canning. The garden plot took up almost a half acre. Weeding alone was a full day's work. Rebecca loved tending the flower beds and garden. If only she could plant and trim and weed all day long, she would be perfectly happy.

They finished what they could before suppertime. Her brothers' help proved invaluable in accomplishing a good chunk of the task. If only she could get them to work without the threat of Fater's wrath hanging over their heads.

Mamm, keeping to her bed, said she had no appetite. The four siblings and their fater ate together at the kitchen table. After a supper eaten in complete silence, Fater went to the bedroom to be with Mamm. Max and Linda washed the dishes while Rebecca and twelve-year-old Danny swept and mopped the floor.

After finishing the dishes, Linda flounced to their bedroom to pout. Rebecca dragged Max and Danny to the garden to finish the weeding in the dimming light. She worked her way around the house, pulling weeds from around the foundation and deadheading roses from the three bushes on the side of the house. She ran her hand gently across one of the pink-and-cream-colored roses then let the silky petals caress her cheek. She breathed in the scent of strawberry taffy wafting from the flower. Rebecca didn't have to force enthusiasm when she worked in the yard. She relished getting in the dirt and making things grow.

At the front of the house, Rebecca squeezed under the porch to eradicate the stubborn bindweed that constantly cropped up there. She flinched when she heard someone trudge up the stairs above her and knock on the door.

Firmly wedged into the small space, she kept weeding. Might as well stay and finish the job. Someone up there would hear the door and answer it.

The screen door creaked open. "Reuben. Hello. *Cum reu*, cum reu," she heard her fater say.

Reuben. Reuben Yutzy? Marvin's father?

"Nae," said the man. "My boots are dirty. I stopped for a talk with you. Can we sit outside?"

She heard the men's heavy steps above her as they tromped to the bench and sat. Should she say something? Call out that she was there, like a voice from space?

No use in suffering the embarrassment of emerging from the depths and interrupting their conversation. Besides, how long could it take? Still lots of weeds. She would make good use of the time while stuck under the porch.

Where Marvin Yutzy loved to linger over a story until his listeners fell asleep, his dat got right to the point. "There is a new housing development planned on the east side of La Crosse. Construction starts in two weeks. We want you to be on our crew."

"Do you?" Fater said.

"It is close enough that we can come home every night."

Rebecca forgot to breathe as the thought of Fater at home every night pressed down on her.

She heard Fater stand and take a few steps away from Reuben. He spoke slowly. "I have a gute job in Milwaukee."

"This one in La Crosse is a gute job."

"My work is steady, and it pays better than what you can find in La Crosse. I supervise five men."

"But you are away from your home so much."

Fater shuffled farther from Reuben and leaned his elbows on the porch railing. Rebecca could see his expressionless face through the wooden slats. "Why should you concern yourself with the time I am away from home?"

"We are thinking of your family."

"Becky manages well."

"Marvin is worried about her. He says her burden is very great."

Marvin? Why did he care? Rebecca almost groaned out loud. She knew exactly why he cared.

"The bishop and the ministers have discussed it," Marvin's dat added.

"Have you?" Fater said.

"Can we send someone over to help on the farm? Every day or two? Or pay for some of the medical expenses so Rebecca does not need to work another job?"

Fater's voice rose, but he did not lose control of his temper. "The Millers do not need help. I am capable of taking care of my family."

"Of course you are."

Rebecca could sense Fater's agitation as he paced around the small porch. "'But if any provide not for his own, and specially for those of his own house, he hath denied the faith, and is worse than an infidel,'" he said. His favorite Scripture. He quoted it almost weekly.

Reuben stayed put on the bench but didn't back down. "No one would ever in a hundred years claim that you do not provide for your own, Amos. But you have special circumstances here. Your wife is ill. She cannot work or even walk most days. You must pay for medicine and doctors. The burden of upkeep of house and farm falls on your eldest daughter."

"She is able—"

"What will you do when she marries?"

A spider crawled across Rebecca's hand. She held perfectly still.

"She is only nineteen," Fater said.

"She is old enough."

"She would not want to leave her mother."

"I think she would not reject marriage to care for Erla," Reuben said. "And Erla would not ask that sacrifice of her. Would you?"

A heavy pause. "I will cross that bridge when I come to it," Fater said quietly.

Rebecca heard Reuben stand and move closer to Fater. "Will you accept help from your neighbors?"

"I have already told you, Reuben. I take care of my own family. Do not shame me by offering charity."

A hint of chastisement crept into Reuben's tone. "Perhaps you confuse shame with humility."

"The Lord humbles me by afflicting my wife. I am sufficiently humble. I will not be humiliated."

Rebecca listened to the crickets chirp as both men fell silent.

Finally, Reuben grunted and tromped down the steps. "We will see you at gmay Sunday?"

"Jah, Lord willing," Fater said.

"Good evening to you, then."

"*Auch vider sehen*, Reuben."

Reuben, with hat in hand, took three steps and turned back. "Think about what I have said. 'The Lord lifteth up the meek.'"

"Good evening, Reuben."

Reuben didn't have to be dismissed a third time. He donned his hat, hitched his thumbs around his suspenders, and ambled down the lane to his buggy. Fater lingered on the porch for a few minutes before resolutely turning and disappearing into the house.

Rebecca breathed a sigh of relief. She was ashamed to admit how grateful she was that Fater had a job in Milwaukee. Running the household by herself overwhelmed her some days, but truth be told, everyone was happier when Fater was away. He was right when he told Reuben that she could manage on her own. When Fater came home, he disrupted her routine and sent the siblings into fits. He yelled and demanded and carried on until they all wished he would stay away. Their life was hard, but it was easier without Fater's interference.

Rebecca never felt so wicked in her life as when she had such thoughts. She should love her fater, when all she could muster was tolerance. *Oh, Father in heaven,* she prayed, *forgive me for my stiff neck and hard heart.*

Fater had always been stern and of a serious disposition. But when his family was younger, he seemed content with his life and satisfied with his oldest daughter. Before Mamm fell ill, Rebecca was Fater's best helper. While she was still too young for grade school, she'd followed him all day long, carrying a tiny pail and a screwdriver. He called her "my little Becky" and let her help with his work. She gathered eggs for Mamm and carried lunch for Fater in her little bucket. Even after she entered school, Fater let her tag along in the afternoons while they helped each other with their chores. She longed for his approval, so she worked extra hard on the farm to earn it. Fater handed out praise sparingly, which only motivated Rebecca to try harder. Rebecca would have done anything to please her fater.

"'Be strong and of a good courage,'" he would tell her. "I depend on you."

Times had changed. Rebecca must have grown unlovable.

When she thought of Marvin Yutzy, her heart sank. Marvin might not have put his dat up to the visit, but Marvin's desires most certainly influenced his father's reasons. Poor, exasperating Marvin. With so many other worthy and available girls in the surrounding districts, how could he find anything attractive about Rebecca?

What would Levi think if he knew Rebecca had a young man interested in her? He would probably laugh or tease her about kissing Amish boys. She loved it when he laughed and she caught a glimpse of those dazzling white teeth.

Was it too soon after their date to send him a text?

Maybe not, but the chores would keep her from her phone past midnight. Levi would have to wait.

Chapter Seven

Levi stirred the foam on the top of his beer with his finger and stared at the TV on the wall. Some baseball game he couldn't care less about flashed across the screen as the announcers droned on about batting averages and trade rumors. He ate another pretzel.

"It'll go flat if you let it sit too long," said the bartender as he stacked menus on the counter.

Levi nodded noncommittally. How long had he been sitting there? Ten minutes? Twenty?

Why had he come tonight? He wasn't really in the mood for a drinking party with friends and perfect strangers. Even in the midst of dozens of people at a bar, alcohol left him feeling utterly alone.

Someone slapped him on the back, and he turned to look.

"Levi, my man!"

"Hey, Jason. Hey, Dax."

His two friends pulled up stools on either side of him. Jason, who was built like an army tank, waved his arm to get the attention of the bartender. "You're not drinking?" he said.

Levi held up his full glass of beer.

"No," Jason said, "I mean *drinking*. By this time of night you're usually on your second or third margarita."

Levi leaned his elbows on the bar. "Just beer tonight."

Jason and Dax stared at each other for a long minute. Jason let whatever he was thinking die on his lips.

"Well, I hope you don't mind if I get totally wasted," Dax said. "It's been one of those days."

Jason ordered a margarita. Dax got a scotch straight up and downed it in five swallows. "Tara texted me," he said, pausing to wipe his mouth with the back of his hand. "She's coming over."

"Here?" Levi said.

"Yeah," Dax said. "She wants to see you."

Levi groaned. "You told her I was going to be here?"

"Chill out, Cooper. She wants to be friends."

Levi lifted his glass to his lips then set it down again. "No, she doesn't."

Dax ordered another drink. "What's wrong with that? For the life of me, I can't figure out why you dumped her."

Frowning, Levi wrapped his hands around his glass and pretended to study the television. "It's not her. It's me."

Jason rolled his eyes. "I've never heard *that* one before."

Levi didn't want to have to justify himself, but he did anyway. "You know that nice new truck Eddie Manville bought?"

Jason nodded.

"Guess who I found making out in the back?"

"Tara and that cowboy?"

Dax hooted with glee.

"So what?" Jason said. "That's just Tara."

Funny, that's exactly what Levi had told Beth.

I'm done with cornflake girls.

Levi glanced at Jason out of the corner of his eyes. He had about ten more minutes of coherent conversation left before both friends were useless. "Why didn't we date any good girls in high school?" he muttered.

Jason laughed out loud. "Because they weren't any fun."

Shaking his head, Dax grinned. "They never would have dated us."

"You're right," Levi said, suddenly glad Rebecca hadn't known him in high school. "The good girls wouldn't have been caught dead associating with us."

"Who wants 'em, when you've got girls like Tara?" Jason said.

"Maybe you could actually have a meaningful relationship with a good girl."

Jason grabbed Levi's arm. "What's gotten into you, man?"

"Nothing. Just thinking."

"Well, quit thinking and start drinking."

Jason and Dax roared with laughter until Jason started into a coughing fit and Dax stood up and pounded him on the back.

Meaningful communication was at an end. Levi surrendered his place at the bar and wandered to the pool table, where a guy was teaching a girl how to hold the cue.

I'll bet Rebecca would like to learn how to play.

Levi shook his head. That girl popped into his mind at the most random moments.

Even amid the noise Levi heard the door squeak open, and he looked over to see Tara saunter in, holding hands with that Eddie guy. Eddie wore a very impressive chocolate-brown cowboy hat complete with a pair of hand-stitched boots and a belt buckle the diameter of a small grapefruit.

Tara was what Beth would call "high-maintenance." Her bright-red fingernails were expertly manicured, and not a strand of her bleached-blond hair was out of place. Her bright-red shoes had impossibly high heels. Levi had no idea how she walked in them. Not easily, because with them on her feet, she bent forward slightly and sort of waddled like a duck. Levi hadn't really thought before about how ridiculous that looked.

Tara quickly surveyed the bar stools and then, not seeing what she came for, scanned the faces around the room.

Levi wasn't a coward, but he didn't want to talk to her. Two dates with Rebecca were enough to compel him to rethink his choices. He didn't want to get back together with Tara again.

But if he informed Tara of that, she'd make a scene and embarrass herself and then he'd feel guilty and angry and trapped all at the same time. No doubt Eddie's presence was meant to provoke jealousy and pressure Levi to beg Tara to take him back. He felt almost sorry for her. How could she know her strategy wasn't going to work?

Levi recognized the moment when Tara spotted him. Her eyes locked briefly on his and then she immediately looked away as if he wasn't anybody she knew. Dragging Eddie along with her, she strode not toward Levi but to the bar, where she greeted Jason and Dax and visited with exaggerated enthusiasm.

Might as well get it over with. Levi hadn't talked to Tara for three weeks. He hadn't called her as he'd intended, hadn't wanted to. At the time, he had left her with every expectation that they would get back together. Man, how things had changed.

Levi marched to the bar and put a hand on Dax's shoulder. "Hey, Tara," he said.

Tara fixed a look of surprise on her face and threw her arms around Levi. "Levi, hi! How are you?"

Eddie looked confused and uncertain at the same time. Levi could see the wheels turning in his head as he wondered whether he should act jealous or angry or neither that Tara hugged another guy. Eddie opted to appear indifferent to Levi's presence. Levi thought that was a good idea. Tara's power increased when she knew she could manipulate someone's feelings.

Nudging her away, Levi told a small lie. "It's good to see you."

"How was the Sports Expo?" Tara asked. "Jason said you had to work it for like twelve hours a day."

"It was fine. Good overtime pay."

"My brother went, but he didn't see you," Tara said.

Eddie, who stood behind Tara, pulled her a little closer to him and put his hands around her waist. Levi looked at Eddie and nodded. "Hey, Eddie."

"Hey."

"I saw the new hubcaps on your truck. Sweet." Levi said.

Eddie kind of smiled. "Birthday present from my dad." He nuzzled his face into Tara's hair.

She pulled away from him and giggled. "Eddie, stop!"

Levi thumped Dax on the shoulder. "I'm leaving. I've got to get up early tomorrow."

"But we just got here," Jason said.

"You're getting along fine without me," Levi said. "I'll talk to you later."

"Wait," Tara said, grabbing his arm. She quickly ordered a beer and pushed Eddie onto the bar stool between Jason and Dax. "I want to talk to Levi alone for a minute. Okay, Eddie? Wait here."

The look of confusion returned to Eddie's face. Tara picked up her beer and tried to take Levi's hand. He avoided her touch. She pretended not to notice then headed for the nearest empty table.

"I don't have much time," Levi said, preparing her for what he hoped was a gentle letdown.

"You're not drinking?" she said.

"I left my beer at the bar."

"Sit," she said. "Just sit for a minute."

He eased slowly into the chair, hoping to make his lack of enthusiasm blatantly evident.

She took a sip of her beer and leaned closer to Levi. "Eddie wants me to get serious with him."

"From what I've seen, you're pretty serious already." He sounded like a bitter ex-boyfriend. He didn't want to sound bitter. He wanted to be done with Tara.

With cornflake girls.

"That was just playing around, Levi. I don't like him like that."

"I don't want to be with you anymore, Tara."

"That's not what you said when we broke up." She clicked her fingernails against the table as if eager to get this chore over so she could move on to something more important. "I've learned my lesson. I'm sorry, and I want you back."

"I've had time to think things out. I'm not mad anymore, and I think you're better off without me. That's all."

Tara folded her arms. "Do you want me to admit that I'm jealous? Okay, I'm jealous. Megan said you were out with some girl the other night."

"I didn't do that to make you jealous." Not entirely true *then*, but entirely true now.

Tara's voice rose with her frustration. "Oh, sure you didn't," she said sarcastically. "That's why you took her to our hangout. You knew at least one of my friends would see you."

Levi stood up. "It's over, Tara. Sorry."

The venom shooting out of her eyes could have killed him. "Maybe I should warn this new girl about you. It's not every day you date a guy with a police record."

Tara knew him too well. Pain scrubbed itself over every surface of his body.

She saw his expression and must have realized she'd gone too far. Jumping to her feet, she grabbed his arm with both her hands. "I didn't mean it, Levi. You know I love you. Sometimes I want to hurt you as bad as you've hurt me."

She snaked her arms around his neck. He was too stunned from her first blow to resist. Pulling him close with amazing strength, she kissed him hard on the mouth.

To avoid touching her, he held up his hands like a bank robber in the sights of a policeman's gun.

When he didn't kiss her back, she took her lips off his but still clung tightly to his neck with her tentacle-like grip. "Come on, Levi."

Levi felt, rather than saw, Eddie behind him. He might have heard Tara scream. Eddie yanked Levi's shoulder and spun him around violently then swung his fist and caught Levi hard in the nose. That was Eddie's first mistake. He should have known that Levi didn't take crap from anybody.

Levi snatched the collar of Eddie's mighty fine Western-style shirt and half-dragged, half-pushed him to the far wall. All it took was one punch to the jaw to lay Eddie flat. Levi had a good right hook.

He shook his hand to drive away the pain and looked down at Eddie on the floor. "You can have her," he said. "But leave me alone."

He grabbed some napkins from the nearest table to soak up the blood pouring from his nose. It stung something awful.

As Levi would have expected, the bartender wasted no time in throwing both of them out of his bar. He dragged Eddie from the floor with one hand and grasped Levi's arm with the other. "No fighting," was all he said as he escorted both men to the door and pushed them out into the night.

As the door slammed behind them, Eddie gave Levi a halfhearted shove before weaving unsteadily to his truck, getting in, and speeding away—his souped-up engine rumbling all the way into the next county. He apparently didn't care that he had brought Tara with him or how she would get home.

"You okay, man?"

Levi turned. He hadn't even heard Jason come out. "Yeah, I'm okay."

Jason already possessed that glassy stare that indicated he wouldn't remember much of anything that happened tonight. "Oh, man. Your nose is bleeding, man. Come in and get some ice or something."

"They won't let me back in," Levi said.

"Oh."

Levi opened the door for Jason and pushed him toward the inside. "I'm good," he said. "Go back inside. I'll call my sister to come get me."

"Okay, man. Take care. We'll see you tomorrow."

Levi sat down on the curb, leaned his head forward, and pinched the bridge of his nose. His blood dripped into the gutter as he peeked through his fingers to dial his sister's cell. He'd sunk pretty low, being forced to call his sister to pick him up like some sixth grader after a playground fight.

His only prayer was that Rebecca wouldn't suddenly decide to drive by in her buggy and see him sitting there.

"Hello, Beth. I'm an idiot. Could you come and get me?"

* * * * *

In less time than Levi would have thought possible, Beth pulled up to Tequilita's Bar and unlocked the passenger door. His nose had stopped bleeding, but he held the napkins to his face so he wouldn't drip on the seats in case it started up again.

Patient, reliable Beth didn't utter a word on the ride home, and Levi didn't volunteer any information. He felt ashamed enough without having to recount every detail to his sister.

She parked the car, and they trudged up the three flights of poorly lit stairs to the apartment. Unlocking the door, she glanced at Levi. "You're lucky Mom had to pull an extra shift."

They walked into the kitchen and Beth turned on the light. "Let me see," she said.

Levi pulled the napkins away from his face.

Grimacing, Beth ran her finger along the bridge of Levi's nose. "You did yourself up a good one."

"You should see the other guy."

"I'll get some ice."

Beth filled a plastic bag with ice cubes, laid it on the counter, and pulverized it with the thick end of a butter knife. She handed it to Levi. "I'm afraid Mom's going to notice this with or without the ice. What are you going to tell her?"

Levi wrapped the ice bag in a towel and laid it gingerly on his nose. "I've never lied to Mom."

"I know. What are you going to tell her?"

"Tara wanted to get back together." Holding the bag carefully, he stretched out on the sofa. His legs hung twelve inches over the side.

"And she hit you?"

"Her boyfriend did. After she kissed me."

Beth sat on the floor next to the couch. "You let her kiss you?"

"She kind of surprised me."

Beth crossed her ankles and leaned back on her hands. "Does this mean you're getting back together?"

"No," Levi said. He went quiet and listened to his own breathing.

Beth threw her head back and looked at the ceiling. "Thanks for all the info."

"You're nosy."

"I'm never nosy."

He glanced at his sister. "You're going to think this is dumb."

"Probably."

"It doesn't seem honorable to go out with Tara anymore. Whether she agrees or not, I've been using her. It's not right. It doesn't feel right."

Beth peered at Levi. "That's not dumb. That's the smartest thing I've heard you say in ages."

"I met somebody," Levi said.

Beth gave him all her attention. "Somebody new?"

"A nice girl."

Struck dumb, Beth stared at Levi for a long time. "Not the type you usually date?"

"Yeah."

"Why are you interested?"

Levi cleared his throat. "At first I felt sorry for her. She crashed a skateboard in front of the store, and I gave her a bandage."

"So, a clutzy, nice girl who rides a skateboard."

Levi lifted the bag of ice off his nose and sat up. "She's different from the other girls. She couldn't care less how good-looking I am."

"That *is* different." Beth grinned. "What else?"

"She doesn't flirt or try to impress me. She's just herself."

"And you probably find that behavior surprisingly refreshing and a bit unnerving at the same time."

"You use too many big words."

"Oh, shut up."

"I've never had to work this hard to get a girl to like me." Levi ran his hand through his hair. "And I don't know if I like it or hate it."

"The emotional roller coaster that we mortals experience all the time," Beth said. She rested her elbows on his knees and looked into his eyes. "You really want her to like you."

Nodding, he furrowed his brow. "Yeah, I do."

"And the uncertainty is killing you."

"Yeah."

Beth smiled and slapped him on the knee. "Good. It's about time you felt nervous about a girl."

"Some sympathetic sister you are."

"Of course I'm sympathetic. I picked you up from the bar, didn't I?"

"Yeah, thanks."

"This still doesn't explain why your preference in girls has suddenly changed."

"You use too many big words," Levi said.

"Answer me."

"Maybe I want to prove to her that not all guys like me are bad. That she doesn't have to be so suspicious of outsiders. Maybe deep down, I'm not a typical guy at all. Maybe at heart I'm still an Amish boy."

Beth raised an eyebrow. "You have more ties to the Amish than I do. I was only three when we left."

"I don't know if I'm anything like them anymore."

"You missed them when Mom married Dad. But you didn't want to feel out of place in the new environment, so you purposefully behaved badly to prove that you didn't belong with the Amish. Especially after Dad left."

Levi shook his head. Beth's logic made little sense to him. "Whatever."

"But I'm all for this new relationship. I'll do anything I can to help you ensnare this poor, unsuspecting girl."

"You will?" Levi said.

"For my brother, anything."

"Do you have a swimsuit I could borrow?"

"I don't think any of mine will fit you."

"I hope not," Levi said.

Chapter Eight

*Sorry about the text. I have to go to work. I found a swimsuit
for you. We are going boating next Monday after work. I will
pick you up at 4:00. Would you like to learn to water ski?*

* * * * *

Levi pulled his 1991 Toyota Celica to the designated meeting spot and
killed the engine. Rebecca insisted on a very strict list of protocols when
it came to their meetings. No engine humming, no horns, and for goodness' sake, no car in her driveway. Levi gazed down the lane and into the
thick growth of bushes that ran along the side of the road. No sign of her.

He almost turned on the radio but then thought better of it. No
noise. Instead, he sang a Muse song in his head and tapped on the
steering wheel to keep the beat. She wouldn't be long. If there was one
thing she wanted to avoid, it was detection. An Englisch boy sitting in
his car a few hundred yards from her house looked too suspicious.

Right on time, she darted through a space in the bushes and ran
to the driver's side of the car. Levi rolled down his window and handed
her Beth's swimsuit. Without a word, she snatched it out of his hand
and disappeared through the bushes again. He smiled to himself. No
precaution was too extreme. She wasn't about to be caught and forced
to give up their outings.

Neither was he. He hadn't expected to have this much fun with an
Amish girl. He contemplated all the places he wanted to take her. Time
to start thinking about another source of income.

She reappeared a few minutes later, draped head to ankle in a fluffy gray robe that was cinched and knotted at the waist with what looked like a black scarf. Clutching the collar around her neck like she wanted to strangle herself, she jumped into the passenger seat and motioned for Levi to drive away. That slight flick of her wrist meant "as fast as possible."

Levi started the car and wasted no time in putting some distance between them and Rebecca's house. "That was a quick change," he said.

"I have a toolshed."

Levi grinned at the cute, sort of panicked look on her face. She worried too much.

With every fence post they passed, Rebecca seemed to relax, but she never released her grip on the robe at her throat.

"Did the suit fit?" Levi asked, trying not to laugh at her discomfort.

"Jah, fine."

"Do you think I will get to see it on you before the day is out, kid?"

Rebecca rolled her eyes and adjusted the robe to cover more of her leg.

Actually exposing herself in that swimsuit might prove to be more of an adventure for Rebecca than waterskiing. Levi had picked the swimsuit of Beth's that had the most fabric—high at the neck and low at the bottom. He was smart enough to know that Rebecca would never agree to a bikini. And he had a great deal of respect for that.

"It might be a little cool in the water. It's still June," Levi said. "I brought you a big towel to wrap up in."

"Ach, I forgot a towel."

Levi stared straight ahead and cleared his throat. "There are going to be other people today. Three or four."

Out of the corners of his eyes, he saw Rebecca pull the robe up past her chin. "In your boat?" she said.

"I don't have a boat. It's my friend Ryan's. He said we could come."

Rebecca took a halting breath and held it for about three years.

"Hey, kid. We don't have to go. There's a swimming pool in Westby. Or the one in Sparta is nicer."

"Nae, I want to go. It will be fun."

Levi almost chuckled. He'd heard that endearing little phrase before. He glanced at her face and then at the road and then back at her again. Her telling expression made his heart swell about three times its normal size. "We really don't have to go."

"I want to go."

He didn't know what came over him, but he couldn't resist putting his hand on top of hers. Initially, she inched slightly away from his touch but seemed to change her mind and left her hand under his. Gratified, he smiled at her. "There. That isn't so bad, is it?"

A reluctant grin appeared on her lips. "Not so bad," she mumbled.

Levi caressed her silky fingers between his own and savored the sensation that coursed through his body. She was the first girl he could remember who invoked not only a strong physical response but a powerful emotional response, as well. What was going on with him?

Levi felt a bit uneasy, himself, about today's adventure. He had purposefully chosen Ryan to take him out on the water, not only because he had a boat, but also because he was the tamest of Levi's friends. Jason and Dax were hard-core drinkers and carousers who would, more likely than not, frighten Rebecca away. His other friends were more of the same. Levi had a different drinking buddy almost every night of the week.

And the girls… The girls were worse—the type you just had to look at to know they had a reputation. Not the kind of kids a nice girl associated with. A nice girl like Rebecca. Funny that Levi's choice of friends hadn't really made him uneasy before.

At least Levi had no fear of Tara making an unwelcome appearance. Ryan was bringing his girlfriend, Ellie, and inviting his newly married brother and his wife. There wasn't room in the boat for other skiers.

Ryan's boat, a small six-seater, was already on the water by the time Levi pulled into the parking lot overlooking the lake. He retrieved his cooler and towels from the trunk and motioned for Rebecca to come.

He reached out his hand to take hers, but she shook her head. "It is not proper in public," she said.

He squinted in her direction and smiled. Some of the notions she held made him scratch his head in confusion.

Ryan must have been watching for them, because he met them halfway to the shoreline, his dark tan evidence that he had already spent a good part of the young summer on the water. He took a gander at Rebecca in her weird cover-up before turning to Levi. "I hope you don't mind," he said. "Ellie invited a couple of friends, and they invited a couple of friends, and it turned into a beach party."

He pointed to the edge of the water by the trees where a couple dozen people had set up beach chairs and towels. Guys threw sticks into a blazing fire pit, and three or four others roasted hot dogs. A radio blared the latest rap song.

Levi groaned inwardly. One girl in a bikini lay flat on her stomach with the strap undone so she wouldn't have an unsightly tan line at the center of her back. Levi had seen it a hundred times before, but this time it annoyed him. Did she have to put it all out there for everybody to see? For Rebecca to see?

He hoped Rebecca hadn't noticed.

It didn't matter. If they proceeded down the beach, she'd see soon enough.

Levi glanced at Rebecca, who had waxed unusually pale in the bright afternoon sun.

Ryan laughed nervously when he saw both their faces. "We'll have to take turns on the boat, but the more the merrier, right? You don't mind, do you?"

To Levi's surprise, Rebecca chimed in. "No, we do not mind. Thank you for letting us ride on your boat."

Ryan's smile widened. "Brady's taken it out, but as soon as he comes back, you two are next." He turned and ran down the beach.

They watched him melt into the crowd at the beach party. "It's really okay if you want to go home, kid."

She took his arm as they walked slowly to the shore. "I am not leaving, bud."

He chuckled at her undaunted stubbornness. "Bud. It sounds like a tobacco-chewing hillbilly. I like it."

Rebecca's fingers tightened around Levi's arm as they got closer to the group of partyers. Curious eyes followed both of them. One guy pointed to Rebecca's robe and snickered with his friends. Levi knew most of the kids there, some from high school, some as friends of friends.

For the hundredth time since he'd met Rebecca, he sincerely regretted the reputation he had made for himself. If Levi Cooper was out with a new girl, everybody wanted to know who she was. They'd make assumptions about her not because of her behavior, but because of his. Levi Cooper only dated a certain type of girl.

As the staring intensified, he wanted to scream at all of them, *Don't you dare think those thoughts about Rebecca! She's a good girl. A nice, decent girl, and I don't deserve her.*

Levi turned his back on the crowd of onlookers and pinned Rebecca with a serious look. "I know you want to go waterskiing," he said, "but people are going to assume things about you because you're with me." He took several steps back the way they had come, and she followed him. "I've done a lot of things I regret, Rebecca, things I shouldn't have. I don't want anyone to think badly of you because you're with me. We should go."

Rebecca folded her arms and planted her feet in the sand. "I am not leaving."

"But I think it would be better for you—"

"I do not care what people think about me."

"I do," Levi said.

Rebecca glanced at the loud party behind Levi. "All Englisch boys fool around with the girls."

Levi shook his head. "That's not true. Some guys do control themselves."

She firmly took his elbow and pulled him farther from the party. But she hadn't decided to leave as Levi hoped. She decided to scold him.

"I try to take people at face value," she said. "Do you know what I see in you?"

Struck dumb, Levi shook his head.

"I see a kind heart and a boy who wants to do right but sometimes does not know how. Is that good enough for you?"

Levi looked out to the lake and cracked a smile. "You forgot to add 'a guy who knows how to ski.'"

In exasperation, she pounded on his chest then chased him around a log at the edge of the water. They laughed and splashed each other.

"Cum," she said, picking up one of the towels Levi had dropped. "Let's go meet your friends."

He again grew serious as he walked beside her. "I still wish I hadn't done those things," he said.

Without looking at him, she whipped the towel up and popped him in the face.

Chapter Nine

Ryan took his girlfriend Ellie's hand and helped her from the water. She squeaked and shivered, and Ryan quickly wrapped an oversized towel around her shoulders. "That was great," she said, her chin already vibrating violently. "Did you see how I caught air off that wake?"

"Way sweet," Ryan said. He hugged Ellie for a minute, rubbing his hands up and down her back to create friction. He guided her to a padded seat on one side of the boat and looked at her reassuringly. "You gonna be warm enough?"

Still shaking uncontrollably, Ellie nodded. "Give me a few minutes."

Ryan turned to Rebecca, cinched up in her life jacket and standing at attention in the very center of the boat. "You ready?"

Rebecca breathed in and out as if she were preparing for a deep-sea dive without oxygen.

"You get used to the water once you've been in for a few minutes," Ellie said.

"I'm good at getting skiers up," Ryan said. "My brother, on the other hand, yanks you up so fast, he about pulls your arms off."

Rebecca forced her grimace into a smile.

Levi came up behind her and stroked her arm gently. "You don't have to do this," he said, already knowing how she would respond to that suggestion.

"Right," said Ryan. "We can give Levi a turn."

Pasting on her cheerful face, Rebecca said, "No, I want to. It will be fun." Her tone of voice could have been referring to some painful medical procedure, for all the enthusiasm it held.

Ryan shrugged. "Okay, then, get in."

Levi guided her to the short ladder that hung over the side of the boat, and she stepped down it backward. When her foot touched the cold water, she squeaked in alarm, lost hold of the ladder, and plunged into the lake. She emerged, flailing her arms and blinking the water from her eyes. The panicked look, the labored breathing, the squeal she gave once her head surfaced from the water propelled Levi into action. He dove into the water, swam to Rebecca, and wrapped his arms firmly around her waist.

She threw her arms around his neck as if he were the only thing between her and a watery grave. "I can't touch the bottom," she said in breathless hysteria. "Don't—don't let go."

Levi tightened his grip around her, if that were possible. "I won't let go until you say. I promise."

"Don't let go."

"Look at my face, kid," Levi said. "Now take a slow, deep breath."

She did as she was told, although she still held on to his neck for dear life.

In the calmest voice he knew, he said, "This life jacket is the best one made. You can't drown when you've got this on. It's impossible." He kept eye contact with her so that she knew he was serious.

She nodded. "Okay."

"Kick your legs," Levi said.

She did.

"You see, just water below. No lake creatures to grab your feet and drag you under."

Rebecca breathed out. "Don't even mention creatures."

Levi loved that her clutching his neck put her face barely inches from his. Good thing the water was cold. It kept his mind off the tantalizing urge to kiss her. "Being surrounded by all this water can make you feel like you're going to be swallowed up. You're doing really good."

Levi glanced at the boat. Ellie and Ryan studied the two of them curiously but were doing their best not to gawk. Ryan was a good guy, patient and nonjudgmental. Levi didn't think either of them would mind the delay.

"Don't let go."

"Believe me, I will not let go until you say."

Still holding on for dear life, she gazed at him doubtfully until her breathing relaxed—a good two minutes. "Thank you for not letting go."

"Of course. I'm very trustworthy."

They bobbed up and down for a few more minutes. Her breathing returned to normal. "Okay, you can let go of me now," she said.

She instinctively tightened her grip around his neck as he released his hands from around her. "I can do this," she said.

Taking one serious look at him, she let her arms slip away. She half-sighed, half-squealed as she sank slightly before her life jacket buoyed her up.

"You're going to cramp up if you tighten your muscles," Levi said. "Try to relax. Think of sitting in a tub and reading your favorite book. Relax."

"The hot water is not working in this tub," Rebecca said, shivering.

Levi waited until she seemed accustomed to being in the vast body of water. "Are you ready to ski?"

"Jah, I am ready."

Levi motioned to Ryan, who slipped the water skis into the water next to Rebecca. Levi helped her get them on her feet, which they managed to do without dunking her under once. He retrieved the towrope and handed it to Rebecca. "Okay, kid. You remember how we showed you to sit with your knees bent and let the boat pull you up?"

"Yes, buster," she said.

Levi laughed. She was going to be all right.

Levi looked at Ryan. "She's ready."

"You'd better get in!" Ryan yelled back.

Levi glanced at Rebecca. "You okay?"

"It will be fun."

"Fun," Levi murmured as he swam back to the boat. "Fun like a root canal."

Once Levi settled into the boat, Ryan gave the signal to Rebecca who, with her fingers still wrapped around the towrope, gave him a thumbs-up to indicate that she was ready. No way was she releasing either hand from her lifeline.

The engine rumbled to life, and Ryan pulled the throttle slowly. The rope went taut and Rebecca slowly rose from the water but then quickly fell over the top of her skis and back into the water, keeping the towrope firmly in her fists. The boat dragged her, water pounding her face, until she got wise and let go of the rope. She came up sputtering and spitting but seemed no worse for the wear.

"If you fall, let go of the rope," Levi called.

"Thanks for the advice."

"Sit in the water and bend your knees right up to your chest." Ryan yelled. "Hold your arms out in front of you. Then relax and don't try to pull yourself up. Let me do that with the boat."

Rebecca dog-paddled back to her lost skis with the towrope in her fist. She put the skis back on her feet and signaled for Ryan to go again.

"You can do it, kid!" Levi yelled. He hated to see her so distressed. Why was she so dead-set on this?

Amazingly enough, she managed to stand on the skis for almost thirty seconds before falling spectacularly into the foamy water. This time she let go of the rope as soon as she hit the surface.

Ryan barked a few more instructions to Rebecca as she once again retrieved her skis.

The third time, with a look of complete concentration on her face, she managed to get on top of the water. Stiff as a board, but staying afloat, she plowed through the water tenaciously. Her ride lasted almost three minutes before she glanced up at Levi with a look of satisfaction and promptly wiped out.

She once again came up sputtering but this time smiling. Levi flexed his arm and realized he had been clutching the side of the boat as he watched her. Did she want to go up again? He didn't think his nerves could take it.

Ryan pulled the boat around to her. "Had enough?" he yelled.

Yes, Levi wanted to say. *At least* I've *had enough.* It was all he could do to sit still and not reach into the water and pull her out. What was she trying to do? Kill him?

"One more time, please," Rebecca said, shivering violently as she reattached the skis to her feet.

The last run, Rebecca popped out of the water like an expert and Ryan towed her around for almost ten minutes before she let go of the rope and glided into the water. She raised her arms in triumph just before she went down.

When he finally pulled her into the boat, Levi breathed normally for the first time in almost an hour.

She would be the death of him.

Chapter Ten

They sat together on the double-seated beach chair close to the fire. Levi had a towel wrapped casually around his shoulders while Rebecca leaned into the heat and held her hands out to the flames. She still shook hard enough to rattle her very bones, even with the thick gray robe wrapped around her. She sat as far away from Levi as she could in the wide chair, but she brushed against him now and then in her search for more heat.

Levi put his arm around her shoulder and tried to pull her close. She resisted. "I want to keep you from freezing to death, kid," he said. "You're going to crack your teeth, they're chattering so hard."

Was this a ploy to take advantage of her in a moment of weakness? Even though he was Englisch, he had proven himself trustworthy thus far. She relaxed against him and let him envelop her in his arms.

"Better?"

"Hmm," she admitted. "But do not kiss me."

He rested his chin against her forehead. "Kid," he said, "I want to kiss you every moment I'm with you. But, as you can see, I know how to control myself."

She patted him on the hand. "More like, I know how to make you behave yourself."

Slowly he traced the back of her hand with his thumb. "I want you to feel safe with me. I haven't always treated girls the way I should, but I want you to know that I would never do anything to hurt you or make you feel uncomfortable."

"I know," she said quietly.

Levi held her tighter.

Out on the water, she knew—knew—she could trust him. She had insisted on going out on the lake in the first place. He wasn't obligated to come to her rescue when she'd gotten herself into her own mess, but he jumped in and held on to her when he could have let go. She hadn't deserved his help, but he'd offered it anyway.

She looked at Levi—really looked at his face. His strong jawline revealed a determination to do anything he set his mind to, and his chocolate-brown eyes danced in the firelight with an intelligence and a warmth she hadn't really appreciated before. Had he changed that much since she first met him?

No. She had changed the way she looked at herself through him.

"Why that look on your face?" Rebecca said.

Levi rubbed his hand up and down her fleecy sleeve. "I'm thinking how lucky I am that you fell on that skateboard in front of my store. If you had fallen in front of the drugstore, Rex Gillis would be cuddling with you in this very seat and I'd probably be out on the boat with some girl who isn't you."

"You are using another line on me, Levi Cooper."

"I swear I'm not."

The sun slowly disappeared below the trees surrounding the lake. Two dozen boys and girls were on their little section of beach, some around the fire, some still messing around in the water. One girl had a guitar, and she strummed a few chords as two or three people helped her sing. All things considered, Levi said, a mellow party.

Rebecca wondered how much longer she could justify sitting here with the warmth of Levi's arms around her. She would be up late tonight, filling lamps and cleaning floors. And probably mucking out, unless Max decided for the first time in his life to do something without being told.

Levi shifted in his seat to get his arms farther around Rebecca. "You're not shivering anymore."

"Toasty warm."

"Did you like the waterskiing? You were pretty good."

Rebecca leaned her head against his shoulder. "I never have to do it again."

"I've heard that before. I wonder if there will ever be anything we do together that you'll want to do again."

"Don't you like to water-ski?" Rebecca said.

"I love to water-ski."

"But you didn't," Rebecca said.

"I had to be focused to keep you safe."

She went silent.

"But it was probably a good preparation for baptism. So you don't hyperventilate when you're dunked into the water," Levi said.

"There's not that much water. It gets poured onto your head."

"Oh. Sounds fun."

Rebecca sat up straighter and folded her arms. "Not really."

"You don't want to get baptized?"

She pulled her knees to her chin and wrapped her arms around her legs. "I do want to get baptized. I—I am simply not looking forward to it."

"That doesn't make sense."

"The bishop preaches that baptism represents a rebirth. We become new creatures in Christ." Rebecca glanced at him. "Ach, never mind."

"No, Rebecca, I want to hear."

Rebecca shook her head. "I am too selfish."

"This coming from the girl who hangs wash at midnight so her brothers will have something to wear the next day?"

Rebecca took a deep breath. He held on to her when he could have let go. "It is…. I feel in some ways, baptism will be like dying. When I am baptized, the walls of my house will close in on me while I watch my mother die and my fater drift further from the family. After baptism, I will be stuck in that life forever."

"Then why be baptized?"

"I want to pledge my life to God."

Levi leaned forward to look into her eyes. "That doesn't sound like the way God would want you to live the rest of your life, like you're stuck in prison."

"That's why I am making my own life right now. I want to feel feelings and have experiences before giving in. Then in the future when I am weighed down by my dull life or pain so severe that I can't crawl out of bed, I can say, *I really lived once.* Then it won't be so bad."

Levi looked at her with something akin to compassion. She didn't want his pity. She didn't want anything from him, did she? Except his skiing abilities.

A boy came near and offered them a can of beer. Levi shook his head. "No, thanks." Then he turned to Rebecca. "Unless you want to."

"Nae," she said.

"Not on your list of things to do before you die?"

"Eating mud is also not on my list," Rebecca said.

"You'll get no argument from me on that one," Levi said. "Most definitely not worth the headache in the morning."

She looked up at him. "You've done a lot of drinking in your life, haven't you?"

"I've done a lot of things I regret." Levi stared at the fire. "Drinking helps to dull my guilty conscience, I guess."

She couldn't resist. She ran the back of her fingers along the stubble of his jaw. "You are holding a lot of pain in there," she said.

"I'm responsible for my own mistakes. Nobody else."

"You don't have to carry it. Jesus will carry it if you give it to Him."

"It's my burden, not His, Rebecca."

"Everything is His burden. You are one of His sheep."

"I'm a lost cause," Levi said.

Rebecca didn't want him to believe that for one more minute. "There are no lost causes."

Levi shook his head.

In alarm, she took his face between her hands. "There are no lost causes."

Their faces were inches apart, and Rebecca felt the intensity in his eyes to her very bones. How could anyone go so low as to think they were lost to God?

Levi put his hands over hers, smiled, and made light of her comment. "Don't kiss me," he said.

The spell broke, and she withdrew her hands. "No kissing," she said, growling in exasperation.

As the sky darkened, the bright fire obscured their surroundings, but Rebecca didn't miss Levi's dumbstruck expression when a thin blond stepped into the light of the flames and came right up to them. Levi recovered and glued an indifferent frown on his face.

"Hey, Levi," the girl said, smiling like the cat who ate the canary while keeping her eyes glued to Rebecca.

Rebecca could feel the muscles in Levi's arm tense. "Hey, Tara," he said.

Tara held hands with a tall boy with hair so black that it shimmered in the firelight. He wore a substantial diamond stud earring in his left ear. Tara pulled her boyfriend closer and whispered something into his ear.

By the set of her jaw and the way she opened her eyes too wide when she spoke, Rebecca could tell that Tara was not pleased with what she saw. An old girlfriend? Rebecca did her best to smile.

Tara motioned to the boy next to her. "This is Shadow," she said. "He's from Chicago."

"Hey," Levi said, his manner discouraging any sort of conversation.

Tara stared at Levi as if she were expecting something from him. "Well," she said, "who's your new girl?"

Rebecca couldn't help but detect the nastiness in her voice. Definitely an old girlfriend. Very pretty. Just the kind of girl Rebecca imagined Levi would be with. Rebecca folded her arms tightly around her waist.

"This is Rebecca. Rebecca, this is Tara."

"You didn't go to our high school," Tara said.

"No," Levi said.

Rebecca and Levi had already discussed it. If they could avoid revealing to anyone that she was Amish, they would do it. If the knowledge of any of her outings got back to Fater, that would be the end of them. Rebecca had insisted that they not lie to anyone, but they didn't have to volunteer any information, either.

Tara plopped on the ground in front of Rebecca and pulled Shadow with her. Then she scrutinized Rebecca's face.

"Where're you from?" Tara said.

"She's from around here," Levi said.

Undeterred, Tara turned to face Levi so her body language completely shut Rebecca out of the conversation. "Oh, she's a deaf mute who can't speak for herself?"

"I can talk," Rebecca said.

"Oh, good," Tara said, returning her attention to Rebecca, "I thought maybe you were too shy. What's your name again?"

"Rebecca Miller."

"Rebecca. You go waterskiing?"

"Yes," Rebecca replied. "It was fun."

Levi tried to divert Tara's attention. "Tara's a great snow skier. She works at a resort in the winter, teaching skiing lessons. She wins races all the time."

"Congratulations," said Rebecca.

Tara stayed on course. "I hang out with Levi a lot, but he's never mentioned you. How long have you been going out?"

"Five weeks or so," Rebecca said, trying to be friendly in the face of an obvious attack.

Tara counted the days in her head. It took her a few seconds. Then she glared at Levi. "You didn't waste any time, did you?"

The muscles in Levi's jaw flexed and the arm around Rebecca's shoulders tightened its viselike grip.

Leaning closer, Tara tried to assume the demeanor of an excited girl wanting to hear some juicy gossip. "So, how did you meet each other?"

"She was on a skateboard—"

"I asked Rebecca, Levi," Tara said. "Man, you can be so overbearing sometimes."

Rebecca slipped her hand into Levi's. "I was riding a skateboard and fell in front of the sporting goods store where Levi works. I hurt my leg, and he drove me home."

Tara studied Rebecca and a lightbulb seemed to go off in Tara's brain. "You're from Apple Lake," she said.

"Yes…yes," Rebecca stuttered, her heart plunging to the ground with the smug look Tara gave her.

"Are you Amish?" Tara asked, her eyes almost bugging out of her head.

Rebecca nodded.

Tara burst into uncomfortable laughter, and her companions sat staring at her until she spoke again. "I recognize the accent," Tara said, very pleased with herself. "We have an Amish lady who cleans house for us sometimes."

They heard Shadow's voice for the first time. "You're Amish? That's cool."

Tara got the giggles and couldn't stop laughing. "What exactly are you going for with this one, Levi?"

"Shut up, Tara," Levi said.

Grabbing Shadow's hand, she stood up and brushed the sand off her swimsuit—still giggling. "If you only knew how ironic that is on so many levels." As she walked away, she waved her hand in Levi's direction. "Watch out for this one. He has trouble with permanent relationships."

Tara stumbled away as her laugh turned angry and spiteful.

Rebecca took a deep breath, let the tension dissipate, and sank back into Levi's arms like she was relaxing into an overstuffed sofa. "That was your old girlfriend, wasn't it?"

"Sorry. She's bitter. But it's nothing personal against you. I broke up with her a few days before I met you. I was even planning on getting back together with her."

"You told me you wanted to make a few girls jealous."

"Tara mostly, but you reeled me in until I didn't know which way was up."

Rebecca smiled and made herself comfortable in Levi's arms. "No manure."

Levi laughed. "How can I make you believe my sincerity?"

"You can't." She closed her eyes and rested her head on his shoulder.

"Tired?" he said.

"Got to get back," she mumbled. "Lots of chores before Fater comes home on Friday."

Levi took his finger and traced the curve of Rebecca's face. She didn't even try to stifle the sensation that accompanied his touch. "That is an aggravatingly plump and puffy robe," he said.

"Uh-huh," she said, too drowsy to form the actual words with her lips.

"You are so pretty," he said.

"Don't kiss me," she mumbled, before she drifted out of consciousness.

She heard him growl—a low, guttural sound deep in his throat. "The death of me," he muttered.

Nudging her until she roused sufficiently to hold herself up, Levi separated himself from all physical contact. "Come on," he said. "Let's get you home safe."

Chapter Eleven

Wednesday morning. Three full days before Fater came home for the weekend. Rebecca mentally made a list of chores for the day. If she could convince Linda to do the laundry and the boys to clean the stalls, she might have enough time to thin the peaches and bake the bread in addition to her daily chores. A full eighteen hours ahead of her gave her hope for a productive day.

Max and Danny were lollygagging by the barn, each holding an empty pail for the milk. She could usually convince them to do the daily milking because they saw how the cows suffered if they neglected their job. But the two of them seemed to be in no hurry today, as they took turns swinging their buckets over their heads to see how far they could send the buckets into the air.

Rebecca hurried to Mamm's room, where she cleared the breakfast tray off the bed and fluffed the pillows. Her mother smiled gratefully and then closed her eyes to concentrate on the pain. "Laundry day," Mamm said.

"Jah."

"Send Linda in."

Seven in the morning, and Linda lay in the bed like a spoiled princess. "Linda," Rebecca said, standing in the doorway and studying the lump in the bed that was her sister. The lump stirred and sighed. "Linda, I know you are awake. Mamm wants you."

Linda stretched and groaned. "What does she want?"

"She wants you."

Rebecca didn't wait to hear arguments or excuses. There was

too much to be done today to wait around for a slothful sister. She marched to the kitchen, filled the sink, and dispatched the breakfast dishes with all due haste. She wiped the table and the cupboards, swept the floor, and spot-mopped the sticky places. Better mop again tonight after supper.

Just as she drained her dishwater, she saw Linda, in her slippers, amble down the hallway with a pile of clothes in her arms. She yawned loudly and made her way into the mudroom where the washer stood. Rebecca did not smile or cheer or jump up and down for her sister, but it was gratifying to see that Linda could still be prevailed upon to get up and work.

A knock on the door inspired more irritation than curiosity. Rebecca had too much to do to be interrupted today.

When she opened the door, she couldn't have been more astonished than if Saint Peter had been floating there. Levi Cooper stood on her porch wearing a bright blue shirt with suspenders, black trousers, work boots, and a big straw Amish hat. He looked more Amish than her brothers usually did. What in the world was he up to?

"Hullo, Rebecca," he said, tipping his hat.

In a panic, Rebecca looked behind her then pushed him backward as she stepped outside and quickly closed the door. "What do you think you are doing here?" she whispered. "Somebody will see you."

He didn't lose the grin. "Well, Miss Miller, that is precisely the point. Why do you think I dressed like this?"

"You will ruin everything."

"No, no, I came to help you. Anyone driving by will see an Amish boy on an Amish farm doing Amish chores. Isn't the outfit good enough?"

Rebecca stood with her mouth wide open. He had rendered her momentarily speechless. "The...the clothes...they are...gute." She got her wits about her and pointed to the road. "You march back home right now, Levi Cooper." She still whispered loudly. "I can't tell my family you are an Amish boy."

Levi still insisted on unabashed cheerfulness. "You don't have to tell them anything. They'll draw their own conclusions." He looked down at himself. "So you like the clothes?"

Rebecca wanted to laugh and cry at the same time. It was just like Levi to pull such a stunt, but what did he mean by showing up at her door dressed in Amish clothes at seven thirty in the morning?

He took one of her hands. "The car is parked about a mile down the road in front of an Englischer's house. No one has to know I drove it."

Rebecca paced back and forth and tried to think. "Why are you here?"

"I came to help with your chores so you won't fall asleep on every date. I'm starting to get a complex about my ability to be entertaining."

She stared at him. What strange dream had she landed in? "You came to help with the chores?"

Levi took a step toward her. "Wednesday is my day off. I came so you could put me to work. I want to help."

"Help me? Why?"

He smiled warmly. "Isn't it obvious?"

She hadn't realized he'd kept one hand behind his back until he produced a long-stemmed red rose and held it out for her. Without hesitation she took it and buried her nose in the silky burgundy petals. How did he know she had a weakness for roses?

"It is beautiful," she said.

"I thought of you when I saw it. I hope it doesn't make you feel uncomfortable. I didn't know if Amish people could get flowers or not."

Rebecca looked away. "No one has ever given me a flower before."

"Does that upset you?"

"Nae, I—I love it." She rubbed the rose against her cheek and smiled at him. "You caught me by surprise, that is all. I didn't expect…"

He took her hand, and she immediately lost her train of thought. "You deserve a rose every day," he said.

He squeezed her arm then clapped his hands together. "Now that I've softened you up, kid, put me to work." He surveyed the barn, the garden, and the yard. "What needs to be done around here?"

"I am not putting you to work," she insisted. "This is ridiculous. You are leaving now."

"Give me a good reason why."

Rebecca tried to shoo him off the porch like a stray cat. "Because if my fater finds out—"

"If your dad finds out, all he'll know is that some Amish boy not from the district came to help Rebecca with her chores."

"And he will forbid it."

Levi threw up his hands. "Then you won't be any worse off than you are now, and he still won't know that I am secretly an Englischer dating his daughter."

Rebecca tried not to crack a smile. She wasn't about to give in yet. "And my mamm and brothers and sister?"

"If I make it easier for them, do you really think they are going to tell your dad? They don't have to lie about it, either. They can conveniently forget to tell him that some boy—again, not from your district—helps with the chores." Levi tapped his foot against the porch pillar. "It's a perfect plan."

She folded her arms and eyed him sternly, but she had already surrendered, and he could tell. "Where did you get those clothes?" she said.

Levi sauntered down the porch steps. "I think I'll mow the lawn if you'll tell me where the mower is."

"It is in the toolshed," she said, pointing to the far side of the barn. She paused. "You didn't steal them off a clothesline, did you?"

Amused at some private joke, Levi thumbed his suspenders. "They were my dat's," he said.

"Your dat's? What are you talking about, Levi Cooper?"

Levi winked. "If you are nice and don't give me any more trouble about being here, I might be persuaded to let you in on my secret."

He turned and left her standing on the porch, clutching her rose, with her mouth wide open. Collecting her scattered wits, she went back inside and slammed the door behind her.

What went on in that boy's brain was a true mystery.

Chapter Twelve

While she kneaded the dough, Rebecca tried to keep her eyes from wandering to the large kitchen window. Levi, perfectly framed between the two panes, sat on the grass tinkering with the lawn mower while Danny, enamored with the presence of a stranger, stood over him watching his every move. Rebecca couldn't hear the conversation, but she guessed Danny had offered suggestions on how to fix the rickety old thing. Levi smiled and nodded and acted as if Danny were the greatest companion in the world for a guy who had to repair the mower before he could cut the lawn.

Levi said something to Danny and Rebecca's little brother took off across the lawn like he was running a footrace. He soon returned with a wrench and a screwdriver. Levi pulled Danny over to sit next to him, and soon the two of them were fiddling busily and laughing and talking as if they had always been friends. Max, true to form, was nowhere to be seen.

There was still hope for Danny. He just needed a little encouragement, maybe someone to show some faith in him. A mentor, a big brother. Rebecca turned from the window. Danny needed a father.

The long-stemmed rose, in a small vase, stood tall on the vast expanse of the kitchen table where Rebecca had placed it. She went to the table and inhaled the sweet fragrance of her flower. She thought of Dottie Mae. No one had ever given her best friend a rose. And she had deserved thousands of them.

After separating the dough into loaves, Rebecca set the bread on the counter to rise. Hearing the halting *putt-putt* of a motor, she looked out the window. Danny pumped his fists in the air and cheered as Levi pushed the mower around the yard. The engine produced a steady hum, not the coughing, choking sound it usually made, and no white smoke puffed from the carburetor.

So, Levi was handy. Did she dare ask him to fix the broken door on the barn or the wobbly buggy wheel? She didn't want to impose on him like that. His being here was a gift. Let him do whatever he wanted to do today.

Linda came padding into the kitchen, no doubt completely worn out from filling the washtub. Dropping crumbs on Rebecca's clean cupboard, she cut herself a piece of bread and plopped a healthy dollop of strawberry freezer jam onto her slice. As she took a sizable bite, something out the window caught her eye.

"*Oh, sis yuscht!*" she murmured. "Oh, sis yuscht!" Laying her bread on the cupboard, she hurried to the window for a better look. "Who is that?" she said in awe, as if she were looking at an angel from heaven.

Rebecca turned her back and pretended to busy herself with the bread dough. "Who?" she said indifferently.

"That handsome boy mowing our lawn."

Rebecca didn't turn around. "Oh, him. He is a—"

Linda seized Rebecca's arm and pulled her to the window. "Do you see?" she said. "That boy. Do you see him?"

"Jah."

Linda rested her forehead against the window. "Oh, Rebecca. Oh, Rebecca. He is handsome. Look how tall he is. Look at the muscles."

She gazed longingly at Levi for a full minute before grabbing Rebecca by the shoulders and shaking her excitedly. "Who is he? Do you know him?"

Rebecca was sorely tempted to tease her sister and plead ignorance, but instead she said, "He is a friend of mine. He came to help with the chores."

Linda turned back to the window. "A friend? Why didn't you ever tell me about this friend? Oh, Rebecca, he is—well, you have eyes to see."

"Jah, he is very handsome."

"How do you know him?"

"I met him in Patton."

Linda glued her eyes to the good-looking boy happily mowing the grass, until, starting from her trance, she smoothed the wrinkles of her dress. "I must get out there and…hang laundry."

Rebecca propped her hands on her hips. "You'd better wash it first."

"Jah. But how long will he be here?"

"All day, he says."

Linda bolted for the mudroom. "I will hurry." She stopped and smoothed the creases of her apron. "How do I look?"

Amused, Rebecca folded her arms and looked at Linda head to toe. "Different shoes. And comb your hair. It is sticking out of your kapp."

Linda nodded seriously and disappeared. Another advantage of Levi's presence—Linda might actually finish the laundry. Rebecca smiled in spite of herself.

When next she looked out the window, Danny pushed the lawn mower while Levi headed to the barn.

What did he plan now? Rebecca scolded herself and retrieved the bathroom cleaning supplies from the cupboard. She'd get nothing done all day if she kept checking on Levi. Resolving not to take one more peek out the window, Rebecca hurried down the hall to scrub the toilets.

A half hour later, Max ambled into the bathroom. With his hands in his pockets, he leaned against the doorjamb and watched Rebecca scrub the tub.

"That boy wants to know where he should dump the manure when he is finished mucking out the barn," Max said, with his devil-may-care attitude.

Rebecca sat up on her heels and brushed an errant lock of hair from her face. "Tell him to spread it in the corn. You can show him the corn rows?"

"Jah, I guess."

"Gute."

Max didn't seem to be inclined to go anywhere, so Rebecca went back her scrubbing.

"Why is he here?" Max said.

Rebecca dipped her sponge into her bucket of water. "He is helping with the chores."

"He is a pest."

"A pest?"

"And he cannot hardly find the words in *Deitsch*. Like he never learned to speak it gute."

Rebecca had to fight hard to hide her astonishment. Levi's father owned a set of Amish clothes and Levi spoke the old language? What exactly was going on? "He is not from Apple Lake. Maybe you do not understand his accent."

"He said he loves to milk cows, but then he didn't do it right. I made him stop and finished by myself. What boy does not know how to milk properly?"

Rebecca kept her face expressionless while she wiped down the walls of the tub. "You finished the milking?"

"Jah, the pails are in the kitchen. He is gute with cleaning out the stalls, but he thinks he knows more about the horse than I do." Rebecca wiped the tub dry, and Max sat on the edge of it. "He says if the stall is not mucked out better, Frankie will get sick. Does he think I don't know how to care for our own horse?"

"He has worked at a stable," Rebecca said. "You would do well to listen to what he says. He cares about the health of the animals."

"So do I," Max said. "I love that horse better than anything."

"Then you best take better care of him so Levi doesn't have to scold you."

"I am not a child. I know how to take care of the horse," Max mumbled.

Rebecca didn't let Max sidetrack her. She sprayed the sink and cupboard and let him do some thinking.

"And then he asked me to fetch the horse brush and soap. I am not his servant."

"Frankie's coat could use a good brushing," Rebecca said, her cheerful tone sending the message that she wasn't going to be persuaded to feel sorry for Max.

"Frankie is our horse. I can brush him."

Rebecca pinned Max with a skeptical eye. "And how long has it been since you brushed him?"

Max looked away guiltily then stood up. "I'll let that boy muck out the stalls. I am going to brush." He left the bathroom and was halfway down the hall when she heard him say, "I can do a better job than anybody on my own horse."

Rebecca almost laughed out loud. Levi was a genius.

For dinner, they ate outside under the big cherry tree in the backyard.

All but Mamm. Today had been a bad day. Rebecca served her lunch in bed and rubbed her legs while she ate. Mealtime was a challenge. Mamm didn't want to eat. Everything tasted like sawdust, she said—but Rebecca wouldn't let Mamm waste away if she had anything to say about it.

Mamm had not even been aware of Levi's presence. The curtains in her bedroom stayed closed all day to block out the light and help her rest. Rebecca knew she had been very lucky. Mamm's curiosity would not be a good thing.

Levi popped the last of his cheese and mayonnaise sandwich into his mouth and chewed with more enjoyment than the sandwich deserved. "Delicious, Rebecca," he said. "I love mayonnaise."

Rebecca gave him an apologetic smile. "I ran out of tuna fish. And lunch meat. The meal would have been better." What she didn't say was that she had no more money to buy groceries until Fater came home on Friday. The week's food supply was always rather thin because the money for groceries and prescriptions and doctors only went so far. The next two days, her family would eat whatever she could scrounge up from the canned goods in the cellar.

"We never have tuna fish, Rebecca," Danny said. "I love tuna fish."

"Hush, Danny. Finish your sandwich."

Levi frowned but didn't say what he was thinking.

Max sat next to Danny, sullenly eating his sandwich but glancing at Levi from time to time. He'd finished brushing Frankie. He'd even helped Levi spread manure in the corn. Rebecca couldn't remember a day when her brother accomplished so much. Still, he made it clear that the presence of a strange boy on the farm displeased him.

Linda sat close to Levi on the blanket, but he didn't seem to notice. She didn't take her eyes off his face for the entire meal and giggled at every word that came out of his mouth. Rebecca didn't know whether to feel amused or annoyed. Levi acted as if Linda's behavior was an everyday occurrence, and Rebecca had to admit that it probably was. A boy like Levi couldn't escape being fawned over by every silly girl in the vicinity.

The good news was, Linda had run the wash with blinding speed and spent a great deal of time and care in hanging the clothes on the line. One of Max's shirts ended up in the dirt with two or three socks when Linda diverted her attention from the laundry to gaze at the handsome boy repairing the hinges on the barn door. Still, what usually took Linda all day to accomplish was completed before noon. Rebecca couldn't help but be pleased.

Levi gulped down his ice water and handed his glass to Linda. "Could I ask for one more glassful?"

Linda leaped from the blanket. "Jah, I will be right back."

They watched her run to the house.

"Thank you for all your work," Rebecca said.

He shook his head. "No thanks necessary. It's been really fun. I had almost forgotten." He knocked Danny's hat off his head and mussed his hair.

"Hey!" Danny protested before snatching his hat and placing it back on his head.

Levi spread his legs in front of him and leaned back on his hands. "What can I help you with, Rebecca?"

"You have already helped so much."

"I've made a list of things I think need to be done around here," Levi said. "But I want to know what you want done. You run this operation."

"I do not want to impose."

Levi held out his hands. "Impose? What kind of a thought is that? I'm here. Use me."

Rebecca stifled a grin. "I am thinning peaches next."

"I don't know how to do that," Levi said. "You'll have to give me lessons."

Rebecca nodded.

"What else?" Levi said.

Sighing, Rebecca recited her list. "Garden weeded, peaches thinned, bathrooms finished, furniture dusted, lamps and propane tanks filled."

Levi threw back his head and looked to the sky. "I'm almost sorry I asked."

"Jah, I knew you would be."

Levi tossed a crumb of bread at Max's head. Max looked up with lidded eyes. "What?"

"Have you guys ever used a power sprayer?" Levi said.

Max took another bite of his sandwich. "What is it?"

"It shoots a stream of water out of a hose and washes stuff down really good," Levi said. "Next week I'll borrow my friend's power sprayer and we'll spray the peeling paint off the barn."

"What good will that do?" Max asked.

"You are coming next week?" Rebecca said.

"Then we can put a new coat of paint on that barn."

"That sounds fun," Danny said. "What would the bishop think if we painted it a crazy color like orange?"

"It looks like it used to be white," Levi said.

"I like blue," Max said.

Levi sobered and studied Rebecca's face. "Do you think you can get some paint? It's expensive."

Rebecca blushed. "Jah, my uncle is in construction. He can get some for cheap. Or he might have some left over from a job."

"Okay," Levi said, brightening. "You pick the color, and we'll get it ready for painting next week."

Linda came back with the water for Levi. "You want to paint the barn?"

"Fater will be so happy," Danny said.

"That's why we don't want him to know anything about me or the power sprayer," Levi said, winking at Rebecca. "He's got to be completely surprised."

"Okay," agreed Danny.

Levi pinned Max with a stern look. "And you?"

"I won't tell," Max said.

Linda smiled flirtatiously. "Me either."

Levi leaned back on his elbows. "There are several side boards that need repair. I can help Max with those. You probably know that barn better than anybody, Max."

Max didn't look happy about being drafted for a job, and he nodded grudgingly. "Jah, okay."

Levi jumped up and clapped his hands together. "Do you guys like McDonald's?"

That got Max's attention. "The hamburger place?"

"Yes," said Levi. "How about I go get McDonald's for supper tonight?"

"Oh, sis yuscht!" Danny yelled. "I have only eaten there once."

Rebecca felt the blood drain from her face, and she hung her head. "We cannot afford—"

"My treat," Levi said, taking her hand and pulling her up from the blanket. "But," he said, "I buy only if Danny and Max weed the garden before supper."

Max groaned, but Danny jumped up and down like the twelve-year-old he was. "Come on, Max. Let's go, let's go."

"And Rebecca has to approve your work," Levi said. "So do a good job."

Danny was halfway to the toolshed when Max slowly stood and brushed the crumbs off his pants. He pointed an accusing finger at Levi. "You do not have to trick me into doing work. I would have weeded anyway."

With all the bravado he could muster, Max walked away from Levi and yelled at Danny to fetch him some gloves and a hoe. Levi smiled and winked at Rebecca, who couldn't help a soft giggle escaping her lips. Max didn't know it, but up against Levi, he was fighting a losing battle.

Chapter Thirteen

Just after five o'clock Levi appeared in the lane, carrying three large McDonald's bags. Rebecca watched from her place at the window as Danny, whooping and hollering, ran to Levi and took one of the bags from him. Levi grinned and, catching sight of Rebecca at the window, raised the bags in triumph as he approached.

Rebecca still puzzled at his behavior. Surely Levi had better things to do than slave away at the Miller farm all day. He had repaired the lawn mower, fixed the hinge on the barn door, mucked out the stalls, cleaned and oiled the buggy, patched holes in the barn siding, thinned peaches, and helped to weed the garden—all this on top of the chores he had convinced Linda and the boys to finish. Never had so much work been done in a single day. Rebecca wanted to weep for joy. Perhaps she would get to bed before midnight.

She ran outside with the picnic blanket and spread it on the lawn. Max and Linda must have been watching for Levi because they appeared in the yard before she even called them. Levi grinned as he clutched his bags of food.

"We're eating outside again?" Max said.

"Jah," Rebecca said, kicking off her shoes and sinking to the blanket. "Then the kitchen will stay clean."

That was true. No dinner dishes was good reason to eat out on the grass. But outdoor dining also meant Mamm wouldn't catch a whiff of the five large cartons of french fries.

Rebecca had made Mamm some potato soup and served it to her before Levi's return. Mamm wasn't expecting McDonald's.

Levi knelt on the blanket and pulled food from the bags the way the Englisch Santa might pull gifts from his red sack.

"Who wants a Big Mac?" Levi said.

"What is it?" Danny asked.

Levi's eyes got big. "A Big Mac is like food from heaven," he said. "Two meat patties and cheese. The best."

"I'll have a Big Mac!" Danny yelled.

"Here," Levi said, pulling another burger and fries from the bag. "Max, you take a Big Mac too. You'll love it. And I bought enough fries so everybody could have their own. My sister and I used to fight over who ate more than their fair share. It was usually me."

Max took the burger, trying hard to hide his eagerness. Linda chose a chicken sandwich.

Levi handed the bag to Rebecca. "You get everything else," he said.

"Ach, no, Levi. Do you think I am a pig?" Rebecca took some fries and a double cheeseburger and gave the bag back to Levi. "Two more burgers in there," she said. "You have them."

Smiling, Levi pulled out another Big Mac and rolled the top of the bag down. "To keep that last burger warm," he said. "When you're ready to eat it."

Danny stuffed about ten french fries into his mouth at once while attempting to talk. "I lub fffench fies," he said.

"Not so fast, Danny," Rebecca said. "You'll choke."

Max polished off his burger in about seven bites. "Is there any more?" he said.

Rebecca grabbed the sack with the extra burger. "You can have this."

Levi tried to snatch the bag from her hands. She giggled and passed it to Max.

"One of us must go hungry, I suppose," she said.

Levi produced the third bag from behind him. "Never fear, I brought dessert." He dumped the contents into the center of the blanket. Five apple pies and five boxes of cookies.

Danny screamed with glee and grabbed one of each.

"Careful," Levi said, "the pies are hot."

Everybody dived into the food, Rebecca noted, like they hadn't eaten well in a long time. And they hadn't. The only time she felt full was when she ate with Levi on a date.

Danny finished the last bite of his apple pie and fell back on the blanket. Putting his hands to his stomach, he groaned softly. "I am so full, I'm going to die."

"Do you want the rest of your fries?" Max said, pointing to Levi's half-full carton.

"Go for it," Levi said.

"Should we play volleyball after?" Danny asked, flat on his back and looking up at the sky.

Levi picked up a fry Max had overlooked and handed it to Rebecca. "I would like to, but I have to be at my job pretty soon. Maybe next week."

"I thought you didn't work on Wednesdays," Rebecca said.

"I got a second job."

Linda munched her cookies daintily while staring persistently at Levi. Her persistence had lasted all day. "Where do you live?" she said. "Why haven't we ever seen you before?"

Levi didn't let the question derail him. He must have been expecting it. "I live on the other side of town. We just moved into our new place."

"So will we see you at the gatherings?"

"The gatherings? I've never been invited. When do you have them?"

"Every week. In the summer sometimes two or three times a week."

Levi's eyes twinkled mischievously. "That sounds like fun. Will you and Rebecca take me?"

Rebecca shook her head in disbelief.

"Can you come on Sunday?" Linda said.

Levi cleared his throat, most likely to hide the laugh Rebecca knew was hidden behind his eyes. "I can't come on Sunday, but I'll go home and ask my mother if she can spare me some other day."

"Okay," Linda said, grabbing Rebecca's arm. "We really want you to come, don't we, Rebecca?"

Rebecca could not muster her sister's enthusiasm for such a scheme, but she also knew that Levi was teasing her behind Linda's back.

Levi gathered all the trash into a bag and handed it to Danny. "Will you go throw this away?"

Danny took off to the trash bin.

Max stood and hooked his thumbs under his suspenders. "Denki for the McDonald's. It tasted gute."

Levi nodded, and Max sauntered to the house.

Gratitude. That was a new development.

Levi Cooper, miracle worker.

Levi stood, took both of Rebecca's hands, and pulled her to her feet. His hands lingered on hers a moment longer than necessary. "I'm sorry I can't stay and do something about that buggy wheel. Maybe next week."

"Do not give it a second thought. You have done so much already."

"Will you walk me down the lane? I want you to show me the pasture."

Linda's smile faded. She hadn't let Levi out of her sight all day. She'd even insisted on thinning peaches with them after the noon meal, which was her least favorite job on the farm. She slumped her shoulders and put on the pathetic expression she used when she wanted Rebecca to feel sorry for her. "I will go check on Mamm," Linda said, trudging toward the house with little enthusiasm.

Rebecca folded the blanket and laid it on the porch steps. Then she and Levi walked toward the pasture.

"I'll bring the power sprayer next week, and then we can paint," he said. "Or we can put off the painting until autumn. That will make it less likely your father will find out about me. At least for a while."

"I do not think we will have that much time. Linda is probably spilling the beans to Mamm right now."

"All your mom will know is that an Amish boy came to help with the chores today. Will she object to that?"

"Nae, but my fater will."

Levi stopped walking and took Rebecca by the shoulders. "Then you'll have to manage things with your mom. She must know how badly you need the help." He was more somber than Rebecca had ever seen him. "She can't expect you to carry the burden of the farm and the house all by yourself. Could you convince her that it is for your family's good not to tell your father?"

"I could try, but she will not feel right about keeping secrets from Fater."

Levi swore under his breath then glanced at Rebecca. "Sorry. Bad habit. But do you have to…?" He didn't finish that thought. "I wish it weren't so hard for you here. They work you to the bone and you get no appreciation."

"I can manage."

Levi took off his hat and ran his fingers through his hair. "What about your Amish neighbors? I know from personal experience how kind they are. They help each other with medical bills and farming and everything. Why won't anybody help you?"

"My fater refuses the help. He thinks it is his Christian duty to care for his own."

"*His* duty?" Levi raised his voice. "He's not doing his duty. *You're* doing his duty."

"Please. I do not want to talk about my fater."

This comment seemed to anger him more than anything else. "Good," he said, "because a problem usually gets solved by not talking about it."

Rebecca broke away from his side and sat on a low stone wall at the edge of the pasture. "I cannot change my fater, Levi. I can either bang my head against the wall every morning or accept what is." She pulled him over to sit next to her. "I accept what is."

"Not me. I like to bang my head against the wall."

"Jah, I can tell there is some brain damage."

"Yep, brain damage."

She studied his face. Did she really want him to know what was in her heart?

Jah, her heart was safer with Levi than anyone else in the world. "I am a wicked girl because, truth be told, I do not want Fater's help. I am happier when he is away."

"You have more freedom."

"I would never be allowed out to see you if he were always at home. And in his mind, I cannot do anything right. The first thing he does when he walks through the door on Friday night is find fault. At least I do not have to hear his criticisms every day."

Levi put his arm around her shoulder. "How could he ever find fault with you? You're perfect."

She couldn't face the honesty in his eyes. "Nae," she said, turning her head away. "No one is perfect. Least of all me."

"I'm sorry I got mad. I'm trying to watch out for you, since nobody else does."

Rebecca sniffed once. "What is it about you that forces me to confess all my wickedness? You know about my fater, my baptism, the skateboarding."

He grinned. "Your secrets are safe with me."

Jah, she knew they were.

With her hand comfortably in his, they continued their stroll through the pasture. Rebecca recovered some of her composure. "A thank-you isn't enough for what you have done today."

"I wanted to come. I'd muck out a hundred barns to be near you."

"You are shoveling manure at me, Levi Cooper."

"Not at all, kid. You're like my porch light, and I'm the moth. I'm naturally drawn to you."

Still walking along, she nudged him so that he lost his balance and tripped into a deep furrow in the pasture. He regained his footing, and they both laughed.

"Okay, okay," he said. "I surrender."

"I have done all the confessing today," Rebecca said. "Now I want to hear your confession."

He grinned. "Um, okay. I get stinking drunk three nights a week.

I have a bad reputation with girls. I forgot to say my prayers this morning. And I don't make my bed. But I've never tried a cigarette, and I'm very good to my mom and my sister, and…" He paused significantly. "I'm thinking of becoming a former drunk. Is that good enough?"

"Do not fool with me, Levi."

"I'm not fooling. I'm a bad guy, Rebecca."

"I want to know about the Amish fater and the Deitsch."

"Jah, I thought you would," he said in Pennsylvania Dutch with a decent accent.

They halted in their progress again when he leaned against a fence post and stared out at the Glicks' cornfield. "Here's my confession. Till I was seven, I was Amish. My dat died in a car accident. My mom… she married an Englischer and left the faith."

Rebecca felt like she'd just crashed into the lake while waterskiing. It was a lot of information to sort out at once. She reached out to the post for support. "Your mamm was shunned, wasn't she?"

"She fell in love. How could that be bad?"

"I do not know," Rebecca said.

Levi looked at her closely. "My mom always defends the shunning. I thought you'd defend it too."

"What do I know about such things?" Rebecca said. "I am sure this has brought much pain to your family."

"Mom's new husband adopted us and everything." A shadow fell across his features. "But when he left us five years ago, we lost our house. Mom's Amish family wouldn't help us because of the shunning."

"I am so wicked," Rebecca said. "At least I have a fater."

"Having no father is better than having a jerk father," Levi said.

"Does he live around here?"

Levi shook his head. "In Chicago with his new wife. Works at some big-time investment firm. Makes a lot of money—not that we ever see any of it."

"Where does your mamm's family live?"

Levi paused then pulled his keys out of his pocket. "That's all the confessing I'm doing today. If you want more info, you'll have to go out on another date with me. How about Friday night?"

Rebecca ran through the list of tasks in her head. "Fater comes home on Friday night."

"What time?"

"The late bus pulls in right after midnight."

Levi jumped over the fence. "I'm thinking laser-tagging. You want to go?"

Rebecca took a deep breath.

He laughed. "Don't worry. Laser tag is pretty tame for a girl who can water-ski."

"Sounds like fun."

"Okay, kid. I'll pick you up at six."

"I will be waiting, Moe," Rebecca said.

"Moe? One of the Three Stooges? I'm honored." Levi bowed respectfully, winked at Rebecca, and disappeared into the bushes.

Rebecca furrowed her brow. Moe was the name of her uncle's horse. What were the Three Stooges?

Chapter Fourteen

That evening after Levi left, they gathered around Mamm's bed and stared at her as if she had just broken out in spots. Mamm sat up slowly and studied each child's face.

Rebecca stood at the foot of the bed with Linda on her right and Max and Danny to her left. The unusual show of unity got Mamm's attention.

"Mamm," Rebecca began, "we want to discuss something with you."

Mamm hesitated then patted the quilt tucked around her legs. "Cum, sit, all of you. There's plenty of room."

The three younger siblings sat on the bed while Rebecca remained standing. "Linda told you about Levi," Rebecca said.

"Of course she did. You would not want to keep that kind of secret from me, would you?" Mamm motioned for Rebecca to sit by her at the head of the bed. Rebecca hesitated then obeyed. "Linda says he worked like an ox."

"Jah, Mamm," Danny said. "He fixed the lawn mower and cleaned out the stalls."

Smiling calmly, Mamm took Rebecca's hand. "It wonders me why he came."

"To help with the chores," Danny said.

"Nae, that is what he did. But *why* did he mow our lawn?"

"It needed mowing," Danny said.

"He likes Rebecca," Max volunteered.

"Now we come to it," Mamm said. "He likes our Rebecca."

Rebecca felt herself blush.

"What district is his family in?" Mamm asked. "Do I know them?"

"I don't think so," Rebecca stammered.

Mamm brushed a wisp of hair behind her daughter's ear. "Linda says he is very handsome."

"And tall." Linda added. "With muscles."

Mamm nodded patiently. "So he can lift the heavy things."

"He wants to come every Wednesday to help us on the farm," Rebecca said.

She saw the weariness appear on her mother's face. "Hmm. I see. And you are wondering what your fater will have to say about that."

Max folded his arms across his chest. "Fater will forbid it."

Mamm sighed and attempted a smile. "You are gute children, and yours is such a burden."

"Fater would never have to know," Danny said.

"Nae, Danny, I will not keep secrets from your fater."

A vein pulsed behind Rebecca's ear. She drew back from her mamm and walked to the door. "Then that's the end of it," she said, anger choking her from the inside out.

"Wait, Rebecca."

Rebecca refused to look at her mamm—didn't want her to sense the disappointment—but she couldn't keep the resentment from creeping into her voice. "I must get to the milking, Mamm. Linda has a sore finger."

"Rebecca," she heard Mamm call from halfway down the hall.

She should have known Levi's helping on the farm was too good to last. But at least she could see him every Friday. She refused to let Fater steal her few hours of freedom every week. At least rumschpringe gave her that much liberty. Mamm may have promised to love and obey Fater, but Rebecca didn't feel the same obligation. Jah, she tried to honor her parents, but was her desire for her own life unreasonable?

Rebecca stormed down the hall.

Why couldn't her fater see reason? Why must Mamm submit to his every wish?

Ach, I am so wicked. At least I have a fater.

Rebecca let the screen door slam behind her, and she snatched the pail from the porch before stomping off to the pasture. She clapped her hands, and the two cows ambled toward her. Slapping their rumps, she guided them into the barn and hooked them to their posts.

After washing the teats, she scooped up the short stool and planted herself next to Snowball. Her hands milked with the speed of second nature. The mundane task left her mind free to ponder her sins. When her resentment subsided, the familiar guilt took its place. How could she be so ungrateful when her life was so gute? She didn't have rheumatoid arthritis like her mother—yet—and she had working hands and legs.

She slipped her hand into her apron pocket and fingered the folded piece of paper she kept there. She thought of Dottie Mae and her list. Her best friend was gone, but Rebecca was alive—living and breathing. How could she be so ungrateful?

Rebecca milked Snowball in record time. She retrieved an empty pail from the corner and moved her stool to milk the second Jersey.

Max startled her when he came up behind her and gently took the stool. "I'll do it," he said, reaching for the pail.

"Nae, I am okay."

"Don't be a martyr, Rebecca. There's plenty more for you to do in the house."

She let him pull the pail from her fingers.

"He is a pest, but it has been a long while since I have seen you smile like that," Max said. "I hope he is allowed to come back."

Rebecca turned her face from him. "I will mop." She left the barn without a second look.

I am so wicked. Yesterday I had a brother who would die before he volunteered for a job. Today is a new day.

Denki, Lord, for a new day.

Before Rebecca reached the house, the screen door opened and Mamm hobbled onto the porch on her cane. The tortured look on Mamm's face made it plain that she moved with great effort.

"Mamm!" Rebecca cried, bolting up the steps. "What are you doing?"

She caught her mother by the arm and tried to lead her back into the house.

Mamm shook her head. "Nae, nae, I came out to have an interview with my daughter."

With Mamm leaning heavily at Rebecca's side, they limped to the bench and sat in unison.

Rebecca sighed. "Mamm, I can come to your room if you want to talk to me. You do not have to put yourself through this."

"I tried to have a talk with you in my room, but you jumped up and ran out the door like the house was on fire."

Rebecca felt her face grow hot. "I suppose I did."

Mamm patted her hand. "I thought perhaps by coming here, you might be convinced that this is as important to me as it is to you."

Rebecca took a deep breath and looked away. She must not say or do anything to upset Mamm. Her burden was heavy enough. "Please do not worry yourself, Mamm." She spoke rapidly so the bitterness would not choke her and Mamm would not detect the fake cheerfulness. "I manage fine here. I am glad Levi came today. He helped very much. But we have gotten along quite well without him before this, and we will get along quite well after. I am sorry I seemed upset. I truly did have to milk the cows."

Stiffly, Mamm lifted her arm and wrapped it around Rebecca's shoulder and pulled her close. "You *are* upset, and if you had an ounce of selfishness in your body, you would jump off this porch and run as far away from here as possible."

The warmth of her mother's touch almost broke through her defenses. At that moment, Rebecca wanted to bury her face into her mother's neck and cry like a baby. But she didn't. No tears of self-pity today.

"Oh, heartzly, you bottle too much inside." Mamm shook her head. "Listen to me. I am trying to comfort you and still I criticize. Poor *buplie*. Poor baby. You get nothing but criticism. Shame on me."

Rebecca swallowed the lump in her throat. "Don't worry, Mamm. I am fine, really." She attempted a smile. "I hate to see you suffer, that's all."

Mamm frowned and rested her chin on the top of Rebecca's head. "This is my own fault. I have been so wrapped up with my own trials that I have not been mindful of my eldest daughter. You do not trust me with the secrets of your heart."

"Nae, Mamm, I am fine." Rebecca's mother winced when Rebecca pulled away from her. "And you should be in bed."

Rebecca stood and held out her hand for her mother to take. A short, relatively harmless conversation. Mamm needed her rest.

Mamm took her hand but, with more strength than Rebecca thought Mamm possessed, pulled her daughter back to the bench. "Sit here with me," Mamm said quietly.

Rebecca held on to her mother's hand as they sat. She began to massage Mamm's knuckles. This always brought Mamm much relief. Mamm furrowed her brow and pulled her hand away. "I have taken advantage of your kindness, Rebecca. We all have."

"Mamm, I am fine," Rebecca insisted. Mamm would be flat on her back for weeks after this ruckus. Why had she not tempered her initial reaction in Mamm's bedroom? So much trouble could have been avoided.

"You've had a long day," Mamm said.

"Jah," Rebecca said, happy for an excuse. "It has been a busy day, and I am tired."

Mamm motioned with her fingers. "Cum, put your legs on my lap, and I will rub your feet."

"How could you even suggest that?"

The wounded expression on Mamm's face spoke for itself. Rebecca chastised herself once again. Somehow she had made things worse.

"My feet feel gute. I do not want you to hurt your hands," Rebecca said.

Mamm ran her fingers along Rebecca's arm. "The Master washed His disciples' feet. Will you not let me do as much for my daughter?"

Her mother gave her such a forlorn look that, instead of refusing, Rebecca hesitated. "Fater would be angry."

There it is, Mamm. Contradict me if you dare.

Mamm looked as if she had just received the news of a death in the family. "Cannot you accept my gift?"

"Why does it mean that much to you?" Rebecca said.

"Because I never do anything for you. You do everything for me. Do you know how worthless I feel?"

"Never, never say that, Mamm. You are the world to me." Rebecca sighed in resignation and took off her shoes. "If it will make you happy to rub my feet, then go ahead and do it."

Giving in to her mother's wishes did not produce the effect Rebecca expected. Mamm slowly kneaded her forehead with the tips of her fingers. "Rebecca," she said, her voice cracking with every syllable, "forgive me. Everything you have done is because you wanted to make me happy. You only now agree to let me rub your feet because it will make me happy." She took Rebecca's face in her palms. "What have I done to you?"

Rebecca didn't want pity, and she didn't want a deep, heartfelt conversation with her mamm. There was too much to hide, too much to distress her mother. "Mamm, I am fine."

Mamm lowered her hands and seemed momentarily confused by what she should do next. Rebecca felt sorry but didn't know what to say. Mamm now felt like she couldn't ask for anything because she believed Rebecca would only do it to please her. Neither could Mamm offer anything, because again, she thought Rebecca would only accept kindness to make her happy.

They sat for a long time, watching the sunset, and Rebecca was about to suggest that Mamm go back to bed when Mamm said, "Do you remember when we set up that quilt under the tree and quilted it with Dottie Mae and her mother?"

"Jah, it was the summer before she died."

"And you hated to quilt, but Dottie Mae loved it."

Rebecca smiled. "She would tease me that I would never make a gute wife because I could not sew a straight stitch."

"We would quilt while you weeded the flower beds." Mamm fidgeted on the bench. "Could you move this pillow behind my back?"

Rebecca picked up the blue quilted pillow that sat permanently on the bench and adjusted it until Mamm said she was comfortable. Mamm closed her eyes and breathed in the fresh summer air. She sat for several seconds with a serene expression on her face. Rebecca leaned and rested her head on her mother's shoulder. She still loved her mother's comfort, even if she seldom accepted it.

"Do you know why your fater stays away so much?" Mamm said.

"His job in Milwaukee pays gute money," Rebecca said.

"You know he could find enough work in Apple Lake to support our family." Mamm turned Rebecca's chin up to look at her. "Don't you?"

"Jah, I know he could."

Mamm squeezed Rebecca's hand. "But he is not strong enough to stay with his family and do what needs to be done."

Rebecca looked at her mother in surprise.

"I do not want you to think I am against your fater, Rebecca. He is a gute man. He works hard for our family, but the responsibility to care for his wife, his children, and the farm is too heavy. He cannot bear it."

"I do not understand," Rebecca said.

"He is ashamed that he does not have your strength. He stays away so he does not have to face his weakness. He rails at you about the farm not being better cared for because he knows deep in his heart that he has not the strength to stay home and take care of it himself. Can you imagine living with that shame? It is a shame that prompts him to refuse every offer of help because he cannot bear to admit that he needs help. Do you see?"

Rebecca nodded slowly. "Jah, I see."

"Your father is the head of our home and we abide by his wishes because it is right to do so, but we also do it because we do not want to compound his shame."

Rebecca's confusion mounted. "Do you love Fater?"

"I love him very much. That is why I will not let him be hurt. But I see his weaknesses just as he sees mine. You have the brunt of the responsibility on the farm. We have taken advantage of your willingness and honest heart. This must stop. This Levi—he is a gute boy?"

"Jah, very gute."

"And he likes you very much."

"I do not know."

"A boy spends a whole day working on your farm, putting up with your little brothers...he likes you. Does he want to marry you?"

Thinking about the answer to that question made Rebecca feel unexpectedly despondent. Marriage was impossible. She was Amish; he, Englisch But the thought that they would be forced to part sometime down the road made her ill. He had become her confidant, the only person to whom she felt comfortable telling her secrets. Could she give him up like a pair of shoes she had outgrown?

"He does not want to marry me," she finally stuttered.

Mamm smiled as if she knew the real answer. "Tell him he will be in trouble on Wednesday if he does not do me the kindness of introducing himself."

"Fater will not approve. You do not have to raise my hopes."

"It is time I put a little more effort into my daughter's happiness," Mamm said. She hugged Rebecca, though Rebecca knew the movement cost her much pain. "You leave it to me. Your fater will see reason, Lord willing. Just because you have never seen my fierce side doesn't mean I do not have one."

Chapter Fifteen

Levi unloaded the last glass from the dishwasher as Beth blew through the door of their apartment, and his heart jumped out of his chest.

Beth stared at the clean cupboard and the empty dishwasher. "Is somebody coming over?"

"No," Levi said, trying to keep the excitement from his voice, "I was just cleaning up."

She gave him a suspicious look. "Who are you, and what have you done with my brother?"

"Hey, just because I never do the dishes doesn't mean I don't know how."

"No complaints from me. I'm all for you taking over dish duty." Beth laid her purse on the table and thumbed through the mail. "What you doing tonight? You going out with the new girl?"

Levi wiped the faucet with a dry towel. "No, she can't go out most nights. Mostly just Fridays."

"What, she only has one night out on work release?"

Levi threw the towel at his sister. It missed by a mile. Unflinching, she stood her ground.

"I have to work tonight," Levi said.

"Work?" Beth said. "You've already been to work today."

"I got a second job."

She looked at him like he was crazy. "A second job?"

"The bicycle place right next to Truckload Sports needed someone to fix bikes."

Beth raised an eyebrow. "Am I missing something here? You got a second job?"

"I can come in anytime I want, so I can work it around my other job. And they pay really well."

"But why would you get a second job?"

"When is tuition due at Northwestern?"

Beth sighed. "Oh, Levi, we've talked about this. I'm never going to come up with enough money."

Levi reached into his jeans pocket and produced an envelope. "I am sorry to say, I committed a federal crime and opened your letter."

She snatched it from his hands and pulled out the paper inside. Her eyes grew as round as buggy wheels as she read. "My grant! They approved my grant." With both arms, she seized Levi by the neck and squeezed tightly. "It's been so many months since I applied, I thought I'd been rejected." Her eyes scanned to the bottom of the page and the wind disappeared from her sails. "It's not enough," she mumbled. "Even with loans, I've still got to come up with five thousand dollars plus figure out a way to pay for housing. It's still not enough." She plopped herself into a kitchen chair.

Levi put a hand on her shoulder.

"It's okay," Beth said. "I've already resigned myself to the fact that I'll be going to the community college."

Levi thought he might burst with excitement. He stuck his hand into his pocket, pulled out a wad of cash, and threw five twenties on the table. "This is for you," he said.

Beth looked at the money as though it might sprout feet and run away. "What for?"

"They pay me by the bike for bike repairs. I think I can muster an extra two hundred dollars a week for the rest of the summer. If you save all the tips you make at MacAffees, I think we can eke out enough for tuition."

Levi looked at the money, which seemed a measly amount compared to what Beth needed. She'd have more if he sold his car and walked to work, but he couldn't bring himself to do it. No car meant no Rebecca. Apple Lake was too far to walk, seven miles, and there weren't enough hours in the day to take the bus. On top of the money he needed to date Rebecca and feed her family once a week, two hundred dollars at a time for Beth was truly all he could manage.

Beth didn't touch the money. "Levi, you already help with the rent and insurance. You want this family to bleed you dry?"

"I can save almost thirty dollars a week if I never buy another margarita again," he said.

She gave him a half smile. "It's a good reason to go sober."

"Please take the money, sis. It'll be like the whole family going to school with you. You have to uphold the family honor, you know."

"The pressure is killing me."

"You'll survive."

With eyes shining, she finally picked up the cash. Clasping it in both hands, she said, "Thank you." She grinned through her tears. "You're the best brother I ever had."

"I'm the only brother you ever had."

"Lucky for you, there's no competition." Beth opened her purse and put the money into her wallet. "When I'm a rich doctor, I'll pay you back every penny."

"No need. Free medical care is all I ask."

She reached over and took his hand. "I wish I could have done the same for you four years ago."

"Nah, the money is much better spent on you." Levi felt that stab of pain again, anger mixed with regret. His dad's abandonment had led Levi down a horrible path he wished he could wipe from his memory. "I never deserved it like you do, Beth."

"Quit with the self-loathing, Levi. You're better than that."

"I wish I were."

Beth picked up her grant letter and put it back into the envelope. "It's this new girl you're dating. You're different since you met her."

"She makes me want to be a better person."

"Well, if she's inspired you to stop drinking, more power to her."

Levi knitted his brows together. "I really like her."

"Don't sound so miserable."

He didn't want to see her reaction, so he went back to the sink, picked up the towel, and wiped the faucet again. "She's Amish."

A shocked silence.

"Does Mom know?" Beth murmured.

"No."

Another long silence.

"She won't like it," Beth said.

Levi simply nodded.

"Does the girl know about all your stuff with the Amish? The accident?" Beth said.

Levi dropped the towel onto the counter. The accident. Would it ever cross his mind without sending a shard of glass shooting through his heart? "She knows we used to be Amish and that Mom has been shunned for almost fifteen years. She doesn't know the worst."

"Are you going to tell her?"

"No. She'd hate me."

Beth frowned. "Of course she won't hate you. Forgiveness is what the Amish do best."

"I'm not taking any chances."

"What if she finds out? Wouldn't it be better coming from you?" Beth said.

"She's not going to find out," Levi said, clenching his teeth. "She's never going to find out."

Chapter Sixteen

Rebecca couldn't help herself. She sat on the floor in the hallway outside her parents' bedroom with her ear plastered against the door. Whether eavesdropping was wicked or not, she simply had to hear this conversation. Mamm seemed so confident that she could win Fater's approval, but Rebecca couldn't feel so secure.

If Fater suddenly decided to open the door, she would be in big trouble—not to mention be left with a splitting headache.

Fater had arrived home on Friday night just before midnight, when everyone but Rebecca was already asleep. She had slipped through the door mere minutes earlier from playing laser tag. Levi had gotten a flat tire and fixed it with lightning speed to get Rebecca home on time.

This morning after breakfast, Fater went back to the bedroom as he always did to get a weekly update from Mamm. When he left the table, Rebecca sneaked down the hall after him. She tuned her ear to the sound of her parents' voices.

"…can save money on chicken feed," Mamm said.

"Danny wastes it," Fater said. "He pours too much at a time."

"He does his best."

"Tell Becky to feed the chickens. She is not as careless as Daniel."

No reply.

"I see the lawn is done. Did Max fix the mower? He probably made it worse," Fater said.

"Nae, someone else fixed it."

Rebecca's heart thumped in her chest so loudly she was sure Fater would hear it.

"A young man came to help us on Wednesday," Mamm said.

Fater lowered his voice. "What young man? I told the ministers we do not need help. Becky knows not to accept charity. I have made that very clear many times."

"There is nothing to be upset about, Amos. This boy is not from our district. The bishop did not send him."

"That does not matter. Becky knows—"

"I would not ask Rebecca to turn this one away."

"I will tell her," Fater insisted.

"He came to see her, Amos."

A pause.

"A suitor?" Fater asked.

"Jah."

"She should not have visitors when she is supposed to be working," Fater said.

"You have not been listening. He came on Wednesday and worked all day. He mowed and mucked out the stalls and fixed the barn door."

"It does not matter. I will not have him or anyone else coming around. We take care of our own family."

Rebecca pursed her lips. She could have predicted exactly what Fater would say. Why did Mamm think she could stand up to him?

"Amos," Mamm said with more authority than Rebecca had ever heard, "close your mouth and bite your tongue and let me speak, or I promise I will hitch up the buggy and go stay with my sister. I have no call for a husband who interrupts me every five seconds."

Rebecca had to strain to hear Fater's answer. "Now you are being childish."

"Bite your tongue now, Amos."

Rebecca couldn't see, couldn't guess the looks exchanged on the other side of the door, but Mamm must have won the contest of wills.

"It is high time we let Rebecca receive suitors," Mamm said.

"That does not mean—"

"Husband," Mamm threatened.

"Just let me say— Erla, what are you doing?"

"Going to hitch up the wagon."

Rebecca moved away from the door as she heard the bed creak.

"Get back into bed," Fater said, his exasperation evident. "I promise I will listen."

"Without interrupting."

"Jah. I will not interrupt."

"With humility," Mamm said.

"Jah. Whatever you want."

Mamm was silent for a minute, probably staring at Fater before she spoke. "It is only natural that Rebecca will have suitors. She is of the right age, and she is very pretty. But she is tied to this house and farm because of all the work. If she cannot go to the boys, then the boys must come to her. This boy wants to prove himself to her. To us. How can he do that if we forbid him from the farm?" Mamm paused. "You may speak."

Fater waited, as if formulating the perfect sentence—the only one he might be allowed to utter. "She can meet boys at gatherings."

"That is not good enough. Rebecca is an unusual girl. She won't be courted in the usual way."

Rebecca almost smiled. Mamm had no idea how accurate her words were.

"Amos, you will allow this boy to come every week and see our Rebecca and work if he is so inclined."

Fater started to speak, and Mamm cut him short. "If you do not, everyone will say you are being selfish with your girl and you are purposefully trying to keep her from marrying."

"Of course I am not keeping her from marriage. She is free to marry."

"Is she?"

"Jah."

"Then do not tell her when she can and cannot see boys."

"I do not approve of boys coming to our house."

The bed creaked as if Mamm were waving her hands in the air.

"You must give her freedom, Amos. Just because it is not your way does not mean it is not right. And if you rob her of this opportunity, the consequences will be on your head."

Rebecca held her breath as the silence lengthened. She waited so long that she began to wonder if they had both fallen asleep.

"I will allow him to come," Fater finally said. "But I want to know more about him. What is his name? Who is his family?"

"I do not know," Mamm said. "I will have Rebecca bring him to meet me."

"I must meet him also."

"You will. Now go make yourself some raspberry-leaf tea. You look to have a sour stomach."

Rebecca stood up and tiptoed to the kitchen. In a daze she started to wash the dishes but felt her knees get weak and sank into a chair instead. Things were worse than ever. Levi would be allowed to come to the farm, but as soon as her parents met him, the farm dates would be over. When Mamm didn't know, when her brothers and sister assumed he was Amish, then Rebecca felt justified in pretending. But after Mamm met him and wanted to know him better, Rebecca could not lie about who Levi really was. She could not make up a family for him or hire parents to adopt him. And Fater would put a stop to the relationship faster than a squirrel could run up a tree.

It shouldn't matter. Once Rebecca learned how to ski, she and Levi would go their separate ways and never cross paths again.

But it did matter.

Rebecca caught her breath when she realized how much it mattered to her. The thought of Levi absent from her life was as painful as the thought of losing her right arm.

She shook her head. Rebecca refused to attach herself to anyone. Levi was an Englischer. An Englischer with a rough past who couldn't possibly take hold of her heart. Rebecca simply regretted losing his company and his strong hands and his skills on her farm. She regularly bore her soul to him, but he wasn't the only friend she had. He was handsome, to be sure, but there were other interested boys. Amish boys. Like Marvin.

Marvin Yutzy—whose company was much like conversing with a cardboard box.

What would it hurt if Levi came one more time? She would at least get to be with him. And once he met Mamm and revealed his true identity, Rebecca could still see him on Friday nights, the one night she reserved to be free of her family. Mamm and Fater need never know whom she met.

Rebecca ran into her bedroom and locked the door. After retrieving her phone from under the windowsill, she sent Levi a text.

Fater is allowing you back. Do you still want to come on Wednesday? You don't have to. Fater wants to meet you and so does Mamm. So I am afraid this visit will be your last.

To her surprise, her phone vibrated almost immediately after she sent her message.

I'm like a beggar. I'll take whatever I can get. Maybe it will work out with your fater. Do you like apricots? I hate them. LOL. Buy some sugar. I'll be there on Wednesday.

Before she could turn off her phone, it vibrated again.

How do you feel about roller coasters?

Chapter Seventeen

On Wednesday morning at six o'clock sharp, Rebecca opened the front door to Levi, who stood on the porch with two red roses and a can of tuna fish in his fist. He smiled so widely, Rebecca thought he might burst into laughter at any moment.

"This is for you," he said, handing her one of the roses.

She gasped with excitement then immediately chided herself. She shouldn't give Levi encouragement by accepting his gift. But Rebecca found roses irresistible. She didn't want to refuse it—even if her acceptance did raise his hopes.

"Oh, denki," she said breathing in the fragrance. "I love roses."

Levi studied her face and grinned. "I can tell." He gave her the can of tuna. "For Danny. And"—he held up the other flower—"this is for your mom."

Rebecca swallowed the oversized lump in her throat. "My mamm?"

"Is she awake?"

"You want to give it to her now?"

Levi screwed his lips into a funny line. "Might as well get kicked off your property early in the day—avoid the suspense that way."

Rebecca instantly felt sick to her stomach. "Jah, the suspense is killing me."

She invited Levi into the living room and directed him to sit on the sofa draped with an afghan Rebecca had crocheted last winter. It was pink and green, the colors of the rosebush outside her window. In the kitchen, she rummaged through the cupboards to find a suitable vase for her flower. Once the rose held a place of honor in the middle of the kitchen table, she went to see if her mamm was awake. With any luck, she had slept in and wouldn't want any visitors today.

Opening the door to Mamm's room, Rebecca abandoned all hope. Mamm sat straight up in her bed, her hair carefully combed and tucked beneath her kapp. She wore her emerald-green dress with the black apron and shoes. Her bed was made, and she sat on top of the quilt as if waiting to be fetched for a party.

Rebecca stared at her mamm. "How did you make your bed?"

Mamm laced her fingers together. "With much effort," she said. "Oh, Rebecca, you look a little pale. Take some cayenne pepper."

"Levi is here."

With trembling fingers, Mamm smoothed the nonexistent wrinkles in her dress. She was nervous? Certainly her anxiety paled in comparison to Rebecca's, who just knew she was going to throw up.

"Is he in the living room?"

"Jah, but I can bring him in."

Mamm frowned at such a thought. "Receive an important guest in my bedroom? What are you thinking, heartzly? Go, go, and I will come out."

"I can help you."

Mamm waved her hand dismissively. "Go and wait for me. I am coming by my own power."

With a doubtful look, Rebecca turned and trudged down the hallway like she was going to her own death.

She entered the living room and sat next to Levi on the sofa.

Levi leaned close to her ear. "Don't worry. In case you haven't noticed, I can be quite charming, kid."

"Charm will not get you very far with a protective Amish *mutter*, Scout."

"Scout? Nice. Like Davy Crockett."

Rebecca let out a sigh that originated from her toes. "Your overconfidence is very comforting."

She listened with growing anxiety as Mamm shuffled her feet

down the hallway. Levi actually put his hand over hers and squeezed reassuringly. She relished the warmth of his touch before snatching her hand away and folding her arms tightly around her waist. No good for Mamm to see them holding hands.

Levi stood as Mamm entered the room, hobbling on her cane with pain etched in the wrinkles of her face. She took one look at Levi and her face brightened considerably. Rebecca should have known. Every mother loved to have a boy pursuing her daughter, but a good-looking boy was reason to be especially proud.

Rebecca stood also. "Mamm, this is Levi Cooper," she said.

Levi handed Mamm the rose, and she breathed in the flower's fragrance. "Denki, Levi. Rebecca tells me you have done good work for us. We are grateful."

Levi flashed those white teeth that made every girl swoon. "I come to help Rebecca with the heavy lifting. She's very capable. I have to work hard to keep up with her."

"Cum," Mamm said. "Sit."

Mamm eased into the rocker and motioned for Rebecca and Levi to sit on the sofa.

"There are other boys interested in my Rebecca. Marvin Yutzy, Peter Stoltzfus, Giddy Yoder…"

Rebecca wanted to crawl under a rock.

"Rebecca's fater does not usually allow others to help with the farm," Mamm said.

"Yes, I understand. Rebecca told me."

Rocking slowly in her chair, Mamm studied Levi's face. "But this is a special circumstance between you and Rebecca."

Rebecca felt her face grow hot. Mamm made it sound like they were a couple.

"My husband has granted his permission for you to be here."

"I'm glad," Levi said, winking at Rebecca.

Rebecca pretended not to notice. How could every gesture, every look from him, prove so unnerving and so invigorating at the same time?

"I brought a power sprayer to remove the chipped paint from the barn. Max and Danny have agreed to help. Rebecca said she could get paint for it next week."

Levi quickly rose to his feet, no doubt in hopes of postponing a conversation that could only end in disaster. "But now I should run and get that power sprayer out of my— I should run and get that sprayer and the apricots. My mother's friend has a tree, and she said I could have all I wanted as long as I picked them."

"Sit, sit," Mamm said. "No need to be in a hurry." She shifted in the rocker and laid the rose in her lap. "Tell me about yourself, Levi. Who is your family? Do I know your parents?"

The moment Rebecca had been dreading had finally come. She wouldn't lie to her mother. A lie was like a hole in the roof. A person had to spend a lot of energy to keep the water from spreading, and like as not, a new leak would appear, and then another and another, and soon there weren't enough buckets to catch the lies.

And Levi wouldn't lie either. He had many flaws that, due to his honesty, Rebecca knew all about. He wasn't perfect, but he wasn't the type to say an untruth. What would he tell Mamm?

She saw Levi look uncertain for the first time, but he charged ahead with a speech he must have rehearsed several times before coming over. "You might know my mother," he said. "My father passed away when I was seven years old."

"Oh, I am sorry," Mamm said.

"My mother is Mary Stutzman. Her parents are Alphy and Nancy Petersheim."

Mamm's eyes widened, and she put her hand to her mouth. "Mary and Isaac's boy," she said softly.

Rebecca stared at Levi. She had never before seen the kind of pain in his eyes that she saw now. Had she not cared enough to look?

"Oh, the poor girl. A sad story, that," Mamm said. She sat quietly for a moment with a strange look in her eye. "She married an Englischer and left the church. Took her two little ones with her."

"I was seven, Beth was three. My father's death crushed my mother; I remember that much. I'd lay awake at night and listen to her crying."

"We felt sorry for her," Mamm said. "But the new man made her very happy."

"My stepdad came on the scene at her lowest point, I think. He got her through a lot." Levi frowned. "Even though he left us, I believe he really loved her."

"He left?" Mamm said.

"Yeah, they're divorced now. Mom works at the hospital, and he lives in Chicago."

"And you?"

"I work two jobs in Patton, and my sister, Beth, is going to college this fall."

Mamm propped her chin in her hand and stared at Levi. He waited for her to say what they all knew she was thinking.

"I do not understand, Levi. You are an Englischer now, aren't you?"

Levi nodded and lowered his gaze. He must not have been counting on that dependable charm to see him through.

"Why do you... I don't understand. Why are you here?"

His matter-of-fact tone almost put Rebecca at ease, but she knew better. "I'm here because"—he glanced at Rebecca—"because I like Rebecca, a lot, and she needs help with the farm."

A pleasant warmth spread through Rebecca's body.

He liked her.

This wasn't big news, was it? But hearing him speak it so plainly to her mother somehow made it finally true.

Rebecca held her breath as she watched the emotions play on her mother's face. Confusion gave way to realization. Outrage followed close behind.

"What do you think you are doing? Are you trying to steal my Rebecca away?"

Levi gazed earnestly at Mamm. "I saw how hard it was for my mom to fit into the Englisch world. I wouldn't do that to Rebecca."

Rebecca put her ice-cold hands to her flushed cheeks. Mamm and Levi were jumping from one very big conclusion to another.

"Then you will break her heart."

"I never want to do that."

In a surge of indignation, Mamm rose to her feet. "I forbid this relationship, Rebecca, for your own good. I absolutely forbid it."

Even though she knew it was coming, Mamm's reaction crashed into Rebecca like a charging bull. She let out her breath and blinked until she subdued the threatening tears.

Levi slumped his shoulders and looked at Rebecca, his face saturated with disappointment. "I will abide by your wishes," he said. "Thank you for listening to what I had to say."

Rebecca fully expected Mamm to storm out of the room. Instead, she fell silent and stared at both of them as her expression softened. "This is for your own good," she said.

If Rebecca could have mustered the composure to speak, she would have reassured her mother. *It will be fine. We will be fine.*

Rebecca stood and took her mother's arm. "Cum," she managed to say. "Back to bed. Levi will go." Her voice cracked once, but with any luck, Mamm did not even notice.

Taking Rebecca's chin in her hand, Mamm looked into her daughter's eyes. "I am only thinking of what is best for you. You understand?"

Rebecca mustered a cheerful expression. "Jah, of course. Do not worry, Mamm. Worrying aggravates your condition, and you have enough on your plate without fretting about me. I will help you back to bed."

"I just wanted to help," Levi said. "I know how hard it is for Rebecca."

Mamm's voice rose in pitch and volume. "You *know* how hard it is? What do you know about our family? Our way of life?"

Levi's expression hardened. "I know that if you keep working your daughter this hard, she'll resent it. How much more can she take before she snaps and leaves you forever?"

"So you do want to steal my daughter away."

A pit formed in Rebecca's stomach. Levi was only making things worse. "I would never leave you, Mamm," she protested. "Never."

Levi sensed Rebecca's distress and hung his head. "I'm sorry. I am out of line for saying that. I will go now." He locked eyes with Mamm. "Could I have your permission to milk the cows before I leave? To help Rebecca one last time?"

"Max has already milked," Mamm said. She turned her back on both of them and started down the hall.

"Max is in bed," Rebecca said quietly.

Mamm stopped short. "And your sister?"

Rebecca hesitated. "Asleep."

Furrowing her brow, Mamm shuffled back into the living room and sank into her chair. "Guide me, Lord."

She rocked back and forth with her head in her hands while Levi and Rebecca stared at her in silence.

"What did you do last night, Rebecca?" Mamm said, not looking up.

"The regular things," Rebecca said, wondering what her mother wanted to hear.

"Laundry?"

"Jah, some laundry."

"And mopping. And dishes."

"Jah," Rebecca said.

"What time did you go to bed, heartzly?"

"I don't know."

Mamm looked up. "It was after midnight, wasn't it?"

"Don't be upset, Mamm. I will try to get to bed earlier."

Mamm held up her hand and shook her head and rocked back and forth, her face pale and a frown on her lips. The wrinkles on her face deepened, and she looked ten years older.

"I have been pretending that things weren't this bad. I thought that if I closed my eyes to the truth, I wouldn't have to do anything about it." Her voice cracked. "I don't have the energy or the strength to do anything about it."

"Mamm, you are sick. Of course you can't—"

"Things here are very hard for you. I have taken advantage of your good heart because the others are not so easily persuaded."

The last thing Rebecca wanted was for Mamm to feel guilty.

"I will be fine," Rebecca said.

"I don't want you to be *fine*. I want you to be happy. You are so concerned for my well-being, and I am too selfish to think about yours." Mamm sighed and massaged her forehead. "You did not go to the gathering on Friday night, did you?"

"Nae, Mamm. I never said I did."

"You were with Levi?"

Rebecca didn't want to further upset her mother, but she couldn't bear the thought of giving up her one source of happiness. "It is only one night a week."

"I don't want to be your enemy," Mamm said. "I want you to share your heart instead of tiptoeing around me for fear I'll ruin your life."

Rebecca couldn't argue. That was precisely how she had been behaving.

Mamm looked at Levi and sighed. "As sure as rain, you are a gute boy, Levi Stutzman. For good or ill, Rebecca likes you. Not only that, but you lighten her burden plenty—one thing I cannot do." She sighed again in surrender. "You have my permission to return to our farm whenever you like."

Levi studied Mamm with undisguised disbelief. "I do?"

"Jah, but it would be better if the children know as little about you as possible."

Levi smiled as if his joy would burst into laughter at any moment.

Rebecca was surprised by her own elation. "But what will you tell Fater?"

Mamm suddenly looked very weary. "I am hoping the subject will not come up for several weeks."

Levi's confidence returned as quickly as it had fled. "I was born Amish," he said. "My parents are Amish. So, technically, I am in rumschpringe. Maybe that is all your husband needs to know."

Mamm managed a half smile. "I will cross that bridge when I come to it."

Grinning widely, Levi squeezed Rebecca's hand and headed for the front door. "Do you want the apricots in my car? Three bushels."

"Jah. We will can them today while you spray the barn," Rebecca said.

"I could drive the car up to the front door here and unload them quick."

"I will help you fetch them. Linda and Max will never believe you are a gute Amish boy if you drive a car."

Levi pointed to his outfit. "Look at me," he said. "Even I'm starting to believe I'm Amish."

* * * * *

Rebecca handed Levi a glass of water. Sweat poured from his face as he gulped the ice-cold liquid like a man in the desert. His clothes were still damp from the power spraying, and the late afternoon sun beat down on his hatless head.

He drained the glass and gasped for air. "Okay, I thought lifting weights was hard, but splitting logs is like the best workout ever."

"I think you have chopped up a whole winter's supply," Rebecca said.

"Gute," Levi said. "Then maybe you won't have to chop another log until spring."

"You said 'gute.'"

Levi grinned and wiped the sweat from his forehead. "Jah, I can speak the local language when I want to."

"You spend a lot of time with the Amish. You dress Amish. Now you are speaking with the accent. Aren't you afraid you will turn Amish?"

He pasted on a peculiar expression and winked at her. "Nae, I'm not afraid of that."

She loved the way her insides curled when he looked at her.

No, no, she didn't. That sort of thing was romantic rot for the wide-eyed teenagers at the gatherings.

"I loved being Amish," he said. "I remember the ice-skating in the winter and the fishing in summertime. We knew how to have fun." He got a faraway look in his eyes before snapping back to the present. "How did the apricots go?"

"Six dozen quarts and little left over for jam tomorrow. Mamm helped. And Linda, a little."

Levi chuckled. "Linda is a gute helper."

"Thank you for bringing the apricots. They will be nice to have this winter."

"I hope so." Levi's face darkened. "I wish I could do more for you."

"Do not say that. I cannot believe what you have done already."

Levi shook his head. "You're half starving out here."

Rebecca took a step back and hardened her face against him. "I know I am full of faults, but I think I manage very well."

"Well? You're a miracle worker, Rebecca."

"Then why do you criticize?"

Levi hung his head. "I'm sorry if it sounds like I am finding fault with you. I would never, never do that."

"Jah, okay," Rebecca said. How could she think Levi was like Fater?

"I care about you. I hate that your life is so hard."

"Life is hard, no matter whose life you are living. But life is gute also. Life is work because work sustains life. And we have many reasons to be happy. Look at that barn. Freshly scrubbed and ready to be painted. What could be better than that?"

Levi handed Rebecca the empty glass. "Getting a glass of water and a smile from Rebecca Miller. That's the best thing to happen to me all day."

"Ach, you are a manure expert, Levi Cooper. You spread flattery like our bishop gives out handshakes."

He held out his hands in surrender. "How will I convince you that every word is true?"

"You won't."

"I guess I'll keep trying, kid."

"You are wasting your efforts, Bub."

"Bub. The fat guy who sits on the bench outside the drugstore and smokes three packs a day. I like it." He put an arm around her shoulder.

She pushed him away playfully.

Levi wiped his hands on his trousers. "Now that the wood's done, I'm hungry. How about Chinese tonight?"

"I've never had it."

"Oh, kid, you're in for a treat."

Chapter Eighteen

Levi snatched his keys from the dresser and practically sprinted down the hallway.

Mom, in her scrubs, stood in the closet-sized kitchen looking into the fridge.

"See ya, Mom. I'm going to the bicycle shop."

"Wait, wait!" Mom practically yelled. "What time do you have to be there?"

"I can be there anytime I want. The sooner I get there, the more bikes I can fix."

"Have you eaten?"

Levi jangled his keys. "No, I'll grab a bite when I get home."

"Let me fix you something before you go."

"No, Mom. Really, I'm fine."

"Give me ten minutes. I'll make you a quesadilla."

"I'm okay."

"It won't hurt you to sit down and eat before you shrink to nothing and blow away."

Levi looked down at himself. "Do I look like I've lost weight?"

"No, but I'm not taking any chances. I haven't made you dinner for weeks."

"We had dinner together on Sunday."

Mom shook her head. "Not counting Sundays."

Levi looked at his phone. He could spare a few minutes for Mom. He pulled a stool from under the counter and sat in silent acquiescence.

Mom opened a cupboard and clattered a few pans around before finding the skillet she was looking for. She thumped it on top of the stove and went to the fridge for tortillas and cheese.

"Do you want help?"

"No, relax. I don't think you've sat for more than five minutes this week."

"Neither have you."

Mom glanced at Levi and shook her head. "I get enough leisure. You're like the Energizer Bunny."

Levi loved to watch his mom cook. She grated and chopped and sautéed as if second nature. Her movements were like a musician conducting an orchestra. Soon the smell of onions and peppers and fried ham permeated the small apartment. Levi breathed deeply and let his mouth water in anticipation.

"Do you want pepper jack?" Mom said.

"Yeah, that's great."

"Are you working late tonight?"

"Probably. Lots of broken bikes."

Mom turned the tortilla on the skillet and sprinkled white and orange cheese over it. "You work tomorrow?"

"I took the day off. I'm going to Wisconsin Dells with some friends."

"And that girl? Beth says you're dating someone."

Levi's "danger" alert perked up. "What did she tell you?"

Mom looked up from her culinary creation and smiled. "No need to panic. She said you broke up with Tara. Says it's a nice girl this time."

He breathed a little easier. "That Beth is such a blabbermouth."

"It's not like I wouldn't have figured it out on my own. You've got so much spring in your step, you could bounce to the moon and back."

Levi stifled a grin by wiping his hand across his mouth. "That's crazy talk, Mom."

"What's her name?"

"Rebecca."

"Where did you meet her?"

"She, uh, she came into the store."

Mom scraped the onions and peppers from the pan into the quesadilla and folded it in half. With one quick flick of her spatula, she slid the quesadilla onto a plate and plopped it in front of Levi.

"Thanks, Mom."

She handed him a fork and watched him eat. "And?"

"What?" he said, sticking the first bite into his mouth.

"And, what about the girl?"

"She's really nice and really pretty." Levi concentrated very hard on cutting his quesadilla. In dread, he knew these pitiful bits of information were not going to fly with Mom.

In a moment she seemed to lose her intensity. She sighed, found the dishrag, and wiped around the stove. "I've never seen so much hemming and hawing in my life," she said.

"There's not much to tell, Mom."

Mom picked up the skillet and used it as a pointer. "Oh, there is a book of details you're not sharing."

"More like a pamphlet."

"I doubt it."

He held up a piece of quesadilla. "This is really good."

"Will I get to meet her sometime?"

"Come on, Mom. I gotta go to work."

"Okay, okay. But don't think you'll be able to avoid the subject forever. I'm persistent. My mamma used to call me 'The Bull.'" A shadow fell across her face then disappeared.

"You miss her."

"Of course. But she writes, and Barbara writes."

"It's not the same," Levi said.

"No. Not the same."

Levi hesitated with the question on his lips he'd been wanting to ask. "Do you wish you could go back?"

The question took her by surprise. "Why do you ask?"

"Do you?"

Mom leaned her elbows on the counter and stared at him. "Does it matter?"

"Yeah, it does."

She sighed and surrendered to his probing. "I wish it every day. When your dat died, I was lonely. Brent was so good to me. I knew he would take care of you children. But I could never quite fit into his world. Remember when we moved to Chicago for, what was it, three months?"

Levi nodded.

"I had a major breakdown. I begged him to move us back."

"To be close to your family, even if they shunned you?"

"That and because I couldn't stand the big city. Too many people, too many buildings, no friends or neighbors. Everyone impersonal and indifferent. Brent was mad, but he moved us back." Mom poured Levi a glass of milk. "It's my fault he left."

"That's not true, Mom. He's a jerk, plain and simple."

"He got frustrated with me. I wallowed in self-pity, and it wore him down. He left because he couldn't live with me anymore."

"He gave up on us, Mom. It wasn't your fault."

She reached over and patted his arm. "No pancake is so thin that it doesn't have two sides, Levi."

"So would you go back to being Amish? If you could?"

"How could I do that to you and Beth? To ask you to live that life?"

"As I remember, it was a pretty good life," Levi said.

"Not after cell phones and cars and computers."

"Beth is going to school. She doesn't have to be baptized. She doesn't even have to live that way, but she could visit all the time."

Mom got a strange look on her face. "And what about you?"

Levi lowered his head and looked at his hands. "I could live there with you. I wouldn't mind."

Mom stared at him for an eternity before sighing plaintively and clearing his plate from the counter. "It would never work. You two are my most important family. I wouldn't do anything that would separate us."

Levi didn't attempt to convince her of an idea that had only been passing through that Swiss-cheese brain of his. Rebecca had completely overtaken any reason or judgment he once had, and the thought of being with her had obviously overruled his common sense.

Me, live among the Amish? Mom's right. It would never work.

Chapter Nineteen

Levi handed Rebecca her ticket. "They'll take this and give you a wrist-band," he told her as they waited in line with what seemed like a million other people. A burly guy in front of him must have been jostled the wrong way because he turned to Levi and scowled.

"Watch it," he said.

Levi glared back at him, and the man backed off. The crowds, the impersonal treatment, were the things Levi never got used to after his mom pulled him from his one-room schoolhouse in Apple Lake and enrolled him in public school. He hadn't spoken English well, and the kids made fun of him. That year he got into a lot of fights. The loneliness he'd felt as a small boy, amid kids who couldn't care less about him, was palpable—kind of how he felt surrounded by hundreds of people trying to get ahead of someone else into the amusement park. Good thing he had Rebecca next to him. He needed her presence more than she could possibly need his.

Levi heard Rebecca's breathing quicken as she caught sight of the roller coaster looming over the park entrance.

He took her hand. "You don't have to ride any ride you don't want to."

She didn't dignify his statement with a response, just kept her eyes glued to the monster thrill ride. Screams from riders pierced the air. Rebecca held her breath.

He leaned over and whispered in her ear. "Rebecca, we don't even have to go in." Levi would have turned around and marched back home without a second thought.

"Ach, Levi, stop it. You already know what I am going to say."

After fifteen minutes of bumping against people in line in the hot sun, they finally made it into the park. Taking a deep breath, Rebecca examined her map. "Where should we start?" she said, trying to sound thrilled but only managing to sound desperate.

Levi took her hand and pulled her in the opposite direction Jason and Tara were headed. "You can go for the big stuff first or do something smaller and work up to the scarier rides."

"Let's work our way up," she said.

"Then we should go to the indoor park first. You know"—he nudged her with his elbow—"to the kiddie rides."

Rebecca didn't even make a face. "I love kiddie rides. And let go of my hand. It is not proper in public."

Levi rolled his eyes but let go of her hand…reluctantly. The feel of her skin sent him to the clouds.

He cheerfully led her to the huge indoor space that echoed with loud voices. Tara wouldn't be found anywhere near here.

"Okay," said Levi. "You're too big for the ball pit, so the next wimpiest thing is probably the tea cups."

Rebecca looked in the direction he pointed. "That looks like fun," she lied.

Levi helped Rebecca into a bright yellow teacup. The average age of a teacup rider was probably eight years old, but Rebecca didn't notice. She sat rigidly with her hands wrapped tightly around the wheel in the center and took deep, cleansing breaths. Levi didn't know whether to laugh or to cry. She was so cute in her determination to scare herself silly, but he couldn't stand to see her in distress. It was going to be a very long day.

The teacups rotated, slowly at first, and then at a speed that pushed Rebecca close to him with the centrifugal force. He liked her closeness but not the miserable look on her face as the teacups whizzed past each other at blurry-eyed speed.

Once everything stopped spinning, Levi took Rebecca's hand as she weaved her way off the ride. They sat on a bench, and she buried her head in her hands.

"That was terrible," she groaned. "Not scary, but sickening."

Levi brushed a lock of hair away from her face. "We can go home if you want."

She mumbled into her hands. "No, this is fun."

Levi couldn't help laughing. She was adorable.

Rebecca snapped her head up. "Don't laugh at me!"

"Oh, weren't you making a joke?"

She cracked a smile. "Okay. It is a great adventure. Is that good enough for you?"

Levi gave in to the urge to touch her hand. "Being with you is good enough for me."

"Manure. Too much manure."

Levi didn't defend himself. He laughed harder.

They sat until Rebecca decided she did not need to throw up and then, with determination, rode the rest of the rides worth doing inside. Once they stepped off the coaster with the ten-year-olds, they made their way to their bench. Rebecca sank onto it as if she would never rise again.

"You know, if you hold your breath on the big roller coaster, you'll pass out," he said.

"I'll remember that." She closed her eyes and rubbed her forehead. "Do you think we could go out and get some fresh air?"

A wall of heat hit them as he led her through the big glass doors to a grassy spot in the shade. She stretched out on the ground and shielded her eyes from the sun. Levi sat next to her and tried not to think about how it would feel to lean over and brush his lips against hers.

"Hey, Levi."

Tara and Levi's friend Jason came toward them. Levi was afraid he might see the two of them today. Jason's dad had gotten them all free tickets through his work. Jason had his hand in Tara's back pocket. Tara grinned smugly. She cupped her hand around her mouth and whispered meaningfully to Jason. Jason looked at Rebecca and then at Levi, his eyes wide.

Great. Levi knew exactly what Tara said so secretly, and Jason was going to freak out. Levi formulated a strategy as the pair got closer.

"Is she okay?" Jason said, looking at Rebecca like she was from another planet.

"Yeah, the last ride made her a little dizzy."

Tara stood over Rebecca. "Weak stomach, huh?"

"A little," Rebecca mumbled, sitting up and smoothing her unruly hair.

Jason stuffed his hands into his pockets and trained his eyes on the ground.

Levi took a deep breath. Might as well put all his cards on the table. "This is my girlfriend, Rebecca Miller," he said. "She's Amish."

Rebecca glanced at Levi and raised her eyebrows.

"Yeah," Jason mumbled. "Tara told me."

Tara tiptoed onto the grass and pulled Jason down to sit with her. "I didn't know Amish girls were allowed at amusement parks," she said.

Rebecca smiled a genuine smile—pretty impressive when faced with Tara's disdain. "Lots of Amish come to amusement parks." She pointed to the building with the kiddie rides. "We saw an Amish family in there."

Tara stopped paying attention after a few seconds, but she seemed disappointed in Rebecca's calm reply. She was obviously looking for a fight, not an olive branch.

Jason, on the other hand, hung on to every word Rebecca uttered. He frowned and studied Levi's face with puzzlement then pulled some grass and played with it absentmindedly. He was tactful enough not to press for answers while Tara and Rebecca were around, but Levi knew he would hear about it later.

Sorry, Jason. How can I make you understand something I can't fathom myself?

Jason did probably the only sensible thing he could. "Hey, I'm going to get one of those slushy drinks. Any of you guys want one?"

"No, thanks," Levi and Rebecca said in unison.

"No," Tara said, "but you go. I'll wait for you here."

Jason took off like a bullet from a gun.

"We're doing the water park," said Tara, "if you want to come. I know Rebecca is allowed in a swimming suit."

"The roller coasters are next for us. Right, Rebecca?"

Rebecca turned as white as a sheet. "I think I should go to the bathroom." She stood but motioned for Levi to stay put.

"It's in that building over there," Tara said.

"Thanks," Rebecca said, already jogging in that direction.

Tara watched her until Rebecca was out of earshot. "Oh, she's so cute," she gushed. "Like your little pet."

Levi expected the viciousness. He didn't even flinch. Tara couldn't help herself, but he didn't have to stick around to take it.

He stood up. "I'll go wait for Rebecca."

Tara grabbed onto his pant leg. "Okay, I'm sorry. I was just kidding. Man, you are sensitive."

"Really, Tara. I'm going to go wait over there."

Tara laid her hands in her lap and stared him down with her pathetic kitten look. "I'll behave, I promise."

Levi hesitated.

"I want to be friends," Tara insisted. "I really want to understand about you and this new girl. You hurt me, Levi."

Levi recognized the manipulation but didn't fight it. Groaning inwardly, he sat down and gave Tara his best no-nonsense expression.

"I've texted you like fifty times," Tara said, "but you never answer. I don't see why we can't be friends, even if you don't like me anymore."

Levi shook his head. "Be honest, Tara. You want to get back together, and I don't."

Frustration flashed in Tara's eyes. "This Amish thing is new and exciting and kind of weird, but I know you too well to think that it's anything serious."

No, Tara, you don't know me at all. How could you, when I'm just beginning to know myself?

"I can't figure out if you feel sorry for her or want to ease your guilty conscience. I don't know what you're trying to prove, but you're not fooling me." Tara suddenly seemed two feet nearer with her face uncomfortably close to his. "We were really good together."

Levi leaned away from her. "Sorry, Tara. Being with you was really fun while it lasted, but I've never been happier in my life."

Tara pulled away. "Never been happier in your life," she said caustically. She stood up and shoved her phone into her back pocket—not leaving much room for Jason's hand. "Remember, you could have had me. Think about that on those cold, lonely nights."

She stormed away, leaving Levi with only pity for her.

When Rebecca got back from the bathroom, Levi was lying on the grass with his hands propped behind his head. "Did you throw up?" he said, peeking at her with one eye closed.

"Nae, but not for lack of trying," Rebecca said, sitting at Levi's feet. "Where is Tara and your friend?"

"Tara is probably in the next state by now."

"Did you make her mad?"

"Furious."

"Why?"

"I told her I've never been happier in my life."

Rebecca didn't say anything, and Levi opened his eyes to see her reaction. She was smiling but looked away when she caught him staring.

"You called me your girlfriend."

Levi leaned up on his elbow. "Does that bother you?"

"I can bear it."

Levi sat up. "Good, because the next phase of my strategy is to get you to hold hands with me in public."

"You will be stuck on that one for quite some time." She laughed, and he saved that sound in his memory. He probably wouldn't hear it again for the rest of the day.

Levi got to his feet and pulled her up with barely a flick of his wrist.

She was still so skinny. "Okay, are you ready for the rest of your day at Misery Park? I'm really looking forward to it."

She let out a breath and nodded. "Where to?"

"I say we do go-carts first and save the big coasters for last. That way, you're more likely to throw up at the end of the day instead of the beginning."

They made their way to the big Trojan horse. The long wait in line proved to be a bad thing, because the longer Rebecca stood there, the more agitated she became. By the time they came to the front of the line, Levi couldn't remember the last time he had heard her take a breath.

Before they got into their little cars, Levi said, "You don't have to—"

"I know," she said.

Not very patiently, the attendant showed Rebecca how to use her feet on the pedals. "Don't slam on the brakes," he said, "or you'll cause a crash."

Dread washed over Levi. One more thing to worry about on a long list of worries. Rebecca hadn't the faintest idea how to maneuver a car, let alone have the instinct to push and release the pedals when she went flying around the track. The other drivers would eat her alive out there. He'd have to stay glued to her like a moth on flypaper. He clenched his teeth. Was it possible to roll the thing if she got going too fast? He said his third prayer in as many hours.

Please, don't let her die.

Rebecca came out of the gates at a snail's pace, but Levi knew her too well to think she'd keep to a conservative speed. She took perverse pleasure in terrorizing herself.

She pushed on the gas too hard, then slammed on the brakes, then punched the gas and squealed her wheels when she tried to slow down. This stop-and-start sequence went on for about a hundred yards before she abandoned the brake altogether and sped through the course with her head hunkered down over the steering wheel.

"Slow down, slow down," Levi muttered as he doggedly followed her trail. She passed three other go-carts. Had she no sense of caution?

By the time she thankfully reached the end of the course, Levi didn't know whether the urge to strangle her or embrace her was stronger.

After she finally braked at the finish line, she unbuckled her seat belt and stumbled out of her go-cart like a drunken sailor. He wanted to throttle her. He didn't.

"Did you see how fast I went?" she said.

"Yeah, I did."

"I even passed three cars." She panted and put her hand to her heart. "I thought I was going to die."

"So did I."

She walked almost deliriously in the direction of the first roller coaster. "That was the worst experience of my life," she said. "But it's off my list. Never, never have to do it again."

Levi finally took pity on her and put his arm around her waist so she wouldn't run into the trees on the edge of the walkway. The roller coasters would be worse for her but better for him. At least she wouldn't be driving.

The long lines couldn't be helped. Summertime in Wisconsin was short. People made the most of it. But it gave Rebecca a chance to recover from each ordeal before plunging into the following one. After each ride, she stumbled to the next, traumatized and shaken, but determined to finish what she set out to do.

Finally, the fastest roller coaster in the park was the only one left. The line for that snaked around the ride itself. After the other rides, Rebecca couldn't fathom why this one was so popular. They sat together, with Rebecca keeping her viselike grip on the bar in front of them. She never held on to him when they did stuff like this. She had to attach herself to something completely immovable.

When the first drop came, she didn't scream, just clamped her eyes shut and held her breath. He knew better than to say or do anything to divert her attention. She had to stay completely focused on survival. It took all his willpower not to gather her up in his arms and hold on for dear life.

When the coaster came to a screeching stop, he took her shaking hand and pulled her from her seat. They walked to the nearest unoccupied bench, where she sat down and buried her head in her hands—a pose she'd taken several times today.

"My head is throbbing," she whispered.

"That was the last roller coaster. Only one more ride to go." Levi studied her with a mixture of sympathy and confusion. Could he convince her, though he hadn't been able to before, to give it up? Self-imposed torture was not his idea of fun.

"Wait here," he said. He went to a concession stand and bought her a Coke. When he came back, she still held her head in her hands, oblivious to what went on around her. "Here, drink this," he said. "It will make your head feel better."

She took a sip and grimaced. "I hate Coke."

Levi parked himself next to her. "We really can go—"

"Do not say it."

"Okay. I just think this is so dumb. I don't mean you're dumb, but you hate this. Why don't you change that insane list? Who cares if you ride a roller coaster before you die?"

"I know it seems crazy." Rebecca looked at him out of the corners of her eyes and frowned. "You won't tell anybody?"

"About your list? No way. You know I wouldn't."

Rebecca looked at the sky then at Levi before closing her eyes and rubbing her forehead. "I am doing it for my friend, Dottie Mae, who passed away."

"How did she die?"

Rebecca trained her attention on the ground in front of her. "She... It was horrible..." Rebecca's voice broke, and she stopped to regain her composure.

"You don't have to talk about it," Levi said, rubbing the back of her hand with his thumb.

Rebecca cleared her throat. "We were best friends. She had a way of getting into trouble because she was always looking for some new excitement. One day while doing laundry, she took a clean sheet to the roof and tried to use it like a parachute. She broke her ankle."

"Ouch."

"We always talked about what we would do when our time came for rumschpringe. She kept a list, an actual list, of things to do when she turned sixteen. I wasn't that interested. I am a chicken at heart."

Rebecca took another sip of her Coke and made a face. She concentrated on her straw as she slid it up and down in the hole in the lid. It squeaked noisily. "When she died, I promised myself I'd do everything on that list because she'd never get a chance." She rubbed her eyes with her fists. "That's why I'm going to finish. I have to do it for her."

Thousand-ton weights pulled Levi's heart to his toes. He wished with every fiber of his being that he didn't know exactly how she felt. He had been responsible for cutting a life short. Someone wouldn't ever have a chance to live her dream—because of him. He'd give anything to have that moment back again.

At times like this, he wished he hadn't stopped drinking.

Why did he ever in a million years think he deserved someone like Rebecca—someone so perfect and innocent, who probably never had a vengeful or impure thought in her life?

Tara was right. He wasn't fooling anybody.

Taking a deep breath, he leaned back on the bench and closed his eyes to let it pass. Rebecca didn't need to see the inner turmoil he'd kept so well hidden. She'd experienced enough of her own.

"You have one last ride before we can get out of here," he said. "I say we get it over with."

Rebecca sucked up the remainder of her Coke with her straw. "Let's go," she said. "It will be fun."

Chapter Twenty

Levi pulled his car in front of the old brick house that must have been eighty years old. But the style and the aging red brick were the only clues that the house was so ancient. The trim had a shiny coat of paint, and the shingles on the roof looked brand new. The front walkway, paved with flagstones, wound through rosebushes and huge pots over-flowing with hostas and impatiens. The yard was shaded with trees and teeming with flora and felt twenty degrees cooler than the rest of the neighborhood.

Levi turned off the car and caressed Rebecca's cheek then wove his fingers through her hair. Warmth pulsated through her body like a cup of hot cocoa...with marshmallows. She closed her eyes and savored his smell, just for a moment.

"You okay?" he said.

"I am sure I will be. Someday. Maybe next week."

He grinned reluctantly. "One of these days, you're going to push me past my ability to endure, Rebecca Miller."

"*Your* ability to endure? Those rides don't even scare you."

"No. *You* scare me when I'm on those rides."

She shook her head. He was teasing again. He grabbed her hand, sending a wave of sparks up her arm.

"I'm okay," she said, trying to ignore the sensation of his hand touching hers.

"At least one of us is." He came around to her side and opened the door. He put his arm around her waist and supported her as they walked to the porch. Her legs still shook after that last ride that catapulted her and Levi into the air and whipped them back again in a matter of seconds. She honestly thought the entire seat was going to come loose from the cables and she and Levi were going to crash into the parking lot at the other end of the park. When they got off the ride, Rebecca felt lucky to have escaped death. Compared to the waterskiing, the roller coasters, and the movie, the catapult had been the worst experience of her life.

Except for losing Dottie Mae. Nothing compared to that.

After Levi peeled her off the sidewalk at the amusement park, they had taken a short twenty-minute drive west into a tree-lined neighborhood.

Rebecca breathed in the fresh air of trees and flowers. "Where are we?"

The door swung open, and a large man with a deeply wrinkled face greeted them with his arms spread wide.

"Levi Cooper! Well, I'll be a monkey's uncle." His booming laughter could probably be heard the next block over. "I guess I am." He attacked Levi with a smothering hug, and Levi barely had time to hug back before the large man released him and turned his attention to Rebecca. "And who is this?" He smiled warmly and held out his hand. "A cute girl. Levi, I didn't know you had such good taste."

He kept hold of Rebecca's hand and pulled her into the entryway. "Come in, come in." Ushering them into his kitchen, he invited them to sit on padded bar stools. He sat next to Levi, and Rebecca couldn't help fearing that the stool would collapse any minute under his significant frame.

"Rebecca," Levi said, "this is my dad's uncle Joe."

Uncle Joe squinted and studied her face. "Rebecca. I have a granddaughter named Rebecca. They call her *Reba*." He waved his hand. "She's their kid. I guess they can call her what they want."

Uncle Joe bounced his fist on the bar. "So, what brings you to my neck of the woods? Come to get my permission to marry?"

Rebecca felt a blush move up her face, but Levi simply flashed his teeth while his eyes danced. "No, not yet. We came from the amusement park, and she feels a little sick. I thought you might let us rest here for a minute or two."

"Amusement park, huh? I haven't been there. Too afraid I'll get stuck in the turnstiles going in."

"It was fun," Rebecca said.

The laughter bubbled out of Levi's mouth. "Yeah, fun. And anyway, Rebecca loves flowers. I wanted her to see your yard."

Uncle Joe smiled big and clapped Levi on the shoulder. "All Tillie's doing. She tells me what to plant and where to move the rocks. I just do what she says."

"It is beautiful," Rebecca said. "I love the climbing roses on the fence out front."

"I built that trellis about six years ago. Tore it down twice because Tillie said it leaned to the left. Now it leans to the right." He slid off his stool. "Come on. I'll show you around."

They went out the back door and stepped into a carpet of impatiens. Rebecca caught her breath at the sight.

"Good shade flowers," said Uncle Joe.

He took them down a path with moss growing between the flagstones. A small pond fed by a trickling stream graced the back of the property, while a gazebo almost completely enshrouded with ivy and clematis straddled the stream. Three benches covered with overstuffed pillows sat in the gazebo, forming a semicircle along the short walls.

Rebecca stepped reverently up the stairs to the gazebo, ran her hands along the ivy, and took a whiff of a purple flower twined around the post. Levi, with his hands in pockets, stood staring at her with an unreadable expression on his face.

Uncle Joe clapped his hands together. "I'll go get some lemonade."

He hurried back to the house with the agility of someone much younger, and Levi slowly walked up the gazebo's steps. He took Rebecca's hand, and they sat on one of the benches. He didn't take his eyes from her face. "*This* is how I want to see you."

"In a garden?"

"Jah," he said, slipping into Pennsylvania Dutch and lowering his voice to a whisper. "This is what you love. You are so beautiful here."

Rebecca hardly had time to realize how close his face was to hers was before he abruptly pulled away, stood up, and moved to the bench across from her. He shook his head and frowned wistfully. "This is going to be the death of me. The death of me."

Uncle Joe came tromping up the steps of the gazebo with two glasses of pink lemonade. He handed one to each of his guests. "You got some color back, Rebecca. In fact, now you look flushed. Have a drink."

"Aren't you having any?" Levi asked.

"Mine's in the house," Uncle Joe said. "You two don't need me out here to ruin your fun. I'm making jambalaya. You wanna stay for dinner?"

Levi looked to Rebecca. She smiled. "Sure we would," he said.

"Okay, good. Tillie will be home at six." He whisked a leaf off the gazebo with his foot. "Sit out here as long as you like. Although, if I were you, Levi, I'd be sitting a whole lot closer to your date."

"I'm trying to be a gentleman," Levi mumbled.

Uncle Joe looked from Levi to Rebecca. "That's the most refreshing thing I've heard all day. Your dad was like that. A good boy, always a gentleman."

Levi rested his elbows on his knees and looked at the floor.

Uncle Joe glanced at Levi. "He still in Chicago?"

Levi nodded. "With Bunny."

Uncle Joe's booming laughter shook the ivy growing up the gazebo. "Bunny. You always knew how to hit my funny bone." He turned toward the house. "Let me know if you need anything else. Do you like your jambalaya spicy?"

He kept talking—to himself or Levi, Rebecca couldn't tell—but his voice disappeared with him into the house.

Rebecca studied Levi, who still had his face pointed to the floor and his elbows planted on his knees. "You do not like to talk about your dad."

"I probably shouldn't have said that about his new wife."

"Said what?"

"Her name is Sherry." Levi stood and paced around the gazebo. He tried to smile at Rebecca, with little success. "I get so mad whenever anybody mentions my dad. His new wife is a bleached blond who gets her nails done twice a month and wears skirts so short, they're almost invisible. She's the complete opposite of my mom. It's like my dad parked my mom in a used car lot and bought a different model. Like Mom doesn't even matter."

"Like you don't even matter."

Levi plopped himself onto a plump pillow. "Yeah, that's how it is."

Rebecca put her legs up on the seat of the bench. "Okay, let's talk about something less upsetting. Like roller coasters."

"Hah," he said. "That's only slightly less painful."

He came over to her again. She swept her legs off the bench and he sat next to her. "I told you, Rebecca, I can't stand it." He rubbed his forehead. "You might think this sounds insincere, but it's not. Everything in my life revolves around you."

She wanted to laugh it off, to tease him about shoveling manure, but the intensity of his gaze made her pause.

"When I'm with you, my protective instincts kick into high gear. Then you force me to watch as you attempt to kill yourself. It ain't fun, kid."

"It's less fun for me, champ."

The ghost of a smile passed over his face. "Like Mohammed Ali." Levi reached out his hand and stroked hers. "I'm asking you to go home and rethink your list. I don't think Dottie Mae would want you to die in the attempt to finish it."

"Dottie Mae would scold me for not having a sense of adventure. She had so much energy. It was like all the lights went out when she died."

"She meant a lot to you."

Rebecca nodded.

"Why don't I ever see you cry?"

"About Dottie Mae?"

"About catapults or lakes or Dottie Mae."

"Crying is weak."

Levi shook his head. "It means you're brave enough to show how you feel. Even if you look like a fool."

"I'd rather show that I'm in complete control of my life."

He maneuvered his arm around her shoulders and stared at her lips.

"Don't kiss me," Rebecca said. "If you kiss me, I'll forever associate kissing with the nausea of the Catapult."

He released his hold, stood up, and started pacing again. "I won't kiss you," he said. "I'm trying to be mad at you."

Had he been about to kiss her?

Gute thing he didn't try. She would never dream of letting Levi Cooper kiss her, no matter how handsome, no matter how kind or generous or wonderful he was. Rebecca frowned at the twinge in her heart that felt something like regret.

"Everything in my life revolves around you."

Rebecca sighed and looked away. Levi had an adorably infuriating habit of holding nothing back. She knew exactly what he thought every minute—exactly how he felt about her. That boy took too many risks with his heart. How did he know that Rebecca wouldn't drop him like a hot potato tomorrow?

He didn't.

He was willing to let his heart get stomped on.

Why?

She was nothing special—a penniless Amish girl who bossed her siblings around and caused nothing but trouble and expense for Levi. And yet he kept coming back for more. The sudden gratitude and tenderness she felt almost took her breath away—gratitude for his caring about her, for being her champion when no one else even noticed. She had a sudden urge to fly into his arms and promise him that she would never shatter the heart he had so freely given her.

But that would mean she would have to show vulnerability, and

Rebecca couldn't bring herself to do it. If she loved someone that much, she gave them the power to hurt her. No one would ever gain that much power over Rebecca. Not even Levi.

New and interesting varieties of flowers were much safer. "Can I go look at the roses over there?" she said.

Levi glanced to the side of the house where a jumble of roses burst from the bushes standing in the sun. He snapped out of whatever contemplative mood he was in. "Okay. I'll come with you to make sure you don't prick your finger on a thorn. With your track record, you'd probably bleed to death. I know how to make a tourniquet."

"Are you a doctor?" she said, happy to be on safe ground.

"Nope."

"Then you are not touching my finger."

Chapter Twenty-One

Rebecca dribbled the last of the paint onto the roller tray and handed it to Levi. "This is it," she said.

Levi looked at her measly offering. "Perfect. Enough to touch up two or three spots and then we're done. I can't believe how precisely you calculated the paint we would need. You got it right, down to the last drop."

"The paint is all!" Max yelled from his ladder.

Rebecca handed the empty paint bucket up to him. "Here, get what you can out of this. That is all we've got."

The barn stood two stories tall, a good stretch for their ladder, but at least it wasn't like some of the barns in the area that towered three or more stories into the air. Max and Levi could reach everything with the ladder and a roller extension.

Mamm sat under the shade of the porch, watching them finish up the painting. A pleasant breeze teased wisps of Rebecca's hair away from her face and kept the painters relatively comfortable in the late August sun. Linda, Levi, and Max each positioned themselves on their own sides of the barn, busily painting, while Danny and Rebecca worked on the fourth wall. They wore painting clothes, and Danny managed to cover more of himself than the trim with bright white paint.

"Cum," Levi said, slipping into Deitsch, as he so often did when he worked on the farm. "Walk around with me and see if there are any spots we missed."

He put down the tray and his brush, and they strolled around the corner of the barn to the side Levi had been painting where they were all alone. Levi slipped his hand into hers with an easy, relaxed motion that seemed as natural as breathing. Hand in hand, they examined the north wall and trim for any flaws.

He pointed to the barn wall. "We patched a hole up there before we painted."

For some reason, Rebecca found it difficult to concentrate on paint coverage after the touch of Levi's hand. She chided herself and pulled away from him. He seemed bent on stretching the bounds of propriety every time he got a chance.

He simply smiled, put his hands behind his back, and kept walking. "This side look okay to you?"

Rebecca nodded.

"And the trim?"

"Jah, very nice."

"Gute, because nothing is finished until it passes your approval," Levi said. "I want this barn to make you smile every time you look at it. Like a picture right off a Hallmark Christmas card. You like it, don't you? The cardinal red with the white trim?"

"The trim makes it look crisp and clean. Like a true Amish barn."

They turned the next corner to find Linda reclining on the grass, her paintbrush sticking out of her empty bucket. "I am never, ever painting anything again," she said, wiping her brow with the back of her forearm. "Ach. I will never get the paint off my hands, and I am supposed to go to the gathering tonight with Mary Jane."

Rebecca pulled Linda off the ground by her paint-encrusted hand. She took the bucket and brush from the grass and handed them to Linda. "Here, go wash these out, and you will still have time to clean up for the gathering."

Linda rolled her eyes and flounced to the hose, where she quickly rinsed the paint off her brush and hands. Leaving the bucket by the hose, no doubt hoping it would put itself away, she stomped up the porch steps and into the house.

"Are you going to the gathering?" Levi said.

"Nae, of course not. I still have floors to mop."

Levi leaned his hand against the red wall of the barn—dry since they'd painted it last week. "Gute, because according to your mom, there are at least three Amish boys competing for your attention, and I don't want anyone else making a play for you."

"Three boys? What boys? That is nonsense."

Levi got that twinkle in his eyes. "Oh, no. Your mom even said their names the other day. Peter, Yiddy, and Melvin or Merlin or something like that."

Rebecca giggled. "That's Peter, Giddy, and Marvin. And they are not interested in me."

He stroked his chin. "Yet you seem to know exactly who I am talking about. Very suspicious."

"They are boys about my age. Mamm thinks everyone wants to marry me."

"They probably do," Levi said. He pushed away from the wall and pinned her with a serious look. "The real question is, are you interested in them?"

"Nae. I don't...I am...I am not," Rebecca stammered, suddenly aware that she couldn't look away from those piercing eyes.

His face relaxed and his eyes crinkled with his smile. "Gute. Because I will not go skiing with a girl who is engaged to someone else."

Max and Danny appeared, each carrying one end of the ladder, with Max kicking the empty can of paint on the ground in front of him.

"School starts on Monday," Max said, "and I've spent my whole summer working."

"Is the trim done on that side?" Levi asked.

"Jah," Max said. "I knocked down three wasps' nests too. Got stung."

Levi opened the barn door so they could put the ladder away. "You're tough. I probably would have cried like a baby."

Danny put his side of the ladder on the ground, and Max hoisted it onto a large hook screwed into the wall of the barn. "Are you bringing supper again?" Max said.

"It is already here," Rebecca said. "It's a great big pizza that I just need to stick into the oven."

Danny gave Levi a high five—a move Levi had taught him last week. "Pizza! I love pizza." He bolted to the house. "I will go shower."

"Hang your clothes outside," Rebecca called. "And don't get paint on the floor."

"I will go wash," Max said. He picked up the empty paint can as he went to the house. "And denki for the pizza," he said over his shoulder.

"No prob," Levi said.

They watched Max go into the house and waved to Mamm, who sat watching them.

"Your mom seems to be feeling better," Levi said.

Rebecca gave a slight smile. "She is especially chipper on Wednesdays. She never sits out this much on other days."

"If her suspicion of me gets her out in the fresh air more often, that can't be bad." Levi took off his hat and scratched his head. "What did she tell your fater about me?"

"As far as I know, the subject hasn't come up. Fater is pleased the work is done and doesn't ask many questions."

Smiling, Levi put his hands into his pockets and nudged her with his elbow. "Let's look at the rest of the barn," he said.

Together they inspected each wall and the trim then walked all the way around again for good measure. When they returned to their original spot, Mamm was gone.

"I am so happy," Rebecca said, making a sweeping gesture. "Denki for this. It is beautiful."

"A beautiful girl deserves a beautiful barn."

She gave him the look that told him he was piling the flattery thick. They both laughed.

"Every girl should have her own barn," she said, wishing she didn't enjoy Levi's company so much. It would make it that much harder when they had to say good-bye. "I should go put the pizza into the oven."

"I'll clean up. If I run out of things to do, I'll muck out the stalls.

The barn always needs to be mucked out. But I'm going to stink for dinner while the rest of you smell nice. I might have to eat outside by myself."

Rebecca didn't know what possessed her, but she picked up a bucket of water sitting near the dirty paintbrushes, and while he was turned, she dumped the water down his back. "You can have a shower out here," she said.

Yelling in surprise, he scanned his surroundings for something to help him retaliate. He sprinted to the hose, snatched Linda's empty bucket, and turned on the spigot full blast. Even at that, the filling was slow.

Giggling like a schoolgirl, Rebecca ran into the barn to the faucet used for watering the animals. Before the water was even an inch deep in her bucket, she heard Levi run into the barn. He paused to locate her among the stalls then let out a whoop and circled in around his prey.

Rebecca took her bucket with its measly supply of water and ran out the other door.

He was hot on her heels, and before she reached the outside hose, he lifted his bucket and doused her.

She squealed as the cold water soaked her hair and splashed down her face. After a hot day in the sun, it was quite a shock.

He dropped his bucket and stood with his hands on his hips, laughing. "Your kapp is all crooked, kid."

She put her hand to her head and straightened the kapp as best she could. "Not fair. I didn't even get your hair wet. You're too tall."

"Here," he said. He pointed to her bucket and leaned over so she could reach the top of his head.

She emptied her inch of water onto his hair.

"Feel better?" he said.

"Not yet." She turned on the hose and filled her bucket. She motioned for him to kneel down then emptied it over him.

He closed his eyes as the water hit him, and he shook his head back and forth like a dog. She protested as water flew everywhere.

"Hey, you started it," he said as he stood up and smoothed his hair back.

"And I finished it," she said. "I should tell you right now, I never surrender."

"Then I surrender to you," he said gallantly. Rebecca never grew tired of that boyish grin.

She stood staring at him and wondered what it would feel like if he kissed her. For a fleeting moment, she wished she knew.

Levi suddenly straightened and fixed his eyes behind her.

"Rebecca."

Rebecca knew who belonged to that voice before she even turned around. "Marvin," she said with a guilty smile, although she wasn't sure what she felt guilty about. Even Marvin couldn't think a water fight was wicked, could he?

Marvin worked very hard to keep his gaze off Levi as sweat beaded on his upper lip. "I came to see if you would like a ride to the gathering tonight."

"Oh, well…" Rebecca smoothed her unruly hair and adjusted her kapp for a second time. "Denki very kindly for the invitation, Marvin, but I had not planned on attending the gathering. The floors need mopping."

Marvin gave a slight nod and kept his eyes on Rebecca. She would have to make the introduction. There was nothing else to be done.

"Marvin, this is Levi. We have been painting the barn today."

Marvin finally looked at Levi straight on, and his frown deepened. "Your fater has refused my help several times," he said. "Or I would have come to paint for you."

Rebecca didn't know what to say. She couldn't very well explain the circumstances to Marvin. She would simply have to let him draw his own conclusions.

Levi stood stone-faced and made no attempt to smooth over the awkward situation. Rebecca had the insane urge to run into the house screaming. Instead she held her ground and tried to dismiss Marvin as gently as possible.

"Thank you for coming over, Marvin. You are very thoughtful. I will come to a singing another time, Lord willing."

Marvin took two steps back then hesitated. "I will see you at gmay then, on Sunday?"

"Jah, to be sure."

He took one last look at Levi before leaving. He reached the lane in a few long strides. She watched him climb into his buggy before turning to Levi. He stood like a statue staring at the spot where Marvin had been.

She grinned mischievously. "That is Marvin Yutzy. He is interested."

Levi didn't even smile. "Oh, yeah. He's very interested." He looked at the bucket in his hand as if he had no idea how it got there. "I've got to go."

He dropped the bucket and walked away from her.

She couldn't have been more surprised if he had picked up a rock and thrown it at her kitchen window. She followed him.

"Levi, I'm sorry. Are you mad at me?"

He stopped dead in his tracks. "Mad at you? Why would I be mad at you?"

"Then are you afraid Fater will get angry?"

"About what?" Levi said, frowning and looking at the ground.

"You and me, playing in the water."

"Why would he be mad about that?"

Rebecca stomped her foot in frustration. "Quit answering my questions with more questions."

"I'm sorry, kid. I could never be mad at you." His lips twitched into an awkward, glum half-smile. "Except when you insist on riding roller coasters." He faked cheerfulness with a wider smile. "I have to go, that's all."

She stepped in his path of retreat. "No, it is not. Do not lie to me, you big baby."

Levi laughed in spite of himself. "Big baby? That's the cruelest nickname I ever heard."

She raised her eyebrows in disbelief as the truth stunned her. "You are jealous of Marvin."

"Jealous? Of course I'm jealous."

"Why? I do not like him."

"I'm jealous because he's part of your world. And I'm not." He ran his fingers through his hair and stared into the distance. "I don't belong, Rebecca, and every time I step onto this farm, I am reminded of how out of place I am."

Emptiness filled Rebecca's stomach. This little game she and Levi played—and it was a game—could only end with two losers. At some point, they would be forced to face reality. He would return to his world, his life, his girlfriends, and she would end up marrying not handsome Levi, but a boy like Marvin Yutzy. Boring, steady, dependable, and Amish. The pit in her stomach expanded to fill her soul.

"We are from two impossibly different places, Levi," she said, keeping the emotion from her voice. "It is no use pretending that things are not really as they are. We cannot let what we want cloud the wisdom of what must be."

"I know, but I wish you didn't have to be so practical about it." He frowned then softened his expression. "So, you want to be with me."

"I never said that."

"*We cannot let what we want cloud what must be.* I heard it. What *we* want."

"That is the point, Levi. It doesn't matter."

"It matters to me," he said. "More than you'll ever know." He tapped his hand against his leg and stared vacantly at the barn. "So, even though our relationship defies wisdom, can I see you on Friday night? We've still got that skiing date." A grin tugged at his lips.

Rebecca breathed a sigh of relief. He wanted to avoid reality as much as she did. "Jah, you bet."

"Gute. Wisdom is so overrated."

Chapter Twenty-Two

Levi opened the car door for Rebecca, and she slipped into the front seat. He smiled to himself as he walked around to the other side of the car. He liked the dates where he didn't have to peel Rebecca off the sidewalk or half carry her to the car or hold her head while she threw up all over the parking lot. Maybe after a day like this, he could convince her to abandon the skiing scheme once and for all.

Rebecca carefully held her newly purchased hosta, making sure it didn't sway with the movements of the car as Levi pulled out of the parking lot. Out of the corners of his eyes, Levi watched Rebecca softly stroke each leaf of the small plant.

"Someday, I'm going to have a whole patch of hostas under that maple tree in our backyard," she said. She looked at him, her eyes shining. "Thank you for buying it for me. I hope you know I don't expect gifts."

"I don't mind bribing you to go out with me."

"Oh, no. I have never thought that—"

Levi reached over and stroked her hand. "How could I not buy it for you? I haven't seen you so excited since the first time I brought you a rose."

Rebecca shook her head and grinned. "You know too many of my secrets."

"What? Like the fact that you love plants and dirt and you have a green thumb? That's no secret."

"To everyone else it is."

Levi felt that familiar stab of indignation on Rebecca's behalf. Her own family depended on her, took advantage of her, and they didn't even know her. "I'm glad you trust me with at least some of your secrets."

She studied his face. "I do. I trust you, mostly."

"Mostly? That's better than sometimes, anyway."

"I would love to see the gardens in the spring. I am sure they are beautiful with the flowering trees," Rebecca said, her eyes back on her hosta. "But the turning trees are so brilliant at the end of the season… like they are on fire."

"I'm glad you liked it," he said.

"Did you like it?"

"It was the best," he said. "I spent a whole three hours watching you smile. Much better than watching the blood drain from your face with that half-crazed look in your eyes."

Rebecca pinned him with a stern eye. "Do not believe for one minute that I don't know what you're up to. Since the roller coasters, we have not done one even slightly terrifying thing."

"That's your opinion, kid. Petunias scare the living daylights out of me."

"In the last three weeks, you have taken me to two greenhouses, an arboretum, and a city park," she said.

"That dog almost bit me at the park. Rabies could be scary."

"Dottie Mae would have been bored stiff."

"So, what besides skiing is left on that psycho list of yours?"

"Driving," Rebecca said.

"I can teach you to drive a golf ball," Levi said. "It's safe. Unless you hit me in the head and kill me."

"Could you teach me to drive your car?"

Levi shook his head. "Lucky for me, it's illegal without a license."

"You said your dad used to take you on the back roads before you got your license. I don't need to drive to Milwaukee. I just want to try it out."

Levi took a deep breath. He knew her well enough to understand that she wouldn't give up until he relented. How hard could it be on the old haul road behind the DeGroots' pasture? A straight, wide dirt road that no one ever used was the perfect place for a driving lesson.

"Okay," he said, "but I pick the place and the speed and the distance. Once we're done, you can't tell me it wasn't good enough."

"Agreed," she said, smiling in satisfaction.

After the hour's drive back to Patton, Levi slowly made his way down the main road, lecturing Rebecca on the finer points of vehicle operation. By the time they got to DeGroots' pasture, he hoped he had her scared to death. A car careening out of control was a bit different than an errant skateboard.

He turned off the car and let Rebecca sit in the driver's seat. He showed her how to start the car then ran around to the passenger seat. "Ease off the brake slowly and let the car roll forward."

As the car moved, Rebecca caught her breath and pressed hard on the brake. They both lurched forward.

"Sorry," she squeaked.

She slowly took her foot from the brake and slammed on it again when the car rolled forward.

"Breathe, kid," Levi said. "We'll crash if you pass out."

For the third time, Rebecca let the car roll forward and abruptly applied the brake.

Levi exhaled. "Okay, you've driven a car. I think that's good enough."

"No, I have the feel of it now."

"One more time, kid."

"Thanks, Pooky."

"Pooky?"

"I heard a lady say that to her son in the store yesterday."

"You might feel stupid calling me Pooky," Levi said.

"Probably."

"Take your foot off the brake and let the car roll. Do you trust me?" Rebecca nodded.

"We're only going about two miles an hour, so we're not going to die. The road is wide enough that you can veer to the right and left a little."

This time by sheer willpower, Levi was sure, Rebecca held her breath and let the car roll. Her foot hovered over the brake, but she resisted the urge to tap on it. The dirt and gravel popped under the tires as they trundled slowly down the lane.

"Turn your wheel slightly to the left," Levi said. "Good, now straighten out."

Rebecca did as she was told. When the car didn't explode, she took a deep breath.

Levi regarded the stretch of road in front of them. A lot of distance to work with. "Okay, now press very slowly on the gas pedal."

The engine revved, and the car jolted forward. Panting heavily, Rebecca lifted her foot.

"Try again," Levi said, hoping he sounded calmer than he felt. He couldn't help his heart racing. When she was upset, he was upset. The sooner they got through this ordeal, the better. Another thing off that darn list.

Rebecca eased her foot onto the gas pedal, and Levi's Toyota gradually, almost imperceptibly, picked up speed.

"Keep the speed right here for a minute. Get used to it."

They couldn't have been going more than ten miles an hour, but the terror on Rebecca's face was plain enough.

"Okay, ready to go faster?"

Rebecca kept her eyes glued to the dirt road but nodded slowly.

The car zoomed to twenty miles an hour—plenty fast for Levi. Any faster and they both might have a heart attack. Rebecca would have to be satisfied that she reached school-zone speed.

Rebecca didn't smile, but she did resume breathing. "This is fun."

"At the end of the road, stop and I'll show you how to put it into PARK."

The dirt road ended at a *T* intersection with a slight drop-off and a grove of trees directly ahead. Rebecca, with her penchant for reckless behavior, put more pressure on the gas pedal and sped to thirty miles an hour.

"Slow down!" Levi yelled, now in full panic mode. He wanted to throttle her.

She took her foot off the gas.

Levi's pried his fist off the door handle. "Stop right here," he insisted. "You're done."

She took her eyes from the road long enough to flash him a sheepish expression as the car slowed considerably. He ran his fingers through his hair. "The death of me," he muttered.

But Rebecca must have missed the brake, because the car suddenly accelerated forward. Levi shouted in surprise as his car plowed off the road, slid down the shallow drop-off, and thudded into a tree.

The impact wasn't huge; she hadn't been going that fast. But the momentum was enough to throw Rebecca forward, so she smacked her head into the steering wheel. Gasping, she clutched her forehead, and Levi saw blood trickle between her fingers.

With his heart sinking to his toes, Levi leaped from his seat and ran around to the driver's side. No seat belt. How could he have been so stupid?

He threw open Rebecca's door and knelt beside her. She had her face buried in her hands.

"Oh, kid. I'm sorry." He pulled her hands from her face to examine the injury. Blood trickled from a relatively small cut above her eyebrow. The size of the cut didn't make Levi feel any better. Reaching into the backseat, he found an old T-shirt, wadded it up, and placed it gently over Rebecca's forehead.

"How do you feel?" he asked.

"Bad," she mumbled.

Her eyes had that glassy look that could only mean a concussion. His heart skipped a beat. He pulled the T-shirt from her head and probed around the wound. She winced in pain.

"Oh, kid. It's going to be okay. I'm so sorry."

Rebecca needed to get to a hospital immediately, but Levi didn't know if the old Toyota could make the trip. The engine was still running, but that didn't mean that the wheels weren't bent or the radiator wasn't cracked. He put the T-shirt into Rebecca's hand and nudged it back over the cut. "Hold this," he said. "I need to check out the car."

Rebecca groaned. "I'm sorry I crashed it. I never should have—"

"Don't worry about it. The car isn't what's important."

He reached over, popped the hood, then walked to the front of the car. The bumper was crumpled but repairable. He lifted the hood to look for damage. No hissing steam or dripping liquids. It looked like the bumper took the brunt of the crash and left the engine unscathed. He patted the front grill. "Good girl," he said. His Toyota—as dependable as man's best friend. The tires looked pretty solid on the ground. With any luck, he would be able to back the car up onto the road without a tow truck. He took a deep breath and said a short prayer of thanks.

Returning to Rebecca, he put her arm around his neck and lifted her out of the car. "Come on," he said. He carried her to the passenger seat and belted her in.

She smiled a groggy smile. "You don't want me to drive anymore?"

"Never again."

"I think I agree."

"Keep the shirt on the bleeding. I'm taking you to the hospital."

She lifted her head and became more lucid. "No, you're not."

"Yeah, I am."

"Levi, I cannot afford a hospital."

"We're going anyway," Levi said.

Her voice rose in panic. "I cannot go to a hospital. My parents will find out. It will cost hundreds of dollars."

Levi clenched his jaw. "You need to see a doctor. We'll work out the payment somehow."

Rebecca reached over and grabbed his arm with her blood-smeared hand. "I do not need a hospital. Hospitals are where people go to die."

Could he bear to put her through one more panic-inducing experience? Hesitating, he stared into those hazel eyes, which depths revealed so many colors at once. His heart melted. How could he refuse her anything?

"Why do I let you talk me into stuff?" He pounded his fist on the steering wheel. Looking behind him, he pressed lightly on the gas pedal and eased the car back onto the dirt road. The three-ton weights on his chest eased considerably.

"No hospital," Levi said, shaking his head. "But against my better judgment. Most of what you've forced me to do in this relationship is against my better judgment."

"I need to go somewhere to clean up before you take me home," Rebecca said, taking the T-shirt from her forehead and feeling the wound. "Do you still have the first-aid kit at work?"

"Hah, very funny. I'm taking you to a professional."

"You said no hospital."

"I'm taking you to a nurse, at her apartment. But when she finds out who you are, she's going to freak out."

* * * * *

Rebecca wouldn't let Levi carry her. In spite of his concern about her head, she thought his carting her up two flights of stairs a ridiculous idea. So he put his arm around her waist and supported her as they slowly made their way up to his apartment.

This meeting between Rebecca and Mom was not exactly how he'd intended it, but he did want them to meet eventually. Levi had a plan, and the accident simply moved up the timing somewhat. This might be the perfect way to broach the subject with Mom—a subject he had been mulling over for weeks, a decision that would dramatically alter his life forever.

He knocked on the door, not wanting to fish around in his pocket for the keys. Mom kept it locked whether she was home or not.

"Who is it?" came a voice from the inside.

"Levi."

Mom opened the door a crack. Since Beth had left for college, she took extra caution. "Levi?" Her eyes widened as she looked at Rebecca. "Oh my, come in. What happened?"

Keeping a firm hold on Rebecca's arm, Levi led her to the kitchen table and pulled out a chair for her. She sat, then sucked in her breath and held it as she studied his mom.

"We were in a minor car accident," he said.

"Have you been drinking?"

She might as well have slapped him in the face. He reeled from the blow then regained his composure. "No, Mom. No way."

She lowered her eyes. "I am sorry, Levi. I shouldn't have assumed—"

"It's okay, Mom. It doesn't matter."

"It's not his fault," Rebecca said quietly. "I was driving."

Mom knelt beside the chair and put a hand to Rebecca's forehead. "You must be Rebecca."

Rebecca nodded.

"Let me see the cut. Levi, go get the first-aid kit. The big one in my room."

Levi jogged to Mom's room and pulled out the box from under her bed. When he returned to the kitchen, Mom and Rebecca were conversing quietly.

"She says she hit the steering wheel," Mom said. "Did you check for signs of a concussion?"

"Yeah, she seemed kind of dazed."

Mom took Rebecca's hand. "You might have a mild concussion, but nothing serious, I think."

She stood and opened the box and donned a pair of latex gloves. With the efficiency of someone who had cleaned many wounds, Mom wiped the blood from Rebecca's forehead and face. "Levi, get a wet rag so she can wipe her hands."

Rebecca held perfectly still and stared at Mom with unguarded curiosity.

"So, you are the girl Levi spends all his time with," Mom said as she poured more mild soap onto a gauze pad. "I can see why he was interested in the first place."

"So can I," said Levi.

Mom rolled her eyes then winked at Rebecca. "Have you noticed that you always know exactly how Levi feels about everything?"

Once the cut was clean, Mom could examine it more closely. "It is small," she said. "Even without stitches, I don't think you will have much of a scar. Right above the eyebrow like that, it will not be as noticeable. I can secure it with a butterfly. But if you wanted to go get stitches at the emergency room, that would be fine too."

"That ain't gonna happen," Levi said. "She refuses to set foot inside a hospital. You were the next best thing."

"I'm glad for that," Mom said, smiling. "I've been wanting to meet you for weeks, and Levi keeps you all to himself." She pulled another gauze pad and some antibacterial ointment from the first-aid kit. "Tell me about yourself. Where do you live? Are you going to school?"

Rebecca glanced at Levi as his mom dressed the cut on her forehead then forged ahead. "The most important thing you should know about me," she said, "is that I am Amish. My family lives in Apple Lake."

Mom was not prepared for such a revelation. She pulled away from her work. The ointment she meant to apply to Rebecca's forehead dangled precariously from the tube as her eyes darted from Levi to Rebecca in shocked disbelief. She plopped down without even checking to see if there was a chair to catch her when she descended.

Mom laid down her medical supplies. "Have you been baptized?"

Rebecca shook her head. "Later on next year, Lord willing."

"How did this happen?" she said, more to herself than either Levi or Rebecca.

"Mom, it's not the end of the world."

She didn't take it as the tease Levi meant it to be. "Yes, it is." Mom propped her elbows on the table, laced her fingers together, and leaned her forehead on her clasped hands. "Do you two understand what you are getting into?"

"We are only dating," Rebecca said.

"That is where the road begins," Mom said. "You have no idea where it ends." She massaged her temples.

"I asked Levi to teach me how to ski. He is going to take me skiing when the snows come."

Mom stared not at Rebecca, but at Levi, with something akin to pity. "I do not know you well, Rebecca," she said, "but I know my son, and this relationship means much more to him than a ski trip."

Rebecca studied her hands in her lap. "It means much more to me too," she said.

Levi's heart did a cartwheel. She had never come so close to expressing some sort of feeling for him. Despite the charged emotions in the room, he wanted to smile.

Mom seemed to think better of whatever she was going to say next. She clamped her mouth shut, picked up the ointment, and began to smear it over Rebecca's cut. They remained in silence until Mom chose to break it. She seemed to suddenly change moods, as if her outburst had never happened. "Who are your parents, Rebecca?

"Amos and Erla Miller."

"Ah, I see the resemblance," Mom said, feigning cheerfulness. "I knew Erla before she married. Beautiful, beautiful girl. How is she?"

"My mamm has been sick since she had my brother Danny. Rheumatoid arthritis."

"Oh, that is too bad. Have they given her good medication for the pain?"

"Some days it works and other days it doesn't."

"And how is your dat?"

"He is a roofer. He works in Milwaukee during the week and comes home on the weekends."

Mom cut some medical tape to the size of the gauze pad. "And brothers and sisters? How many?"

"One sister, two brothers. I am the eldest."

"Your mamm was a bit younger than me, but we met at *singeons* and such," she said as she finished securing the pad over Rebecca's cut. "There now. I will give you some extra pads and tape. Change the gauze every few hours but leave the butterfly bandage in place for at least five days, if you can. It might fall off on its own."

"I will," Rebecca said.

Levi pulled his keys from his pocket. "I'd better get her home."

Mom nodded. "Don't be too late tonight," she said, flashing him a we-need-to-talk look.

Yep, Levi had been expecting it. He flashed the same look right back at her.

She fished a packet from the first-aid kit and handed it to Rebecca. "Take some ibuprofen for the headache. If it's worse in the morning, go see a doctor. No excuses."

"I will."

Levi took Rebecca's hand and tugged her to the door.

"Denki for taking care of my head, Mrs. Cooper," Rebecca said.

"It is best to have someone wake you up every two hours tonight, just in case," Mom said.

"I will call you on your phone," Levi said. "Keep it on, okay?"

Rebecca nodded and turned to Levi's mom. "I am very happy we could meet."

"So am I," she said, giving Rebecca a half smile that did nothing to mask the pity in her eyes. "May the good Lord smile upon you all your days."

It sounded like Mom never planned on seeing Rebecca again.

Chapter Twenty-Three

Levi parked his crippled car in the usual place next to the bushes that separated the Millers' property from the road and turned off the engine. They sat in silence as they watched the last bit of dusk disappear into darkness.

"Please let me walk you to your door," he said.

"Nae, I will be fine."

He stroked her cheek with his thumb. "You're injured. What if you collapse in the field and I'm not there to pick you up?"

"I will call you on my cell phone."

"What if you drop your cell phone and lose it in the dark?"

"I can crawl to my house. It is not that far."

"You might think this is funny," Levi said, running his fingers through his hair, "but it's not. I make myself sick worrying about you. Today was the worst."

"Levi, I am nineteen years old. I will be fine."

"How will you explain the bandage to your family?" Levi said.

Rebecca shrugged. "I don't know. Fater will be mad that I got myself hurt."

"I should stick around."

"I don't want him to see you. It will make things worse."

"Worse? How?" A sickening thought slapped Levi upside the head. "Does he hit you?" He almost spit out the words.

Her eyes got wide. "No, never. How could you even ask?" She abruptly opened her door and leaped out of the car.

Levi followed her through the bushes, not caring how much noise he made.

She got as far as the toolshed before he caught up with her. "Rebecca, I'm sorry. I didn't mean to offend you. Please don't leave this way."

Withering, Rebecca slumped her shoulders and folded her arms tightly around her waist. "Go home. It's cold, and I don't want anyone to see you."

Levi rubbed his forehead. "I shouldn't have said that. It's none of my business. I hate thinking you're in danger, that's all."

She turned her face away from him and stared at the side of the shed. "I have never told anyone before," she said in a whisper.

Levi's throat tightened and he clenched his fists, fighting off his suddenly keen curiosity. "You don't have to."

"I'm ashamed."

"You don't have to tell me, Rebecca."

She took his hand—a first for her. Levi usually made the first move. "You are the only person who never thinks badly of me, even when I deserve it."

"You don't deserve it."

"After Dottie Mae died, I went to her grave every day and sat there for hours in the cold, crying. I shouldn't have neglected my chores like that. Or Mamm. She needed me. Things were bad for Fater too. He lost his job and Mamm was sick."

Levi bit his tongue and tried not to be angry with Rebecca's parents. They had placed the weight of the world on Rebecca's very young shoulders.

"One morning I forgot to load coal into the stove before going to the grave. Mamm is so sensitive to the cold, and she tried to load the stove herself. She fell down the cellar stairs and lay there for three hours before Fater and my siblings came home and found her. After the ambulance took her away, he came to find me."

Levi rubbed his hand up and down her arm. She trembled with emotion.

"I didn't even hear him come. He yanked me from the ground at the graveside and slapped me hard across the face. 'Stop your crying. Stop it,' he said. I remember it like yesterday. 'Your mamm was injured because you have been here wallowing in self-pity. Get yourself home and ask the Lord for forgiveness, because you almost killed her.' He wouldn't even let me visit her in the hospital. I sat home racked with guilt, not even sure if Mamm would live, and he wouldn't let me go to her. 'A wicked child like you don't deserve to see her mother,' he said. He's hated me ever since."

She didn't surrender to the tears, but Levi did. After he wiped the wetness from his face, he reached out and pulled Rebecca into his arms. He wished he had about ten arms to embrace her. She wrapped her arms around his waist, and he propped his chin on top of her head. He could feel the rapid rhythm of her heart.

"Fater brought Mamm home two days later. She had a broken leg and a broken wrist and a bruised kidney. She looked so pale. I remember standing in her doorway watching her sleep. Fater caught me looking. 'This is your fault, Becky. If she dies, it will be because you cared more about yourself than your mamm. Mend your ways.' That is the one and only time he ever struck me. And that is the last time I ever cried."

Levi held her close and tried to shield her from the chill. "I'm so sorry, kid. I wish I'd been there."

She held on to him for another lingering minute then pulled away and took a step back. Her sense of propriety seldom took a vacation.

"You won't tell anybody?"

"All your secrets are safe with me."

She put her hand to the bandage on her forehead. "I've got to go."

Although this seemed like rotten timing, Levi couldn't string Rebecca along with false hope. He ran his fingers through his hair again. "I don't think I can take you skiing."

"Why not?"

"Because after what happened today with the car, I will never forgive myself if you get hurt."

"But—"

"People break their necks skiing. People die. You don't know how to ski, and you aren't exactly the most coordinated person in the world."

"I can do it."

"When have I heard that before?"

Rebecca's voice rose with her agitation. "You promised. This is what I have been waiting for all these months."

She couldn't know how those words stung. Was it all about skiing? After he took her to the slopes, would she cut him out of her life?

Of course she would. He didn't belong in her world.

"Maybe it was a promise I never should have made," he said.

"Please, Levi. I've got to do it for Dottie Mae."

"I think Dottie Mae would have wanted you to be happy and live your own life. Not hers."

Rebecca paused to think about that. "They put you in a box when you die. A little box that holds your whole life, your whole existence. Dottie Mae was fourteen years old. She died with nothing to show for her life except a friendship quilt she made with her mother. They wrapped her in it and buried her. No matter how much I wished or prayed or cried, I couldn't bring her back. I promised Dottie Mae, on her grave, that I would finish what she never got to do."

Levi didn't know what to say. His pool of answers to life's most pressing questions was very shallow.

He only knew he didn't want to take her skiing.

He caught his breath. He knew more than that. He had come face-to-face with his true desires just as Rebecca had hit her head against the steering wheel.

He loved her. He couldn't bear to lose her.

He wanted to marry her.

And he was willing to do whatever it took to make that happen.

The thought sent his spirit soaring to the sky and crashing to the ground at the same time.

He would do whatever it took to be with Rebecca.

His life was about to change drastically.

"I've… I gotta go," he stammered.

"What about the skiing?"

"We'll talk about it later," he said. "I gotta go." He turned back to her. "Call me if you have any trouble or need anything, okay? I'll be here in a heartbeat."

Doubt filled her eyes.

"I gotta go," he said.

She frowned, folded her arms, and quickly walked away from him.

"Don't worry, kid," Levi whispered as she disappeared into the house. "Everything is going to be okay."

* * * * *

It was two o'clock in the morning, but Levi knew his mom would be waiting for him. Sure enough, as he silently walked through the door, she sat at the kitchen table clutching a cup of coffee. The apartment was dark except for the single light that hung above the table, casting shadows around the dim room.

"Sorry, Mom. You know I didn't want you to wait up."

Her eyes held that exhausted look that Levi had seen so many times. "You want some coffee?" she said.

"I'll get it."

He stepped into the kitchen and poured himself a cup then sat at the table across from his mom. He had things to say. She had things to say. They'd probably be up the rest of the night.

She looked into his face and frowned. "You've been crying."

Levi lowered his head. "Yeah, all night."

"Are you all right?"

He put his hand over hers. "I'm good, Mom. It was a good kind of crying."

Mom studied his face for several seconds before taking a sip of her coffee. "She is a beautiful girl, Levi."

"Yeah."

"I know she is in rumschpringe, but what do her parents think?"

"Her mother is okay with it. Her father thinks I'm Amish."

Mom shook her head. "Oh, Levi, deception is a dangerous thing. The lies pile up until you are buried in them."

"He hasn't even met me. He just assumes I'm Amish."

"You are still deceiving him."

"Rebecca does everything at that house. I help her so she doesn't keel over from exhaustion. Her father would never let me come if he knew who I really am."

"I guess it doesn't matter," Mom said. "You know this relationship must end before you both get hurt."

"It's not like that."

"I wish I would have known. I would have put a stop to it long before now." Mom took a deep breath. "You love her."

Levi snapped his head up. "Yeah, I do."

"And you are going to be devastated when you are forced to go your separate ways."

"I don't want to go separate ways."

Mom leaned her elbows on the table and clutched Levi's arm. "Don't do that to her. If you pull her away from her community, she will end up miserable. Don't make the biggest mistake of your life."

Levi stood and took his mother's hand. "Come here," he said. He pulled her to the sofa, and they sat with his arm draped around her shoulder.

"Mom, I want to tell you something. Or ask you something. Just don't think I'm crazy, okay?"

"I can't promise anything."

He squeezed her shoulder. "Mom, what would you say if you and I—okay, this sounds crazy—but, Mom, I think I want to join the Amish church."

He could have heard a pin drop. In Africa.

With a look of utter perplexity, Mom sat up straight and fixed her eyes on Levi. "What are you—? Are you—I don't—"

He leaned forward. "You want to go back more than anything else in the world."

"No, I don't. I want my family more than anything else in the world."

"Most of them are in Apple Lake. And they are shunning you. What kind of family life is that?"

She frowned. "You and Beth are my family."

"I want to come with you. Beth could live with us too, Mom. She'd just have to manage without electricity. It's not like she's going to be with us much anyway. She's got four years of undergrad and then medical school." He took both her hands. "Mom, this is going to work."

"Oh, Levi, it is much harder than you think to fit into the Amish way of life. You have to give up cars and electricity and cell phones. You'd be as miserable as Rebecca would be, trying to fit into your world."

"It's different with me. I was Amish until I was seven. I have good memories. I'm pretty good at the language, and I spend one day a week immersed in the culture. I want to do this."

His mom stared at him with her brows furrowed. "If this is all for Rebecca, it's not enough. You have to understand, Levi. Love is not enough. I learned that the hard way."

"I understand that. It is hard to separate my feelings for Rebecca from this decision. But, Mom, I love her. I would live on the moon if that's the only way I could be with her."

"I can't let you do this, Levi."

"Don't even think about me for a minute. Think about yourself. You want to go."

"It doesn't matter what I want."

Levi leaned back and pulled his mom with him. "Let's go talk to a bishop. Get details about what you'd need to do to get back in. It can't hurt to get some information. I kind of sprung this on you. Let it marinate for a few days."

Mom grinned. "Marinate. Good idea. You'd better marinate, yourself."

"Don't worry about that. I've been marinating for weeks. I'm ready for roasting."

"Out of the frying pan, into the fire. Have you told Rebecca?"

"No, I have to figure out how to break the news to her." Levi pulled out his phone. "Speaking of the girl of my dreams, I've got to call her so she doesn't fall into a coma. That would make the relationship more difficult."

"No," Mom said, "your relationship is already about as impossible as it gets."

Chapter Twenty-Four

Rebecca woke with a splitting headache and a stiff neck. Linda slept beside her, her deep breathing a sure sign that she would not be waking soon.

Had it really only been twelve hours since the car accident? Rebecca felt as if seventy years had passed and she was now an old lady ready to die.

Luckily all the siblings and Mamm had been in bed and Fater's bus hadn't come yet when she got home last night. She could avoid the questions and awkward explanations until morning. But twelve hours wasn't enough time to determine exactly what to tell Fater about the mountainous goose egg on her forehead. Should she stay in her room and tell him she was ill? That wouldn't be a lie. She felt as if her head might explode if she sat up.

The pain of the accident wasn't even what ailed her the most. She puzzled over Levi's sudden change of mood last night. Would he take her skiing? That barely mattered this morning. Did he share Fater's opinion about her fault in Mamm's accident? Or had he decided to be done with her because she insisted he take her where he didn't want to go?

She rolled over in bed and curled up into a little ball. Tightening every muscle, she tried to squeeze the unwelcome emotions from her body. How could one boy make her feel so whole and so torn to pieces all at once?

When they were apart, she thought of nothing but him—his eyes, his smile, the way he looked at her as if she were the only person in the whole world. Levi monopolized every corner of her life so that chores and responsibilities were almost impossible to complete.

When they were together, she wanted to fly over the clouds and shout at the top of her lungs how happy she was—how wonderfully, deliriously happy—just being with him, just sitting by him in the grass while he laughed and teased her.

But how much more time did they have together, really? Once he took her skiing, he might not want to end it, but she would. Reluctantly. Very reluctantly. But what else could she do? Levi was not Amish, and Rebecca would never leave her community. They would have to break from each other eventually.

She knew it was the only possible decision, but thinking about doing the right thing had never made her feel so miserable.

Rebecca pulled herself from the bed and ran her fingers through her hair. It didn't matter how rotten she felt, she would do what had to be done. Rebecca always found the strength that others did not. Regardless of Levi's pleading or her own heart's sorrow, she would not waver.

She had to be strong.

After pinning her kapp into place partially over her bandage, Rebecca tied her shoes and ventured into the kitchen. Fater might be sleeping in. After arriving home so late on Fridays, he often slept until seven or eight on Saturday mornings.

No matter. Rebecca determined to face his wrath head-on. She would tell him the truth about the bump on her head, regardless of how he may react. She couldn't think up a truthful explanation that would appease him, so she opted for the whole, unedited story. She wearied of tiptoeing around her fater.

Fater stood with his back to her, scrambling eggs at the stove. He turned his head to glance at her. "Did the apples get picked?"

"Jah, they are out on the back porch. I will do applesauce this week, Lord willing."

He didn't turn around. "Gute. The two trees did well this year. I milked the cows, but have Max strain the milk."

Rebecca didn't call attention to herself, just retrieved the broom from the closet and started sweeping the floor. Might as well get along with the chores.

"I am pleased with the way the barn turned out," Fater said. "Your mamm says the new young man did most of it."

Fater wasn't one to throw out a compliment lightly. He seldom remembered Levi's name—quite all right with Rebecca—and usually referred to him as "the new young man" whom he had never met. But whatever disapproval Fater felt for Levi's presence on the farm melted when Fater saw the difference Levi's work was making—hinges that creaked for years happily silenced, the horses' coats cleaned and brushed like proper Amish animals, the yard groomed with nary a leaf out of place, the barn crisply painted.... Levi's labor had turned their place into the kind of farm tourists passed and said, "Amish people must live there. Look how well kept it is."

"Jah, he works very hard." Rebecca's heart shrank. Only for a few more weeks. Then he would be gone.

Fater scooped the eggs onto two plates and put the plates on a tray with forks and napkins. Without looking up, he said, "I am taking breakfast to your mamm. Wake Linda and the boys for chores."

Rebecca smiled to herself. This was going well. With any luck, Fater would neglect to look at her all day and a lengthy explanation would be unnecessary.

A knock at the door interrupted Rebecca's sweeping. Who could that be on a Saturday morning?

Levi stood on her porch, as she had seen him so many times before, in full Amish garb with a red rose in his hand. He looked weary but content, like a farmer after the hay was successfully harvested and safely stacked in the barn.

"What are you doing here?" she said in a hissed whisper.

"How's the head?" he said, handing her the rose and stroking her cheek. "Have you changed the gauze yet?"

The flower distracted her for a second, and she buried her nose in its petals. Then she snapped up her head and glared at Levi. "You have to get out of here. Fater is in the other room. If he sees you, he will ask too many questions that have the wrong answers."

"How is your head?" he repeated patiently.

"It feels like a cracked egg," she said dismissively. "You could have asked me this in a text. Now go away."

"Did you take something for the pain?"

Rebecca sighed. Didn't Levi realize what he was risking here? "Please, go."

Levi reached into his pocket and pulled out a packet of two orange pills. "Ibuprofen. Take them."

"Will you go away if I promise to take them?"

Levi's smile did not quite reach his eyes. "I've come to have a talk with your fater."

Panic rose into her throat. "Not about what I told you?"

"No, no, of course not. I would never—"

"Then what? Fater will put an end to us faster than the chickens run from the cat. We can't risk it before we go skiing."

A frown flickered across Levi's face. "I need to talk to him. Could you ask?"

"I know you don't want to take me skiing, but if this is your way to make sure I can't go, don't bother. I will find a way to ski with or without you."

For once she couldn't determine the emotion in his expression. "I swear to you, Rebecca, I will take you skiing. Can I talk to your fater now?"

In confusion, Rebecca turned from Levi and went to fetch her fater. It irritated her that he seemed always so confident and sure of himself when she was certain the floor was going to open up beneath her and swallow her whole.

She knocked on her parents' door. "There is someone to see Fater," she said.

A pause before the door opened, and then Fater slipped from the room. For the first time today, he took a good look at her. "Becky, what happened to your head?"

"I had an accident."

"Mamm did not mention it."

Rebecca fingered the bandage. "I think you should meet your visitor."

Fater frowned and turned his gaze down the hall. "Who is it?"

"Cum and see," was all she could say.

He followed her to the front door. When he laid eyes on Levi, Fater studied him with unguarded suspicion.

"Fater, this is Levi. He is the boy who has been helping us."

Some of Fater's icy exterior melted, and he shook Levi's hand. "You have done much good for us, Levi. You could be working your own farm, but you choose to help Rebecca."

"I am glad to help her," Levi said.

"Do I know your parents?"

"I wonder if there is a private place we could go to talk," Levi said.

Fater looked surprised and puzzled at the same time.

"A place we could discuss a serious matter," Levi added.

Fater's eyes darted from Rebecca to Levi, and Rebecca could almost see the wheels turning in his head.

Had Levi come to ask for her hand in marriage? Her heart did a joyful somersault before she yanked it down to earth.

Of course not. What could be more absurd?

"The barn will be warm enough," Fater said.

Levi glanced at Rebecca and nodded. "Very gute."

Fater lifted his jacket from the hook by the front door. "Keep everyone from the barn until I come back."

"Jah," Rebecca said, resisting the urge to tackle Levi and demand an explanation.

She watched from the door as they trudged away side by side. She wished she were a fly on the wall of that bright red barn.

Chapter Twenty-Five

Levi walked next to Rebecca's fater with his head lowered and his hands clasped behind his back, much like a prisoner going to his execution. Or perhaps his reprieve. He couldn't be sure how Rebecca's fater would react.

Who was he kidding? Levi knew exactly how he would react. From what he knew already, Rebecca's fater was not an understanding man.

They entered the barn and Rebecca's fater closed the door behind them, shutting out the bright light. They stood three feet from two milk cans, but her fater didn't sit down and didn't ask Levi to sit, either. Through the dimness, he scrutinized Levi with a frown on his face. With one look at that stern expression, Levi's throat constricted and he found it impossible to speak. He hadn't expected to be terrified out of his mind.

"What is the serious matter you wish to discuss?" her fater said.

Levi cleared his throat and wished he were sitting. It wouldn't be good to pass out right now. "I have come to ask for forgiveness."

"Forgiveness?"

"Jah, for the injury to Rebecca's head."

Her fater narrowed his eyes. "What happened?"

"We were riding in my car and got into a small accident."

Rebecca's fater took a step forward to study Levi more closely. "Your car? A good Amish boy does not own a car."

Levi took a deep breath. With the next words out of his mouth, he might destroy his own future and seal his doom. But it had to be done, come what may. "My name is Levi Cooper," he said. "My dat was Isaac Stutzman, and he died when I was seven years old. My mamm married an Englischer, who adopted me and gave me his name. I have been raised outside of the community ever since."

Rebecca's fater slowly folded his arms across his chest. "You are not Amish?"

"No."

Her fater's face darkened, and he shoved his finger into Levi's chest. "What do you want with my Rebecca?" Then, louder, "What do you want with my daughter?"

"It's not what you think."

"You think my daughter is an easy target for an Englisch boy?" He pointed to the door and yelled, "Get out and never come back!"

Levi lifted his hands in surrender. "Will you listen to what I have to say?"

"You mock us by coming on our farm in these Amish clothes, making us believe you are something you are not. How far have you pulled Rebecca down?"

"I do not mock anyone," Levi said, unable to keep the tears from sliding down his face. "And I would never harm Rebecca. I love her."

The lines in her fater's face deepened. "What have you done?"

Levi dared to take a step forward. "I want to explain everything to you. I mean no harm." He motioned to the two milk cans. "Can we sit?"

Rebecca's fater didn't budge. He stood with his fists clenched at his sides, a pillar of stone frowning at Levi.

Levi opted to sit—hopefully a less-threatening position than towering over Rebecca's dat. "I want to be baptized," he said.

"Is this a joke?" her fater said, scowling.

"My life changed when I met Rebecca, and now she is the only thing that matters to me. I want to join the church and marry her."

Her fater flinched. "Do not even suggest that."

"I'm more serious about this than I have ever been about anything in my life. I want to be baptized."

Her fater folded his arms. "You pretended to be Amish. Why should I believe anything you say?"

"Because I'm telling you the truth now. If she were my daughter, I would want to know. I met Rebecca in May, and we have been seeing each other ever since."

"So she has been deceiving me also."

"It is her rumschpringe. I didn't want you to know. I thought you would put a stop to it."

Her fater glared at Levi. "I would have."

"I convinced her that it would be okay during rumschpringe."

"Rumschpringe is no excuse for wickedness."

"Rebecca has done nothing to shame herself. She won't let me kiss her or hold hands in public."

Rebecca's fater rubbed his chin, and the frown seemed to soften a bit.

"She always behaves like the virtuous woman she is," Levi said. "Believe me, she has done nothing wrong." He ran his fingers through his hair. "I want to marry your daughter, but things must be right between us first. How can I make all things right?"

Rebecca's fater folded his arms and looked away. "I do not for one minute believe your sincerity."

"Try me."

He pinned Levi with an icy gaze. "You will not work on the farm or see Rebecca until you are baptized. Then we will see if you truly mean what you say."

Even though he was expecting it, Levi felt as if his heart might crumble into a million pieces. How could he bear the thought of not seeing Rebecca? "I will agree to that," Levi said, keeping his voice steady. "But I have two requests for you. I ask that you not tell Rebecca that I plan on being baptized. I want it to be a surprise."

Her fater snorted in bitter laughter. "A surprise? I will be surprised if it comes to pass."

"Will you keep it a secret?"

"Why the secrecy?"

"I want to have all my plans in place before I tell her. It must be the perfect time."

"As you wish. It won't amount to anything anyway," said her fater.

Levi's heart beat harder. "There is one more thing. Rebecca wants to go skiing. More than anything else in the world before she is baptized. And she wants me to take her."

"Nae," said her fater. "I have already said no."

Levi stood and held out his hands. "You must understand. To her, it is almost a matter of life and death."

"Why?"

He had said too much already. Rebecca would not want her fater to know about the list. "I am a good skier. I can keep her safe. If I'm not allowed, I promise she'll find a way to go by herself. And she could get badly hurt."

Her fater shook his head. "She will not go if I forbid it."

Levi took a breath and chose his words carefully. "You are gone from home every week. Rebecca is a gute girl, obedient and strong. But in this one thing, she will defy you. Are you willing to take that risk with her life?"

Anger flashed in Rebecca's fater's eyes. "She would not dare."

Levi's eyes stung with tears of frustration. "Mr. Miller, I made Rebecca a solemn promise that I would take her skiing, and I intend to keep it. Please don't ask me to break one promise to keep another."

Rebecca's fater had no immediate argument. He sat down on one of the milk cans and rubbed his forehead with the tips of his fingers.

He was silent for nearly five minutes.

Levi felt sick to his stomach. He couldn't do anything but pray.

"She wants to go skiing," her fater said.

Not an argument or an accusation. Levi saw a ray of hope. "Jah, it is the last thing she wants to do before she is baptized, and she says she will not let Jacob Glick take her."

"Jacob Glick is thirty years old and unbaptized. I will not let Jacob Glick take her either."

Levi dared a half smile. "Just for one day. I will watch out for her and bring her safely back. And I will keep my promise about not seeing her otherwise."

Rebecca's fater grunted. "When she sets her mind to something, she cannot be talked out of it. It would be just like her to break her neck in stubbornness." He shook his head. "I will find someone else to take her."

Levi stood and squared his shoulders. "I will take her. I would appreciate your approval."

Rebecca's fater lifted his chin and folded his arms across his chest. His eyes bored into Levi's skull as if hoping to extract the secrets there. They stared at each other in breathless suspense until her fater turned away. "See that she is safe," he said.

Levi grabbed her fater's hand and shook it vigorously even though her fater didn't return his enthusiasm. "Denki. I will never forget your kindness," he said, elated that he ranked slightly higher than Jacob Glick in Rebecca's fater's opinion.

It was a start.

Chapter Twenty-Six

After practically slamming the front door on Fater and Levi, Rebecca swept and mopped with unusual speed. If she didn't work herself to death, the curiosity would kill her.

She had just hung the mop in the closet when she heard another knock. What? Had her house suddenly become more popular than the bus station?

She must be a very wicked girl for God to punish her so.

With hat in hand, Marvin Yutzy stood staring at her with a mixture of determination and stubbornness on his face. His eyes widened when he saw the bandage. "What happened to your head?"

Again her hand instinctively went to the cut. "I had an accident," she said, hoping to put an end to the questions with her tone of voice. She certainly wasn't going to bare her soul to Marvin Yutzy.

Marvin cleared his throat and hung that determined look on his face again. "Is your dat home?" he said. "I came to speak with him."

Rebecca took a deep breath. Had Levi and Marvin conspired to humiliate her today? "He is in the barn," she said.

"I will go find him."

"Nae, Marvin, he is…someone else is talking to him. You had best wait your turn."

"My turn?"

"Jah."

Marvin pointed to the bench on the porch. "I will wait here."

Reluctant as she was, Rebecca remembered her manners. "Nae, cum reu. Come in and sit. It is too chilly for sitting outside."

Marvin wasted no time in planting himself on the sofa and inviting Rebecca to sit next to him. She couldn't very well avoid his invitation without being rude, so she sat down on the end of the sofa farthest from him.

Ever since the day he discovered Levi and Rebecca in the middle of the water fight, Marvin had redoubled his efforts with Rebecca. Besides continuing to pick her up on Tuesdays from Mrs. Johnson's house, he personally invited her to every singing and gathering and often came by on a Sunday evening to sit with the family.

"I saw your buggy wheel is fixed," Marvin said. "I am glad you did not have to buy a new one. They are expensive. We bought a new buggy three years ago, and my dat hopes it is the last one we have. I think as long as you take good care of your buggy, it can last for several years, unless it gets hit in an accident."

Marvin gave Rebecca a tutorial on the best way to clean buggy seats and windows. She listened intently simply because there was nothing else for her to do. She couldn't very well leave Marvin in the living room talking to himself while she refilled the propane lamps and gathered the eggs.

Max and Danny both wandered into the room at some point but left after a few minutes of listening to Marvin talk about the color of the milk from the cows at the dairy. No doubt they went to find a more exciting pastime, like staring at the ceiling.

A half hour must have passed before, through the window, Rebecca saw Levi and Fater emerge from the barn and march resolutely toward the house.

Rebecca jumped to her feet, happy that she had been able to stay awake through Marvin's droning. "Here comes Fater now."

Fater stomped into the house, followed by Levi. Levi gave her a weak smile.

"Fater, Marvin has come to see you."

Fater practically tripped over his feet in an effort to shake Marvin's hand. "Marvin Yutzy," he said with exaggerated friendliness.

Rebecca glanced at Levi, who seemed to bear Marvin's presence with composure. He watched them but didn't change expressions.

Marvin shook hands with Fater while keeping his eyes glued to Levi. "I wish to speak with you, Amos," he said. "In private."

Fater forced a jovial laugh and took Marvin by the elbow. "Well, then," he said, "step into my office." He opened the door and led Marvin to the barn. Good thing the cows had already been milked. No one else would see the inside of that barn this morning.

Rebecca glanced at Levi. He stared out the window and pursed his lips. For some reason she wanted to give him comfort—for what, she couldn't say.

Levi glanced at her. "The vultures are circling. And your fater would much rather have him for a son-in-law."

"My fater will not pick my husband."

"But your future husband must have your fater's approval. Marvin has already won your fater to his side."

"Fater does not wish for me to marry. I am needed at home."

"With such a pretty daughter, I think he's resigned himself to the inevitable."

Rebecca folded her arms. "You two had a lot to say to each other."

To her surprise, he reached out and gently drew her in for an embrace. She had absolutely no desire to pull away. "Oh, Rebecca, I had to do it."

She felt a tear splash on her cheek. She looked up. He was crying. "Do what?"

"My mom said I needed to, and she was right. I told your fater everything."

"Everything?"

He squeezed her tighter. "Not what we talked about last night. I told him about how you hurt your head. I told him about my Amish parents and my Englisch stepfather. He was very angry. We shouldn't have kept that from him, kid. I rationalized that it was better to deceive him because you needed the help. But he is your fater. He deserves to know."

Rebecca's eyes stung with tears that she refused to shed. She knew what was coming.

"He won't allow me to set foot on this farm," Levi said, "until…"

"Until what?"

"Until pigs fly, I guess."

She pulled away from his warm embrace and turned her back on him. "Why did you come? I told you not to come."

"I have to make right what I can."

"Did you tell him about the list?"

He shook his head. "That is between you and Dottie Mae."

"What about the skiing?"

His voice was mild but held undercurrents of profound pain. "Is that all I am to you? A means to an end? A skiing trip?"

Rebecca couldn't look into his eyes. "What does it matter?"

He sighed, sat down, and buried his face in his hands. "He gave me permission to take you skiing."

"He did?"

"I told him I'd take you whether he agreed or not."

The news that she had permission to go skiing should have made her ecstatic. But all she saw in the skiing trip was an end to her relationship with Levi.

It is better this way.

I have to be strong.

"Isn't it great?" he said, his voice cracking. "You get to go skiing."

She sat down next to him. "Great," she replied flatly.

They sat together, the silence cramming into Rebecca's ears.

"When will I see you again?" she said.

"Could I call you every day?"

"Jah. But can I see you ever?"

"When we go skiing."

"But when else?" she said.

He studied her face. "Does it matter?"

She took a deep breath to clear the grief filling up her chest. "Jah," she said. "It matters."

He let the air out of his lungs as if he had been holding it for a long time. "Denki," he said. He took her hand then released it just as suddenly. "But I want to gain your fater's approval."

"It is my rumschpringe. Fater may be able to keep you off this farm, but he cannot keep me on it."

"Just the thought of being away from you until the snows fall is enough to make me miserable," he said. "But more than anything, I want to do this the right way. To honor your fater and your traditions. It's the only way."

"The only way what? Levi, you are making me frustrated."

He chuckled. "I promise, when I sort this all out, you'll be the first to know. Just trust me, okay?"

"No, I won't. I can look after myself."

He stood up. She followed him to the door. He reached for her then pulled back before he made contact. "This is killing me, kid. But I'll call every night. Will you answer the phone if you're not too frustrated?"

"Jah."

He took a long look at her, as if memorizing her face. "Let's hope the snows come soon," he said.

She could have no such wish. Falling snow meant the end of her perfect summer.

Before she said another word, he was gone. She watched through the window until his long strides took him from her view. Could he have walked a little slower?

Not until after she mixed the bread dough did Fater and Marvin appear in the kitchen demanding Rebecca's attention. Fater looked no less pleased with himself than Marvin did.

"Marvin wants to come help you on the farm, Becky," Fater said, as if it were the best, most original idea to ever cross his mind. "And I have given him my permission."

Marvin grinned and fiddled with the brim of his hat. "I would like to come on Wednesdays after work at the dairy."

Wednesdays. How convenient.

Rebecca's throat tightened. "I am grateful for your help."

"Since your fater cannot be here, you must put me to work doing anything you need," Marvin said. "I want to lighten your burden."

Why did Marvin's kindness make Rebecca want to pull out all her hair? She thought of Levi with his old car and faded blue jeans. An Englischer, plain and simple. Nothing would change that.

Marvin, on the other hand, would make the perfect Amish husband: hardworking, loyal, faithful, predictable.

Rebecca suddenly saw the long years of her life laid out before her. Excusing herself as best she could, she hurried out of the room as it began to spin.

Chapter Twenty-Seven

Bishop Bender pulled the buggy up in front of the white clapboard house. From the backseat, Levi heard Mom catch her breath.

"It is just like I remember," she said.

"Your fater has been feeling poorly," said the bishop.

Mom nodded. "Jah, Mamm wrote about it in her last letter. The diabetes."

"His feet are bad."

Levi let his eyes travel over the house and bare trees standing sentinel in the yard. A thousand memories of Mammi's house flooded his mind. He never entered that house without paying with a hug and a kiss. The cookie jar was always full, and Mammi never, ever scolded him, even when he carried a squawking chicken by the leg right into the house.

No one loved him like his mammi did.

His heart thumped wildly as he stepped out of the buggy. Would they remember him? Accept him? Or had their love died when Mom left the church?

Mom grabbed his hand and squeezed hard. From the look on her face, she was more terrified than he. Levi squeezed back. Come what may, they had each other.

The bishop knocked firmly. A short, plump woman, who hadn't aged a day since Levi last saw her, threw open the door and halted in her tracks when she got a good look at her visitors.

She popped her hand over her mouth. "Well, bless my soul. Bless my soul." After glancing at the bishop, she reached out her arms to

Mom and pulled her in for a bone-crushing embrace. Mom got her height from Mammi. The older woman couldn't have been more than five feet tall.

"My Mary, my Mary," she moaned as she rocked her daughter back and forth in a sort of welcome-home dance. The surge of emotion was too much for Mom. Her tears flowed. They embraced for an eternity before Mammi wiped a tear from her eye and ushered the three into her house.

"And little Levi," she said, reaching up and taking his face in her hands. "I always knew you would be a handsome man." She put her arms around his waist, held on tightly, and wept. Her unbridled acceptance broke his heart, and Levi bawled right along with her.

After sniffling in his arms for a few minutes, she retrieved a handkerchief from her pocket and mopped her face. "You are not little Levi anymore. Luckily you did not inherit your height from your mutter's side."

They laughed through their tears.

"And where is Beth?"

"Away at school," Mom said.

Mammi nodded. "She was always a smart girl, my Beth." She gestured to the sofa. "Cum reu and sit. I have some whoopie pies in the fridge."

"Nancy," the bishop said, "we have come to ask you something."

"Everybody sit," Mammi said. "With the bishop's approval, we can give you money, if you need. That other time you asked—"

"I did not think it wise," the bishop said.

"I understood," Mom said. She sat between Levi and Mammi on the sofa and took both of their hands before pausing to choose her words. "Mamm, I want to come back to the church."

Mammi's mouth fell open. Then there was another round of tears as she buried her face in Mom's neck and couldn't speak for a full minute. When she regained her composure, she patted Mom on the cheek. "I will fetch Alphy." She jumped up from her place and disappeared into the other room, but they could still hear her voice. "He told me, 'Prayer works, Nancy. Prayer works.'"

The bishop smiled. "I do not think this will be a problem."

Whereas Mammi hadn't changed a bit, Levi barely recognized *Dawdi*. His peppered-black beard had filled in snowy white, and a maze of wrinkles lined his face. Leaning heavily on a cane, he slowly shuffled into the room, stooped and arthritic. Mammi followed close behind with her hand on his back in case he stumbled.

"Look what we have here," he said, his booming voice shaking the rafters. "A sight for sore eyes, I'd say."

Mom stood to embrace him and then Levi took his turn. Dawdi had always been larger than life, but now his arms looked like matchsticks and he had shrunk at least three inches.

Dawdi shook his finger at Levi. "If I did not know better, I would say you is Isaac Stutzman alive and well. Only taller. You is the spitting image of your dat."

Levi felt like his heart might swell right out of his chest.

"Mary wants to come home," Mammi said. "Back to the church."

Dawdi threw his head back and almost fell over. Mammi caught him by the arm. "Prayer works, Nancy," he said.

They settled onto the two sofas, and Dawdi sank into his lumpy recliner.

"Mary is wondering if she and Levi could move into the dawdi house. At least until they can work out a place of their own," Bishop Bender said.

Mammi's eyes got as big as saucers. "You coming too, Levi?"

"Yeah. I want to be baptized."

Dawdi pointed his finger at the ceiling. "Prayer works, Nancy."

"Ruth and Ben want to move in when the new baby comes in the spring. Ben is Barbara's oldest boy. But we can put them off if you need the apartment."

"No," Mom said, "just for a few months. We want to buy our own place once we get settled."

"I'd just as soon you stay with us," Mammi said. "I have missed out on fifteen years with you."

"We will find something very close, Lord willing," Mom said.

"Mary must still be shunned for six weeks before being accepted into full fellowship," said the bishop, turning to Mom. "You cannot eat at the same table or associate with the community. This is done out of love for one who is baptized, and out of concern for your soul. To remind you of your sins and motivate you to repentance."

"I understand the conditions," Mom said.

The bishop inclined his head. "Levi has not been baptized and will not be shunned. He must take the baptism classes, and then, Lord willing, his baptism can take place after the new year."

Blood raced through Levi's veins. Is this what he wanted?

Yes. Rebecca's love drove him forward.

"When do you want to move in?" Mammi asked. "The brothers can help move your things tomorrow if you like."

"We need a few weeks to settle our affairs. Beth is coming for a visit next weekend, and we will tell her the news then. I must give notice at the hospital, and we need to work out payment with our landlord." Mom looked at Levi. "And Levi wants to wait until the first snow."

"An inconvenient time to move furniture," Dawdi said.

"This is the hardest part," Levi said, leaning closer to Dawdi. "We don't want you to tell anybody until the day we move in."

"But the family will be thrilled. I cannot keep the good news bottled up," Mammi protested.

Levi reached across his mom and took Mammi's hand. "This is very important to me. There is someone else who needs to hear the news first."

Mammi bit her lip then patted Levi's hand. "Right as rain, then. I will not say a word, and neither will Alphy."

"Jah," Dawdi said. "Nancy has the loose tongue. Not me."

"Alphy, don't you talk about your wife that way," Mammi said.

Levi nodded. Rebecca had to be the first to know.

He dialed her phone number several times a day even when he knew she wouldn't have her phone on, just to hear her on the voice mail.

Even though being away from her made him feel as if an empty hole gaped right in the middle of his chest, he was determined to honor her father's wishes.

"*We will see if you truly mean what you say.*"

I do, Mr. Miller. Nothing will keep me from loving Rebecca.

Levi had his strategy planned to the last detail. He would take her skiing in the morning and then out to dinner at Chez Henrie in the evening. Sitting in the priciest café in town, he would tell her he was joining the Amish church.

He pictured her laughing with pure joy and throwing her arms around his neck—the best moment of his life, and it hadn't even happened yet.

"We was planning to fix the plumbing in the old place," Dawdi said. "I will get Titus to look at it right away."

"But no spilling the beans," Mammi said.

"I am not the gossip in this house."

Levi grinned. He looked forward to knowing his grandparents again.

Dawdi clapped his hands together. "Let's talk about what you have been doing for the last eight years."

"Fifteen years, Alphy," Mammi said.

"I know that," Dawdi said.

"Oh, Alphy, dear, you did not."

"Yes, I did, but maybe I only want to hear about the last eight."

Oh, yes, Levi wanted to know his grandparents again. In the meantime, he waited impatiently for the first good skiing weather.

Chapter Twenty-Eight

Rebecca stared out the window with her hands in the sink, unable to muster the energy to finish the dishes. She gazed at the exact spot where Levi and Danny had fixed the lawn mower, what seemed like three years ago. She thought of Linda's reaction when she laid eyes on Levi—much the same as hers. Levi was good-looking, but Rebecca knew his heart. And she missed him mighty terrible, grieving for his loss as if it had already happened. Might as well have happened. She never saw him.

Slowly swishing the rag around the inside of a cup, Rebecca imagined Levi standing outside the window beckoning her to come and look at the barn or the garden or the apple trees.

The cup slipped from her fingers and into the soapy dishwater, where it cracked another cup. Rebecca growled.

Max lugged the full milk pails into the kitchen and set them on the floor. Rebecca washed with renewed vigor when Max came through the door.

"All done with the milking, then?" she said.

"Marvin did it," Max said. "Levi never milked the cows for me. He tricked me into finishing the job myself. Don't think for a minute that I didn't know what he was doing. I let him trick me because I knew I should do the milking myself and not let a stranger take over the job." He stared out the window at the barn. "I wish he was back."

Rebecca concentrated on her dishwater. "Do you?"

Max grabbed an apple from the basket and took a monstrous bite.

"You will ruin your supper," Rebecca said.

"My supper is ruined every Wednesday," Max said. "All we do is sit and listen to Marvin talk about the dairy. I used to think working at the dairy sounded like fun. Not anymore. It wonders me how someone can make chocolate ice cream sound as dull as dishwater." Max draped his arm around Rebecca's shoulder. "Take my advice. On the day you marry him, buy some earplugs. You will be much happier."

Reality crept up on Rebecca and squeezed the air out of her lungs. Even Max expected a wedding to come of this. Was there any use in fighting it?

The only groom she wanted was a boy she couldn't marry. She should quit this childish pining for him and surrender to her fate.

But she needn't be in a hurry. With Mamm feeling poorly and the work piling up, Rebecca could put off marriage for three or four more years. That thought cheered her considerably. Perhaps it would be enough time to get used to the idea of Marvin Yutzy as a husband.

If Fater thought that separating her from Levi would bring an end to her feelings for him, he was mistaken. Every day she didn't see Levi only heightened her longing. Although he called every day, she hadn't laid eyes on him for three weeks. Could she bear being away from him for the rest of her life?

What was the alternative?

Chapter Twenty-Nine

Texting you isn't near as good as seeing you. I wish I were there to chop firewood. The days are so cold.

> *Marvin chopped a whole cord yesterday.*
> *Levi, are you there?*

> *Does he come every week?*

> *Yes. So far four times.*

> *I'm glad you have help.*

> *I can also tell you how much milk every cow at Eicher's Dairy gives. To the gallon. LOL*

> *Yesterday I watched a video on YouTube about how to milk a cow so I could feel close to you.*

> *You don't have to suffer. I will ride the bus to town and come to your work.*

> *No, I want to do this right. I want your dad to approve.*

> *My fater will never approve.*
> *Levi, are you there?*

When Levi didn't answer her text after a few minutes, Rebecca reluctantly left her phone in her room and went to the kitchen to fetch Mamm's food. It had been almost six weeks since she had seen Levi. Thanksgiving was next week. Perhaps the extra work would take her mind off him. She could only hope.

She marched into Mamm's room with a tray of food. "Supper," she trilled.

"Ah, Rebecca, you are too gute to me."

Mamm slowly sat up and fixed the pillow at her back. "Two plates?" she said. "You must think I am very hungry."

"I thought I would eat with you tonight," Rebecca said. "We can talk."

Mamm's eyes twinkled, and she nodded slowly. "Marvin is still here, isn't he?"

Rebecca sighed. "Some days I am afraid I will be unkind and say something I should not. Better to hide in here than to be rude to Marvin."

"It is good of him to help with the chores."

"Jah. I am so wicked to have these feelings against him."

"Feelings are not wicked. It is how we express those feelings that is important."

"So, it is gute I am sitting here with you while Marvin is at the table with Max and Danny and Linda, telling them how records are kept on dairy cows."

"Jah, very gute. I would hate to have you insult Marvin's cows."

"I wish he would not come," Rebecca said. "It is too cold for him to stay outside all afternoon, and when he is in the house, I cannot get any work done for his talking."

"Levi came to work on the farm," Mamm said. "Marvin, it seems, comes to work on you."

"Levi let me be." Rebecca's voice broke. "Marvin loves the sound of his own voice."

Mamm did not take her eyes from Rebecca's face. "You seem so blue. I have St. John's wort if you want to take some."

"Nae, I am fine. Do not worry about me."

Mamm pursed her lips. "I saw this coming. I should have done more to stop it. But he made you so happy."

"My feelings do not matter. I will do my duty."

"Your happiness matters very much."

"Enough for you to see me marry an Englischer and leave the community?"

Mamm didn't answer.

"You see, my happiness is not that important."

"I do not think marrying this Englischer will make you happy in the long run," Mamm said.

"Of course you are right, but it does not matter what will make me happy. I will always care for you, Mamm." Rebecca decided she might like the conversation in the kitchen better. "I will go to see if Linda has started the dishes and come fetch your plate when you are done."

She bent over and kissed her mamm on the forehead then trudged out of the room, leaving her plate with the food untouched.

Chapter Thirty

She opened the door before he knocked. There he stood, as if summoned from her store of good memories, with a rose in his hand and an irresistible smile on his face.

"You're even more beautiful than I remember," Levi said.

Rebecca leaped forward and almost bowled him over when she threw her arms around his neck. Let Fater chastise and Max tease her. She didn't care. She could have tucked herself right next to his heart and died there.

"Hey, kid," he said softly as he wrapped his arms as far around her as they would go.

She melted into his warm embrace.

"We don't even have to go skiing," Levi said. "I would rather just stand like this all day." He stroked the braid that she had fashioned under her white beanie. She breathed in his clean scent as they stood holding each other.

"Me too." She didn't want to face the inevitable end.

After a few glorious minutes, Levi broke contact. He handed her the rose and took her hand. "Let's get going," he said. "This is what we've both been waiting for."

* * * * *

Encased in a white ski suit that Levi had borrowed from…she couldn't remember who, Rebecca felt as if she were made of marshmallows—roly-poly with lots of padding. The boots, skis, and poles were rentals, which she had insisted on paying for. She hadn't saved up all that money for nothing. Besides, Levi usually paid for everything.

With her hands buried in thick gloves, she clutched her ski poles in case they decided to leap out of her hands and leave her defenseless against the formidable hill. The bunny hill, Levi called it, but there was nothing cute and cuddly about it.

The only good thing about her day so far—no, the only gloriously wonderful thing about her day so far—was that after fifty-eight long days, she got to see Levi. How could she bear to be out of his sight ever again?

The long two months of Levi's exile had been what Rebecca imagined hell to be like.

Hell is knowing what might have been.

"Remember the wedge. Keep your knees apart. That'll slow you down. Then widen it out when you need to stop."

Levi had already made her watch the ski movie at the lodge, where she mostly stared at Levi instead of the screen. He wouldn't even think of letting her on a chairlift until he spent a half hour on the flatland teaching her what to do on the slopes. She was ready to go. Terrified, but ready.

"Don't go too fast," he warned. "I'll be right beside you." He practically glowed with excitement. "Breathe, kid. This is what you've waited for. Enjoy it."

She looked into his eyes to see if he was teasing. Nope. He brimmed with enthusiasm. Was he no longer worried she'd get hurt? Or was he ready to move on with his own life?

The despair that had been her constant companion these two months reemerged. She did not want to move on with her life. She wanted things to be exactly as they had been—with Levi, not Marvin, coming to the farm every Wednesday and her Friday nights filled with marvelous and horrifying adventures. She could bear anything if Levi was with her.

Instead, this was quite possibly the last day she would ever see him, and he acted happy about it.

Holding her breath, she pushed herself over the crest of the hill and slid slowly toward the bottom. She squealed weakly in panic as she gained speed, but her intense focus left no energy for a hearty scream. As promised, Levi stayed glued to her side, as closely as possible without getting their skis tangled. She teetered three times on the way down but didn't fall. Snow from other people's skis whipped her face, but her own efforts didn't kick up much ice. So be it. Skiing like a snail was still skiing.

Dodging several small children, she let her momentum take her all the way to the fence at the bottom of the hill. She took a deep breath as she swiped snow from her goggles. Although she wouldn't break any speed records, at least she'd made it down without crashing.

Levi growled and wrapped her in a bear hug. "You did it! What did you think?"

"It was fun," she said.

He laughed as if she had told the funniest joke in the world. "That's what I like to hear. Pure, unadulterated lying. So, can we go now?"

"We just got here."

"We came, we skied. Good enough for me."

She tried to make her voice sound carefree. "Trying to get rid of me?"

"I'd rather spend every hour of this day staring at you instead of fearing for your life. When we get out of here, the weight of the whole mountain will lift from my shoulders."

"It's been a very heavy weight, hasn't it? Dragging me around the state, babysitting my every move." she said.

"I've loved every minute of it. Except the times you almost died."

She couldn't match his high spirits. His behavior didn't make sense unless he was very happy to be rid of her.

He led her to a group of benches near a small shack that housed a refreshment stand. "Would you like some hot chocolate?"

"Jah," she said, maneuvering her skis so she could sit. "A nice break before we go back out."

He rolled his eyes, released his skis, and stabbed his poles into the snow. "I'll be right back." He looked back at her as he walked away and flashed her a smile that melted the snow ten feet in every direction.

"The Amish girl skis too?"

Rebecca turned to see Tara in a sleek black snowsuit with an electric blue beanie. She studied Rebecca with that devil-may-care look Rebecca had seen more times than she cared to remember. "First time skiing?" she said.

"Yes," Rebecca said.

"I figured," Tara said. "Levi's never done the bunny hill in his life."

"It was fun," Rebecca said. "Do you ski the bunny hill too?"

Tara laughed at Rebecca's ignorance. "I'm an instructor. I live at the lodge all winter and teach little kids how to ski. You did pretty well, but you need to loosen up. Stay as stiff as a board and you'll wipe out every time."

"Levi told me. It is easier said than done."

"The skiing was probably Levi's idea, huh? He loves to ski. We came up all the time last winter. I'm kinda surprised you're still dating. Nothing personal, but Amish girls aren't really his type."

"As you have said before."

"I guess maybe a guilty conscience keeps him around," Tara said.

Against her better judgment, Rebecca took the bait. "What do you mean?"

"He hasn't told you, has he? Isn't that just like a guy? Get what they can and lie to you while doing it."

"He has told me about the things he used to do."

"You don't know the worst, Becky. Believe me, if you did, you'd have been long gone by now," Tara said. "Levi is not the good guy you think he is. He's been in lots of trouble. Lots."

Rebecca wouldn't give Tara the satisfaction of thinking she was the least bit curious. Levi's face was an open book. He couldn't hide anything from her.

"Like a week after his dad packed up and moved to Chicago, Levi raided the liquor his dad had left behind, and he and three friends got stinking drunk," Tara said. "He hated his dad so bad."

He still does.

"Levi has told me all about his drinking," Rebecca said. "He hasn't had a drink in almost five months."

"That's not the worst of it."

Rebecca looked up. Levi trudged toward her empty-handed. She recognized the moment he caught sight of Tara. Quickening his pace, he closed the distance between them in record time.

"Tara," he said. "You worked at a different resort last year." He stood next to Rebecca and popped his boots into his skis.

"Didn't expect to see me?"

Levi tried to ignore his old girlfriend. "Sorry about the hot chocolate, Rebecca. The machine broke."

Rebecca stood up. "That's okay. It's better I don't risk spilling it."

Levi put his hand on Rebecca's elbow. "Nice to see you, Tara. We're going now."

"I just got off," Tara said. "If you want, Rebecca, I'll take you on one of the steeper runs. Not real hard, but better than this Mickey Mouse hill."

"No, that's okay, Tara," Levi said. "We were leaving."

Tara glared at Levi. "You have this bad habit of answering for Rebecca when she should answer for herself. What do you say, Rebecca? I'm a good instructor. I can show you what to do."

Rebecca should have declined Tara's offer immediately. But Levi's cheerful mood had left Rebecca completely out of sorts. Every smile, every gesture made her want to lash out at him. Didn't he care that this was their last day together?

"I would like to do something a little faster," she said.

"Okay," Tara said. "We'll do Backbone Ridge."

"No way, Tara," Levi protested. "It's too hard for Rebecca."

"Now you're telling her what she can and can't do? You're such a jerk, Levi."

Rebecca should have defended Levi and backed out of this stupid plan. Levi, always so careful, knew what she could handle.

Shouldn't their last day together be filled with good memories?

Jah, there would be memories. Memories of Levi's couldn't-be-happier face when he told her good-bye forever. Memories of her burying her head in the pillow, trying to shut out the sound of his voice in her head.

Gliding on their skis, they followed Tara to the chairlift.

"You need about two more weeks of skiing before you try this," Levi said.

"I don't have two weeks."

"I promised your fater I would keep you safe, kid. If you get hurt, he's never going to trust me again."

Rebecca pushed aside her irritation. "It doesn't matter what Tara says. I want to do a steeper hill. The kids' hill doesn't really count as skiing to me."

Levi looked away and let out a deep breath. "I knew you'd say that."

"We can take it slow. Then we can get ourselves lost at the bottom so Tara can't find us."

He looked up the hill to the top of the run—probably calculating how far she was likely to fall. "Okay," he said. "If you promise to do the snowplow thing the entire way down."

"I promise that no matter what I do, you will be in a panic by the time we get to the bottom."

"I guarantee that," Levi said.

They let Tara go ahead of them. Rebecca held her breath as the chair sneaked up behind them and lifted them off the ground. She held the cross bar with an iron grip as they rose higher off the ground.

"We're almost there," Levi said. "Put the tips of your skis into the air when you meet the ground and slide off."

Rebecca watched the people in front of them easily glide off the lift. How hard could it be? Her skis clonked the snow-covered ground below her, and she pushed off the chair with sufficient force. Unfortunately, her pole clamped itself around the back of the chair and she crashed spectacularly, face-first into the snow.

Levi hooked his arm under Rebecca's armpit and lifted her out of the way of the oncoming chairs.

Tara, who waited for them at the side of the run, grabbed Rebecca's other arm and pulled her along. The muscles in Levi's arm tightened around her, and he growled under his breath.

They found a flat boulder to sit on while Rebecca regained what little pride she had left.

"Don't worry," Levi said, "people do that all the time."

Tara smirked. "Not often."

Levi snapped his head up and scowled at Tara, but it didn't matter to Rebecca. Tara's bitterness slid off her like skis over the snow.

Rebecca pulled her gloves tighter around her wrists and zipped her coat to her chin. She watched as skiers practically leaped off the edge of the trail and raced down the mountain at dizzying speeds. She was going to be sick.

What did she think she was doing here? It wasn't like a roller coaster where she sat as a passive participant in complete terror but never really risked injury. Watching the other skiers fly down the hill, she considered the very real possibility of her death.

Rebecca closed her eyes and willed her heartbeat to slow to a gallop. She had never given up on any of their adventures before. She couldn't quit at the last one. She just couldn't. Besides, how many people actually ever died on a ski slope?

Levi pulled her to her feet. "Are you breathing? Breathe, Rebecca." He put his skis parallel to hers and pulled her into his arms. "We are not doing this," he said. "I've never seen you this bad. We did the bunny hill. That's enough."

Rebecca pulled away from him. "Nae, I've got to do it."

"I can help her all the way down," Tara said. "People pay big bucks for my instructions."

Levi's voice was mild even though his words were sharp. "I don't trust you, Tara. Stay away."

Rebecca tried to calm her breathing even as she felt beads of sweat slide down the back of her neck. "Tomorrow is the five-year anniversary of Dottie Mae's accident. I have to finish it. For her."

Even through their thick jackets, Rebecca could feel Levi's arms tense. "What did you say?"

Tara clapped her hand over her mouth, and her eyes grew rounder than platters. "Oh, ho. It just gets worse and worse for you, doesn't it?"

A wild, confused look jumped into Levi's eyes. Even with his skis on, he staggered backward in the snow. "Don't say another word, Tara."

"December sixteenth," Tara said. "I remember it well because it is my brother's birthday."

"Shut up, Tara!" Levi yelled. "Shut up." He took Rebecca's arm as if to move her away from Tara, but there was nowhere for them to go but down.

Tara somehow managed to slide between Levi and Rebecca. "Five years ago. That's the night Levi and Derek and the other guys got drunk and plowed Derek's car into an Amish buggy. Killed the little girl instantly. Her dad had to get like four surgeries on his leg."

Wild-eyed, Levi backed away from Rebecca, sank to the boulder, and buried his face in his hands. "I didn't know. I didn't know it was her."

A high-pitched ringing started in Rebecca's ears as her surroundings blurred. This…the voices…she could barely make sense of anything. "Was Levi driving?"

"No, Derek was. Lucky they were all underage, or Derek would have seen some serious prison time. Levi got juvey overnight for giving Derek the alcohol." Tara gave Rebecca's shoulder a pat. "Was that girl a friend of yours?"

Rebecca stood motionless. On the inside, she experienced the perfect storm as a thousand shards of ice pierced her heart.

Dottie Mae. My best friend.

Lost when four drunken boys ignored a stop sign and crashed into her buggy, reducing it to kindling. Four boys who cared more about the trouble they'd be in than my best friend's life. My friend who would never ride a roller coaster, never ski, and never kiss a boy.

She had spent five years hating those boys. They had killed Dottie Mae. They didn't deserve to go on enjoying their lives while having robbed Dottie Mae of hers. Rebecca's heart almost exploded out of her chest with anger and despair.

Nothing would atone for what Levi and his friends had done to Dottie Mae. He couldn't begin to repay such a debt by a few weak attempts to show an Amish girl a good time.

"Vengeance is mine, saith the Lord."

God will make him pay for what he did.

The stifling heat of the bright snow made her catch her breath. She was going to suffocate. The ringing in her ears became unbearable, and Tara said something Rebecca didn't hear.

Levi stood up, and even on his skis, he seemed to stumble as he came toward her. "I didn't know, Rebecca. I didn't know."

Rebecca recoiled at his touch. Her only thought was to get far away from that boy who'd killed Dottie Mae.

That boy she had trusted with her deepest secrets.

That boy she loved with every breath she took.

With her meager skill, Rebecca pushed with all her might to the edge of the drop. She heard both Tara and Levi yell as she plunged down the hill at a reckless speed. With no one ahead of her for several yards, she managed to stay upright, keeping both skis pointed downhill and concentrating every bit of energy on staying on her feet. But almost halfway down the hill, she encountered a tall lump of ice and flew wildly through the air. She hit the ground, and her feet flew out from under her, hurtling her into the trees on the side of the run. A sickening *crack* was followed by a nauseating pain traveling from her shoulder to her neck. Coming to a stop, she moaned and then managed to roll onto her back so she wouldn't get a mouthful of snow.

"Are you okay?"

Two boys had their skis off and knelt beside her almost before she stopped rolling. One of the boys touched her arm, and she screamed in pain.

"She broke something," he said.

"Rebecca!"

Levi and Tara got to her at the same moment. Levi released his skis and crawled to her head. "Rebecca. Where are you hurt? Can you feel your legs? What about your neck?"

Rebecca didn't answer, although she wanted to scream at Levi to get away. She panted as the pain threatened to send her into unconsciousness.

"I think she broke her collarbone," said the first boy. "We need a rescue crew up here." He pulled a cell phone from his pocket and dialed a few numbers.

"No," Rebecca said, trying to sit up. The searing fire in her shoulder sent her to the ground again. "I cannot afford it."

"I'm taking you to the hospital," Levi said.

This time she did sit up, in spite of the efforts of three boys to keep her down. "No hospital," she said, before the trees, the faces, the sky became a cloud of snow and fog.

Levi gently took her by her good arm and put his hand around her neck. "Lay back, kid."

She didn't argue. She couldn't argue. When she made any movement, the pain almost overwhelmed her. She sank to the ground with Levi's hand still under her head.

"It'll be all right. You'll be okay, kid."

"Stay away from me," she said weakly.

The tortured look on his face did nothing to lessen her contempt.

She tried to push his hand away with her good arm. He wouldn't budge. "Don't touch me." She talked to the boy with the cell phone. "Get him away from me."

Levi and the other boy looked at each other in confusion. "Hey," the boy said mildly, "I don't think she wants to be touched. The pain is making her punchy."

Rebecca took a deep breath and let a wave of pain subside. "You killed Dottie Mae."

Levi's face twisted in pain. "I'm so sorry, Rebecca. I was going to tell you about the accident. I didn't know it was Dottie Mae."

Tara folded her arms and flashed Levi a superior look. "You forgot to share that minor detail about your past."

Rebecca's shoulder burned and froze at the same time. "Go away, Levi. I never want to see you ever again."

The ski patrol announced themselves on two growling snow-mobiles. They quickly assessed the damage and wrapped her shoulder and arm while Levi and Tara stood watch. Levi wouldn't leave but stayed far enough away that she couldn't complain that he was harassing her.

The medics lifted her onto a strange sort of medical sled to transport her to the bottom of the hill, where Rebecca suspected an ambulance waited.

Tara folded her arms and glanced smugly at Rebecca. "I told you she was a self-righteous little prig."

"Save it, Tara," Levi said. "I'm not listening anymore."

Chapter Thirty-One

Rebecca never felt more forsaken than when she lay on that examination table staring at the dingy white ceiling and waiting for the results of her X-rays. Her arm and shoulder felt like they were on fire. If only Mamm were here to hold her hand and reassure her that everything would be okay. At this moment, Rebecca would have settled for Linda or Danny. Even Max would be better company than her thoughts. She wished she could erase the last seven months of her life and forget she ever knew Levi Cooper. She would be content if the thought of him never crossed her mind again.

The nurse pulled back the curtain and handed her a cup of ice water with a straw. "Here you go," she said.

Rebecca wiped the sweat from her forehead. "I've got to get out of here," she said. "Please let me out of here."

The nurse rubbed her hand up and down Rebecca's leg. "The doctor should be back in just a few minutes, honey. You're almost done. Everything will be all right."

Rebecca took a long sip of water and tried to breathe normally.

The nurse picked up a towel and sponged off Rebecca's head. "I hate to ask again, but that boy in the waiting room is wondering if he could come in and see you. I know you've already said no, but he looks so upset. I thought you might change your mind."

Rebecca frowned and closed her eyes. Thank goodness for hospital privacy rules. "I won't see him."

The nurse forced a smile. "Okay, I'll tell him."

"Tell him to go home."

"He says he's your ride."

"I've already called someone else to come and get me."

"Can I tell him how you're doing?"

Rebecca turned her head from the nurse and stared at the wall. "Tell him I'm much better off without him."

* * * * *

Mrs. Johnson pulled the car in front of Rebecca's house. "I'll help you in," she said.

In spite of the searing pain up her arm and shoulder, Rebecca popped the door open and jumped out. "I can manage."

"You sure?"

"I'll be fine."

The hospital ordeal was finally over. After the doctor gave her a crisp sling and discharge instructions, Rebecca had sneaked out the back way to Mrs. Johnson's waiting van. Undeterred, Levi tracked Rebecca's escape and tenaciously followed in his Toyota, back to Apple Lake like a stray puppy.

Glancing behind her, she saw Levi sitting in his dented car at the entrance to the long driveway, leaning as far forward as he could and waiting for Mrs. Johnson to back out. "Thank you a million times for the ride, Mrs. Johnson. You saved me today."

"You called at a good time. My soap was over, and I had nothing else to do all afternoon. Get some rest, and I'll see if one of the Newswenger girls can clean for me until you're better."

Rebecca made her way to the house as rapidly as she could without jarring her shoulder. She must be safely hidden inside before Levi could intercept her. Oh, that she had never asked him to take her skiing!

Rebecca slammed the front door behind her and stormed into the kitchen. She stopped short, and her heart sank. Wednesday afternoon. Marvin was here.

He sat at the table with Linda, Max, and Danny. Linda must have been in charge of dinner. They were eating hot dogs and dill pickles, and the cupboards practically sagged with dirty dishes.

They stared at her in silent disbelief. She must look a sight. Englisch clothes, hair askew, arm in a sling… She chastised herself for not sneaking through the back door.

"What happened to your arm?" Danny asked with his mouthful of pickles.

"Where have you been?" Linda said.

Rebecca ignored the questions and Marvin's shocked expression and went to the sink. She turned her back on her family, filled a pot with water, and put it on the stove to heat up. Then she put the plug in the drain and turned on the faucet. She poured dish soap under the cold running water and filled the sink with dishes left from breakfast and lunch. Disregarding her throbbing shoulder and the deafening silence behind her, Rebecca started washing dishes with her one good hand.

As expected, she heard a knock at the door.

She looked at Marvin and tried to remove any emotion from her voice. "Tell him I will not see him."

Without taking his eyes off her, Marvin rose deliberately from his chair, laid his napkin on the table, then disappeared into the living room. Rebecca could imagine his smug expression when he opened the door and discovered who stood on the porch.

Levi's voice cut through her soul. "I need to talk to Rebecca."

A long pause. "What did you do to her arm?"

"I would never hurt her."

"She will not see you."

"I'll wait."

"Go away," Marvin said. "She does not want to see you."

Rebecca heard Marvin shut the door partway and Levi put out a hand to stop it. "Please," he said, talking louder. He must have suspected she could hear him. "Someone as good-hearted as Rebecca would give even her worst enemy a chance to explain and ask for forgiveness."

"So you *did* hurt her arm."

"Please ask her to come out."

Marvin shut the door, and Rebecca heard him slide the dead bolt into place. When he came into the kitchen, she picked up the frenetic pace of her pot-scrubbing.

"What did he do to you?" Marvin asked, his words charged with indignation.

Rebecca winced as her sudden movements pulled at her shoulder.

Max jumped to his feet. "Sit, Rebecca. Danny, finish the dishes." He pulled Rebecca gently by her good arm and led her to his chair at the table. Kneeling beside her, he laid his hand over hers. "You're as pale as a sheet," he said. "Is your arm broken?"

Rebecca shook her head. "Collarbone."

Marvin towered over her and folded his arms. "Why are you dressed like that? Your fater warned me that boy would be trouble."

Rebecca met eyes with Max in unspoken communication. Max stood and gave Marvin a firm pat on the shoulder. "Denki for coming today, Marvin," Max said. "But it is time for you to leave. Rebecca needs rest."

"I will stay," Marvin said, straining for the bravado he didn't have. "He won't dare threaten you while I am here."

"Levi would never harm us," Max said. "And we will take care of our own."

Marvin looked to Rebecca for support. She averted her eyes and grabbed on to Max's hand. Fourteen-year-old Max stared Marvin down until Marvin surrendered. After a brief hesitation, he lifted his hat from the stand and reluctantly put on his coat.

"Send to my house if you need help," he said.

Rebecca nodded and tried to hide her relief that Marvin was going. Max turned to her, and she mouthed a "Thank you."

Marvin frowned in frustration and stomped out of the kitchen. The door closed with a loud *bang*, and they heard his heavy steps on the porch.

"What happened, Rebecca?" Max said. "And what does it have to do with Levi?"

Rebecca covered her face with her hand. "I fell, skiing. It's starting to hurt terrible."

All heads turned when they heard another knock at the door. Rebecca couldn't find her breath.

"Do you want me to make him leave?" asked Max.

"Jah, please."

Max walked out of the kitchen, and Rebecca heard him go outside.

"You went skiing?" Danny said, abandoning his dish duty and sitting next to Rebecca.

"Did they take you to the hospital?" Linda asked.

Rebecca nodded.

"How will we pay?"

"I don't know," said Rebecca.

"It's not coming out of my money," Linda insisted. "I am saving for a scooter."

"Did Levi go skiing with you?" Danny asked.

They heard the door open. Max walked through the kitchen and down the hall. He came back carrying a thick quilt from his bed.

"What are you doing?" Rebecca said.

"He won't leave. He says he will stay on that porch until you come out. I'm taking him a blanket because it's cold out there, and from the set of your mouth, it looks like he'll be out there a long time."

Rebecca took deep gulps of air to keep from breaking down. "He can freeze to death out there, for all I care."

Max's dark expression made him appear years older. "He's crying, Rebecca. Crying. What happened?"

"He's a liar and a fake. An Englischer, Max. He pretended to be Amish so Fater would let him come to the farm."

"That is no reason to leave him out in the cold," Max said, raising his voice. "Levi is a gute person, Englisch or not."

"You don't know what he did!" Rebecca yelled back.

Max pulled Danny off his chair and sat next to Rebecca. "Whatever it was, as a Christian, you should hear him out. Get off your high horse and go out there."

"You don't know, Max. Stay out of it."

Still clutching the quilt, Max scowled and stormed out of the house.

Danny immediately slid into the chair beside her. Tears filled his eyes. "He will get real cold out there."

Rebecca's resistance slackened. Danny was a better Christian than she. "He will leave when it gets cold enough," she said.

"I don't think so," Danny said. "Remember how he stayed until midnight painting the last of the red on the barn? He won't quit easy. I don't think he'll go away unless you talk to him."

The thought of facing Levi made Rebecca sick to her stomach. How could she look into those penetrating brown eyes that stunned her senses with their depth, knowing what he had done? But Danny was right. Levi refused to give up on Rebecca. He loved her too much to ever quit trying.

She caught her breath. He loved her—she knew it beyond a doubt. Her heart pounded with miserable longing. That was why he would wait on her porch until he turned to dust and the wind blew him away. He loved her, and she could not bear the thought of it.

Keeping his eyes glued to Rebecca's face, Danny wiped a tear from his cheek. "Do you want me to come out with you? I don't mind the cold."

Rebecca sighed. "Nae, I will go myself."

Danny supported her arm as she slowly rose to her feet. Every movement sent shock waves through her body. "Are you okay?" he said.

"I will call if I need you," she said.

Danny helped her walk to the door and opened it for her. She let go of his shoulder and stepped out onto the porch.

Levi sat on the bench, his knees to his chin, with his arms wrapped around his legs. His forehead rested on his knees with the blanket draped around his shoulders. When Rebecca emerged, he jumped to his feet. He grabbed a stunning bouquet of long red roses from the bench and held them out to her. "Rebecca," he said, his eyes brimming with sorrow.

She stood her ground. "I don't want your roses."

Dejected, he laid them on the bench. "You must be cold," he said. She stood motionless as he took the quilt from his shoulders and wrapped it around her, taking care not to bump her arm in the process. She refused to be moved by his singular kindness. She shrugged the quilt off her shoulders and set it down on the bench, smothering his roses.

The gesture was not lost on him. He riveted her attention with a tormented look. His eyes were too brilliant. She couldn't look away. "What do you want, Levi?"

"Tell me what words to say so you won't hate me." He took a step closer. "I'll do anything."

She didn't answer. He reached out and grabbed her good hand. She snatched it away. "Don't touch me."

"Rebecca, you have to believe how sorry I am about the accident. That memory tortures me every day of my life. I relive it over and over, wishing like crazy that I could change the past. Please forgive me."

"Forgive you? Dottie Mae is dead. *Dead*. And you and your friends drove off and let her die because you didn't want to get caught."

"That's not true—"

"You will answer to God."

Levi hung his head. "You told me once that you always take people at face value. That you see what I really am inside. Can't you see that now?"

"How can I ever love you? You are a liar and a drunk. And a— and a murderer."

Rebecca immediately chastised herself for that part about loving him. Where had that come from? Of course she didn't love him. She never had. The thought of loving such a person repulsed her.

Her words struck him dumb. They stared at each other for a thirty-second eternity.

"Please, Rebecca," he said.

She turned to go back into the house. "I have chores."

"I can't change it, Rebecca," he said in one last-ditch effort to sway her. "I wish it had been me in that buggy instead of Dottie Mae."

"So do I."

Her words found their mark. Levi caught his breath and stumbled a few steps backward. His chest heaved up and down as the tears rolled down his cheeks. "I'm sorry, Rebecca," he whispered. "I'm so sorry."

"So you've said. Now go away."

He backed slowly down the steps, never taking his eyes from her face. And then he was gone. Rebecca stood motionless on the porch, staring in the direction Levi had gone, listening as the rumbling echo of his Toyota slowly faded to nothing.

She didn't realize she'd been holding her breath. She took air into her lungs in spasms, as if she had just spent hours weeping bitterly for what might have been. Closing her eyes, she bit her lower lip. Hard. *Block out every other pain, no matter how intense. Don't scream in frustration or guilt or heartbreak.*

Don't cry.

Never, ever cry.

Why would she ever waste tears on Levi Cooper? Dottie Mae would scold her harshly.

Did our friendship mean nothing? she would say. *Spend your tears on me, not on one of my killers. No matter that he has stolen your heart. Do not love him.*

I don't. I won't love him. He is dead to me now.

With her good hand, Rebecca scooped up the quilt and the bouquet of roses from the bench. They probably cost Levi upwards of sixty dollars. He shouldn't have bothered. She thudded her foot a couple of times against the front door, and Danny immediately opened for her.

"Where's Levi?" he said.

Rebecca pushed past her eager brother, marched to the kitchen, and shoved the roses into the garbage bin.

"He's gone," she said. "Gone for good."

* * * * *

Levi stumbled to his car, slammed the door, and tore out of Rebecca's driveway. He drove in whatever direction the road took him until his vision blurred and he couldn't seem to find his way.

He was going to lose it.

After pulling into an ancient gas station spotted with rust, he parked his car and rested his head on the steering wheel to stop the world from going in circles.

Her name was Dorothy. Levi hadn't even made the connection.

Oh, please, dear heavenly Father. Anything but this. Could You hate me any more than You do? I can't bear this punishment.

He felt as if he were plunging from a jagged cliff into a river of stones that tumbled and crushed and pulverized him into dust. He longed for a stiff wind to blow him into oblivion.

"I wish it had been me in that buggy instead of Dottie Mae."

"So do I."

Crying out in pain, he put his car into Drive and squealed the tires in an effort to get away. He had to find a drink. He had to have a drink.

* * * * *

The gravel crackled under Levi's tires as he pulled up along the side of the road. He parked far enough from the shoulder that there was no risk of a passing motorist hitting his car in the dark. The cold night air felt good after sitting in his stifling car. Clutching the neck of his unopened bottle, he staggered to the rocky bank of the half-frozen river where he and his dad used to spend lazy afternoons, fishing.

For a moment, Levi forgot his self-loathing. Anger at his dad welled up inside him. If it hadn't been for Dad, Levi wouldn't have been so reckless, wouldn't have been in the wrong place at the wrong time. If Dad were still around, none of this would have happened.

But rage at his dad couldn't hold Levi for long. He knew precisely where to lay the blame. Oh, how he hated himself for what he had done! The despair engulfed him. Now Rebecca hated him too. There were no words of comfort that would sway her. She despised the very sight of him. How could he bear her contempt?

He had lost her.

He raised his bottle of whiskey in the moonlight. This was the only thing that ever gave him comfort. It dulled the pain enough to let him function, let him forget for a few hours what he was. He eagerly peeled the wrapping off the lid. In his carelessness, he pulled the wrong way, and the sharp foil sliced through his finger. Good. A new pain to dull the old one. He tried to twist off the lid, but it wouldn't budge. No matter. He'd never met a liquor bottle he couldn't open.

Doubling his efforts, he grasped the bottle tightly, but his hand slipped around the lid as if it were greased.

Growling, he took a deep breath and contemplated bashing the thing with a rock, when a glint of light on the river caught his eye. A cloudless night in Wisconsin in December was rare, and the moon glowed unhindered in the sky, bathing the frosty water in a sparkling glow. Momentarily captivated by the brilliance, he gazed out over the water, and Rebecca's bright eyes seemed to appear in the reflection. He heard her voice.

"Jesus will carry it for you if you give it to Him."

"It's my burden, Rebecca, not His."

"Everything is His burden."

He wished he could believe it. He wanted to believe it with all his heart. But how could God ever love, ever forgive him? He tapped a knuckle between his eyebrows in an attempt to drum Rebecca's voice out of his head.

"Can a woman forget her sucking child? ...yea, they may forget, yet will I not forget thee. Behold, I have graven thee upon the palms of my hands."

Levi didn't know how that Scripture found its way into his brain, but he heard it again and again. Focusing his eyes across the river, he pictured Jesus standing on the other side with His arms outstretched.

"I have graven thee upon the palms of my hands."

What did that mean?

In a flash of insight, Levi knew exactly what it meant. The Lord had paid a high price for sinners like him. Anyone could see the price if they looked at His hands.

Rebecca's voice rang inside his head like a bell.

"There are no lost causes."

Just look at the hands.

He felt as if he were standing on the railroad tracks as a train came full speed and bowled him over. The weight of his life, his mistakes, hit him and threw him into an imaginary brick wall. Unable to support himself, he groped his way to the nearest tree and wrapped his arm around it.

Bowing his head and letting the grief overcome him, he wept, spilling out tears with every emotion he had buried deep.

That poor girl. Her death threw countless lives tossing and rolling in its wake: her family, her friends, his old friend Derek who was with him in the car that night, his family, Rebecca, his own…. Tonight, more than ever, the weight of consequences crushed him. How could Jesus ever lift it? It was too heavy.

"Come unto me, all ye that labour and are heavy laden, and I will give you rest."

He moaned in exhaustion, his strength spent.

Levi looked down through tear-filled eyes. He still had the bottle. Again he tried to unscrew the lid. This time it opened with ease. He tipped the bottle upside down and poured out every drop. The whiskey sloshed and splashed on the rocks.

It was time to let God, not the liquor, take control of his life.

The sharp rocks of the riverbank cut into his skin as he fell to his knees.

"Dear God," he said, tears still streaking down his face, "I think I'm ready for a rest."

* * * * *

Early the next morning, Rebecca stepped out on the front porch to attempt to sweep with one hand. She looked down.

A single red rose lay on the welcome mat at her feet.

Her heart drummed a wild cadence as she looked down her driveway and across the pasture. Not a sign of him. The disappointment almost overwhelmed her.

She picked up the rose, closed her eyes, and stroked her cheek with the soft petals. She stopped herself before she put the flower to her nose. How could she ever think about accepting a gift from him?

She crushed the rose until it fell apart in her hand then cast the petals onto the snowdrift in front of her porch.

Her hand smelled like rose milk the rest of the day.

Chapter Thirty-Two

Levi crunched through the snow in heavy boots with two full pails of milk. His breath hung on the air as he paused between the barn and the house to savor the quiet stillness of dusk on Christmas evening. It had started snowing early in the morning as the houseful of guests stirred from sleep. Flakes heavy enough to catch on his tongue still drifted to the ground as he stood gazing at the frosted windows of the house. A white Christmas—like the ones he remembered from his childhood.

On a day like this, Dat would hitch Beauty to the sleigh and they would glide around the snowy lanes to the pond for some ice-skating. Levi's cheeks would grow numb and bright red before Mom made him bundle up in the sleigh and Dat drove them to Mammi's house for Christmas dinner.

Levi and his mom had moved into the dawdi house almost a week ago. Relatives by the buggy-ful came to their apartment to help them move out, while a houseful of more relatives greeted them at their new place to help them settle in. The dawdi house was attached to the main house. It had two bedrooms and a nice, big living area with a complete kitchen.

Today, Mammi's house was nicely crammed from cellar to attic with out-of-town visitors—Mom's sisters Barbara and Eva and their husbands, plus Uncle Jonas with his family, and, ach, too many cousins to count.

Surely they made up half the population of Amish people in Wisconsin.

That morning after breakfast, the uncles and cousins went sledding on the big hill beyond Mammi and Dawdi's pasture. Levi took several of the little cousins for rides down the hill. Cousin Rachel, who was four, would go only if Levi sat behind her, held on tight, and dragged his feet in the snow the whole way down.

Rachel reminded Levi of Rebecca. Rebecca would hate sledding.

Thinking of Rebecca always left Levi panting for air. He closed his eyes and waited for the raw pain to subside. Thoughts of her swirled in his brain constantly, rendering him unable to sleep or eat or carry on a coherent conversation.

The look in her eyes last week on the ski hill was riveted to his memory. Her rejection was a pocketknife right to the gut.

She wishes I had died instead of Dottie Mae.

The cruelty of her declaration struck Levi as if Rebecca were standing right there and saying those words to him again. His legs shook. He placed his milk pails on the ground and knelt in the ankle-deep snow. The wet cold crept up his legs and into his heart.

He wished the tears didn't come so easily. He bowed his head and whispered a prayer. "Lord, please help me get through this. And please let Rebecca heal. She deserves to be happy."

He knelt there motionless with tears streaming down his face, trying to lift his vision to heaven, until his knees throbbed and his teeth chattered with cold. He swiped away the tears, stumbled to his feet, and picked up his pails, determined that his troubles wouldn't ruin his first Amish Christmas in fifteen years.

The first for many years to come, Lord willing.

Because in spite of it all, Levi knew he wanted to be baptized. That night at the river, faced with the reality of losing Rebecca, his heart changed and he found another, better motivation. A permanent Rock-of-Ages reason to give his life to God.

Levi poured the milk into the large metal container sitting outside the back door and then went inside, leaving his boots on the rug in the mudroom.

Mammi, Aunt Barbara, Levi's sister, Beth, and five older cousins bustled around the kitchen preparing a Christmas feast. Beth had come from school to spend Christmas with them, and even though she was in her Englisch clothes, she seemed to fit in perfectly with her Amish relatives. She chopped carrots while chatting merrily to Mammi about her time at the university.

Mom sat in the corner with her eyes shining and her hands clasped below her chin. While the family included her in what they could, certain formalities of shunning would still be observed for another few weeks. She didn't seem to mind being excluded from the food preparation.

When she caught sight of Levi, she leaped from her stool and came to him.

"Oh, Levi, isn't this wonderful-gute? Mammi made *stollen* and pecan pie. And you should see the size of the turkey in the cookstove."

She squeezed his hand and smiled so big that Levi could see the little girl she used to be. At times like this, his heartache evaporated. Levi had never seen his mother so radiant.

Mammi, with a dot of flour on her cheek, pulled a plate of pickles and olives from the fridge. "It's high time to wash up, Levi. Dinner will be ready in two shakes of a lamb's tail."

Levi helped *Onkel* Titus and the cousins move the big furniture out of the front room and set up two columns of long tables and benches. The older girl cousins spread silky tablecloths over the tables and arranged tall candles and pine greenery down the centers.

Mammi pulled out the good china, and the tables soon looked like something Levi would have seen in *Better Homes and Gardens* magazine.

The food measured up to the festive table. After silent grace, Mammi and the aunts brought out platters and bowls piled high with turkey, chestnut stuffing, corn, green beans with bacon, rolls, pickles, and olives. Mammi's fluted, long-stemmed glasses were filled with a layered pudding dessert that made Levi's mouth water just looking at it. There were at least five varieties of cookies and Mammi's special Christmas punch.

Levi, Beth, and Mom sat at the end of the table, an arrangement that seemed to satisfy everyone's requirement for shunning, even though the relatives talked to Mom as much as anybody else.

Levi sat in amused silence and listened to several conversations at once. There was a great deal of teasing cousin Eliza about a new boy she was seeing. Toby showed the cousins sitting next to him the scrape he got while sledding this morning, and the middle-aged men talked about what they always talked about: the weather and farming.

Beth was admiring the new work boots Dawdi received for Christmas. "They look sturdy," she said.

"They'll do," Dawdi said. "I'm partial to my old boots, but they is ruined."

Mammi laughed and nudged Beth with her elbow. "His own fault."

"I greased them up gute and put them in the cookstove for a quick dry," Dawdi said.

"He forgot about them," said Mammi. She tapped a finger to her forehead. "Memory's going, ya know."

Dawdi harrumphed and thumbed his suspenders. "I am still as sharp as a tack, Nancy. It just went out of my mind, is all. Next morning I got up and lit a fire and them boots was burned to a crisp."

Everyone laughed, and Dawdi cracked a smile. "It wasn't all bad. I got a new pair of boots." He lifted his foot in an attempt to show off his gift and almost tumbled backward. Beth and Eliza steadied him before he picked up his fork and took a healthy bite of stuffing.

After dinner, the school-aged grandchildren presented the Christmas story. King Herod's scepter looked suspiciously like one of Mammi's spatulas, and "the Mother Mary" became "the Motho Mawy" because Annie couldn't say her *R*s. Levi loved every minute of it.

After the presentation, the family sang their favorite Christmas songs. The Christmas spirit permeated the very air, and Levi didn't hear a sour note in the bunch. Singing must have been a genetic inheritance of the Amish.

When strains of "The First Noel" died away, Dawdi, who'd sat perfectly still in his plump recliner, slapped his knee. "Let's bundle up and go a-caroling to the shut-ins. They ain't nothing that would make them so happy as to hear us sing."

"Caroling is for *die youngie*," Onkel Titus said. "John can take them around to the shut-ins, and we can eat a piece of pie while they are gone."

Dawdi sank back into his chair. "Do you have pumpkin, Nancy?"

"With real whipped cream," Mammi said.

Dawdi nodded. "I'll wait here."

Just like this morning, getting out the door proved to be a huge production. Each caroler needed a hat and gloves, coat and boots. They finally made it outside and down the lane with John leading the way. Levi held hands with his nine-year-old cousin, Sissy, until she stubbed her toe on a rock. Then he lifted her for a piggyback ride, singing and laughing all the way down the road.

Levi paid no attention to where they were going until they stopped in front of a house with a long driveway and a bright red barn with white trim. Of course they'd come here; Rebecca's mother was a shut-in. His heart sank to his toes and did a tap dance at the same time. He hadn't laid eyes on Rebecca since the ski trip last week. He'd been to her house every day to leave a rose on her porch but hadn't been fortunate enough to even catch a glimpse of her.

Once he and Mom moved into the dawdi house, Levi looked for Rebecca everywhere. He went to a gathering when he heard that she would attend, only to be heartbroken when she left as soon as she caught sight of him.

The Petersheim cousins, oblivious to Levi's history with Rebecca, trekked through the deep snow covering the Millers' sidewalk and tromped up to Rebecca's porch en masse. Levi momentarily hung back. Would Rebecca's fater see this visit as a broken promise? Would Levi ruin Rebecca's Christmas by showing up at her house? Or would she see him and remember the gute times they had together?

Small red circles dotted the snow in front of Rebecca's house.

Rose petals, no doubt from the rose he had delivered early this morning, were strewn about like a handful of chicken feed tossed into the snow. He swung Sissy to the ground and pretended to ignore the hurt that bubbled up inside him.

He'd seen it before—rose petals from the previous day's rose when he came to deliver the next one. But tonight, on Christmas, the sting of rejection felt especially acute.

Levi found himself standing on the porch but couldn't remember moving his feet to get there. He melted in behind John and Ize, not sure if he wanted to be seen. He didn't think he could endure the contempt in Rebecca's eyes.

One of the cousins knocked, and they began to sing "Away in a Manger." Danny threw open the door and stood listening with a wide grin on his face. Soon Linda joined him, and Max and Rebecca were close behind. Rebecca's arm was still in a sling. Levi winced.

Like a sophisticated radar device, Rebecca zeroed in on Levi immediately, as if he were the only one standing on the porch. She hadn't been smiling in the first place, but her frown deepened when she saw him, and she quickly averted her eyes. He held his breath, glued his gaze to her face, and drank in her features like a very thirsty man. She looked thin and pale and ten years older. Her eyes held none of the light that had reeled him in from the first day he met her. Still, she was the most beautiful girl he had ever known. His heart broke again and again as he stood there. Would she ever forgive him? Could he ever hope to win her back?

The thought of the accident no longer brought him to his knees. Jesus had taken his pain away. And if he had forgiven himself, surely she would forgive him too. Wasn't that what the Amish did best?

After one verse of the song, Rebecca's mother appeared at the door. "Cum reu, all of you, and get warm. How thoughtful of you to come and see me."

Rebecca's mamm ushered all seventeen of them into the front room, where a fire blazed merrily in the hearth and pine boughs decked the mantel and door frames. The house smelled of cinnamon and apple cider.

Rebecca's mamm squeezed Levi's hand as he stepped over the threshold. "Welcome into the community, Levi Cooper. We are very glad to have you back." She winked at him and half smiled. She knew what an uphill battle this was going to be.

Both Max and Linda caught sight of Levi. Max furrowed his brow and looked away. Linda turned red in confusion and busied herself by stoking the fire.

Rebecca's fater sauntered into the room and frowned when his eyes met Levi's. His response almost perfectly mirrored Rebecca's. They both refused to look at him and surveyed their guests with expressionless faces, as if they were reading some dull newspaper article. But Levi could see the tension in Rebecca's shoulders and hands as she stood against the wall and pressed her good fist into it, as if it would fall over if she relaxed.

"Levi!" Danny opened his arms wide and threw himself at Levi. At least he had one ally in the Miller family.

"Hey, Danny."

"We have missed you so much." He looked at his sister for confirmation, but Rebecca studied the floor intently. Danny motioned for Levi to lean closer. "Rebecca said you weren't ever going to come back, but I wish you would. Rebecca misses you something terrible even though she never says your name ever."

Levi swallowed hard and tried not to let a spark of hope ignite. Better to be cautious with his deepest desires. "Thanks, Danny. I miss you too. And I really miss Rebecca."

Danny smiled. "I told her you did. She shook her finger and told me to go milk the cows."

Levi and his cousins sat on the sofas and the floor. Rebecca didn't surrender her wall while they sang Christmas songs even though she looked like she'd rather be anywhere else. After "Silent Night," she grabbed Linda's hand and they bolted into the kitchen. Linda brought out hot cocoa and whoopie pies while Rebecca stayed hidden.

After everyone had cocoa, cousin John stood up. "Merry Christmas to you. May the good Lord bless you in the coming year."

Rebecca's mamm didn't try to stand, but she held out her hand to John. "Lord willing. Thank you for coming."

Each cousin stood and took her hand before walking out the front door. When it was Levi's turn, she pulled him toward her until he felt compelled to kneel beside her rocker. She stared into Levi's face and patted his hand. "Come and visit us again," she said. "We could use some cheering up around here."

Levi smiled weakly and nodded. He could use some cheering up too. But unless Rebecca quit ignoring him or her fater softened his heart, he held out little hope.

As the group moved on down the driveway, Levi stopped to lift a petal from the snow. He rubbed it between his fingers and thought of Rebecca's silky skin. The longing to feel her hand in his overwhelmed every other sense. He didn't even notice the cold.

The front door opened, and the light from within cast a shimmering glow on the snow. Danny leaped down the stairs and held out a small brown box to Levi.

"What's this?" Levi asked.

"It's a Christmas present," Danny said. "Rebecca threw it in the trash, and I was spying. I kept it because I thought someday she might be sad she threw it away." He stared at Levi with a mixture of childlike innocence and wisdom beyond his years. "I think you should have it. Merry Christmas."

Levi took the box from him, and Danny ran back into the house.

The cousins were already far down the road.

"You coming?" John yelled.

"I'll catch up," Levi said.

"Don't get lost," said John. "Dawdi will scold me if you never come back."

Levi loosened the crudely tied ribbon from around the box and lifted the lid. Inside was a small pile of tickets and papers. He picked up the top one.

DECEMBER 15. ALL-DAY SKI PASS. ROCKY SPINE SKI RESORT.

Levi felt his legs go weak. He stumbled to the porch steps and sat down before he collapsed into a heap in the snow.

December fifteenth. The day Rebecca decided to hate him. The worst day of his life—and he'd had some pretty bad ones. He pulled out the next ticket.

FOXFIRE BOTANICAL GARDENS. A receipt for one hosta plant was taped to the ticket. Warmth spread through Levi's body as he remembered the way Rebecca cradled that plant like a baby. That was the day she drove his car into a gulley. He cringed as the memory of Rebecca's pale face and bleeding head assaulted him.

In addition to the Mt. Olympus amusement park ticket, Rebecca had kept the snapshot Uncle Joe had given her of his backyard. Levi smiled.

A small plastic bag full of sand. A pressed wildflower. And the movie ticket from their very first date. Levi unfolded a large piece of paper underneath the tickets.

THE TETANUS IMMUNIZATION AND YOU—WHAT YOU SHOULD KNOW.

Levi pressed the paper to his chest and chuckled. Why she would ever want to remember that experience, he'd never know.

The dry remains of several rose petals lay in the bottom of the box. Levi thought the lining of the box was crinkled, but when he looked closer, he realized it was a piece of notepaper clinging to the bottom.

He tipped the box upside down, and the paper fell into his hand.

Live in my very own house.
Plant an acre of roses.
Make Fater love me again.

And in very small letters in a different color of pen—

Kiss Levi Cooper.

Levi set Rebecca's things on the porch step as if they had burned him. He shouldn't have opened that box. Rebecca had a right to keep her deepest wishes and dreams private.

Kiss Levi Cooper.

Those three words made him almost giddy, as if he were soaring effortlessly above the tallest mountains. Despite all her protests, he held a place in her heart. Or at least he had before she found out the truth about him.

Levi looked at the pile of tickets and papers, picked up her list, and read it again. All Rebecca wanted was a little love. She was not only going physically hungry in this house, she was also starving for affection. Tears stung Levi's eyes. All he wanted to do was love her. Why wouldn't she let him?

He quickly stuffed the tickets and petals and memories into the box, put the lid on, and took it with him as he sprinted down the driveway. He wanted to get far enough away before anyone heard the sobs that threatened to overtake him.

Why wouldn't she let him love her?

Chapter Thirty-Three

Levi sat on the hard bench wedged between two old men. His first Amish wedding. The groom hadn't stopped smiling since the service began. Levi had never seen any two people so happy. The groom couldn't keep his eyes off his bride. He gazed at her and grinned through four songs, two long sermons, and a prayer. However, Levi's attention was divided between the ecstatic groom and the face of Rebecca Miller, who was sitting across the room with her back rigid and a frown pasted on her face. The sight of her always stole his breath and his reason.

It had been five weeks since the skiing trip, and still she refused to see him. At least he held hope that she would not bolt from the wedding. Someone had told him that she was related to the bride.

Finally the bishop invited the bride and groom to stand. Levi didn't catch much of the ceremony itself. High German had completely escaped his memory. But the adoration and joy radiating from the bride and groom were evident enough as they stood clutching hands while the bishop performed the ceremony. When he finished, the couple sat down. Levi was a little disappointed. No kiss.

Tears coursed down the bride's cheeks. The groom looked only slightly more composed. Ultimate joy, it seemed, was difficult to contain.

Levi let his gaze return to Rebecca. He would have to thank the groom profusely for inviting him, for giving him a chance to stare at the girl he loved without her hiding her face in disgust. Being new to the community, Levi hadn't expected to attend the wedding, but the groom had insisted he come. The groom, Nathaniel King, was Levi's new employer.

Another prayer and a song. The large room, built with a temporary addition for the occasion, echoed with the music of hundreds of voices. Levi estimated there must have been over three hundred people stuffed into the limited space.

As soon as the last strains of the song floated up to the rafters, the place exploded into action. Everyone jumped to their feet. Levi saw Rebecca lead her mamm to a padded chair then bustle out of the room with the other women. Her mother looked as frail as ever, moving slowly and painfully to her seat.

Some of the men began setting up tables between the benches. The whole operation ran like a well-oiled machine, but Levi couldn't discover anyone in particular to be in charge.

He approached a middle-aged man and offered his help with the tables. The man looked doubtful for a fraction of a second then smiled and motioned for Levi to follow. The man's hesitation wasn't unexpected. Levi had encountered it many times in the last five weeks, mostly at gmay. Understandably, some of the community regarded him with suspicion as an outsider. Some in the district had other misgivings. Surely many of them knew about his part in the accident. Did they forgive him or hold him in contempt like Rebecca did?

Anger at his father reared its ugly head, as it did every time Levi thought of that night. He pushed the feeling aside and squared his shoulders. The Lord had forgiven him, and he had forgiven himself. He could only hope that the others would offer mercy and that Rebecca would offer her heart. He would show her, prove his worth. He could not bear if she, in the end, condemned him. Hope was the only thread he had left.

In the meantime, he would endure whatever rejection she chose to heap upon him. What else could he do? He loved her.

Levi and another man grabbed either end of a table leaning against the wall. Levi looked up to see Marvin Yutzy sharing his table.

Marvin frowned, averted his eyes, and acted as if he were setting up the table by himself. As soon as they placed the table, Marvin disappeared into the crowd. Levi almost smiled. There was absolutely no hope for a friendly relationship with Marvin. Not when Levi was trying to steal Marvin's girl.

The bride and groom sat at one of the tables surrounded by family and friends. About eighty people fit around the tables. They would have to eat in shifts. Levi guessed that was already part of the plan.

Once people settled onto the seats, teenage girls and young couples brought out heavenly smelling dishes of turkey and stuffing, cooked celery, mashed potatoes, and cabbage rolls. Levi leaned against the wall and never took his eyes from Rebecca as she dished up mashed potatoes from a huge serving bowl that Linda carried. He sighed in exasperation and admiration. Rebecca would never let something as trivial as one hand stop her from thrusting in her sickle. Could she not betray the slightest weakness?

She must have felt his gaze upon her because she glanced up and locked eyes with him. Only for a second. Then, frowning, she looked away and never let her eyes stray to his side of the room again. She liked to pretend he didn't exist.

The ache overpowered him, and he couldn't resist. He strode forward and tapped Linda on the shoulder.

"Levi," Linda said, glancing at Rebecca and blushing.

Rebecca scowled but didn't let his closeness distract her. She dished up potatoes with determined efficiency. But was she holding her breath?

"Do you know who you are coupled-up with for the singing?" Linda said.

Levi shook his head.

"Mamm says you are joining the church. I am very glad."

"That looks like a heavy bowl. Aren't your arms tired?" Levi said.

"Ach, sure are. But Rebecca cannot do it by herself."

"Here," he said, lifting the bowl out of Linda's arms. "I will help Rebecca."

Linda flashed a perplexed expression. "Okay, I guess. I don't like serving." She skipped off in the direction of three boys standing by the window.

Rebecca glared at him with hooded eyes. "What do you think you are doing?"

Even though the ache was deep, he still felt elation at standing so close to her. "I'm helping the poor, one-armed girl since she won't let people with two arms carry their weight."

"Everyone around here pulls his weight."

"This way, you can't run and hide. I'll hold your potatoes hostage."

"My mamm and the bride's mamm are sisters. I have to be here. Or believe me, the minute I saw you come strutting in here, I would have been headed to the next county." Rebecca plopped a dollop of potatoes onto the next plate.

Levi gave her a weak smile. "Thank goodness for cousins, then."

"Why do you bother me? There are plenty of girls here who want a try with you—all staring at you like you were the archangel himself. It's sickening."

"I hadn't noticed."

"You never do." Using her spoon as a pointer, she motioned to his clothes. "What game do you think you are playing?"

"I'm not playing a game, Rebecca. As soon as I finish baptism classes, I'll be baptized."

"And leave the Englisch world for this dull existence?"

"You think it's dull?"

"Don't you?"

"It's not frantic like Englisch life, if that's what you mean. But peaceful is not the same thing as dull. It's basic living. And people here are happy."

He gazed at her until she looked away.

"You do not have to bring a rose every day," she said.

"Would you prefer every other day?"

"I would prefer not at all."

"You deserve a thousand roses."

"I deserve nothing," she said, so quietly Levi had to strain to hear.

"Are you kidding? You are the reason I'm here, kid. I'm making myself better for you. I want to be with you."

"I can never forget Dottie Mae," she said, her voice cracking.

His hand brushed hers as she reached for another spoonful of potatoes. Her touch felt heavenly. "I don't want you to forget, but I'm begging you to forgive," he said.

"I'm dating Marvin," she said, pulling from his touch. "I'm not interested."

Trying to quell the sting of jealousy, Levi took the spoon from her fingers and placed it in the now-empty bowl. "I love you like no one is capable of loving you, Rebecca. So until you marry Marvin or some other guy you don't really love, there will be a rose at your doorstep every morning. Because you deserve it and I still have hope."

The urge to kiss her attacked all five senses and two or three he didn't know he had. Levi turned on his heels and walked away with her empty bowl and spoon.

He looked like an idiot. He felt like one too.

* * * * *

Rebecca marched back to the kitchen to get another plate of—anything. And another spoon. Levi had stolen her spoon too. Why didn't he go back where he belonged, to Tara and his old car and the alcohol? He didn't deserve to be here, where people treated him kindly and acted as if nothing had happened.

She tripped past her cousin Kate, who was the bride, and Miriam Bontrager, another cousin, deep in conversation. Rebecca forced a smile. This was a wedding, for heaven's sake. She'd better put on a happy face for the happy couple. Kate and Miriam made a beeline toward Rebecca the minute they saw her.

"Rebecca, wait," Kate said.

Being careful of her injured arm, first Miriam and then Kate gave Rebecca hugs.

Rebecca's sour mood softened in Kate's embrace. Her cousin accepted and loved everyone freely. "Oh, Kate, I am so happy for you."

"I never imagined that anyone could be this happy," Kate said, her eyes shining. She gazed at Nathaniel, who stood a few feet away visiting with two of his relatives. "The Almighty has blessed me beyond measure." Kate took Rebecca's good hand. "But I am worried for you."

"Jah," Miriam said. "Has your mamm taken a turn for the worse?"

"Nae. Considering it is wintertime, Mamm has been doing very well."

"I am glad to hear that," Miriam said.

Kate was not put off so easily. "You seemed upset just now, Rebecca. Can I do something to help you?"

"I am fine," Rebecca said. She had said that phrase so many times, she was thinking of embroidering it onto a pillow.

Kate withdrew her hand and managed a half smile. "Oh. Gute."

Miriam furrowed her brow. "You look so gloomy for such a happy occasion."

Rebecca cleared her throat. She couldn't close out her favorite cousins like this. "There is a certain young man at the wedding who is making a pest of himself."

"So many young men are flighty these days," Miriam said.

Kate studied Rebecca's face and frowned. "By the look on your face, I'd say that whoever he is, he has done something cruel." She gasped. "We shouldn't have coupled you up with Marvin."

"It is not Marvin Yutzy."

"Then who?" Kate said. "Shall I have Nathaniel speak to him?"

"Goodness gracious, no," Miriam said. "What would people think?"

Rebecca blanched at the thought. "I can take care of myself."

"I know you can," Kate said. "But if you have trouble, go right to Nathaniel. He will help you any way he can."

Rebecca hugged her cousins again and retreated to the kitchen.

Nathaniel was a gute man who would do anything for anybody, but he couldn't do the one thing she needed. He couldn't pluck the ice-cold pain from her heart.

* * * * *

Nathaniel hovered around his bride, Kate, like a moon in orbit.

The young people coupled up after lunch and sat in the large front room singing song after song. Levi was coupled with a girl named Priscilla, whom he couldn't coax to say one word. Priscilla smiled at him shyly but blushed profusely when he asked her any questions. Thank goodness the singing meant they didn't have to converse very much.

The newlyweds might as well have been the only people at the wedding, for all they paid attention to anyone else. They sat together on a bench in the corner exchanging whispers and meaningful looks. Levi's heart swelled so large, he thought it might pop out of his chest as he watched them. His longing for Rebecca grew with every moment he spent at the other man's wedding.

Emma Weaver, Kate's mamm, interrupted the singing when she and two of her daughters came into the room bearing trays of fruit and bread, soft pretzels, and chocolate for the singers. Someone handed Levi a cup and proceeded to pour him a helping of warm apple cider. Rebecca sat next to Marvin, who grinned smugly in Levi's direction whenever he thought Levi was watching. Levi tried not to look at either of them. The sight of Rebecca pretending to be happy with Marvin felt like someone stabbing a dull pencil right between Levi's shoulder blades.

He felt a firm hand on his shoulder and turned to see Nathaniel King smiling at him. "Are you enjoying the gathering?" he said.

"Someone pried you away from your wife?"

"My mother-in-law stole her," Nathaniel said. "But if she's not back in five minutes, I'll go searching."

Priscilla jumped up from her seat and moved to the safety of three friends across the room. Levi had just been dumped.

Nathaniel grabbed the arms of two young men behind him. "Adam, William, you remember Levi Cooper, don't you."

"Oh, jah," Adam said, "the new man at the shop."

Levi stood up and shook hands with both young men. "I've only worked there three days," he said. "It might take me a little time to learn all the names."

"He is very gute with his hands," Nathaniel said. "He came in the shop just as my nail gun jammed and fixed it, no problem. I hired him on the spot."

Levi smiled. Going into the shop five days before the boss's wedding turned out to be a terrific idea. Levi would do a good job for Nathaniel, but he wasn't sure if he got the job because of his skills or because Nathaniel's lovesick stupor compelled him to do good to the whole world—to offer a poor, fatherless outsider a much-needed job.

"You got moved in okay?" William said.

"My mom's family came by the buggyload. It only took us about an hour to move everything out and another hour to clean the old place. You Amish sure know how to do a job right."

"Don't say 'You Amish,'" Nathaniel said, putting a brotherly arm around Levi's shoulders. "You're one of us now."

"Even if your accent is a little rusty," William said. "But we promise not to tease you about your speech impediment."

Levi grinned. Maybe he could make a few friends among his neighbors.

"Is where you are staying a gute place?" Adam asked.

"Yeah, it's the perfect size for me and my mamm. But we want to move into our own house as soon as we get some money." He nodded to Nathaniel. "I am grateful for the job."

"Do not thank me yet. The work is hard. You'll earn your money."

"I'm not afraid of hard work."

"Jah, I can tell. That is why I hired you." Nathaniel looked around the room. "Where is your mamm?"

"She is probably in the kitchen watching them prepare the evening meal," Levi said. She was still not allowed to help because of the shunning, but it did not seem to bother her. "She is very, very happy to be back."

Two girls diverted Adam and William's attention and left Levi and Nathaniel standing alone.

To Levi's surprise, Nathaniel pointed to Rebecca. "That is Rebecca Miller, my wife's cousin. Would you like me to introduce you? You were staring at her like a piece of butterscotch pie. She *is* pretty."

"She's beautiful," Levi said, hoping his despair didn't make him sound like a slobbering puppy. "And I'm in love with her."

Nathaniel laughed at what he thought was Levi's teasing. "What? You have been to the wedding half a day and you already love my wife's cousin?" He nudged Levi with his elbow. "She's with Marvin Yutzy."

The lump in Levi's throat rendered him mute. He nodded.

Nathaniel took one look at Levi's face and the eternal smile left him. "You are serious," he said. "How do you know Rebecca?"

Levi took a deep breath. "It's too long a story for a groom on his wedding day."

Nathaniel studied Levi's face. "She's broken your heart, hasn't she?" He closed his eyes and massaged his forehead. "I know how that feels, and I never want to go there again."

"This is a very bad topic for your wedding day."

Nathaniel saw the bride almost before she walked into the room, like he had some sort of radar only for her. He smiled sadly at Levi. "I want to help," he said. "When I get back from visiting relatives in Ohio, we will talk."

Unconvinced, Levi inclined his head as he watched Nathaniel resume his orbit around his wife.

You can't help me, Nathaniel. No one can.

Chapter Thirty-Four

February second. Groundhog Day. The snow fell in bushels all night, burying the farm's already-deep layer of snow in still more snow. Rebecca watched from the window in the dismal light of dawn as Max and Danny tried to make a path up the sidewalk with their oversized shovels. A full scoop of the wet snow probably weighed thirty pounds. Max stuffed a handful of snow down Danny's back, and Rebecca heard his screams muffled through the window.

Most likely, today the groundhog wouldn't even come out of his hole long enough to be scared away by his shadow. It didn't matter. Rebecca held no hope for an early spring. Winter would probably last until May, followed by a scorching-hot summer and a miserable, soggy autumn. Why did anyone want to live in Wisconsin?

Rebecca wrapped her shawl around her shoulders as she tended the pancakes on the griddle. The woodstove in the basement had started smoking something terrible this morning, and Rebecca dared not stoke a fire. The house seemed almost as cold as the outdoors. Mamm would have to be moved to the front room near the fireplace if the old cast-iron stove wasn't up and running soon.

She glanced at the thermometer hanging outside the kitchen window. Fifteen degrees. Jah, that stove must be fixed right quick.

Rebecca carried Mamm's breakfast into her bedroom. Mamm lay wrapped in her quilt, shivering quietly.

"The stove is smoking again," Rebecca said.

"I should have known. It's freezing."

"I started a fire in the fireplace. Max will fetch Menno Glick as soon as he and Danny clear a path."

"Jah. I think I will go to the front room. Will you help me up?"

Rebecca placed the breakfast tray on the side table and took her mother's hand. It was cold as ice. "I will make up a bed for you right by the fire."

Max knocked then stuck his head in the room. "I found someone to fix the stove," he said, avoiding Rebecca's eyes.

"Already? Good work."

Rebecca followed him to the entryway, where Levi Cooper stood smiling sheepishly and holding a red rose.

She glared at Max.

"He was passing by," Max whispered. "You want the stove fixed, don't you?"

Levi didn't take his eyes from her face. She saw such tenderness in his expression that she almost ran into his arms. She knew she would find comfort there. Comfort from the sorrow of losing Dottie Mae and losing him. Comfort from the miserable chore that was her life.

Rebecca cleared the lump in her throat. She didn't need comfort. She needed a good kick in the *hinnerdale*.

Levi held out the rose, and she took it out of reflex and tossed it onto the sofa.

"I was walking to work," he said. "Max said you needed help."

Max nodded. "You are persistent to deliver roses in this weather."

"How is the shoulder?" Levi asked.

"Healed fine," Rebecca replied.

"What can I do?"

"We—our stove is smoking something awful," Rebecca said, prying her gaze from Levi's handsome face and turning quickly on her heels. "In the basement."

Both Levi and Max followed her down the steep stairs. Rebecca felt the sting of embarrassment that Levi should see the poor condition of the basement, even though she tried not to care. The bare cement floor was riddled with cracks and holes, and cobwebs floated in the air like dandelion parachutes. An unruly pile of coal spread itself in the corner. And the mildew smell wouldn't disappear, no matter how much bleach Rebecca swabbed the floor with.

Levi didn't seem to notice anything amiss with the room. Holding the lantern Max had given him, he silently studied the stove. He ran his fingers carefully over the top and around the flue and its joints. Squatting at the front, he opened and closed the door and checked the seal around the edges. Rebecca loved watching those capable hands— the shape of his long fingers, the veins that pulsed under the skin, the muscles flexing up his arms. Levi seemed to know what needed to be done simply by touching something.

"It's an old stove," he said, looking at Rebecca with concern. "Years past its expiration date."

"We cannot afford—"

Levi smiled at her. "I didn't mean to make you uncomfortable. I can fix it, but we'll have to light a fire to check for leaks. Do you have something to block the light from the windows? The room needs to be completely dark."

Rebecca tromped upstairs and pulled two old blankets out of the closet. When she returned, Levi and Max had the stove filled with newspaper and kindling.

Tuesday had been her last day in the sling, but her shoulder still felt sore as she strained on tiptoes to stuff the bulky blanket into the small window nearest the stove.

As she struggled, she felt Levi's warm hands cover hers and his breath on her cheek. "Here, let me," he said.

Trembling, she backed away as he took the blankets and, with his superior height, easily smothered the first window and then the second.

The room went black except for the small lantern in Max's hand. Levi lit a match, and the fire danced on the newspaper before spreading to the kindling. He shut the door and held the lantern close to the flue. Rebecca heard the fire crackle in the stove and smelled the burning hickory.

Holding the lantern aloft, Levi concentrated intently on the stove. Rebecca could see the muscles in his arm and shoulder rippling under his shirt. She felt the familiar, tortuous tug on her heart. Why hadn't Max fetched old Menno Glick to fix the stove instead of the boy she was trying to forget, the boy who was so hard to shake from her soul?

"There it is," Levi said, holding the lantern higher. "Do you see it?"

The beam of light illuminated a continuous puff of smoke coming from the top flue.

"Easy to fix," he said. "Oh, wait—look." He pointed to another spot farther down the stovepipe that also emitted a steady stream of smoke. "Two leaks."

He pulled a pen out of his pocket and marked the flue then pulled the blankets from the windows before saying, "Max, will you put out the fire?"

His hand brushed against her arm as he handed her the blankets. She determined to ignore the sensation.

"If you don't mind," he said, in perfect mildness, "I'll get what I need from the toolshed."

"I don't mind."

When Levi returned to the basement, Danny came with him. Levi worked a full hour on the stove while Rebecca's brothers watched. He explained his repairs to both Max and Danny, so they could fix it next time. Rebecca could tell the minute he lit the fire in the repaired stove. The house warmed up immediately.

Then, true to form, Levi slipped outside and spent another hour in the cold, chopping wood. Rebecca kept to the kitchen as her brothers paraded through the back door and down the steps, their arms laden with logs. Max and Danny hauled enough wood into the basement to last the rest of the winter.

When he finished, Levi tapped on the back door. Rebecca ushered him into the warm kitchen.

"I'd better get to the shop," he said, wiping drops of sweat from his face. "Nathaniel is back from Ohio, and he'll wonder why I am late on his first day home."

Rebecca heard Mamm shuffle in from the front room. She put her arm around Rebecca's waist. "Levi, you are a blessing to us. My husband will know how kind you have been. Thank you."

Levi frowned and hung his head. "I hope your husband knows that I mean no disrespect by coming here. He forbade me from working on the farm until I am baptized. I want to honor his wishes. Hopefully he will understand that today was an emergency."

Rebecca didn't know what to say. Why did he have to be so perfect? Perfect except for that one glaring flaw that made him impossible to love.

"Oh, posh!" Mamm said. "My husband will sing your praises to the sky when he finds out."

"I will stop by tonight to make sure it's still working," Levi said.

"No need," Rebecca said. "We will be fine."

She might as well have told him that his entire family was dead. The hurt flashed in his eyes before his expression went hard. "Okay, then. I'm glad I could help." Giving her one last glance, he put on his hat and walked out the back door.

Mamm squeezed her closer. "He doesn't deserve that, Rebecca."

"We don't need him, Mamm."

"Only if we want to freeze to death."

Rebecca put her arm around her mamm and led her back to the front room. "It was nice of him to come," she admitted.

"He sacrificed two hours of wages, and he deserves a little kindness from you," Mamm said.

"Dottie Mae is dead because of him."

Mamm furrowed her brow and studied Rebecca's face with concern. "Cannot you offer forgiveness to the poor boy?"

"Let him bring Dottie Mae back, and then I will forgive him."

Mamm lowered herself to the sofa and pulled Rebecca with her. "This bitterness is making you miserable."

Rebecca frowned. "Why does everyone think I am so unhappy?"

Kate and Miriam had noticed at the wedding. Frieda Yoder thought she looked pale, and even Marvin had asked her doubtfully if she was having a good time.

She should have done a better job of burying her feelings. Mamm couldn't help her, and no one could possibly understand her pain. Her world had gone cold and dark, like a barren, rocky wasteland never touched by the sun. She was convinced that if she sat perfectly still, she would freeze to death.

She wanted to remember the sunlight—to close her eyes and soak up the warmth on her face.

Then, as quickly as the thought came, she chided herself for giving in to weakness. The summer heat would never lull her into complacency again. Levi had burst into her life like a brilliant star, warming everything he touched with the gift of spring. But those who played with fire got burned. Better to stay in her icy cocoon than be consumed by the heat.

"Do I give you reason to believe that I am unhappy, Mamm? Do I mope around the house, crying my eyes out?"

"You never cry. I haven't seen you cry since Dottie Mae's funeral."

Of course not. Those tears didn't bring Dottie Mae back. "Crying is a luxury."

"Crying means you're not afraid to show your heart."

"I'm not afraid of anything."

"Nae, you are always so brave." The familiar look of resignation flitted across Mamm's face. She sighed and looked out the window. "I think the house is warm enough now. Will you take me back to bed?"

Chapter Thirty-Five

Luke Miller—no relation to Rebecca—slapped his knee and abruptly stood up. "The whistling must stop."

"Ach, was I doing it again?" Nathaniel said, scratching his chin and fingering the short whiskers of his new beard. "Sorry."

Luke curled his lips into a pained grimace. "I hoped that once you got married, you'd give up the constant cheerfulness."

"He's only been back a week," Zeke said.

"The cheerfulness will never be over," Nathaniel replied, grinning like a fool.

"The whistling had better cease soon, or you will have to cart me off to an institution," Luke said.

Levi looked up in curious amusement. Luke found something to complain about almost every day at work. If it wasn't Nathaniel's whistling, it was Zeke's tracking mud on the floor with his boots or Adam's walking in and out and letting all the warm air escape the shop.

"Bring some earplugs next time," Zeke said. "It's his place. The man can whistle if he wants to."

While he finished tightening the screws on the cabinet door, Levi thought of Nathaniel and wondered if he himself would ever be that happy. It all depended on Rebecca, and that prospect looked bleaker and bleaker with each passing day.

Nathaniel looked Levi's way, smiled, and shrugged. Not even Luke's sour disposition could mar Nathaniel's perfect bliss.

He came over to inspect Levi's work. "Have a problem?" he said.

"The last of the screws is in."

"You look as if you needed some help," Nathaniel said.

"Nae, it's ready to finish up."

Nathaniel slapped his forehead. "Ach, I forgot about you and Kate's cousin. Some friend I am."

"You've been preoccupied."

"I should never be that preoccupied." Nathaniel pulled two chairs together and invited Levi to sit. "I don't mean to offend you, but you look miserable. Is this for Kate's cousin?"

Levi couldn't answer. For some reason, his throat chose that very moment to tighten up.

"How are you adjusting to Amish life?"

"It is harder than I thought. I feel like I'm back in first grade, asking for help because I don't even know how to tie my shoes."

"I thought you could fix anything."

"I can usually figure out mechanical things, but I have yet to grasp the details of being Amish, like where to buy propane or who to call for a ride or how to butcher a pig. Those are beyond my abilities."

"No one minds lending a hand," Nathaniel said.

"I know, but I hate to impose like that. I want to be able to take care of myself and my mom, not depend on people who are already busy enough with their own lives."

"The Englisch are busy. The Amish don't look at life that way. Your work is my work," Nathaniel said.

Levi shook his head and frowned. "I wish I didn't need the help, that's all."

"Did your mamm find a job?"

"Jah, no problem there. There's a lady in Patton who needs twenty-four-hour care in her home. It's the closest thing to nursing Mom can do without being a nurse. The pay is good. Not as good as a nurse, but okay. We're saving up for a house."

"Am I paying you enough?"

"You are very generous," Levi said. "Living is a lot cheaper with no car or cell phone to pay for. And I have a second job on Saturdays. We manage okay."

"Another job?"

"I take the bus into town early on Saturdays to repair bikes and come back late on Saturday night. I get almost twelve hours in."

Nathaniel wrinkled his forehead. "We'll have to see what we can do about that. You'll wear yourself down to a stub." He smiled. "What about friends? Are you making any friends?"

"Counting you," Levi said, pretending to make a tally in his head and on his fingers, "I have one friend."

Nathaniel laughed. "It will come with time."

"I'm an outsider. And most of the guys are siding with Marvin Yutzy."

Nathaniel put a hand on Levi's shoulder. "Tell me about you and Rebecca Miller."

Levi's tears sprang up like dandelions. Why did he have to break down the minute someone showed him a little kindness?

Nathaniel pulled him out of the chair and steered him to a door at the back of the workshop. "We need a little privacy."

Levi numbly followed Nathaniel's lead into a smaller workshop. He sat on the chair offered him while Nathaniel lit a propane lamp. The room was not dark, but the lamp brightened it considerably.

"I'm very discouraged," Levi said.

"Anybody not preoccupied with a new wife can see that," Nathaniel said.

"We started dating last summer. I don't know what I was thinking at first. I guess I felt sorry for her." Levi folded his arms around his chest to try to keep the pain at bay. "No, that's not it. I wanted to know her better."

"Rebecca most certainly has a mind of her own, but I admit, I'm surprised she agreed to go with you. We're wary of outsiders."

"She wanted to do some non-typical Amish things, and she needed an Englischer to help her do them. I was her only option."

Levi took a deep breath. That's all he was to her—a means to an end. How had he been so blind?

Love is blind.

"And now you love her," Nathaniel said, his voice thick with compassion.

"I love her." Levi pressed his hands over his eyes and wiped away all the offending tears.

"Does she love you?"

"Five years ago I was in an accident—"

"Jah," said Nathaniel quietly. "We all know about that."

"Another reason I don't have any friends."

To Levi's surprise, Nathaniel grabbed his shoulders. "No, no, Levi. Never believe that. The Wengerds have forgiven you. We have all forgiven you. You must know that."

"Rebecca hasn't. I love her, and she hates the very sight of me."

"Have you talked to her about it?"

"She says she wishes I had died instead of Dottie Mae." Levi's voice shook, but he pinched his arm to keep the tears from multiplying.

Nathaniel rubbed his whiskers. "She was Dottie Mae's best friend."

"One of the reasons I joined the community is because I want to marry her."

"That is real love, I think," Nathaniel said. "You are giving up a lot for her."

"I'd give so much more...if she'd only forgive me."

"I think we cannot ask for forgiveness unless we have forgiven. Have you forgiven yourself?"

"The memory still brings me to my knees," Levi said. "But, yes, I have forgiven myself. The Lord has taken away my guilt."

"What about the other boys involved?"

Levi hadn't ever thought about that before. "I don't blame them. The fault is mine. I was so angry at my dad that I—" His heart skipped a beat then sank to his toes. He frowned and looked away. "I guess I haven't forgiven everybody."

"Your dat?"

Realization slapped Levi upside the head, and he couldn't stem the tide any longer. He let the tears go unhindered down his face. "Wow. I'm so blind. I keep praying for Rebecca to find it in her heart to forgive me, but I find it impossible to do anything but hate my dad. Why should I ask more of her than I am capable of doing myself?" He threw up his hands as the weight of his predicament smothered him. "I give up," he said. "I can't forgive my dad." He buried his face in his hands.

Nathaniel put a comforting hand on Levi's shoulder.

"I can't do it," Levi said. "I hate him, Nathaniel. I hate him."

Nathaniel let him wallow in his self-pity for a minute before he went to a small desk and pulled a Bible from one of the drawers. His soft voice, both clear and deep, felt like a blanket around Levi's shoulders. "With God, all things are possible."

"I know," Levi said. "But I don't know how to tap in to that grace."

"Do you believe that Jesus suffered and died to pay for our sins?"

"Jah."

"Including your dat's sins?"

"I suppose so."

"Then you either choose to accept Jesus' payment for those sins or you decide that what Jesus did was not good enough, that his sacrifice doesn't work for your dat. Which is it?"

"I believe," Levi stuttered. "But my dad should suffer for what he did to me."

"Just as you should suffer for what you did to Dottie Mae?"

"I have suffered."

"Not like Jesus did. You said He took away your guilt." Nathaniel opened his Bible. "'Be not overcome of evil, but overcome evil with good,'" he read then looked at Levi. "When we don't forgive, the evil that was done to us multiplies. What would have happened if you had forgiven your father instead of letting your anger lead you that night?"

"I wish. Oh, I wish," Levi said, still unable to control his emotions.

"The cycle of evil is broken when we choose to absorb a hurt instead of hurting in return, Levi. Refusing to forgive is great wickedness because we are rejecting Jesus' sacrifice."

"I never thought of it that way."

Nathaniel pulled his chair closer. "Picture Jesus in your mind, immediately after being scourged by Roman soldiers. The cross lies ahead—greater suffering than either of us can imagine. The blood runs down His face from the wounds made by the crown of thorns. His back is bloody, His flesh torn by the cruel whip meant to torment the very life out of a man. But look into His eyes. When I look, I see nothing but love...love for the very men who torture Him. Love and forgiveness. Do you see Him?"

"Jah, I can picture His face."

"Listen. Can you hear Him? 'Levi,' He says, 'I will take the punishment for your father. I love him so dearly. How many stripes will you have Me take for him until you are satisfied? I do it willingly. I love you. I love him. How much more suffering will you ask Me to take for him?'"

They were both weeping now, Levi's body taut with the sobs that racked his very soul. "None," he cried out.

Nathaniel got to his feet and pulled Levi with him into a rib-crushing embrace. "No more," he said. "It is enough."

Chapter Thirty-Six

Levi stuffed his hands into his pockets and started across the empty pasture. He needed to do one more thing before heading to Chicago tomorrow. The cold still pierced his bones, but he smelled a bit of spring in the air. *Thank You, God, for the rebirth of spring.* Spring reminded the world to have hope.

The man Levi sought stood at the far end of the pasture mending the barbed wire at the top of his fence. His cane rested against his leg as he struggled to bend the wire with a pair of pliers.

"Can I help?" Levi called.

The man's face lit with recognition but was followed by a look of puzzlement. "Just one more twist should do it," he said.

Levi came closer, and the man held out his hand. "Levi Cooper," the man said. "I am honored that you would visit me."

Levi lowered his eyes. The man's enthusiastic welcome shamed him. "The honor is mine," he said. "You're very kind."

"How is your mother?"

"She is doing really well. She's back into full fellowship. Doesn't stop smiling."

"And you?" asked the man. "When will you be baptized?"

"Next week, Lord willing. That's why I'm here."

The man closed his eyes and took a deep breath. "There is no need."

"I don't want to be baptized until I am sure that I have done everything in my power to make amends—"

"You have done plenty. You paid for the buggy, as I recall, with money you didn't have."

Levi laid a hand on Vernon Wengerd's arm. "Will you allow me to ask your forgiveness? One more time?"

Vernon nodded, sorrow suddenly appearing in his eyes.

"I am sorry for getting drunk that night. I am sorry that I gave my friends alcohol and that we let Derek drive. I am sorry we were laughing when we hit your buggy." Levi wiped a tear from his face. "I am sorry about your leg. Mostly I am sorry that Dottie Mae is dead."

Vernon put his hands on Levi's shoulders. "My Dottie Mae is safe in the arms of Jesus, happier than she ever would have been on earth. God must have needed another angel. I forgive you with all my heart. I did that very night."

"Thank you," Levi whispered, not trusting his voice to be steady.

"You asked my wife for forgiveness again, didn't you?"

"I wanted to be thorough."

Vernon laughed. "There is a difference between being thorough and making a pest of yourself." He clapped Levi on the shoulder. "We will speak no more of this between us, agreed?"

"Jah," said Levi.

"Then come in and have some pie. Jane's pies make you glad you have a mouth."

"She already invited me."

"See? If you praise Jane's pies, she will be your best friend forever."

"I would like that," Levi said.

"So would I," Vernon said. "You are a gute boy, Levi. You've turned out right well."

* * * * *

The office machines hummed in a sea of cubicles. Curious faces turned toward Levi as he followed the assistant down the rows to the corner office. His dad was one of the bigwigs. He got an office with walls and a door.

The assistant made his way to a secretary guarding the entrance to Dad's office. Dad's secretary had a full head of auburn hair that sat on top of her head in a tight bun. Freckles dotted her nose, and she couldn't have been a day over twenty-five. Did Dad's wife, Sherry, ever worry about Dad having an affair with his secretary? It would serve her right.

Levi wanted to smack himself. *Leave those thoughts in the past. "Charity thinketh no evil."*

Dad's secretary never stopped typing as she glanced over her glasses. She didn't even pause when she laid eyes on Levi, in typical Amish attire, standing before her desk.

"Sorry to bother you, Ami," said the assistant. "He doesn't have an appointment, but he wants to see Mr. Cooper."

"He's on the phone," Ami said, still typing.

"What do you want me to do?" said the assistant.

"Make an appointment for next week."

"I can't come back next week," Levi said.

"Sorry, his whole week is booked," Ami insisted.

Amish or not, Levi still possessed a particle of irresistible charm. He took off his hat and leaned close enough to Ami to compel her to look up. He recognized the moment she decided he was good-looking. Her frantic keystrokes wound down before she stopped typing altogether.

"I'm Levi," he said, flashing her an enchanting smile.

"I don't date Amish guys," she said. A look of horror flitted across her face as if she couldn't believe she said that out loud.

Levi stifled a laugh. "Too bad."

She blushed.

Levi leaned on her desk. "I know he's busy. He works harder than anybody I know."

"Tell me about it."

"But I'm his son."

She knitted her brows together and looked Levi up and down as if she were just now seeing him. "He never said anything about a son."

Levi ignored the pinprick of pain poking at his heart. "I got up this morning at three a.m. and rode the bus for an eternity. I have to get back on the bus at six tonight. Can't you cut me a break?"

Ami's mouth twitched in surrender, and she pointed to the phone sitting on her desk. "You see that light? He's on the phone with Mr. Heinzelmann. They've been at it for forty-five minutes. When that light goes off, you can go in. And tell him I tried to stop you."

"Okay," Levi said, bestowing one of his nicest smiles on her. "Thanks. You're the best."

He stood at Ami's desk with his arms folded, staring at the red light on her phone, until she insisted he take a seat. "I can't work with you looking over my shoulder."

Another twenty minutes passed before she snapped her head up. "You're in," she said. "Go, go, before he gets another call."

Levi hadn't expected the wild pounding of his heart. It was his dad, for crying out loud.

The office, rich with dark wood and brass trim, commanded a panoramic view of Lake Michigan outside the floor-to-ceiling window. Rebecca wouldn't be able to set foot in this office without a major panic attack. Levi's father sat at his desk, his back to the door, as he stared out his thirtieth-floor window.

"Hi, Dad."

His dad whirled around in his leather swivel chair and came to a dead stop when he laid eyes on Levi. A look of utter shock spread over his features, and he began to chuckle quietly. The chuckling soon turned to all-out unabated laughter. He propped his elbow on his desk and buried his face in his hand to stifle his amusement.

The hurt flared up inside Levi like gasoline on a fire. What had he expected? That his dad would leap from his desk and smother him with affection?

As the laughing continued, anger reared its ugly head. *What right does he have to mock me?*

"*Charity is not easily provoked. Charity beareth all things, endureth all things.*"

The Lord was testing Levi's resolve. Had he really forgiven his father? Could he purge the anger from his heart and make room for love?

Levi pictured the face of Christ in his mind and let the anger pass through him as if he were a sieve. He wasn't perfect yet—the wound still festered—but he got control of his emotions and looked on his father with empathy. He thought of treasured memories. The times he and Dad worked on the old Toyota together and played catch in the backyard. The images of Dad coaching him from the dugout and teaching him how to throw a perfect spiral. The memories of how much Dad loved Mom and how much he gave up for her.

The laughing finally subsided, and Dad sighed and wiped his eyes. "You took me by surprise," he said. "So, Mom dragged you back to the community."

"I wanted to join."

Dad propped his elbows on the table and laced his fingers together. "I'm not giving you any money, if that's what you want."

"I came to talk."

Dad picked up a pen and wrote something in his notebook as if the conversation were already over. "We don't have anything to talk about."

Levi winced. The relationship had been strained for too long. He had pushed his father away the minute Dad packed up his things and moved out. With his dad, Levi had returned evil for evil, and today he was reaping the consequences.

"Dad?"

"Forget about a poignant father-son moment, Levi."

"I came to apologize."

"You came to apologize?" Dad shook his head. "What you really want is an apology from me. You're not going to get one."

Without being invited, Levi sat in the overstuffed chair across from his dad. "Dad, just listen."

Dad hesitated then tapped his pen on the desk. "I'm listening."

"When you left, I let my temper get the better of me. I've had a lot of bad feelings toward you. I've been angry and resentful, and I ruined our relationship. I'm sorry."

Dad briefly paused the tapping. "You wouldn't even let me explain."

"I know. I'm sorry."

"That e-mail you sent—"

"I never should have said those things."

"I gave up. I did my best with you, Levi."

"Can you forgive me?"

"It's too late for that." Bitterness tinged every word. "There's no relationship. You're a stranger to me." He motioned in Levi's direction. "Even more with that Amish stuff on."

Ami, the secretary, knocked lightly and stuck her head around the door. "Julie Pantell's on line one," she whispered, as if speaking softly would be less of an interruption.

Without another word, Dad glanced at Levi and picked up the phone. "Julie, what did you think of those projections?" he said.

Levi was being dismissed. Just like that. After two minutes of a heart-to-heart with the most important man in his life, they were finished.

Levi stood and placed a hand on the desk, leaning in and demanding his father's attention.

"Hold on one second, Julie," Dad said. He put his hand over the mouthpiece. "There's really nothing left to say."

"I want to say that I love you. You're my dad. I'll always love you."

Dad sprouted a peculiar look on his face before turning away from Levi to the window. "You've done your duty," he said. "You can go home with a clear conscience." That was all he had to give. He removed his hand from the phone and continued his analysis with Julie as if he had never been interrupted.

The disappointment almost rendered Levi immobile. He stood like a statue until his dad rolled to his computer and started clicking. Blinking back the stupid, ever-ready tears, Levi turned on his heels and marched through the doorway.

After his talk with Nathaniel and a long night of soul-searching,

JENNIFER BECKSTRAND | REBECCA'S ROSE

Levi had felt so light, so free from resentment and malice, that he forgot the rest of the world might not share his enthusiasm.

In his imagination, the scene between him and his father played out like a sappy made-for-TV movie, where everything got nicely resolved in ninety minutes or less. Life proved more complicated. He should have known that. Look at how he'd managed things so far with Rebecca.

Walking in unprepared for his dad's hostility made the sting that much worse.

And it really hurt.

Levi found a nice tree on a grassy spot across from Dad's building and cried his eyes out for a quarter of an hour. Dad remembered the e-mail, written to him in a horrible state of mind right after he moved out. Levi had called Dad and his new girlfriend, Sherry, every foul name he could think of. He'd practically declared war. They never communicated again. Dad surrendered complete custody of Levi and Beth, moved to Chicago, and never spoke to either of them again. The only way they knew he was still alive was by the child-support check that came on the first of every month without fail.

Levi found himself slipping into the old patterns, the condemnation, the self-loathing, that had consumed him for five years. If he had been a better son, Dad wouldn't have left. If he had tried to see his father's point of view, he wouldn't have abandoned them. All of it was his fault.

Levi swallowed hard and actually tasted alcohol on his tongue. The desire for a drink caught him off guard. He dug his fists into his eyes, said a quick prayer, and pulled Mom's old Bible out of his backpack.

Knowing exactly what he searched for, Levi turned to the book of Revelation. Things got awfully dark in Revelation before they got better.

"And God shall wipe away all tears from their eyes; and there shall be no more death, neither sorrow, nor crying, neither shall there be any more pain: for the former things are passed away."

He'd made a complete mess of things with his dad five years ago, and no amount of wishing would change that. It was time to let Jesus take care of the past and make everything right through His grace.

Would Rebecca be willing to tap in to that grace too?

Chapter Thirty-Seven

Vernon Wengerd was a big man—almost as tall as Levi, with thick arms and a barrel chest. Dottie Mae took after him. When she died at fourteen, she was five feet, ten inches tall and could wrestle her little brother to the ground with one hand.

Rebecca always felt extra short standing next to her, as she did now when Dottie Mae's dat opened the door and gave her a big hug.

"Rebecca Miller, you are a sight for sore eyes," he said. "I was told you never come to gatherings."

"I would never miss a gathering at your house," Rebecca said. "And I got my chores done early."

"Whatever the reason, we are honored. And Linda, how nice to see you. Cum reu. Jane and the boys are setting up the Ping-Pong tables." He still walked with a cane. The buggy accident had permanently damaged nerves in his leg.

Rebecca glanced around the family room. She and Linda were the first ones there, but Marvin would arrive soon. He was unfailingly prompt—an excellent quality for a husband. Rebecca massaged the back of her neck; she felt as if every muscle were pulled as tight as a cable.

She'd planned the early arrival on purpose so she could spend a few minutes with the Wengerds. The Wengerd house had always been a second home to her. The exposed wooden rafters tapered down the walls to an ancient wooden floor polished until it shown like glass. Jane, Dottie Mae's mamm, loved plants as Rebecca did, and pots and planters of exotic and common houseplants sat on every unused surface. The purple afghan crocheted by Dottie Mae still had a place of honor on the sofa underneath Dottie Mae's cross-stitched pillow that read, THE LORD IS MY LIGHT AND MY SALVATION; WHOM SHALL I FEAR?

Behind the sofa, a set of accordion doors opened into the large space where the Wengerds held church services. The doors were open now, and Jane Wengerd and her sons set up two Ping-Pong tables there for the gathering.

After Dottie Mae's death, Jane and Vernon cared more for Rebecca's grieving than they did for their own. They brought her small mementos of Dottie Mae and invited her over every Sunday evening to sit.

The Wengerds were more than a second family; they were Rebecca's ideal family. In many ways, Vernon was the father Rebecca longed for—accepting, kind, and at home. And Jane labored dawn to dusk for the good of her ten children. Nothing was ever too much work if it benefited her family.

Rebecca didn't dwell on those sentiments very often. The good Lord had blessed her with a hardworking fater and a mother who loved her children fiercely. And Rebecca knew how ungrateful her comparisons were.

Jane bustled to Rebecca's side and embraced her warmly. "It has been ages since we saw you. Why must you be a stranger? You work too hard, I think."

"Not as hard as you," Rebecca said.

"The chores, your mother's illness, they all wear on you. I can see it in your eyes."

"Nae, I am fine."

Jane took Rebecca's hand. "Cum in the kitchen and help us finish the pretzels."

Jane always had a task for Rebecca whenever she came to visit. Being asked to do something in Jane's kitchen meant that Rebecca was part of the inner circle of the family instead of a mere guest who wouldn't be asked to help at all.

The kitchen and family room were separated by a long wall with a wide opening so that the people in either room could see each other.

Potted plants lined the ledge of the opening and trailed their leaves in cascades down either side.

A flurry of activity greeted Rebecca. Jane's four daughters—Ruth, Naomi, Esther, and Hannah—bustled around the kitchen in a pretzel-making dance, laughing and chattering like they'd never had so much fun in their lives.

Hannah glanced up. "Rebecca, thank goodness you are here. Mamm insisted the pretzels be hot out of the oven for the gathering, but now we have to scramble to finish in time. Can you poach?"

"Jah, sure," Rebecca said. She took the skimmer from Hannah and marched to the cookstove, where a pot of soda water boiled merrily. She loosened the frozen dough, already formed into pretzels, from the baking sheet and plopped two pretzels into the water. After a minute, she pulled them out of the water with the skimmer and placed them on the greased baking sheet manned by Esther. Esther brushed each pretzel with an egg wash and sprinkled it with salt. When the sheet was full, she popped it into the oven.

The Wengerds' kitchen had two cookstoves that stood side by side, a luxury to be sure. But at a time like this, with pretzels to be made, the extra stove became a necessity. As quickly as Rebecca and Esther could fill a pan with pretzels, it went into the belly of the stove. When the timer rang at periodic intervals, Naomi whisked the golden brown pretzels out of the oven and into a basket, which she covered with a clean dish towel to keep them warm.

Esther nudged Rebecca's arm. "Albert says Marvin Yutzy's mamm told your mamm to plant celery this spring. Is there something you want to tell us?"

Rebecca blushed. Celery was a traditional wedding food. The bride's mamm planted celery to prepare for the big day. Marvin hadn't shared his wedding plans with her. Not that he needed to. His intent to marry her next fall was plain enough. But she had other plans. She could probably stall him for another two years before she committed herself.

"Maybe Marvin's sister is planning to wed," she said.

Esther and Hannah giggled.

"Eva? She's fifteen," Hannah said. "Oh, Rebecca, you know how to bust me up laughing."

Once the last of the frozen pretzels was poached, Rebecca poured the water into the sink and washed the pan. Then she wiped the cupboards while Ruth and Hannah prepared bowls of jam, honey, and mustard for dipping.

Hannah placed her bowl on the counter and leaned close to Rebecca. "Marvin's here, ready for some fun. Don't let him sit too close," she teased.

Rebecca looked into the family room as newly arrived young people greeted each other and visited before prayer. Adam and Davie Eicher played Ping-Pong at one table while two younger girls played at the other.

Marvin sat on the sofa talking with Abner. "Manure can be a good source of income for the dairy," she heard him say.

She looked away—didn't care much about that conversation.

The front door squeaked open, and Rebecca caught her breath as Levi walked into the room. Her heart leaped out of her chest, and she promptly shoved it back into place. She would get over this childish fascination with Levi Cooper.

Levi shook hands with two boys near the door as the eyes of every girl in the house seemed to follow him and drink him in like the dry ground soaks up rain. He flashed that one-of-a-kind smile and the girls practically swooned. Rebecca knew every line of his face, every emotion expressed in his eyes so well that she could almost read his thoughts. She could see that he wasn't even aware of the attention.

Indignation soon replaced those unwanted feelings. How could he? She almost didn't have words for his audacity. She stared at him as a thousand violent emotions warred inside her head.

Dottie Mae's dat came into the kitchen lugging a bag of ice. She didn't even acknowledge him—just kept staring at that impertinent young man standing in the Wengerds' family room, who acted as if he had every right to be there.

"What's wrong, Rebecca?" Vernon asked. "You all right?"

"I can't believe he would show up here," she murmured. "After what he did, how dare he set foot in your house? I will tell him to leave right now."

Vernon saw where she was looking and furrowed his brow. "Don't do that," he said. "I invited him."

"Don't you know he is one of the boys who—"

"Of course I know. He is a gute boy. He came over last week and helped me fix my fences."

Rebecca's voice rose with her agitation. "But how can you stand to look at him? Because of him, Dottie Mae is gone. Your daughter. He killed your daughter."

Vernon frowned, and pain flashed in his eyes. "Do not talk like that. All is forgiven."

Her breathing became rapid; her hands felt ice-cold. "How can you forgive him? What he did was wrong."

Vernon put down his bag and wrapped an arm around Rebecca's shoulder. "Cum," he said.

He led her up the stairs, and they sat on the top step looking down on the gathering…far enough away they wouldn't be heard, high above where no one would think to look.

Vernon grabbed Rebecca's hand and held it tightly. "Last week he came to ask my forgiveness again. He feels it very deeply."

"Again?"

"The day after the accident, he came to the hospital and begged for my forgiveness. I never saw such remorse. How could I not forgive him?"

"Those four boys ruined your life."

Vernon shook his head. "After the accident, do you know what Levi did? He jumped out of the car while the other three screamed at him to get back in. They were afraid they would get caught. He refused, and they drove away without him. When he saw that Dottie Mae was dead, he cried out like he was the one who had been hurt. After he called an ambulance, he stayed with me. He put pressure on my leg. If he hadn't stayed, I would have bled to death. The doctor said as much. Levi saved my life."

Of course he did. That was exactly what Levi would have done. Wouldn't have worried about the trouble he was in, wouldn't have tried to save his own skin, just would have seen what needed to be done and did it. If she had searched her heart earlier, she could have guessed the story before Vernon even told it. Rebecca couldn't speak.

Vernon squeezed her hand. "When Dottie Mae died, our hearts were broken. But God has a plan for everyone. I must trust in that plan. God chose to take my daughter. We must not punish Levi for that."

Emotions washed over Rebecca like waves on a beach. At first she resisted what they were telling her, but then she gave in and listened.

She had forgiven Levi a long time ago.

The realization didn't make her feel better.

She loved him.

She didn't merely love him. She breathed him in and out with every heartbeat.

And he would break her heart over and over again if she didn't guard it.

Rebecca's heart shattered into a million pieces that day on the slopes because she finally crashed against the truth that she had given her heart completely to Levi, and she felt as weak as a kitten because she loved him too much. When she found out about his connection to Dottie Mae, she resolved to never put her full faith in anybody ever again. The consequences proved intensely painful.

Not trusting her voice to remain steady, Rebecca nodded to Dottie Mae's dat. More than anything in the world, she wanted to be alone. Could she slip out of the house without being noticed? She patted Vernon's hand and tiptoed down the stairs to the family room full of young people. Marvin saw her from across the room and motioned for her to sit by him. She shook her head slightly and ducked into the kitchen. Rebecca tiptoed down the back hall, through the mudroom, and out the back door. Linda could drive the buggy home.

Wrapping her arms tightly around herself against the cold, she trudged up the muddy lane to the main road. The horses, standing patiently with their buggies, twitched their ears as they watched her pass.

The dirt-packed road made for easier travel. Rebecca had always been a fast walker. The Wengerds' house was soon several hundred yards behind her.

Footfalls on the gravel told her someone sprinted to catch up. She knew who it was even before she heard her name. She quickened her pace.

"Rebecca!"

Reluctantly, Rebecca turned around. Levi jogged the rest of the distance between them, his muscular body especially graceful when he ran. His cheeks and nose were red and he panted for air, but he had that dazzling smile on his face that always stabbed through her heart. Why did she have to love him so?

"You forgot your coat," he said, first holding it out to her and then helping her into it. Even the slightest touch from his hand seemed to leave an impression on her skin.

"Denki," she said.

He slowly pulled his hands from her shoulders and cleared his throat. "I'm starting to get a complex. I walk into a room, and you walk out. You're not avoiding me, are you, kid?"

"You should know me well enough by now, Bucky. Jah, I am avoiding you."

"Bucky. Like the beaver. My teeth aren't that bad."

She loved the sound of his laugh.

Refusing to be taken in by his charm, she opted for a quick dismissal. "Good-bye, Levi."

He smiled sadly. "Please, don't leave. You go to so few gatherings. I'll go so you can stay."

"No need. I have to get to some chores."

"I thought maybe enough time had passed. I hoped you'd be able to tolerate my presence."

"You can join every youth group in Apple Lake, for all I care," she said. "It doesn't matter to me."

"But it does matter. A lot. I want to give you all the time you need."

"I do not need more time," she countered. "I forgive you for Dottie Mae. You don't need to keep asking and wondering. It's done." Her voice sounded harsh, even to herself.

He searched her face. "I believe you. You have too good a heart to punish me forever."

"What do you know of my heart?"

"I know that you are suffering terribly. I know that Marvin doesn't understand you well enough to see it."

"How can Marvin see what isn't there?"

"The suffering is all my fault. I want to make it better."

"Don't feel obligated to do anything for me. You owe me nothing."

He came closer and gently stroked her arms. She wasn't sure why she didn't pull away. His voice caressed her with its tenderness. "I used to think that water and heights frightened you. Now I know the only thing you are truly, truly afraid of is love."

"I'm not afraid. I'm realistic. Love makes people vulnerable."

The intensity of his gaze held her hostage. "You don't know how much I regret all the hurt I ever caused you."

"That's what happens when you love somebody. They rip your heart out and throw it on the sidewalk. Sometimes they don't even mean to. They get sick or die or ignore you, but the result is still the same."

Levi nodded, too eager. "So you admit you love me."

"No, I am saying that's what would happen if I let myself love you."

"You love me, Rebecca. Why won't you say it?"

"Because I never want to feel so terrible again."

"I promise I will never give you reason. I will make you so happy, you won't even notice bad weather."

"What happens to me next week or next year when you decide you are tired of the Plain life?"

"That won't happen." He lowered his eyes. "Not if you share it with me. Any relationship worth having or caring deeply about has ups and downs, like a roller coaster."

"I hate roller coasters."

"Bad analogy." In frustration, he released her arms, placed his hands on the nearest post, and gazed out at the Wengerds' orchard beyond the fence. "So you'll marry Marvin Yutzy out of spite."

"Marvin is the perfect husband for me. I have no expectations, so he will never disappoint me. I don't love him, so he will never break my heart."

"Perfect," Levi said. "I'm sure he'd be happy to know how much he means to you."

"I will be a gute wife to him. I know how to work hard."

"What every man wants, a wife he can work to death."

"I will do my duty."

"And be miserable."

"And be content," Rebecca insisted. "I will never fear losing him."

With lightning speed, he took her into his arms. She trembled involuntarily at his closeness and felt the masculine power in his embrace. She tilted her head back to look at him. His lips were inches from hers.

"Don't marry Marvin," he said. "I love you."

The vapors from his breath and hers mingled together before floating away into the air. Could he feel her heart hammering out an unfamiliar and dangerous cadence?

"Don't kiss me," she whispered.

He froze and, for several breathless seconds, stared at her mouth. She saw the turmoil in his eyes and then the final, agonizing surrender. He slowly released his hold and moved away from her. "I wouldn't think of it," he said.

His face became an emotionless mask as he stuffed his hands into his pockets and looked anywhere but at her. "There won't be anymore gatherings for me. You can come and go without fear of my being there. I won't bother you again. May God bless you with a long and happy life."

He turned and walked slowly in the direction of the Wengerds'. She walked the other way, chancing one more look back.

Chapter Thirty-Eight

Warmth washed over Levi as he and his grandpa came in the house and stomped the snow off their boots. Heavenly smells of bacon and pumpkin waffles wafted from the kitchen.

"Your mammi has a way with a skillet, to be sure," Dawdi said, grunting as he slowly sank to the bench. "But with your mamm here, theys is the best pair of cooks in Apple Lake."

"Here, Dawdi, let me." Levi knelt down and loosened the laces on Dawdi's boots before pulling them off his feet. "I wish you would let me do the milking on my own. The cold can't be good for your hands."

Dawdi waved off the suggestion. "Ach, I've done the milking for going on seventy years. Mammi wants us to sell the cows, but I ain't ready to give it up yet."

Levi didn't argue. That Dawdi even managed to get up in the mornings was a miracle. If the milking kept him going, who was Levi to rob him of the experience? Still, he was glad he could relieve some of the burden for his grandparents. The milking machine proved temperamental at times, and Levi gladly kept it in working order.

Levi had expected a mighty struggle in adjusting to Amish life, but his kind neighbors had made the transition much less painful. Mom was right. The Amish were the most charitable people he'd ever met.

If it weren't for the fact that he'd lost the only girl he would ever love, he could be quite content with his life. Rebecca's rejection cast a pall over everything in the world.

Once his own boots were off, Levi helped Dawdi from his bench, and they hobbled into the kitchen. Ever since Mom had made her public confession and they reinstated her as a member, they had taken all their meals with Levi's grandparents. Mammi was adamant. To make up for lost time, she said.

Mom set a heaping plate of waffles on the table while Mammi poured orange juice. "Sit, sit," Mammi said. "The waffles will get cold."

Dawdi insisted on pulling out a chair for Mammi before sitting himself. With his arthritic body, the effort took some time. Mom sat next to Levi. She pursed her lips doubtfully and squeezed his hand.

After prayer, Levi poured a generous helping of Mammi's legendary maple cream syrup over everything on his plate and made short work of his waffles.

Once he cleaned his plate, he sipped his orange juice while he listened to his grandparents talk about the holes in the fence that must be mended before spring.

"We had a horse get through the fence last year," Mammi told him.

Levi said something in reply, but he wasn't even sure what. He wondered if Marvin had mended those fences at Rebecca's place. There were two gaps in the pasture fence Levi hadn't gotten to before winter. Max might be able to help, but Rebecca probably couldn't fix them on her own.

Mom pounded her fist on the table and startled Levi from his stupor. "I'm not letting you go through with it," she said.

"Through with what?"

"You're not getting baptized."

"Mom, yes, I am. This Sunday. Don't freak out on me."

Dawdi turned to Mammi in confusion. "What does she mean, Nancy?"

Mammi put down her fork. "Don't you want Levi to be baptized, Mary?"

"You might as well know," Mom said. "Levi is in love with a girl—"

"Jah, Rebecca Miller," said Mammi. "We all heard."

Dawdi groaned and rolled his eyes. "What a tattletale you are!"

"You are the one who told me, Alphy," Mammi said. "From Gabe Zook, remember?"

"I don't tattle," Dawdi said. He picked up a piece of bacon and pointed it at Levi. "Gabe says you take her a rose every day."

"Rebecca was the reason Levi wanted to join the community," Mom said.

Mammi nodded. "Now she's lost her senses and won't have him." She looked at Dawdi. "I heard from Izzy Herschberger."

"You have no reason to be baptized," Mom said. "If you're baptized before you leave the community, I'll either have to shun you or join you. So, I'll join you because I can't bear to lose you and then I'll be shunned and we'll be right back where we started."

Levi groaned and tried to put Rebecca out of his mind. If he could just get over the stabbing pain he felt every time he thought of her. He took an unenthusiastic swig of orange juice.

"Don't leave us, Mary," Mammi said. "I think my poor heart would break."

"You could stay without being baptized," Dawdi said. "That's been done before. It's when you make your promise to God and then leave that things get tricky."

Levi had already replayed this debate in his head too many times to count. He looked around the table at people he loved most. "I will love Rebecca until the day I die, and she won't have me. I can't make somebody love me who doesn't love me. But I want to be baptized. I want to make my commitment to God. He has done so much for me. I want to pledge my life to Him."

"The only good reason to be baptized," Mammi said.

"I like it here," Levi said. "I have a good job with a great boss. Once Rebecca marries Marvin, I will probably be able to make a friend or two. Besides, there's too much noise out there in the Englisch world. I couldn't hear myself think. For the first time in a long time, I feel at peace. Mostly."

Mammi wrung her hands. "Oh, my poor boy."

Levi felt the stinging tears. This propensity to weep at every thought of Rebecca was getting ridiculous. "Sorry," he said, rubbing his eyes.

"You take after the Petersheims," Mammi said. "Your dawdi can't hold back tears for anything."

"Why do you say this about your own husband?" Dawdi said.

"I might as well be miserable among the Plain folks rather than miserable in the Englisch world," Levi said. "At least here I have my mom and grandparents."

"I know plenty of girls you could marry," Dawdi said.

"I'm content because I've made my peace with myself and Dad and God. Everything is going to be all right." He reached over and grabbed Mom's wrist. "I really want to join the church. Even if Rebecca is out of the picture."

"Sue Ann Yoder is a pretty girl. She lives down the lane," Dawdi said.

Levi cracked a smile. "I'm afraid Sue Anne Yoder doesn't interest me."

"Barty Mast has three or four daughters, unmarried."

"Oh, Alphy, stop it. The poor boy doesn't need your matchmaking," Mammi said.

Grandpa frowned between bites. "I want to know what Rebecca Miller has that Sue Anne Yoder don't."

"Rebecca is...she's everything. She's smart and feisty. And brave. She made me take her skiing once, and she's afraid of heights. And speed. And pretty much everything else. You know how hard she works on that farm, without complaint, caring for her siblings and her mom. She's like an angel." Okay, enough. The grandparents had seen plenty of blubbering.

"All I can say is, if the girl is too blind to see what's right in front of her, she don't deserve you," Dawdi said, wiping his eyes.

"Nae, Dawdi. I don't deserve her. I never did."

"Ha," Mammi said. "Not likely."

They heard the car horn. Mom growled. "There's my ride." She stood and snatched her bonnet and coat from the hook. "We're not done talking about this," she said, shaking her finger at Levi.

"I didn't dare hope we were," Levi said.

"I'll see you after work." Mom rushed through the door as the horn honked for a second time.

Levi took his plate to the sink.

"Never mind that," Mammi said. "Go to work."

"Mammi, I can help with the dishes. It'll take three minutes."

Mammi gave in and handed him her plate. "Go sit, Alphy, before you fall over and break something."

Levi filled the sink with soapy water and quickly washed the dishes while Mammi wiped counters and the table.

"What did we ever do without you?" she said.

Dawdi shambled into the kitchen mere minutes after he had managed to plant himself in his special chair in the living room.

"Alphy, go sit," Mammi insisted, hands on hips. "I won't have you taking a tumble."

One side of Dawdi's mouth turned down. "The door is for Levi."

Levi pulled the plug in the sink. He noticed a tear making its way down Dawdi's face. "You did not get your crying gene from me," he said. "I only cry on special occasions."

If Levi had expectations of whom he would meet at the door, he certainly never imagined *this* in his wildest dreams. His dad stood on the porch, hands in his jeans pockets, intently studying the welcome mat at his feet.

Levi couldn't help it. His heart raced on ahead of him. "Dad."

"Hey."

"Come in," Levi said.

Dad shook his head. "Can we talk out here?"

"Sure, okay." Levi was accustomed to having serious conversations on people's porches. He grabbed his coat and closed the door behind him.

Dad took a step back and gazed down the road. "I think it's colder here than in Chicago. The gauge in the car said twenty-five."

"It's supposed to warm into the thirties next week."

Levi went silent, waiting for whatever Dad had come all this way to say. Besides that short meeting in Chicago two weeks ago, Levi hadn't seen his father in five years. He hadn't changed except for a few more strands of gray at his temples and an extra pound or two around the middle.

Keeping his gaze on the road running in front of the house, Dad said, "I loved your mother so much. The day I laid eyes on her when she was working at the market, I didn't care if she was Amish or Russian or Martian. I knew I wanted to marry her. And she had these two little kids I couldn't get enough of."

He smiled at some distant memory. Levi bit the side of his cheek and tried not to get emotional.

"It was really good for a while," Dad said, "but your mom started missing her own people. A woman needs her mother, I guess, at any age. She got depressed. Some days she wouldn't get out of bed. She didn't want to go anywhere or do anything, and she wasn't interested in my friends. Can you imagine how I felt every day, watching this woman I loved be so unhappy, knowing it was all my fault?"

"Mom chose to leave the community."

"What did she know? She was a sheltered Amish girl. She'd just lost her husband, and I came along to save her. Who wouldn't have chosen what she did?" Dad kneaded his forehead. "It started wearing on me. It's not a good enough reason, but that's what happened. I worked later and later so I wouldn't have to come home to her. Sherry understood me. She helped me to be happy again."

Levi wanted to point out that darling Sherry had destroyed another woman's home.

Clenching his fists inside his pockets, he said a silent prayer. How could he spurn such an overture from his father? Ach, he was yet so weak.

"I told myself that it was better for your mom if I left. Without me holding her back, she could return to the community and the life she knew best." He finally looked at Levi and placed a tentative hand on his shoulder. "You were the only reason I stayed around so long. The best son a father ever had."

Their eyes met, and they communicated emotions both had buried deep.

Levi propelled himself into his dad's embrace. "Oh, Dad, I'm so sorry."

Weeping in unison, they held each other in an attempt to make up for five lost years.

"I shouldn't have cut off contact when you sent that e-mail. My own son, whom I loved more than anything in the world, despised me. I couldn't face you again. I chose to replace my hurt with anger."

"I wish I hadn't written that. I want to take it back so bad."

Dad pulled away and held Levi's shoulders firmly. "You were a kid. I wanted to blame it all on you. That way I didn't have to face the fact that I was a complete jerk when I left my wife and kids to fend for themselves."

"It's okay, Dad. We can't go back."

"I want you to be my son again. More than I've ever wanted anything in my life."

Levi squeezed his dad tightly enough to crush some ribs. "I love you, Dad. I wouldn't have stayed so mad if I didn't love you so much."

"Sherry urged me several times to contact you. She really is a good lady." Dad finally broke away and fished around in the inside pocket of his coat. "I started a savings account for you when your mom and I got married. It's been sitting in a bank in La Crosse for fourteen years. I want you to have it."

He handed Levi a check. Levi felt dizzy, looking at all those zeros. Thirty-thousand dollars? Was this for real?

"I talked to Beth," Dad said. "We agreed I'd pay her tuition if you promise to never send her another dime."

"She said that?"

"She says you need money for a house. Says you've got an Amish girlfriend."

Levi lowered his eyes as a bed of quicksand engulfed his heart. "Not anymore. But I do need money for a house."

"Your mom deserves a house."

They embraced again. So much could be said with a good stiff hug.

Dad smiled. "Hey, your grandpa said you were going to work. I don't want to impose, but could you get the day off? I'd like to spend some time with my son."

"I can't think of anything I'd rather do," Levi said. "Will you drive me over there, and we'll ask Nathaniel? He'll be very happy to meet you."

"Sure, anything you want."

"And Dad?"

Dad closed his eyes and took a deep, cleansing breath. "You don't know how much I love hearing you call me *Dad*."

"You don't know how much I love saying it. Dad, could we stop one other place before work? I have a rose I need to deliver."

Chapter Thirty-Nine

Levi sat on the front row of benches with five other young people. His heart thumped so loudly, he was sure the bishop and the preacher and all the congregants could hear it. And it wouldn't let up, either. Even while he sat through songs and prayers and sermons his heart kept a frantic pace, until he thought he might die of a heart attack before he had the chance to be baptized.

The doubts pounded in his head and kept time with his heartbeat. Did his life in the community mean anything without Rebecca? Was he ready for this life? Did he want to live and die Amish? Was he ready?

To calm himself, he reviewed the "Confession of Faith" in his head—all eighteen articles. It didn't help. What if he wasn't ready? His internal heater went into overdrive.

The regular service came to an end, and the bishop and the preacher stood to begin the baptisms. Smiling, the bishop motioned to Levi.

Levi wanted to smack himself. Couldn't he have sat in the middle of the group so he didn't have to go first? What if he messed up? With heart still trying to break some sort of speed record, Levi slid off the bench and onto his knees. The bishop cupped his hands together and the preacher poured water into them. Levi bowed his head. The bishop said a blessing in High German and sprinkled the water on his head.

The water felt like a fresh spring rain after a dry spell. Someone handed him a towel, and he sat on the bench and dried his hair while the bishop performed the same ceremony with the other five.

Levi took a deep breath. He didn't feel much different, except that his hair was wet and his heart had slowed to a normal pace.

He glanced back at his mom and Beth sitting with Dad's wife, Sherry. Beth gave him the thumbs-up. Even in her Englisch clothes, Beth seemed to fit in well with the Amish women surrounding her. Sherry, on the other hand, stood out in her floral print dress and bright red lipstick. Dad sat on the men's side in the very back, pulling his collar and fiddling with his tie.

Levi looked at his dad, then at Nathaniel King sitting a row in front of him. Unexpectedly, an overpowering sense of peace spread through Levi's body. He loved his dad, but he didn't fit into that world anymore. Tara, Jason, the cars, the drinking, all seemed like a dream. Today, he was waking up.

He belonged with these people.

And he was finally home.

* * * * *

Rebecca leaped out of Marvin's buggy without saying good-bye and practically ran to the house. Tuesday evenings after cleaning at Mrs. Johnson's were a scramble. She had to catch up on all the work she missed at home. And with the worst possible timing, Fater was due to arrive home tonight. Because of bad weather, the contractor had held up his roofing job in Milwaukee. With the unexpected loss of income for the week, Fater would already be in a bad mood. Everything must be in perfect order. She could really use some help on a night like this.

Not Marvin Yutzy's help. Levi Cooper's help. Levi worked hard and competently, and he had a knack for getting her siblings to work hard too.

Rebecca caught her breath for the hundredth time that day as she thought of him once more.

Hoping against hope that Linda had started supper, Rebecca burst into the kitchen and looked into the cookstove. No such luck. She'd like to give that girl a good talking-to.

Rebecca untied her bonnet and removed her coat as she rushed down the hall. A propane lamp burned brightly in Mamm's room. Mamm sat on the bed reading. "Hi, Mamm. I'm home."

"Gute day?"

"Jah, for you?"

"I feel better. The new medication helps."

"Gute." Rebecca tapped on the doorjamb. "I need to get supper on. We can talk later."

After depositing her overclothes in her room, she ran to the kitchen. Six long-stemmed red roses sat in a vase on the table. She had surrendered to the gifts weeks ago. If he insisted on depositing them on her doorstep every morning, she might as well enjoy them. They were the only beautiful things in the dreary kitchen in the wintertime. Rebecca buried her nose in the blooms before pulling six frozen chicken cordon bleu packages from the icebox. A luxury item, to be sure, but on a day like today when the family and Fater expected to be fed right quick, it was her only option.

Max and Danny burst through the back door, each carrying a bucket of milk.

"Rebecca," Max said, looking at her as if she'd just materialized from thin air. "You are home too early."

"This is the time I always get home."

"Jah, Max," Danny said. "You should have planned better."

Max and Danny laughed nervously at some private joke Rebecca wasn't interested in hearing.

"I suppose that means you didn't get to the mucking out," she said. If the boys had only finished cleaning the stalls, Fater would be satisfied with the condition of the barn.

"The mucking out is done," Max said. "And the fence is mended and the buggy hitch repaired."

Rebecca sighed in relief. "Oh, you really saved my bacon. Fater would not have been happy about the buggy. Denki."

"No thanks necessary," Max said. "Here is the milk. I need to finish some things in the barn, and then I will be in for supper."

"Stay warm," Rebecca said. March had come in like a lion and proved as cold as February. Rebecca hung her hopes on April.

Danny put the milk through the strainer then poured it into the separator jars while Rebecca sliced potatoes and onions and laid them in the skillet.

"What did you do at school today?"

"Esther tripped me at recess, and then Teacher said no singing today because we didn't finish our lessons. It wonders me why we have to learn math. I won't need it to work at the mill."

"Do your lessons. You don't want to be a lazybones."

"Remember Levi Cooper?" Danny said.

Unbidden heart somersaults. "Of course I remember. He was here in February to fix our stove, silly goose."

"Abe says Levi bought the house and farm next to the old highway. You know that one by the Zooks'?"

"It's mighty run-down."

"Abe says he'll have to burn the old thing to the ground and start over."

"Set the table, will you, Danny?"

"Abe says Levi is sweet on Sue Ann Yoder."

The spatula slipped from Rebecca's hand, and she burned her palm on the edge of the skillet. She gasped and tried to shake the pain away. "Don't forget the napkins," she said.

"But I told Abe right quick that Levi is sweet on you."

Rebecca ran her throbbing hand under the faucet. "Don't go spreading tales to your friends."

"It ain't tales. He brings a rose every morning."

"Fill a pitcher with water."

"Abe says you won't have Levi, and Sue Ann visits an awful lot."

Rebecca scraped the potatoes now stuck to the bottom of the pan. The spatula screeched gratingly against the skillet. "What does Abe know?"

"He lives right across from Levi. They're friends." Danny set the last cup on the table. "If you are not nicer to Levi, he won't bring roses. That's what Abe says. Do you want him to stop bringing the roses?"

Of course she wanted him to stop with the roses. He shouldn't waste his money. They meant nothing to her.

Nothing except knowing that someone, anyone, cared about her. Cared if she lived or died. Cared for her beyond what she could do for them.

Stop with the self-pity. Mamm cares. The Wengerds care.

"Why don't you like Levi?" Danny said, looking at her with those big brown eyes that always broke her resistance.

What could she say?

I do like him. I love him. But love is too painful. I don't want more pain.

Before she could formulate an insincere answer to his honest question, the front door flew open and Fater stormed into the kitchen like a tornado.

Dark clouds loomed in his expression. "What have you been doing behind my back, Becky?"

"What do you mean?"

"The elders know better what is going on in my home than I do. I look like a fool!" he yelled. "I have forbidden this relationship. How dare you defy me?"

Rebecca didn't risk a reply. Pleading ignorance would further enrage her fater.

The racket brought Mamm from her room. She appeared in the doorway in her slippers and robe. "Amos, what is the matter?"

He pointed at Rebecca. "She's been seeing that Englisch boy again." He took Rebecca's arm and yanked her toward him. "I will not stand for disobedience."

Terrified of his father's rage, Danny stepped back and bolted out the door.

Dumbfounded, Rebecca opened her mouth and closed it again.

She'd only seen Fater so angry once before. She couldn't help her trembling. "I'm not," she managed to stammer.

"Don't compound your sin by lying," Fater said. "You cannot hide it from me. I met the bishop just as I got off the bus. He saw that boy working here. And I have made it clear that he is not allowed on our farm."

"You jump to conclusions, Amos," Mamm said. "I told you. Levi came the day our stove went out. He apologized even though he saved us from freezing."

"Nae, the bishop saw him today!" Fater yelled. "This afternoon, mending fences in our pasture. What do you have to say, Becky?"

Rebecca stared at her fater in confusion. "That's impossible."

"What must I do to weed the disobedience out of you?" he growled, his face inches from Rebecca's.

The back door swung open and banged against the wall behind it. To Rebecca's complete astonishment, Levi rushed into the kitchen, with Max and Danny close behind. His expression was every bit as dark as Fater's. He took one look at Rebecca and immediately moved himself between her and Fater.

Panting, Rebecca retreated a step and stared at Levi's back, at his fists clenched and the muscles taut under his navy shirt. She couldn't help herself. Relief washed over her even as her hands shook.

Levi's size and demeanor commanded respect. "Don't hurt Rebecca. I'm responsible. She knows nothing."

Fater stood his ground. "I would never lay a hand on my daughter."

Rebecca held her breath. Would Levi share her secret and contradict her fater? *Please don't, please don't,* she thought over and over. Maybe Levi would hear the words reverberating inside her skull.

Levi glanced her direction but otherwise didn't betray that he knew the truth. "You told me not to set foot on this farm until I had been baptized," he said. "I made my covenant to God three weeks ago. You said I could come back then, so I came."

"I wouldn't have given my permission had I known."

"I assumed it was already given."

Fater stepped to the side to look at Rebecca. Levi moved to stay between them. Fater scowled. "And you still claim to know nothing about this, Becky?"

"She didn't know," Levi said. "She is uncomfortable when I'm around, so I've been leaving work early on Tuesdays to help here while she is at Mrs. Johnson's."

Rebecca caught her breath in amazement.

Fater had no answer to that. He sputtered and grunted until he gathered his wits. "Marvin Yutzy already comes on Wednesdays. We don't want your charity."

Rebecca wanted to bury her head in shame. How could Fater be so ungrateful for all Levi had done for them?

The truth fell on her head like a splash of water from the eaves of the house. No one was more ungrateful than herself. She had treated Levi so contemptibly that her father's behavior paled in comparison.

Say something, a voice inside her head urged. *Defend him.*

Mamm's soft voice overpowered Fater's yelling. "Amos, the boy has done nothing wrong."

Fater turned down the volume, if not the intensity. "You know I do not want you working here, and you have gone behind my back. I want you off my property—for good."

"Okay," Levi said. Rebecca heard the sorrow, the resignation. "I would never intentionally do anything to cause you embarrassment. Please don't take your anger out on Rebecca."

"Becky will marry Marvin Yutzy."

"Becky?" Levi murmured. "Becky."

"My girl is none of your concern," Fater said.

Levi nodded curtly and turned to Rebecca. She couldn't look into his eyes for fear of what she would see there. Keeping her gaze to the ground, she tried to swallow the lump in her throat.

He wouldn't let her get away with that. He nudged a finger under her chin until she looked at him. "I'm never far away, kid. If you need anything, if you're ever in any trouble, I'll be right there." He brushed his thumb against her cheek then took his hat from Danny, and just like that, he was gone.

Rebecca felt like she might never breathe again.

* * * * *

Rebecca hadn't slept well since the ski accident, but last night broke some sort of record. Thinking of Levi kept her tossing and turning all night. If she slept at all, her dreams haunted her with memories of his pain-filled eyes pleading with her to show a little kindness. Could she even remember him with a smile on his face? Her restlessness amplified the sounds of the night, a howling dog, the creaks of the house, and the distant moaning of police sirens on the highway.

Her waking hours weren't much better. Fater had given her a tongue-lashing at dinner for buying such expensive chicken and then burning it. Had she possessed a weaker will, she might have escaped to Levi's house and sought his comfort. But the best way to handle Fater was simply to endure, and he soon gave up his ranting and went to bed.

Unable to sleep, Rebecca rose an hour earlier than usual. She tiptoed downstairs and stoked the fire in the woodstove that, thanks to Levi, still worked. Upstairs, she made herself a cup of cocoa and sat alone in the early morning silence as she watched the sky lighten. An icicle hanging from the eaves dripped slowly. Rebecca went to the window and peered into the half light. The ice was actually melting. She looked at the outside thermometer. Forty degrees. Practically a heat wave. She closed her eyes and thanked the good Lord for spring even as winter lingered in her heart.

Max and Danny stumbled into the kitchen, and she made them each a bowl of oatmeal. Linda emerged after the boys left for school, and Rebecca served her a heaping helping of oatmeal with a few raisins sprinkled in. Fater came out of the bedroom long enough to scoop two bowls of oatmeal for himself and Mamm. "This floor is filthy," he said, before disappearing down the hall.

After breakfast, Rebecca piled the kitchen rugs by the door and mopped the floor. Linda washed the dishes and tidied the kitchen before hibernating in their bedroom with a book.

When she finished mopping, Rebecca scooped up the rugs and stepped onto the porch to shake them out. She looked down at the welcome mat—black rubber molded in an elegant cursive WELCOME, upon which Levi had laid a rose every day for the last three months.

Except for today. The mat was empty today.

Fater mustn't see her cry. No one would ever see her cry. Rebecca thought she might explode as she bolted off the porch and sprinted to the toolshed. Panting in an effort to delay the tears, she rushed into her tiny sanctuary, slammed the door behind her, and wedged the shovel under the handle to keep intruders out. She threw herself to the ground as the dam burst and great sobs shook her body.

Levi had given up.

Lying on the cold ground, she shattered into a million pieces. The pain left her so broken, she could barely breathe. This was how it felt to lose Levi. Really lose him.

Without her realizing it, the rose had become a lifeline of sorts, connecting her to Levi like a single golden thread. Now she had nothing to hold on to.

The voice inside her head urged her to be strong—for Mamm's sake.

She moaned and buried her face in the crook of her elbow.

Rebecca felt like that fourteen-year-old girl again, crying at Dottie Mae's grave—unable to think of anything but her all-encompassing pain. Would Fater break down the door and rebuke her for indulging in selfishness?

She bawled in the shed for over an hour, until the cold forced her to pay attention to her shaking limbs and numb fingers. Soon they would wonder where she was and come searching. But how could she face anyone?

She wiped the tears from her face and straightened the hair under her kapp. Cracking open the door a few inches, she peeked into the yard. All clear. Keeping a sharp eye on the house, Rebecca bent over and picked up a handful of snow. She took some in either hand and pressed it to her eyes to lessen the swelling. Hopefully she could pass herself off as fatigued. No one ever need know she'd watered the tool-shed with her tears. Taking a deep breath, she trudged up the steps and through the front door.

The slosh of water from the back of the house told her that Linda had started the laundry. Rebecca rolled up her sleeves and made her way to the washroom.

Linda bent over the basin, pouring soap into the water. "Fater is furious," she said without looking up. "Where have you been? He made me start the laundry."

"I'll help."

"He and Mamm went to Walmart. They'll be back after lunch."

"Mamm must be feeling gute this morning."

"Good enough, I guess," Linda said. "I'll feed if you turn the crank."

Rebecca wasn't sure how she passed the morning. Had she scrubbed the toilet? Or just the shower? She must have helped Linda finish the wash, because a row of half-frozen clothes hung on the line outside. She recalled making dinner, because Linda complained that they had no butter for the bread and refused to eat another apricot for as long as she lived.

After dinner when Linda went to visit Sadie Bieler, Rebecca sat at the table and fingered the roses from previous days. She could barely breathe through the paralyzing ache in her chest.

When she heard the front door open, she jumped to her feet and busied herself by wiping the counter for a second time. No good to let Fater see a hint of idleness. She came in from the kitchen as Fater led Mamm to the sofa.

Panting with exertion, Mamm took the quilt folded over the sofa and draped it over her legs.

"Becky, cum. Help bring the groceries," Fater said.

Rebecca hurried to the buggy and slung half a dozen plastic grocery bags over her arms. She and Fater carried the supplies into the house and made two more trips before the buggy was empty. She deposited the groceries in the kitchen and went back to the front room to check on Mamm.

Max and Danny burst through the front door from school.

"Did you hear about Levi?" Max said.

Chapter Forty

"Levi, stop. Put on the harness before going down there," Silas said. "High-moisture corn this year."

Levi quickly slipped into the body harness that fit between his legs and clipped around his chest. He and Silas were removing the crop, and frozen grain kept clumping and gumming up the augur. It was his first week on the job. The late-night work paid well, and he needed the money if he was going to fix up that house.

With one hand wrapped around the harness rope, he climbed into the silo and gingerly walked across the top of the corn. It seemed solid enough to support his weight. The grain crunched under his feet as he slowly made his way around the wall.

The air inside the silo was stifling, pungent and stagnant, like a cold sauna with too many sweaty bodies hanging around.

Breathe normally.

He was a little spooked about all those people on the news who'd died in silo accidents. He had a harness. He'd be fine. Just new-job jitters.

He bent over and picked up a clump of frozen corn then pounded it against the side of the silo to break it up. The harness line went taut. He wasn't going to die with this thing strapped around him. He risked letting go of the line, shifted his weight, and reached out with both hands. Suddenly, as if a giant underground snake opened its mouth to swallow him, he plunged into the grain. He screamed in terror and was soon buried up to his chest and struggling for breath.

The invisible snake clamped itself around his upper body and squeezed the air right out of him. He felt the crack of his ribs, accompanied by a searing pain.

Above him, he heard Silas shouting words he couldn't understand in his pain-induced state. The harness tightened, and it felt like a tourniquet squeezing the blood out of all his extremities.

Our Father who art in heaven, spare my life.

The walls of the silo and the light overhead swirled in dizzying patterns around him. He couldn't catch his breath. He was going to die.

"Rebecca," he gasped. "Rebecca."

A loud *bang* and then blackness.

Levi sat up with a start and groaned as blistering pain tore through his chest. He lay back down. All was quiet. The heart monitor bleeped in predictable cadence as he gazed around his dark hospital room.

Only a nightmare. He was still alive.

* * * * *

Dread filled every space in Rebecca's body as she stared at Max.

"He was working at the granary last night when he fell into the silo. Firemen worked almost two hours to pull him out," Max said.

"Is—is he hurt?" Rebecca stuttered.

"The pressure broke some ribs, and he might have a collapsed lung. Yoders say they took him to the emergency room late last night. They almost lost him."

Almost lost him.

An invisible hand clamped around Rebecca's throat.

"The boy had no business taking a second job at the grain elevators. He does not know how dangerous they are. This is what comes of setting his heart on riches," Fater said.

"He wants to save money to fix up his house," Mamm said.

"And almost got himself killed," Fater finished. He patted Rebecca on the elbow and acted as if he had already forgotten the whole affair. "Cum, I will help you put away the food."

Danny wrapped his arms around Rebecca's waist. "He fell in the grain elevator. He had to have a chest tube. Do you think he will die?"

Rebecca knew that if she spoke, she would disintegrate into dust, so she stared into Danny's eyes and shook her head.

Max marched to the closet and pulled out some work gloves. "Nathaniel is organizing some men to work on Levi's house—to see if we can get it into shape before he gets out of the hospital. I'm going over there to help."

"You have plenty of work of your own," Fater said. "Charity begins at home. The wood needs chopping, and the cows must be milked."

"I will milk," Danny said, still clinging to Rebecca.

"I'm going," said Max.

"You are fourteen, Max. You do not know how to help," Fater said.

"Why don't you come with me, Fater? We can work together. That roof is about to collapse."

Fater turned to walk into the kitchen. "Stay here and help your sister."

The muscles in Max's jaw tightened. "I am going," he said. "I do not care if you don't want me to go."

Max and Fater stared at each other for a few seconds. Fater blinked first. "Then you'll have to walk," he said.

Without another word, Max bolted out the door and slammed it behind him.

Fater shoved a finger into Danny's face. "You better be mighty sure you finish that milking." He turned on his heels and disappeared into the kitchen.

Danny burst into tears and buried his face into Rebecca's apron. "I don't want Levi to die," he said.

Still incapable of speech, Rebecca put her arm around him and stroked his hair.

"Hush, now," Mamm said. "It will turn around right, Lord willing. We will keep him in our prayers every minute." She studied Rebecca's face and furrowed her brow. "He is in God's hands."

Rebecca nodded and wiped away whatever expression alarmed

Mamm. She patted Danny's head then escaped into the kitchen. Fater's indifference made it easier to keep her composure than Mamm's sympathy.

Because Fater would never see her cry again.

* * * * *

When night finally cast its shadow over the house, Rebecca could no longer avoid being saturated with grief. Everyone retired to bed, and the skeleton of the house creaked as other noises faded in the darkness. Lying in the blackness next to Linda, Rebecca imprisoned the sobs inside her for fear of waking her sister. Ach, how she longed to be completely alone! With no fater scrutinizing her work, no siblings demanding her care.

Afraid the feeling would smother her, she sat upright in bed. She had to get out. The toolshed was impossibly cold this time of night, so she snatched a quilt from the closet and tiptoed down the stairs to the cellar.

She spread the quilt on the cold floor and sat cross-legged on the bottom half, wrapping the rest around her shoulders and legs. Sitting perfectly still, she stared into the glowing woodstove.

She imagined Levi's athletic hands caressing the stove's door, searching for leaks. Then she pictured the shock on his face the first time she'd refused to kiss him. She loved that expression, when she threw him off balance and took his confidence down a notch. Now she had chopped his ego about as low as it could go.

Rebecca finally let the tears flow freely. Five years of pent-up heartache rolled unhindered down her face. An unexpected sob escaped her lips.

Every part of her body screamed for Levi.

He hadn't brought her a rose this morning because of the accident, but she couldn't bear the thought of his lying in the hospital not knowing how she felt.

The self-condemnation multiplied as she silently cataloged her transgressions.

She was afraid she had lost him, and even though she wanted to be strong, the pain of that possible loss overpowered her. This was exactly what she had tried so hard to avoid every day since Dottie Mae's death.

The door at the top of the stairs creaked open, and Rebecca's heart plummeted to the floor. She did not have the strength to face Fater's anger. But it was too late. She had nowhere to hide.

She swiped a hand across her eyes to clear the tears.

To her surprise, her mamm slowly lumbered down the stairs.

"Mamm? Did I wake you? I'm sorry. Cum, I'll help you back to bed."

"Nae, stay there," Mamm said. She held a lantern in one hand and the stair rail in the other. "Am I disturbing you, or would you like some company? I could get you some melatonin if you are having trouble sleeping."

"You should be in bed."

"Scoot over," Mamm said, "and I'll sit by you."

"You can't sit comfortably on the floor. We can go back to bed."

"I am feeling better tonight. I can sit."

"Fater will not like it."

"He won't know."

Reluctantly, Rebecca opened her blanket and moved over to share with her mother. Mamm set the lantern on the floor beside them and tucked herself nicely inside the quilt.

They sat in silence for several minutes, Rebecca unsure what her mother wanted and unwilling to bring up any subject that might upset her.

Mamm took Rebecca's hand and studied her face. "It wonders me," she said, "whether the sun would fall from the sky if you stopped trying to live up to everyone's expectations. If you gave up doing your duty and simply searched for happiness."

This time the emotions were already close to the surface and

Rebecca was too weak to put up her guard. She burst into tears for the third time today and rested her head on Mamm's shoulder.

"I would be very selfish," she replied.

"You do not have a selfish bone in your body," Mamm said. "Everyone deserves happiness, especially my daughter. It would break my heart to see you wallow in misery your whole life." Mamm took Rebecca's face in her hands. "Be honest, heartzly. What do you want? What do you truly want?"

Rebecca cried so hard that the words came out more like a sob. "I don't want to be afraid anymore."

"What are you afraid of?"

"I'm afraid of losing you, like I lost Dottie Mae."

"And what about Levi?" Mamm prompted.

"If he dies, I will not be able to bear it, but even if he survives…" Rebecca took a deep breath and looked Mamm in the eyes. "Remember when Fater used to take me ice-skating? He'd hold my hand and whip me around the ice, and we'd laugh and laugh. Now all he does is criticize and hurt my feelings whenever he's home. I do not love him anymore." She averted her gaze. "Now you know my wickedness."

"Emotions are not wicked."

"What if I give my love to Levi and he rejects me? What if he turns out like Fater? What if he dies? I would rather lose him now than be hurt like that."

"I believe you love Fater, but you shield yourself against him and call it indifference."

Rebecca nodded. "That is how I have treated Levi."

"But Levi loves as if he has no fear of being hurt."

"He jumps into the pool without checking to see if it has water in it."

"Could be very painful indeed," Mamm said. She embraced Rebecca and held her tightly. "Rebecca, if there is no pain in losing someone, there is no love in life. If you hadn't loved Dottie Mae so deeply, you would not have been so sad when she died. Pain is part of love."

Mamm's shoulder was soaked with tears by the time Rebecca pulled away. "I love him, Mamm. I love him so much."

"Then go to him. Marry him."

"What if he has rejected me?"

"You might be able to change his mind," Mamm said.

"How can I leave when you need me here?"

"A true mother would never hold her child hostage. I have three other children and a capable husband who will remember his duty. And you will not be far. Levi's property is only twenty minutes by buggy. Go and be happy. That is my greatest joy."

Rebecca felt the weight of the world slip from her shoulders even as a thrill of fear ran through her veins. "I am so afraid."

"Love is only for the courageous."

Rebecca squared her shoulders. "I am very good at trying things that scare me to death."

Chapter Forty-One

Rebecca felt like she passed several tests of bravery before she even got to Levi's room on the fourth floor. The smell of sterilized air was bad enough, but the sight of nurses and doctors in scrubs and lab coats almost sent her running for the exit. Every beep of every machine attacked her calm facade until she was a nervous wreck.

As hard as it was to be in a hospital, Rebecca's bigger worries involved Levi. Word had come early this morning that Levi's surgery was successful and he had been moved out of intensive care but would have to remain in the hospital for a few days until the chest tube could be removed. What if his accident had knocked some sense into him and he had decided to give up on her? What if he wouldn't accept her love? How was she going to approach him?

Hi. I've changed my mind. Will you marry me?

Maybe his pain medication would render him incoherent and he wouldn't remember she even visited.

Ach, she was driving herself crazy.

She quietly stepped down the hall to Levi's room. Levi's bishop and Luke Miller stood in the corridor conversing softly. Rebecca nodded to them as she passed. The door was closed, but Rebecca could see Levi through the window. His eyes were shut, but even in sleep he wore a look of discomfort on his face. Rebecca flinched. She'd give anything to see that smile again. Tubes grew from his arms and chest like dandelions, and the green lines on one monitor tracked the rhythms of his heart. She swallowed hard and clamped her eyes shut. This image of Levi in such pain would haunt her forever.

No fear. Pain is part of love.

I love him. I will accept the pain.

Preacher Zook came out of the room.

"Is it okay for me to come in?" she said quietly.

The preacher flashed a weary smile. "Jah, he is awake but heavily medicated. There is a lot of pain. A visit from a pretty girl like you will probably perk him up a bit." He walked away, looking almost too tired to lift his feet.

Rebecca clamped her fingers around the door handle, but before she could turn it, Levi's mother rushed to the door from inside Levi's room. Frowning, she nudged Rebecca back into the hall and quickly closed the door behind her.

"Rebecca. I didn't expect to see you."

"How is he?"

"He broke three ribs and collapsed a lung, but considering that we almost lost him, his injuries are a miracle. Praise the Lord."

"Does he have to stay here very long?"

"The chest tube must be in for a few more days, but he is young and in good physical shape, so the doctor thinks his hospital stay will be short."

"Do you think I could see him?" Rebecca said, suddenly feeling shy.

Levi's mother put an arm around Rebecca's shoulder and slowly guided her down the hall away from Levi's room. "Oh, Rebecca. You are so kind to do your Christian duty and visit my son. Levi always tells me what a gute girl you are. But I don't think it would be a good thing for him to see you right now—the way he has been treated by you and your family."

"My fater—"

Levi's mamm shook her head. "I hold no ill will toward your fater or you, Rebecca, but I am a mother bear, I suppose. I have to protect my cub. Seeing you might upset Levi and worsen his condition. You understand, don't you? I am only thinking of my son's health. You understand."

Finding it impossible to speak, Rebecca looked down at her shoes and nodded.

Levi's mother actually gave her a hasty hug before walking back to Levi's room.

Her surroundings blurred, and Rebecca made a beeline for the elevators. Once inside she pounded her finger against the button three times before the doors finally came together. In consternation, she realized that her dry-eyed days were over. She pressed herself into the corner of the elevator and wept.

* * * * *

Holding her basket tightly, Rebecca tiptoed across the muddy yard to the old house. The crumbling sidewalk led directly to the front door—no steps and no porch. Before she was born, an old bishop lived in this house, and it was already falling into disrepair back then. Once the bishop died and his wife moved away, no one wanted the house, and the property lay dormant for a quarter of a century. Levi had probably landed a terrific bargain.

The wood siding looked like Rebecca's barn before Levi painted it. Most of the windows were broken, and the roof looked thin in more than one place. But according to Max, Nathaniel said the foundation was solid and the outer walls well-built. A good shell to work with.

There must have been thirty men working on Levi's new—or ancient—house that evening. Some crouched on the roof repairing holes and installing new shingles. Others measured and squared window casings while two ladies covered gaping holes in the glass with plastic—at least to keep the inside dry until new windows could be installed.

Could Levi afford new windows?

The sound of hammers and other noises rang inside the house, and Rebecca cautiously stuck her head through the doorway. Max and Luke Miller held Sheetrock while Marvin Yutzy used a power drill to secure it into place.

Max caught sight of Rebecca first. "Come in," he said, grinning from ear to ear. He gestured around the small front room. "You should have seen this yesterday. It was a mighty mess." Even though the room couldn't have been warmer than fifty degrees, he wiped sweat from his face.

"You have done gute work," Rebecca said. "It smells like a new house."

"By the time we are finished it will be a new house." Max laughed. "Beneath this dust, the wood floors have the most interesting pattern. Luke says once we polish them up, they'll be fit for a king's castle."

Though still stinging from her visit to the hospital this morning, Max's enthusiasm wrapped itself around Rebecca. She fully expected him to break into song.

"I brought supper," she said, holding up her basket. "For you and Marvin."

For the first time since she entered the room, Marvin looked up. "Denki," he said. "I am sorry I did not come to your house to work yesterday. We want to finish the walls yet before Levi leaves the hospital. And his mamm will be over tomorrow night to see our work."

Rebecca nodded. "If you had come to our place, I would have sent you over here. Should we sit on the floor?"

She found a broom in the corner and swept away the worst of the dust. The three sat down together, and Rebecca pulled out cold fried chicken and boiled eggs. She studied Marvin out of the corner of her eyes. As soon as he ate, she would ask him to walk her to the buggy and then break the news to him. She dreaded hurting his feelings, but she had to put a stop to his expectations.

Since the moment yesterday when there was no rose on her welcome mat, Rebecca determined that no matter what else befell her, she could not marry Marvin Yutzy. Marvin needed a companion who adored him and adored the dairy business. It was unfair to pretend to love him when he could have the real thing. Rebecca knew how the real thing felt, and Marvin deserved it.

Once Max and Marvin wolfed down the chicken, Rebecca pulled out the whoopie pies. Marvin loved whoopie pies, especially ones made with pumpkin cake. Max ate with gusto, but Marvin nibbled on his until half was gone. He wrapped the other half in a napkin and put it in his pocket. "Very gute," he mumbled.

"I must get back to finish the milking," Rebecca said. "But when the walls are done, I will help paint."

"And clean," said Max. "We need lots of cleaning."

"I will carry your basket to the buggy," Marvin said.

Perfect.

She gave Max a quick hug. "What time will you be home tonight?"

"Ach, late. Very late."

"Not too late to make Fater angry."

"I will do my best."

Marvin scooped up the basket and took Rebecca by the elbow. "Cum," he said.

She tightened the shawl around her as they walked outside.

"Could I talk to you about something?" Marvin said.

"Jah, I would like to talk to you too."

They reached Rebecca's buggy, and Marvin frowned. "I am afraid this will hurt your feelings," he said. "I do not mean to make you unhappy. You are a wonderful-gute girl and very pretty. And a hard worker. But I am not interested in dating you anymore. I am sorry."

Rebecca wanted to clap her hands and jump for joy. She opted for a slight nod.

He misinterpreted her restrained silence and took her hand. "I know this is very sudden. We have always been gute friends, and I know I am your fater's choice. But Martha Zook works at the dairy store, and she loves cheese."

Rebecca stifled a grin. Why hadn't she seen it before? Martha barely put two words together in a conversation, and Marvin could chatter for hours without drawing breath. They were perfect for each other.

"I appreciate you telling me this. It is better to know how you feel now so that my fater's hopes are not raised. Can you imagine if we had been published before you realized how you feel about Martha? All things work out according to the will of the Lord."

He gazed at her sympathetically. "You are always so brave, Rebecca. I know you will find true love someday. Don't give up hope."

Rebecca put her hand to her chest and pressed down on the gaping hole there.

I won't.

Until hope gives up on me.

Chapter Forty-Two

Rebecca sat in an inconspicuous corner of the hospital lobby until she saw Levi's mamm emerge from the elevator with Luke Miller and walk out the automatic doors. Mary was leaving Levi's side to inspect the new house. Now was Rebecca's chance to throw herself on Levi's mercy. Her heart made so much noise, Levi's mamm would surely hear it from the parking lot.

Quickly, she hopped into the elevator and held down the fourth-floor button until the doors closed. Once off the elevator, she practically tiptoed down the hall to Levi's room, afraid of being captured but filled with dread at the reception she might receive. The fear squeezed her until she thought she might be sick, a fear worse than the roller coaster or the deep lake—the fear of rejection. It was almost unbearable.

She peeked through the window in Levi's door. Levi lay in the bed awake, a peaceful expression on his whiskery face. His color was better, but there were still machines and tubes and bandages everywhere. He said something to someone else in the room before leaning back and closing his eyes.

To the right, where she could barely see them, Levi's grandparents sat next to each other. His grandmother read a magazine. Rebecca cracked open the door and got Alphy Petersheim's attention. She motioned for him to come to her. Puzzled, he stood up with some effort and came into the hall.

"Rebecca Miller?" he said.

"This is a great favor," she said, "but could I speak with Levi alone for a minute?"

Alphy rubbed his gray beard. "You will be nice?" he said with a twinkle in his eyes.

Rebecca nodded.

"'Tain't no problem. Me and Nancy will get something to eat. But this hospital food, ach—a gute Amish wife should come in and teach them a thing or two."

He went back inside, whispered to Nancy, and took her hand. They helped each other out the door.

Levi's mammi stared curiously at Rebecca. In amusement, Alphy winked at Rebecca and led Nancy down the hall.

Rebecca took several deep breaths. If she did pass out with fright, what better place to be than a hospital?

She slowly opened the door and shut it loudly enough that Levi would notice. He opened his eyes and looked at her. Was he happy to see her? Or miserable? She had always been able to read him like a book, but today his feelings were a mystery to her.

"Hey, kid," he said.

"Hey, Gimpy."

His smile sent her reeling. "Gimpy. I like it. Very appropriate to my situation at the moment." He studied her face. "That bad, huh? And Mom says I'm looking better."

Even lying there, Levi looked so handsome that her heart broke all over again. And as frightening as it was, honesty was her new policy. "You look so wonderful."

He looked at her in puzzlement then gave her an uncertain grin. He held out his hand, and Rebecca watched the pain flit across his face. "Would you like to sit down?" He lightly patted the edge of his bed.

When she got close enough, he grabbed her hand. He closed his eyes for a second and smiled. "I love how this feels. Do you mind? It's my therapy."

Rebecca's heart did a somersault. He had the uncanny ability to send her twirling to the ceiling.

"I've come to register a complaint," she said, unable to keep her voice steady.

His face clouded over. "Okay."

"I have not received my promised rose for three days, and I want an explanation."

He cracked a smile. "I'm being held hostage by the doctors, and I begged and begged my mom to take you roses, but she doesn't see the big picture."

"Excuses, excuses. If a boy says he loves me and then doesn't show it, I start to worry that I'll get my heart broken. Especially by this one. Because I really love this boy."

She couldn't help herself. The emotion overpowered her, and she promptly burst into tears.

The heart monitor went crazy. "I've never seen you cry before," Levi said.

"I cry all the time now. At singeons, grand openings, cow milkings…"

"You've gone weak, huh?"

"As a baby. I'm giving my whole heart to you, Levi Cooper. Do what you want with it."

His warm hand squeezed hers. "So does this mean you'll marry me?"

She laughed through her tears. "With all my heart."

When he smiled, it was as if light radiated from his entire body. "It's shameful to profess my undying love in a hospital gown," he said. "But I have no pride left, and I do love you, Rebecca. From now on, my only desire is to make you deliriously happy. You'll have no reason to ever cry again."

Rebecca caught her breath as the thrill engulfed her. Was this much joy even possible?

She rested her palm gently on his chest and stared at his lips. He got the message and slowly pulled her into him so she could feel his breath on her cheek. They sat like that for a few breathless seconds. She ached for a kiss and leaned closer.

"Don't kiss me," he said, so near that his lips almost touched hers.

She heard the amusement in his voice and didn't back away. "Why not?"

"I've got three broken ribs and a newly inflated lung, and you expect a kiss?"

"I don't see any blood. How serious can it be?"

"If you kiss me, I'll forever associate kissing with hospitals and pain medication. How could you do that to my future wife?"

She leaned a fraction of an inch forward and kissed his jawline. He trembled. "Perhaps you could forever associate kissing with the moment your future wife told you how deeply she loves you and how she can't bear to live another day without you."

Even with all the tubes and needles, he wrapped his arms all the way around her and held her so tightly that she couldn't possibly pull away. "That's a great idea."

And suddenly, his lips were on top of hers with a gentleness Rebecca had never expected and never knew existed. The exhilaration spread down her arms and hands, legs and feet, saturating her with warmth. This was surely what heaven felt like.

She sighed. "*Now* I've done everything on the list."

"Kissing me was on Dottie Mae's list?"

Rebecca laughed.

"I'm glad that list is done," Levi said. "Because I think my health would suffer if we had to do any more dangerous things."

He kept his gaze on her mouth. "Do you know what I was thinking just before I passed out in that grain elevator?"

Rebecca shook her head.

"It was like quicksand, pulling me under. I couldn't do anything but scream my guts out and hope I wouldn't die before the weight crushed my lungs and I stopped breathing."

Rebecca ceased breathing at the thought of it.

"I kept thinking, I'll never get to kiss Rebecca Miller. That was the only thing on my list of things to do before I died."

A sympathetic moan escaped her lips before he stopped it with another feather-soft kiss. Rebecca wanted to shout in elation. She would never want for another thing in her entire life.

She leaned more heavily on his chest and felt him flinch. "Does it hurt?"

"Like crazy. But don't stop," he said.

With her heart beating wildly, she reluctantly pulled from his grasp. "People will be shocked if Rebecca Miller puts Levi Cooper back in intensive care by kissing."

"Yeah, but what a way to go."

"You need time to heal."

He fell back onto his pillow. "The day the pain in these ribs is bearable is the day I marry you."

"Most Amish couples don't get married until winter."

"I won't wait that long. April is a great month for a wedding." He looked at her doubtfully. "Unless you want to wait. You just agreed to marry me. I'll do anything you want."

"I want to be with you every hour of every day starting now."

Levi smacked his forehead with his palm and immediately recoiled in pain. "*Oh, sis yuscht!* I can't take my bride home to a dawdi house." He took both her hands. "Look, Rebecca, I bought a piece of property with some money my dad gave me."

"Your dad?"

"It's good pastureland with room for a huge garden. But it's a pathetic little house. I promise, I'll work like a crazy man to get it ready for you, but with all the stuff that needs doing, we probably won't be married for another three years."

Rebecca did her best to wipe the smile off her face and to appear sufficiently troubled.

"I think if I provide a sturdy roof over your head, your fater might give his permission to marry you. Unless he's still hanging his hopes on Marvin Yutzy."

"Marvin is not interested anymore," Rebecca said. "Fater will have to settle for you or risk having an old-maid daughter. He couldn't bear the shame."

"Marvin gave up? So I'm your second choice?"

"You have always been my first choice."

"I don't care if I'm your twenty-seventh choice, as long as you choose me." He sighed. "How can I be in so much pain and be so happy at the same time?"

"Must be the medication."

"There is no drug or drink that can make me feel this way." He pulled her to him again. "The only thing better will be when I finish that house and I never have to let you go."

His lips found hers once more, and she thought she could die quite happily in that exact position. Being careful not to bump any tubes, she put her hands on his shoulders.

"I've changed my mind," he said between kisses. "I'll bet there's a hospital chaplain who'll marry us right now."

She heard the door open behind her and pulled away from Levi with blinding speed. Her sudden movement left him groaning in pain.

Levi's grandparents stood in the doorway, staring at the two of them with jaws almost to the floor. Alphy was the first to recover.

"See, I told you, Nancy. From the look of things, she's doing him a world of good."

Nancy nudged his elbow. "Oh, hush now, Alphy. Don't embarrass him."

"If he don't want to be embarrassed, he should not do his kissing in public."

Rebecca covered her mouth with her hand and tried not to giggle.

"Sorry," Levi said. "We didn't mean to embarrass you."

"Embarrass me?" Alphy shrugged off that suggestion. "I seen plenty of kissing in my day, young man. I done plenty of kissing in my day."

"Alphy, you hush," Nancy said.

"It takes more than a little spooning to ruffle my feathers."

Nancy helped Alphy to his chair. "Pay no never mind to my husband, Rebecca. He is an old man."

"And you are an old woman, last time I looked," Alphy said.

"Hush."

Alphy leaned forward in his chair and pointed his cane at Levi. "Do I hear wedding bells for you two?"

Nancy put her hands on her hips. "Alphy, if you don't quiet this minute, I will call Titus to come fetch us home."

Levi put his hand over Rebecca's and squeezed tight. "Jah, Dawdi. Rebecca says she'll marry me."

Levi's mammi clapped her hands in delight and didn't hesitate to give Rebecca a hearty embrace. "Such a handsome couple you'll be."

"But," Levi said, pinning Alphy with a look of mock sternness, "no one must know. I haven't talked to her fater."

"Jah, you must get permission yet," Alphy said.

"I will not say anything to anyone," Nancy said. "And you won't either, will you, Alphy?"

"I can keep a secret 'til the cows come home," said Alphy. "Nancy is the tattletale in the family."

Nancy shook her finger at her husband. "Don't you talk about your wife that way."

Chapter Forty-Three

With the sun playing at the tops of the trees, Rebecca stood on her porch and watched as the Petersheims' buggy slowly made its way up the driveway. Levi had promised Rebecca that on the very day of his release from the hospital, he would ask for permission to marry her. Rebecca had come home from the hospital only an hour earlier to put the house in some semblance of order for Levi's arrival.

She had spent every possible moment of the last two days with Levi in the hospital, watching him grow stronger, feeling happier than she ever had in her life. Levi's mother had no objections once she saw that Rebecca returned Levi's affection. The three of them spent visiting hours making plans for the future and joyfully anticipating becoming a family.

Rebecca and Levi decided that Levi would petition Rebecca's fater as soon as he got out of the hospital. After that, he wanted to take Rebecca to see his new property.

"I'm seriously considering not letting you come to the house until I've fixed it up," he had said. "If you see it in the condition it is now, you might reconsider our engagement."

Rebecca smiled in anticipation. Levi didn't know about the work the community had done on the house. The surprise would bowl him over.

Levi's mom drove the buggy, because Levi was under strict orders to limit his activity. Rebecca knew how it galled him to be forced to bring his mom along for such an important visit.

Levi gingerly lowered himself from the buggy. His mom stayed put, trying to be as inconspicuous as possible. He took the steps in slow motion but grinned with excitement when he finally reached the porch.

Rebecca smiled back at him. She wasn't as nervous as she probably should be. Fater might not give his approval, but she was determined to marry Levi with or without it. Arranged marriages had never been the Amish way, and Fater didn't have power to keep her from marrying the man she loved to distraction, especially since Levi was a fine, upstanding Amish man with a newly renovated house.

He moved close to embrace her, but she stepped back slightly and took his hand.

His eyes twinkled. "You are holding my hand in public."

"This is not public. This is my porch."

"It's still progress, kid."

"Dream on, lung boy."

Levi laughed and immediately groaned and wrapped an arm around his rib cage. "I'm not supposed to laugh. But I don't know how they expect me to keep from laughing. I'm so darn happy."

"Are you nervous?" Rebecca said.

"Terrified," he said.

"It doesn't matter what Fater says."

"It does to me. I want to start off on the right foot."

"It's too late for that."

"Probably."

Rebecca led Levi into the front room, where Fater sat in the rocker reading *Die Botschaft*, the Amish newspaper. He looked over his glasses and made no secret of his displeasure at who stood in his front hallway. Frowning, he glanced at their hands, still clasped, and wadded his paper into a twisted mess before trying to refold it and then giving up altogether and tossing it onto the sofa.

"What does he want?" Fater said.

His tone of voice summoned the agitation that Rebecca hadn't experienced earlier. Better explain before her airway closed. "He wants to talk to you, Fater."

Fater removed his glasses and eyed Levi with distaste as he lifted his chin and dared Levi to make a friendly overture. "Sit down, then."

Levi cleared his throat and sat, his back as rigid as a board.

Rebecca gave him one last resigned look and tiptoed out of the room. She should have gone straight to her bedroom to give them some privacy. Instead, she ducked around the corner into the kitchen and stood with her ear to the wall. Mamm sneaked up behind her, laid both hands on her shoulders, and leaned close. Rebecca gave her a look of shock, and Mamm put her finger to her lips to hush her.

In unison, Danny, Max, and Linda appeared from nowhere and gathered quickly and quietly around Rebecca. Rebecca wanted to shoo them away but couldn't manage it without making too much noise. Danny smiled sheepishly, shrugged his shoulders, and knelt on the floor. He put his ear to the wall. Linda and Max leaned in to hear what was going on in the other room.

They stood in complete silence, straining to hear the conversation in the front room.

Levi got right to the point. "I have come to ask permission to marry your daughter."

The ensuing silence grew thick.

"I am baptized," Levi said. "I have employment, and I bought some property next to the old highway. I will take gute care of Rebecca, and I love her as if she were already flesh of my flesh."

Rebecca's heart fluttered. It was a good strategy to quote Scripture. Fater loved to quote Scripture.

"She will marry Marvin Yutzy," Fater said.

"She wants to marry me," Levi insisted. "We love each other. We would really like your permission."

Again Fater drew out the silence. "I do not give it. Rebecca will marry one of our boys."

"I know I am an outsider," Levi said with calm humility. "But I have made my commitment to God."

"You will decide you are tired of the Amish life and leave the community. I will not take that risk with my daughter's heart. I do not give my permission."

To Rebecca's horror, Mamm sprang from her hiding place and stormed into the front room.

"Amos, I will not allow this," she said. Her voice was strong and clear. Mamm could muster incredible courage in an emergency.

"Erla, this is a private conversation. Go back to bed."

"You will not sabotage our daughter's happiness," Mamm said.

"I am not—"

"Husband, do not interrupt your wife."

"Let me speak before—"

"You will listen to me," Mamm said.

Fater sighed in frustration, but he kept quiet. Rebecca could only imagine what Levi must be thinking.

"Levi is a gute boy who has stuck by Rebecca for many months. They love each other. Don't you dare separate what God has joined together."

"The Almighty has nothing to do with this."

"If you do not give permission for this marriage, I will pack up the buggy with the children and stay with my sister Emma. She has three extra rooms in that house, and she said I could come anytime my husband decided to be unreasonable. Are you eager to cook your own meals and wash your own clothes?"

"You wouldn't do that. What will people say?"

Mamm's voice increased in volume. "What will people say when it gets around that you think our daughter is too good for Levi Cooper? You have already sent the message that you are too good for their help. How much pride can you shoulder, Amos?"

Rebecca could imagine her fater squinting his eyes and lifting his chin in indignation. "That is not how I feel."

"Make your decision wisely, Amos, or you will be living like a bachelor."

Again, the quiet in the front room proved deafening. Levi was probably racking his brain desperately for something appropriate to say.

Fater finally spoke. "It is hard for a father to let another man take his daughter. He wonders if she will be treated well and taken care of. Little Becky is my jewel, and you are asking me to hand her over to you as if it were as easy as whistling. What you want requires a great deal of trust on my side. This is not a minor request."

"I will never hurt her," Levi said softly.

"We used to do everything together—fishing, chores, gardening. Then Dottie Mae died, and I got discouraged when I couldn't make it better for her. I hope you will do better than I did."

Rebecca felt the tears slip down her face. Her fater still loved her, as best he could.

Fater paused. Rebecca wished she could see what looks passed between them before he spoke again. "You have my permission to marry my daughter."

Linda involuntarily let a soft squeal escape her lips. The four siblings looked at each other then tiptoed out the back door and sprinted to the front of the house where Levi stepped through the door with a big smile on his face.

Danny ran up the steps and threw himself into Levi's arms. Levi grunted in pain but kept smiling so as not to discourage Danny's enthusiasm. They walked down the stairs with Levi's arm around Danny's shoulder.

"We spied on you," Danny said, unable to stop giggling. "We heard every word. I almost cheered out loud when Fater said yes."

"Me too," said Levi.

He shook Max's hand and gave Linda a brotherly hug, his face starched into a permanent smile amd his movements slow and deliberate. With a wink, he wrapped his arm around Rebecca's shoulders and squeezed her tightly when she tried to pull away.

Oh, very well. Let the whole world see. Two people as in love as they were couldn't be expected to act rationally. Engagement was the perfect excuse to throw caution to the wind.

"When will you be married?" Max said.

Linda's cheerful expression faded. She slumped her shoulders and sank to the porch step. "I'll be stuck doing all the chores, won't I?"

Levi put a hand on Max's shoulder. "Max and Danny know how to be men. They'll pull their weight."

"I guess," said Max with a groan, but then he grinned, and Levi nodded back with unspoken understanding.

"I can be here several times a week to help with Mamm," Rebecca said. "I'll be married, not dead."

"I want to show Rebecca my new house," Levi said. "Well, my very old house. More of a shack, really. Do you all want to come? My mom said she could take us as soon as I secured your fater's permission."

"She was confident, then?" Rebecca said.

"No, she honestly didn't think she'd ever be taking you to see the house. She was even less confident than I was."

"So, in the depths of despair, basically?"

"Basically."

"Five o'clock would be a good time to go over there," Max said.

"It's about four thirty. Let's go now," Levi said.

"Five o'clock is much better," Max insisted. "You don't want to rush anything."

Levi raised an eyebrow. "What am I rushing?"

"You want to enjoy the first time Rebecca lays eyes on the house."

"I don't think so," Levi said. "Better to get the horror over with sooner than later."

"Danny, go ask Mamm and Fater if they would like to join us. We will hitch up our buggy," Rebecca said.

"That will take a few minutes," Max said.

"And Linda will want to fix her kapp, and I must find my green shawl and freshen up."

"Hurry it up," Levi said. "The sooner we get there, the more time you'll have to get over your disappointment."

Rebecca smiled to herself and bounded up the porch steps to show Levi that she was properly motivated. Mamm and Fater sat together in the front room. Mamm's eyes were moist, and Fater looked as if he'd eaten something that disagreed with him.

"Your fater has agreed to find a work crew closer to home," Mamm said.

Fater chewed on his words before he spit them out. "Now that you will be married."

Rebecca didn't know whether to rejoice or mourn at that decision. She felt sorry for Linda and the boys, but Mamm would have more help and Rebecca wouldn't feel so bad about leaving. And perhaps Fater would not have so much to criticize once Rebecca was gone.

"We are going to see Levi's house," Rebecca said. "Would you like to come?"

"Your mother has had a long day," Fater said.

Mamm laid a hand on Fater's knee and patted twice. "We would be pleased to see it. Max has done so much work on it."

Fater looked at Mamm's hand then up at Rebecca. "I will hitch the buggy."

"Levi doesn't know about the work on the house. Don't tell him anything until he sees it."

Rebecca slowly washed her face and fixed her kapp just so. They needed to stall for a good fifteen minutes before getting underway. Fater helped quite a bit by taking his good time in hitching up the buggy—clearly a last-ditch effort to exert control, as he must have sensed it slipping through his fingers.

Once Fater brought the buggy around, another five minutes was necessary to load Mamm and see that she was comfortable. Rebecca rode with Levi and his mom. The others followed in the Millers' buggy. They had taken enough time to get moving that their arrival at Levi's place would be exactly on time.

Rebecca could barely contain her excitement. She was going to her house—her very own house to share with her beloved husband, to bear and raise little ones, to make precious memories with the people she loved. Levi's joy would make hers that much greater.

Buggies lined the old highway a quarter mile from Levi's property. "What's all this?" Levi said. His jaw dropped lower and lower, the more buggies they passed.

Once they passed a stand of trees, Levi's house came into view—as did dozens of people waiting in his front yard.

He looked at his grinning mother and then at Rebecca. "Why are all these people here? And why is my roof a different color?"

His mom guided the horse over the deep ruts in the front yard and halted the buggy in the midst of Levi's neighbors and friends. Kate and Nathaniel King stood out from the crowd, as did cousin Miriam, Luke Miller, Levi's grandparents, and the men from the wood shop, in addition to other Amish and Englisch neighbors. Rebecca jumped from the buggy first. When Levi emerged, the crowd cheered.

Levi was rendered speechless, but the shock on his face was plain enough. "I—I don't believe this," he said.

Nathaniel shook his hand. "We've been meaning to fix up this old place. Glad we could finally do it. We wanted you to have a place to bring your bride, if you are ever able to talk someone into marrying you."

Levi's smile was a mile wide. "I have managed to do that." He stared at the freshly painted siding and new windows. "The Amish really are the best people in the world."

"You are one of us, remember? So don't get a big head about it," Nathaniel said.

"I never dreamed..." Levi's voice cracked, and he burst into tears. "Thank you all so much."

Nathaniel laughed. "*Oh, sis yuscht,* I've never met a man who cries so much."

Levi wiped his eyes. "And you never will. I am a baby."

Several people laughed with them as Nathaniel opened the door and motioned for Levi and Rebecca to go inside. "You two can walk through by yourselves. If you want the grand tour, come get me."

"I helped with the Sheetrock," Max said.

Levi and Rebecca stepped over the threshold, and Nathaniel closed the door behind them. They found themselves alone in the empty front room, a refinished hardwood floor under their feet. The rich darker and lighter shades of wood formed an intricate lattice pattern, and Rebecca felt as if she had stepped into a mansion.

"Look at the floor," she said.

Levi stared in awe at the smooth finish that practically glowed at their feet. "When I bought the place, I didn't think it would be salvageable. Nathaniel's work, no doubt."

They walked through the archway to the empty kitchen, where the walls sparkled a crisp white. Spaces stood open for a stove and an icebox, and the cabinets looked brand new.

"Nathaniel's doing, again," Levi said, wiping another tear away. "I have a little money left over from the house payment. I'm not letting him foot the bill for this."

Rebecca ran her hand along the smooth countertops. What would it be like to cook in such luxury? Her heart swelled. To cook for Levi.

Levi took her hand, and they floated up the steep, narrow stairs to the three bedrooms. The two smaller rooms stood empty like all the other rooms in the house, but the larger room contained a bed made up with a stunning Amish quilt appliquéd with red roses.

Rebecca gasped and ran her hands along the quilt, caressing the petals of the abundant flowers, fingering the tiny stitches that outlined every rose.

She looked up to see Levi watching her. When their eyes met, he promptly turned on his heels and tromped down the stairs.

"Levi," she said, quickly following him to the front room.

He stood looking out the window.

"Did something upset you?"

To her surprise, he gathered her in his arms and sighed in contentment. "I don't believe that anyone has ever loved someone as much as I love you. I think my heart will leap out of my chest if we don't marry soon." He pointed out the window. "Plant a thousand roses if you want."

"What about pasture for the cows?"

"Only if there is room left over. I'll buy you every hosta you ever dreamed of, and we'll fill this room with seed catalogs. What else can I do for you?"

"Nothing. If I never touched another rose in my life, I would be perfectly, absolutely happy with only you."

"From now on, your happiness is the only thing on my list."

"Then you can successfully cross that one off."

Rebecca shivered as he tightened his arms around her and brought his lips to hers.

She was home.

About the Author

JENNIFER BECKSTRAND grew up with a steady diet of William Shakespeare and Jane Austen. After all that literary immersion, she naturally decided to get a degree in mathematics, which came in handy when one of her six children needed help with homework. When daughter number four was born, she began writing, and between juggling diaper changes, soccer games, music lessons, and dinner preparations, Jennifer finished her first manuscript in just under fourteen years. *Rachel's Angel*, a historical western, won first place in two writing contests. Soon Jennifer turned her attention to the Forever After in Apple Lake series, about three cousins who find love in Wisconsin's Amish country. Her debut novel, *Kate's Song*, was the first book in the series and released in 2012. *Rebecca's Rose* is the second book in the series, and the third, *Miriam's Quilt*, will release in 2013.

Jennifer has two Amish readers who make sure her stories are authentic. No matter the setting, she hopes to pen deliriously romantic stories with captivating characters and soar-to-the-sky happy endings.

A member of RWA, Jennifer is the PAN liaison in her Utah RWA chapter. She lives in the foothills of the Wasatch Front in Utah with her husband and two children left at home. She has four daughters, two sons, three sons-in-law, and one grandson.